HIS GODS WERE
HIS SWORD AND BLOODY BATTLE.

There was a look of sheer ecstasy in Calgaich's eyes. Cairenn watched fascinated as he swung the heavy, balanced blade in slashes, thrusts, parries, crosscuts and a curious weaving pattern that was so swift in its execution that she could have sworn she saw the reflection of the blade tip still hanging in the smoky air even after it had passed on....

Now Cairenn knew why Cuill had once spoken of Calgaich with awe and deep-seated fear. "Don't you know who he is?" he had asked with astonishment when she inquired about her new master.

"Calgaich the Swordsman! One of the wild Novantae from southwestern Caledonia, who have no peers in the red wet work of the blades! Calgaich, son of Lellan, who is lord of five hundred war spears and deadliest of all enemies to the Romans! Calgaich mac Lellan, grandson of Evicatos the Spearman! Calgaich the Swordsman!"

GORDON D. SHIRREFFS

CALGAICH
THE SWORDSMAN

PLAYBOY PRESS
PAPERBACKS

CALGAICH THE SWORDSMAN

PRODUCED BY LYLE KENYON ENGEL

Published simultaneously in the United States and Canada by Playboy Press Paperbacks, New York, New York. Printed in the United States of America. Library of Congress Catalog Card Number: 79-89959. First edition.

Books are available at quantity discounts for promotional and industrial use. For further information, write our sales promotion agency: Ventura Associates, 40 East 49th Street, New York, New York 10017.

ISBN: 0-872-16605-8

First printing March 1980.

*To Scotland
the Brave*

—————————— **LEGEND** ——————————

••>••>••Route of Calgaich and Cairenn from Eriu to Albu (Caledonia).

——>——>Route of Calgaich and prisoners from Britannia through Gaul to Massalia, and sea route aboard trireme *Neptunus* to Ostia, the port of Rome.

—·—>·—·—>Route of Calgaich and escaped barbarians from Ostia to Albu.

Albu is present-day Scotland.
Britannia is present-day England.
Eriu is present-day Ireland.
Gaul is present-day France.
Iberia is present-day Spain.
Luguvallum is present-day Carlisle, England.
Massalia is present-day Marseilles, France.
Ostia, the ancient port of Rome, at one time had 50,000 population; today practically nothing exists there. At the mouth of the Tiber River, about 22 miles by river, 13 miles by road from Rome.
Rioghaine, the *rath*, or town, of the chieftain of the Novantae, situated in Galloway, southwestern Scotland.
Tyrrhenian Sea, present-day Italian Mare Tirreno, an arm of the Mediterranean.

Massalia

ROME

Tyrrhenian Sea　 Ostia

Raid on the *Fortunata*

Mare Nostrum

Caledonia is a mysterious land of mists and dark woods. The people are brave in battle with a wild, undisciplined courage. They have a love of bright colors, of feasting and of drunkenness, and they love praise. They quarrel much among themselves, and their honor is a touchy thing, not to be trifled with at any time. Aye, they are brave in battle but fearful of their dark gods and of the restless spirits of the dead.

CHAPTER 1

Caledonia, Fourth Century A.D.

The rising wind was beginning to shriek again. It beat its wild wings beyond the thick and low layer of clouds that concealed the rock-fanged southwest coast of Caledonia. The cold gray sea writhed in thick convolutions as Nodons, the feared god of darkness and water, gathered his terrible strength anew to try once more to overwhelm the blue-sailed Hibernian *birlinn* that was drawing precariously nearer to the unseen coast. All that gloomy day and the dark night before, the storm had driven the small bark farther north and away from the great firth, or estuary, that cut deeply into the land of southwestern Caledonia.

Calgaich mac Lellan stood in the bow of the storm-driven *birlinn*, steadying himself with one hand on the forestay while with his other hand he gripped the long shaft of his *laigen*, or great war spear. The wind swept back his tartan woolen cloak and tore at his long, reddish-blond hair and untrimmed mustache. The vessel plunged deeply, showering him with spray that sparkled on his salt-whitened cloak and violet knee-length linen tunic. A great iron sword hung at his left side. It was sheathed in a beautifully figured bronze scabbard wrapped in part of a wolf pelt. A long dirk hung at the right of his narrow waist. His long, sinewy legs were covered with loose saffron-colored trousers, cross-gartered from his ankles to just below his knees. The damp tunic clung to his wide chest. His muscular arms showed bare as his cloak whipped out behind him, held at his throat by a bronze *fibula*, or brooch. A heavy torque twisted from soft Hibernian gold circled his neck, and matching arm rings were above each of his elbows.

His face was as taut as a death mask. Nothing moved on that mask except the curiously twisted scar on his left

9

cheek, which ran from the corner of his eye to the strong line of his jawbone and which no amount of sun or exposure would ever darken. The hard gray eyes, like glacial ice, seemed to probe into the opaqueness ahead of the craft as if he could see his beloved homeland of Caledonia beyond the mist and flying spindrift.

Cuill, the Hibernian helmsman and owner of the *birlinn*, glanced fearfully at the rising seas and looked desperately at the tall Celt in the bow. Here and there on the pitching deck, huddled in their dirty cloaks, crouched half a dozen crewmen. Behind Calgaich, seated against a timberhead, was the Ordovician *cumal*, or bondswoman, who had boarded the craft with Calgaich two days past. The wind was playing with her thick, lustrous dark hair, whipping it over the low rail of the struggling *birlinn*. Spray glistened on her pale, heart-shaped face, while her large green eyes with thick lashes watched the broad back of Calgaich.

Calgaich could sense the fear of the crewmen. There was no need for him to turn and look at them. Fear was no stranger to a *fian* such as he—a roaming warrior, divorced from the society of his own clan, a man who sells his spear and sword to the highest bidder and who has few peers in the red wet work of the blades. But this time there was no fear in his heart, just respect for Nodons and that confederate of his, Taranis the Roarer, god of the stormy sky.

Somewhere beyond the shrouding sea mist was Calgaich's homeland, unseen by him for three years, ever since his sword blade had death-spitted his cousin Fergus. Because of that Calgaich had incurred the *galanas*, or blood debt, and had been forced to flee from his clan. Calgaich released his grasp on the forestay so that he could finger the twisted white scar on his taut bronzed face. He grinned wryly. Fergus had fought well, he thought grudgingly; his cousin had left his serpent's mark on the face of his killer. Nothing could ever erase that scar.

Death was also familiar to Calgaich the Swordsman, as he was called not only in his own country of the Novantae in southwestern Caledonia but also far to the south of that land and into the land of the Britons occupied for three hundred and fifty years by the Romans, the hated Red Crests. A hunted man runs with the hounds if he can. Therefore Calgaich, wanted by both the Romans and even his own people, had fled to Hibernia, there to serve the highest bidder, knowing full well that death now walked the southwestern coast of wild Caledonia. It waited patiently for the sight of him, the son of a chief, the murderer of his cousin, and the hired killer of an Hibernian king.

"The Hibernians mean you harm, *fian*," the woman said in her clear, musical voice.

Calgaich glanced behind him at the woman seated against the timberhead, surprised that she had addressed him. Then he turned back to the rail and laughed into the cold teeth of the wind. "Let the Hibernian dogs growl and show their yellow fangs behind the back of Calgaich, Cairenn, woman."

"You are indeed *An Fear Mor*," she murmured to his back.

Calgaich again looked at her. Her eyes were like emeralds set in her flawless heart-shaped face. *An Fear Mor* —The Big Man. She had spoken very little to him since he had taken her from the court of Crann, King of the Five Hostages, as a parting gift from Crann to a *fian* whom he had grown to love like a son.

"There is death in the wind," Calgaich murmured, as though to himself. He studied her. She was a beautiful chattel. "It might have been better for you to have stayed at the court of Crann."

She shivered a little and shook her head. "A slave such as myself is oftentimes nothing but bed sport for the king and his kin, only to be thrown to the drunken *fianna* and thence to the common herd when they are through with her. Their horny hands are always up beneath her skirts, and she can be rutted by any hound in the pack, like a bitch in heat."

"Do you think it will be any better in Caledonia?" he asked her harshly, still watching her.

"Perhaps so and perhaps not. I will likely live in body if not in spirit once we arrive at the *rath* of your clansmen. That can't be said for you, *fian*. Why do you court death by returning? You are an outdweller, outlawed and exiled by your deed. You are not wanted there. Even the mad sea seems to conspire against you to prevent you from returning. Turn back to Hibernia, Calgaich mac Lellan."

There was foreboding in her voice. Calgaich looked

away from her. The Ordovician woman must have known she had been hated and feared at the court of Crann of the Five Hostages. She had been one of the spoils of a great raid by the Scotti on the Ordovician coast near the holy island of Mona, once the greatest sanctuary and center of the Druids, since almost wiped out, man, woman and child by the Romans because of their fear of those strange and mystical people with their dark secrets. Because of her exceptional beauty and youth she had been brought back unharmed to King Crann and given quarters in his *rath*. Calgaich suspected that the men had been afraid of her. Her eyes, those living emeralds in a face of exquisite ivory, were thought to have masked the fearsome, ravaged face of a witch, so that no living being, held entranced by those same eyes, could see anything but the shape and semblance of the face the witch herself *wanted* them to see. It would have been only a matter of time before she would have died horribly, perhaps burned alive in a wickerwork cage, accused most probably by the jealous wife of some man who had become infatuated with Cairenn's evil beauty.

Calgaich himself was beginning to wonder why he had taken her as a parting gift from King Crann. As he was leaving, King Crann had bade him wait and sent a slave back to the settlement to fetch her. "She's yours for serving me well," he told Calgaich, and together they had watched the woman walk toward them—a slave, yet bearing her departure with dignity. Had there been a sly look on the face of aging Queen Creide as Calgaich pulled the slave woman up behind him on the war horse to ride to the sea for passage to Caledonia?

"You return because of your father, don't you, *fian?*" Cairenn asked.

Her words brought Calgaich back to the present. His powerful hands closed tighter about the forestay and the ashen shaft of his *laigen*. A cold trickle of sweat worked its way down his sides. He could not look at the *cumal*. It was not the first time Cairenn had spoken casually to him of things she could not possibly have known. Calgaich had not told her or anyone else at the court of Crann the reason why he had left the well-paid service of the king. Perhaps Paralus, the Greek trader who annually crossed the Hibernian Sea from Caledonia to trade throughout Eriu, as the Hibernians called their country, had spoken to others of what he had learned in Caledonia. Paralus was welcomed throughout Britannia, Caledonia and Hibernia, not only for the fine trade goods he carried from the continent but also for the fund of news he always brought with him. It was Paralus who had taken Calgaich aside to warn him that all was not well in the clan of the Novantae, that Lellan, the father of Calgaich and hereditary chief of the clan, had been betrayed into the hands of the Romans by Bruidge of the Battle-Axe, the younger brother of Lellan and father of Fergus, whom Calgaich had slain in fair combat.

How could she have known? She had hardly been in Crann's *rath,* or settlement, for more than a few days and then only after Paralus had already left for the most northern boundaries of the wild Scotti in Eriu.

"Look, *fian!*" Cuill cried, suddenly pointing south.

Calgaich turned. A low-lying vessel was moving swiftly through the mist tatters. Its long oars beat against the white waves, while its faded square sail was belly-swollen with wind from the howling mouth of Taranis the Pᵣ.rer. The craft was moving fast—too fast for such weather—and it was between the *birlinn* and her planned course to the south. Calgaich knew they could not be fishermen, for their boat was far too large and well manned for a simple fishing *birlinn.* There was a lean and hungry look about it. Parts of the western coast of Caledonia were infested with such predatory sea reivers.

"Who are they, *fian?*" Cairenn asked.

Swift as the strange vessel was, the smaller Hibernian *birlinn* seemed to be holding her own as she fought her way in toward the unseen coast.

Cairenn stood up and joined Calgaich at the rail. The keening wind whipped her woolen cloak back from her body, flattening her long green linen tunic and her undergown against every curve of her young form.

"Get down, fool!" Calgaich shouted to her.

A thin and eerie wailing cry arose from the other vessel. It sounded like hunting hounds who have at last seen their prey. The approaching oars beat faster and the craft began to gain, plunging deeply and showering back glittering diamond sea spray.

"It's too late, woman." Calgaich shook his head. "You have been seen. That was a foolish thing to do."

"Who are they?" she asked again, staring past him at the oncoming vessel.

Calgaich looked slowly at her, then away. His face was set like carved granite. "A reiving ship. Sea raiders."

"Britons?"

"Too far north for them. I am not sure."

She drew her damp cloak about her. "It does not matter that they've seen me. They were after us before they knew there was a woman aboard this *birlinn*."

"So?" Calgaich would not look at the witch.

"It is in my heart that they know *you* are aboard, *fian*."

He glanced sideways at her. There it was again, that accursed knowledge of hers.

She smiled faintly. "I heard it said before we left Hibernia that a fast *birlinn* had departed from there for the country of the Novantae in worse weather than that which we are facing on this wild passage. Someone there *knows* you are coming home, Calgaich mac Lellan. They do not mean to let you land in your own country."

He looked at the reiving craft. "There is nothing and *no* one who can stop me from landing in my own country."

"Even though you'd face possible death to land there?"

"Yes. I must find out whether my father is still alive."

"He is not dead," she asserted.

His eyes widened and he hastily averted his face from her. He spoke to her over his shoulder. "How do you know that?"

"I don't know how I feel these things," she replied simply. "It is a gift, or perhaps a curse."

"But you do know that he is still alive?"

She nodded. "He is alive."

He looked at her. "It was told to me by the Greek trader Paralus that my father had been betrayed into the hands of the Romans, his deadly enemies, and that he is now their prisoner and hostage. He is a frail old man and his sight is nearly gone. The Romans have a way of making a man die mysteriously just to get him out of the way."

"If he is so close to death, why do you want to get him out of the hands of the Romans?"

Calgaich spat over the side. "A womanish question," he sneered.

"You did not answer it."

"It is good for a man to die among his own people and in his own country. If he must die among his enemies, it is better that he dies on his feet, reddened blade in hand."

"And if he is dead? If I am wrong?"

Calgaich's eyes were fierce and unblinking. "Then, I am hereditary chief of the clan!"

"Who leads the clan now?"

"My father's younger brother," he replied bitterly. "Bruidge of the Battle-Axe, with whom I served my fosterage and from whom I learned the arts of the hunter and warrior."

"Then, whether your father is dead or not, what can you, one man alone, do against such a man?"

The scar on Calgaich's face twitched. The reiving vessel was getting closer to the stern of the *birlinn*. "Cuill!" he called, ignoring her question. "Stand by to come about at my signal!"

"In this wind and sea, *fian?*" Cuill shook his head.

"Do you know who they are in that boat?"

"I don't, *fian.*"

"Cruithne," Calgaich said. That and no more. He unfastened the *fibula* that held his cloak about his neck and let the heavy garment drop to the deck.

None of the ashen-faced crewmen moved. They would not look at the pursuing craft. Instead, their eyes were on the warrior in the bow of the pitching *birlinn*.

"We're doomed!" a crewman cried out. "We can't even see yonder rocky coast and yet we drive into the blinding mist like madmen!"

Calgaich again spat contemptuously over the side. He picked up his wooden, lime-whitened shield from the deck and slung it over his left shoulder. He picked up his war spear. It was a fearsome thing and yet a work of art. The foot-and-a-half-long, leaf-shaped blade was socketed and riveted to a stout ash shaft. The length of the spear was a foot taller than Calgaich. Just below the shaft socket of the blade a ruff of heron's feathers fluttered in the wind. At the butt of the shaft was a bronze balancing ball, chased and enameled blue and green in the fantastic and uncanny style of the skilled Celtish metalsmith.

Calgaich walked aft.

"Calgaich, who are the Cruithne?" Cairenn asked, following him.

He stopped and looked down at her. "The Painted People. The Picts," he replied quietly.

"We are doomed!" the crewman repeated. He lay down on the deck and covered his head with a corner of his cloak. He shivered like a frightened dog, ready to die rather than resist.

Calgaich looked at Cuill. "Have those Hibernian dogs get up. We'll need their help if we want to live."

"They are not warriors like yourself, *fian,*" Cuill reminded Calgaich.

Calgaich laughed. "I do not need warriors. I need seamen. I am Calgaich mac Lellan, son of that Lellan who once led five hundred war spears! I was a fighting man, a *fian* for King Crann of the Five Hostages. I will do all the fighting here this day!" he boasted loudly.

Cairenn could not take her eyes from Calgaich. She knew there were at least a score of ferocious Picts in the fast-closing reiving vessel. They were formidable fighters, raiders and killers. Their fierceness and savagery in battle had won for them the grudging respect of the Roman legions and of the auxiliary troops who manned the Great Wall of Hadrian, which spanned eighty miles across the full width of northern Britannia to hold back the barbarian hordes of Caledonia. Cairenn had heard much of these people in her native country. Man for man, in single-combat open battle, the Picts and the Celts could take the match of even the tough legionnaires of Rome, although they had never learned how to cope with the disciplined maneuvers of those same legionnaires, who had conquered all of the known world, with the single exception of Caledonia. Now this madman, this long-haired braggart Calgaich, seemed willing and even eager to face a score of the Picts alone.

Calgaich pushed Cuill away from the tiller bar of the steering oar. "Stand by to come about!" he ordered.

"In this wind and sea?" Cuill demanded. "It can't be done and we won't do it!"

Suddenly Calgaich's left hand slashed full across the mouth of the Hibernian, smashing him down on the deck in a spray of blood and broken teeth. Cuill rolled into the larboard waterway with blood leaking from his slack mouth. His glazed eyes stared dazedly up at Calgaich. Cairenn turned away.

"You stupid bastard!" Calgaich's voice grated. "Don't you know who those men are? If I let them take you and your chamber pot of a *birlinn*, our heads will hang in a row from their railings! They hunt heads like other men hunt hares! Now, damn you into the pit of everlasting darkness, get those shivering dogs to their feet and wait for my commands!"

Cuill staggered up to his feet. He wiped the blood from his mouth and set swiftly to work with foot and fist until his frightened crewmen stood to their lines with their fearful eyes on Calgaich. Now and then Calgaich looked back at the pursuing Pictish craft. It was hardly a good spear's throw away from the Hibernian vessel.

The *birlinn* plunged deeply, rolling wildly as it fought for its normal buoyancy. Spray showered high over its sides to drench both craft and crew alike. Cairenn felt her hands slipping on the rough wet wood. The timbers of the boat groaned as they worked in the wrenching seas.

A hail came from the approaching vessel. "Let us come alongside!" a Pict yelled hoarsely.

The words of the Pict sounded different from that of the Hibernians, the Novantae and her own people, Cairenn thought. There was an alien quality in the speech that made her shiver. She looked at the squat, helmeted man who stood in the bow of the reiving craft. There was something peculiar about the face of the helmeted Pict. He had bands of blue paint, or perhaps tattooing, on his cheeks and forehead, and the wings of his nostrils had bluish curves and spandrils about them in an intricate design. The fierce yellowish eyes peering from his grotesque manmade mask were as cold and penetrating as those of a hunting wolf. They seemed to linger on her as he surveyed their craft.

"*Fian!*" the Pict shouted.

Calgaich turned quickly. *It is in my heart that they know you are aboard, fian,* the slave woman had prophesied. Then it *was* true! A cold feeling came over Calgaich, not because of the nearness of the Picts, but because the woman had prophesied this very thing and in so doing had made it plain to Calgaich that *someone* did not want him in Caledonia—someone who had most likely made a deal with these bloody Picts to stop Calgaich from landing there.

"*Fian!*" the Pict repeated. He quickly tapped the edge of his naked sword against the small, square, blue-painted shield he carried. "Let us come alongside or you will all die!"

"For the love of all the gods, *fian*," Cuill pleaded through his bloody, broken mouth, "do as he says." He cringed at the wolf's look in Calgaich's eyes.

Calgaich eye-gauged the oncoming vessel. "Now!" he commanded, throwing his weight against the tiller bar to force over the steering oar. The *birlinn* shuddered and creaked. Cuill swiftly drove his crewmen to their work. The sails lost wind and fluttered madly, with the wet lines beating a drum tattoo against the canvas. The *birlinn* slowly heeled until the wind caught her, filling her sails with a powerful blast. She plunged deeply, as though intent on diving down to meet Nodons in his dark lair beneath the sea.

The Picts yelled wildly. Their boat lost speed as the *birlinn* cloaked the wind from them. For an instant the Pictish vessel wallowed with little way on her, and then the lean prow of the *birlinn* poked closer as Calgaich leaned full on the tiller bar. He bent his head as a spear flashed toward him. The blade swept through his hair and its shaft rapped his shoulders as it sped past into the chest of one of the crewmen. His mouth squared. He coughed thickly as blood poured from his mouth. He fell backward over the side of the vessel with the spear still sticking from his chest like some strange leafless growth.

The prow of the *birlinn* struck the bow oar on the larboard side of the other craft and snapped it like a twig, lifting the rower helplessly from the bench. The handle of the oar drove up into his chest, and hurled him upward and then over the side of the boat.

One after another the long oars were snapped off or smashed back against the side of the vessel as the *birlinn* surged close alongside it. Screaming, cursing Picts were caught by the handles of the oars and flung about within the craft. As the stern of the *birlinn* neared the stern of the other vessel a trio of Picts who had been standing near their helmsman beat their swords against their wooden shields to avert evil and readied themselves to leap aboard the slow-moving Hibernian boat.

"Cuill!" Calgaich shouted. He leaped to the side of the *birlinn* as Cuill took over the tiller bar. A Pict jumped the narrow gap between the two vessels. Swiftly the tip of Calgaich's spear met the oncoming Pict to brush aside his shield. The keen iron struck deep into the man's chest. His momentum still drove him on. Calgaich braced his legs and swung with the impetus of the Pict to lift him high into the air, squirming like a live hare on a spit. He pitchforked him clear over the far side of the *birlinn*.

A second Pict leaped the gap between the boats. He drove in hard under the downcoming spear with his shield close up under his chin while he probed eagerly for Calgaich's guts with his sword blade. An instant before the Pict's sword tip could plunge into Calgaich's belly, Calgaich brought the bronze balancing ball at the end of his spear shaft down in a smashing blow atop the Pict's battered helmet and drove it down over his eyes. He staggered blindly toward the far side of the *birlinn*. Calgaich whirled. He set himself and drove his bloody leaf-shaped spear blade into the Pict's back. The Pict shrieked just once as he plunged over the side. Calgaich drew back, letting the weight of the dying Pict withdraw the spear blade.

Lines with barbed grappling hooks were thrown over from the enemy craft. They sank into the deck of the *birlinn*. The two vessels swung close together. Three Picts readied themselves to leap as the grapnels caught fast.

Calgaich dropped his war spear and whipped out his long sword. The iron blade hissed as it cleared the bronze sheath. Calgaich swung his shield from his left shoulder to his left arm and thrust his forearm through the loops. He cut through the nearest of the grapnel lines. A Pict jumped onto the deck of the *birlinn*. He slashed wildly at Calgaich's grinning face. Calgaich's shield struck the shield of the Pict with a grinding of the metal bosses. The reiver was staggered. The sword tip flicked in once, hardly a few inches, and the Pict was dead before he hit the deck. He rolled against Calgaich's legs. Calgaich leaped high over the fallen Pict and met another reiver with a downsweep of his sword. At the same time he raised the metal edge of his shield under the chin of the Pict. The man died instantly between the two surfaces.

Calgaich jumped back. He screamed above the rising fury of the storm wind. *"Abu! Abu!* To victory! To victory!" He leaped to the low railing while thrusting once into the thigh of a charging Pict. He reversed his blow and slashed the man's contorted face open from temple to chin.

Calgaich then leaped like a cat across to the pitching afterdeck of the Pictish craft. He met the determined rush of half a dozen tattooed killers. His great sword blade whirled high and came down like a flash of solid lightning, again and again, battering on shields and helmets, striking musically from the blades of the Picts, darting and hissing like a thing alive and drawing blood at almost every stroke, spattering the droplets in a reddish haze about the knot of fighting, cursing men.

"Do you hear the wild fowl calling?" Calgaich the Swordsman chanted. He was *fey,* with the mystical battle madness of the Celt. "The ravens gather for your flesh! Come to the sword welcoming, Cruithne! A red welcome for a feast of sea-wolves! Do not stand back, you who come unbidden! Is my welcome to you the doorway to sudden death?" He laughed wildly.

"He is *fey!* The battle madness is on him!" Cuill screamed hysterically to the crew. "He cares not whether he lives or dies just so he can keep on killing! Cut loose the lines, Usnect! Let the mad *fian* die!"

Cairenn could remain still no more. Overcoming her fear, she ran along the full length of the deck. She snatched up Calgaich's war spear, the bloodied weapon, the mighty *laigen.* It felt strange in her hands, heavy, wet with blood, but she had to learn its use *now.* She leaned the tip of the blade lightly against Cuill's chest so as to draw a little of the red, just a very little. Her stomach heaved, but she must not falter. "Do not move, Cuill." The words grated between her even white teeth. Her emerald eyes never left his face. "If you move, I will do thus." She leaned on the spear, and Cuill shrieked in pain and hysteria far greater than her own. The crewmen slowly backed away from the lines, hypnotized by Cairenn's threats and the sight of a woman armed.

Calgaich's shield was splintered from top to boss; blood splattered its whitewashed surface. A Pict went down screaming and struck up at Calgaich's crotch with a broken-bladed sword. Calgaich caught him full in the face with a smashing heel, and then he leaped back to parry a vicious sword blow from another burly Pict. He calmly swept his sword sideways to shear through the tough wooden shield of the Pict. The man's sight was destroyed in the red jelly left in the blade's deadly track. Calgaich slammed his shield into that of the blinded man and drove him back against three of his cursing mates who called hysterically for a sword stroke or two at this stinging gadfly who had landed in their midst.

Calgaich retreated to the railing of the Picts' vessel, holding them in check with reddened sword. He swiftly looked back over his shoulder at the pitching *birlinn* just yards away. "Cut loose," he shouted.

Cairenn hesitated, slightly lessening her pressure on the war spear piercing Cuill's chest.

"He tells us to cut loose himself," Cuill wailed. "We must obey."

But Cairenn shook her head. The wind whipped her long dark hair back from her face. "Not without you, *fian*," she called to Calgaich above the wrath of the waves.

"Now!" Calgaich roared at her again.

But again Cairenn held firm, allowing Cuill to feel her weight behind the bloody spear. The crewmen remained motionless, caught in time between two forces they did not understand.

Calgaich thrust hard and missed. He then recovered and slashed his blade into a Pict's unprotected crotch to emasculate him. The man reeled back against his screaming mates. Calgaich then hurled his blood-dripping sword like a javelin across the widening gap between the boats and leaped across to catch up the sword as the tip of it struck quivering into the deck. Whirling about he thrust out the sword just as a last Pict, blood-maddened and heedless of sudden death, jumped after him. The sword point darted into the Pict's chest and was withdrawn as the Pict fell backward into the water between the two vessels.

Cuill, released from the point of the war spear, worked frantically to free the lines. Gradually the *birlinn* fell away. It wallowed in the vicious crosswaves, wind filling the mainsail. Light throwing spears, the deadly *slegs,* arced across the widening gap between the two boats. Calgaich laughed as he swung his sword in rhythm, first to one side and then to the other, striking the light *slegs* and spinning them away into the whitecapped waters.

Cuill stared at Calgaich. "He is not human," he muttered. Cairenn, too, gazed in wonder at Calgaich as she wiped her hands on her wet woolen cloak, as if to wipe away all memory of the bloody war spear that she had held only moments before. She had disobeyed him—for a warrior in battle the punishment was certain death. Yet she would do it again.

Finally, as the *birlinn* left the reiving craft behind, Calgaich caught one of the light spears in a show of strength and threw it back to find the heart of one last Pict. He stood at the rail in a solemn moment of triumph before he came aft to where Cuill had once again taken over the tiller bar. He looked sternly at Cairenn, as if he were about to speak, but then strode past her to the steering oar. Resting his sword tip on the deck beside Cuill, he spoke. "Sail for the coast," he ordered. The wildness of bloody battle had left him. He was no longer *fey.* Once again he was the calm and confident *fian.*

This time there was no denial from Cuill.

CHAPTER 2

Hours after the battle, fear came down from the low overcast sky and settled silently on the deck of the pitching *birlinn*. It had come to stay.

"*Fian!*" Cuill screamed from the afterdeck. "We must turn back to the open sea. We can try for the coast when the weather changes; we are too far north of your landing place now. It is two days' sail to the south. If we don't turn back, we'll lose my *birlinn* and our lives as well."

Calgaich did not answer him. Instead, he untwisted his left arm torque of gold and tossed it the full length of the vessel so that it clattered on the deck at the feet of Cuill, who scooped it up despite his paralyzing fear of the dangerous coast in the mist somewhere ahead of them. It had been King Crann's gift to one of his favorite *fianna*, as the woman, Cairenn, had been. Crann paid his warriors well. The arm torque could keep Cuill in comfort for many years to come. He slid it inside his tunic.

Cairenn looked up into the face of her master. "Cuill is right. The gods do not mean to let you return home."

"Quiet!" Calgaich snapped. "The sea will hear you!"

As though the sea had indeed heard, it began to work itself into an increased white-maned fury. The timbers of the *birlinn* creaked and groaned in the powerful grip of the waves. Despite the beating of the wind the mist had not dissipated. It was almost as though it were semisolid in content. Perhaps the gods had placed it there to prevent the *birlinn* from making a landfall.

Calgaich pointed with his spear. "There! Nodons shows his teeth!"

Black-fanged rocks wreathed in foaming white rivulets that streamed back into the dark waves had appeared

23

on both sides of the vessel. Beyond them were more rocks in serried ranks, as though Nodons had ringed the *birlinn* with sharpened stakes that could pierce her wooden sides as easily as a bone needle pierces cloth.

"Turn back! Turn back!" the crewmen screamed in unison.

It was too late.

No vessel in the known world could have turned within the scope of those grinning rock teeth and won free to the open sea. Nodons was playing his bitter game to the death well. He would win as he almost always had won. The rock jaws seemed to close in on the *birlinn*. A pointed needle of a rock ripped into the thin bottom planking and raked its way from stem to stern with a sickening crunching sound. The sound passed into the very souls of the humans aboard the *birlinn*.

There was one exception to the fear that seemed to paralyze all the others—the tall warrior. He peered eagerly into the wreathing mist. His nostrils were drawn wide like those of a questing hound. He could smell the land. "There she looms!" Calgaich cried in an exultant voice. He pointed with his spear. "Albu! Albu!" he shouted. There was great longing in his voice.

Cairenn, forgetting her own fear for a moment, looked with wonder at Calgaich. His face was drawn as though he were in great pain, and yet it was alive with the same eagerness she had noticed on his face when he had fought *fey*, like a madman, on the deck of the Pictish reiving craft. It was almost as if Calgaich spoke of a woman he had known and loved well and for whom he had hungered during the long years he had been outlawed from Caledonia. It was the desperate, longing cry of the exiled Celt.

A dark headland showed through the mist. Another sound more terrible than the incessant whine of the wind came to the people on the doomed *birlinn*. It was the grinding of the surf boiling against the rocks and shale of the shore and the great dragging withdrawals of the waves that battered at the coast. Rocks stabbed at the slowly sinking hull of the vessel. The driving waves savagely worried at her like unsated hounds at their meat. Suddenly the *birlinn* struck hard, tilting wearily to one side like a stricken thing seeking its last resting place. She began to settle. Waves swept freely over the weather rail and carried some of the screaming crewmen over the lee side. The mast tilted and then cracked at the deck line to collapse over the side.

Cairenn watched in horror as Calgaich threw off his tartan cloak, unbuckled his belt and dropped it and the heavy-sheathed sword to the deck. He withdrew his dirk from its sheath and thrust it inside his tunic. He poised the magnificent war spear and cast it toward the beach. It flashed through the tatters of mist and struck into the dark sands to quiver there like a living thing.

The *birlinn* was breaking up. Waves flowed knee-deep over the deck. All of the crewmen had vanished into the sea. Cairenn waited for the sea to claim her next. Only Cuill clung to the useless tiller, while staring ahead to see his own death approaching, unable to save himself while his beloved *birlinn* died first, broken beneath his feet.

Calgaich undid his thick gold neck torque. He hurled it into the sea. "Nodons!" he cried. "Take this as an offering for a safe passage to shore for myself and the woman!"

He slid over the prow into the sea. For a moment his hard gray eyes held the emerald-hued eyes of Cairenn. In that moment she was almost sure he meant to leave her to drown. It was his right. His own life came first. She was only a *cumal*, a chattel to be dealt with like any other piece of property.

"Can you swim, woman?" he shouted.

She nodded. "I can, *fian*."

"Then strip and get into the bath." He grinned.

She hesitated. Her eyes were wide with fear.

"Now!" he snapped. "Or, by the gods, Nodons shall have a tasty morsel this night in his black cavern beneath the sea."

She had no choice. She stripped off her cloak, long tunic and undergown to reveal full young breasts budded with pink, fine hips and shapely thighs, and the soft curling mat of darkness where her long legs met the flatness of her belly. She stood there naked to the biting teeth of the wind and the icy pelting of the sea spray.

Calgaich's admiring gaze shifted. He ripped a plank loose from the disintegrating hull and beckoned to her. She let herself down into the cold water and felt his hard hands pass along her body to help her straddle the rough plank. Calgaich struck out for the shore while he guided the plank with his left hand. Waves flowed over Cairenn's shivering nakedness and it seemed as though she could never get enough air into her lungs to breathe. Twice Calgaich went fully under, only to emerge with his long hair plastered across his face. The second time he came up his temple skin was split and there was a faint pink tint of blood in the wetness on his features.

Rocks seemed to drift past. Then the surf took charge of them, changing momentarily from a frothing maelstrom into a gentle surging that swung them safely past the rocks and then tumbled them over and over again in a melee of water and churning sand to carry them to the beach.

Cairenn opened her eyes. She lay on the hard wet shingle covered by Calgaich's cloak. His spear was still thrust into the sand close beside her. Spindrift blew horizontally from the sea toward the gloomy shoreline, where Calgaich stood knee-deep in the surf looking out to sea. There was no sign of the *birlinn*.

Calgaich turned toward her as he wiped the blood from his face. He could not resist smiling at her. She was enveloped in the tartan cloak with just her pale face and those great green eyes of hers looking up at him like a frightened hare peering from its hole.

"Nodons threw me back my cloak," Calgaich said. "Perhaps it was a wager between us. Nodons lost."

"Not by much, *fian*." She shivered a little.

"But still a victory."

"Must there always be victories for you?"

He studied her. She had a way of disarming him from his trained viewpoint of life. "There is glory and honor in good battle."

"And in death?"

He shrugged. "What is there to lose? There is a better life hereafter in *Tir na n'Og* for a warrior such as myself."

She smiled faintly. "The Beautiful Land of Youth, where there is no pain, disease or death. Where a warrior may feast and drink, fornicate and fight to his heart's content throughout eternity."

Calgaich nodded his head absentmindedly. "West-Over-Seas," he murmured. He looked at her suddenly, trying to gauge whether or not she was subtly baiting him. "Get up. The storm is still rising. We'll need shelter to survive this night." He withdrew his spear from the sand and wiped the blade on his tunic.

"Where are we?" Cairenn asked, rising awkwardly from the sand.

"Too damned far north for comfort. Perhaps in the land of the Fir Domnann, the Damnonii. We can't be far from the land of the Picts."

She shivered. "Such as those in the reiving vessel?"

He nodded. "There has been bad blood between the Damnonii and my people of the Novantae for some years."

"And the Picts as well?"

Calgaich smiled crookedly. "Most of the time we are at war with them. There have been several times in the past when we were allied with them but only for short periods. Paralus, the Greek trader, told me there are rumors in Caledonia that the border clans—the Novantae, Selgovae and the Votadini—may ally themselves with the Damnonii, the Picts and the Older People of Caledonia against the Romans. It was done in the past, in the time of my grandfather, Evicatos the Spearman, and even in the days of my father Lellan, when I was very young. It was Evicatos who led the alliance against the Great Wall of the Romans, to cross it and raid almost to Londinium. My father and my uncle were young warriors then." His voice faded and a faraway look came into his eyes.

"And this new alliance, do you think it will take place?"

"Who knows? I find it hard to believe. The Damnonii might be agreeable to it if they believed in any one leader. The Picts likely not. That has always been the trouble with the Caledonians. We've never learned to unify and work together against our hated common enemy—the Romans!"

"You need a new leader, like your grandfather Evicatos the Spearman."

He nodded. "But where is he?"

She studied him for a moment. "Perhaps I know," she said quietly.

He reached out a big hand to her damp shoulder and

drew her close to look down at her. His face was hard and set like amber. "Listen, woman! Only by the grace of the gods did you get to leave Eriu alive!" He bent closer to her face, trying to see through the beauty of it into the real face of this feminine creature whom men suspected of being a witch. It was no use. Her loveliness and great eyes effectively concealed whatever fearsome sight might lay hidden behind them. "I will tell you only once," Calgaich added. "Do not prophesy in this country of mine, or your death will come so swiftly you will not know that it's coming. Or perhaps they will sentence you to the long death, with hours of agony and hell before you die. Do you understand?"

She nodded. "I will remember," she promised.

He turned away. "We've got to find shelter. We can't survive on this open beach."

Calgaich led the way up from the lonely strand, which was haunted by the screaming of the low-wheeling gulls as they hovered over the place where the *birlinn* had gone down. Cairenn trudged after Calgaich, bruising her slender feet on the rounded pebbles of the shingle. Now and again she would look up at his broad back. She remembered all too well the look on his face as he had eyed her naked body when she had stood on the deck of the *birlinn*. She remembered, too, the touch of his hands as he helped her straddle the plank that carried her ashore. She shivered a little thinking of the harsh rape that was bound to come sooner or later. Was that why he had saved her? Yet she shivered not only from fear but also from a strange anticipation of his body on hers, forcing her to his will. Yes, that time would come. She pulled the tartan cloak more tightly around her shoulders and hurried to catch up to him.

They stopped at the crest of a low hillock that overlooked the sea. The gray-bearded waves rolled in against the shoreline in serried ranks, and a thundering shock could be felt through the trembling earth at their feet.

She looked up at his taut face. "What is it, *fian?* The Picts again?"

Calgaich shook his head. "The *birlinn* was a good craft. She was as swift as a seal, and she rode the white-maned sea horses like a gull. It was a terrible sight to see her die like that, a broken thing at the mercy of the seas." It was almost as though he spoke of a once living thing.

"And the men who died with her, *fian?* Do you not think of them?"

He looked at her. "They were there by choice, woman. The *birlinn* was not." He turned away from her and strode on across the sandy, hummocked ground, wigged here and there with coarse furze bushes.

A great land-cup lay within a grim circle of lowering hills whose tops were crowned with thick low-lying clouds of dark gray that seemed to be racing inland, driven by the powerful western wind. A sea loch of leaden-colored water probed into the land. Drifting mist hung throughout the great land-cup within the embrace of the hills. The strong salt smell of the sea hung in the air. A light drizzling of cold rain began to descend.

A humped earthen mound stood not far from the steep slope of one of the hills, as though a giant of nature had lain down to rest and covered himself with a thick cloak of bracken and heather. The sea wind ruffled the growths as if beneath them the huge chest of the giant were rising and falling in his deep sleep.

Calgaich stopped short. He quested with eyes, ears and nose as if he were a hunting hound. His hands tightened, white-knuckled, on the shaft of his spear.

"What is it?" Cairenn whispered.

He shook his head. His eyes were fixed almost hypnotically on the huge earthen mound.

Caireen waited uneasily, puzzled and shivering. She looked curiously about herself and made out a rough circle of great, lichen-covered stones standing on end, half-sunken in the thick turf. The stones encircled the mound. She eyed the mound more closely. A cold and eerie feeling came over her. This was no curious feat of nature. The mound was manmade. Between the upright stones at one end of the mound were the remains of a paved open court that reached to the front of the mound. Slowly Cairenn perceived a rough doorway set into the end of the mound. It had uprights and a lintel of age-eaten, lichened granite. Bracken hung about the shadowed doorway like a ragged beard around the mouth of a toothless old man.

She could not help herself. "Calgaich?" she cried.

He did not move. He had been unafraid of the hungry sea between Hibernia and Caledonia. He had not feared to turn back the *birlinn* to face the pursuing Pictish reivers. He had not been fearful of casting himself into the watery domain of mighty Nodons. Now something deeply frightening had come silently through the overcast to roost on the broad back of the *fian*. It was something that had swiftly woven a slimy green thread of fear through the bright red fabric of his great courage.

"Calgaich?" Cairenn drew closer to him.

There was no sign of life within that foggy land-cup encircled by the gloomy hills. The only things that moved were the drifting mist and clouds, and the uneasy gray waters of the mysterious-looking sea loch.

He turned slowly to look down at her, hidden fear lurking within his eyes. "It is a Holy Place," he murmured.

"Then there is nothing to fear."

He shook his head. "You don't understand. It is a barrow. The Ancient Ones, the Little Dark People, left such places. *This is the place of the Horned One,* woman."

A cold feeling like the tracing of a sharp icicle tip went down her spine. She hesitated, then said softly, "I did not think you feared the Old Ones, *fian*."

"It is not them!" he lied hastily. "It is the men who might still worship here that are to be feared."

"The Painted Ones?"

He shook his head. "More likely the Damnonii. They came from the south long, long ago, and either killed or drove away the Little Dark People." He looked beyond the mound toward the distant hills. "The Damnonii do not like trespassers," he added.

"I see no one." Cairenn moved closer to him.

Calgaich fingered his spear shaft. "No one that can be *seen*," he murmured softly. "Can't you smell the evil? There is a stench of old blood about this place."

"If the Damnonii think so much of it, why isn't it guarded?"

Calgaich wet his dry lips. "It *is* guarded," he whispered.

"I see no one. I hear no one."

"The Horned One."

Cairenn asked no more questions. She knew by the tone of his voice that he felt something alive and evil lurking here, something he could not or would not explain to her. The faint howling of a wolf came from far across the great cup of land shielded by the mist-haunted hills. The howling did not sound real to her.

Calgaich bent his head. His hands tightened on his spear shaft, as though in doing so he would gain spiritual strength from it. "Lugh of the Shining Spear," he prayed, calling on his god. Cairenn waited quietly, her head bowed, for him to finish. The wolf howled again.

Calgaich raised his head. He strode purposefully toward the mound as though he had gained that strength for which he had just prayed. Without hesitation he passed between two of the ancient ring stones. Cairenn came just behind him. Calgaich approached the furze-shrouded doorway of the barrow. An old hide studded with age-greened bronze bosses hung in the doorway. He thrust out his left hand with the first and little fingers extended and the two middle fingers bent within the palm—the sign to avert evil. He pulled aside the hide. The bronze bosses clashed dully together as he did so. Calgaich looked quickly about as though someone else other than Cairenn might have heard the sound. Then he motioned for her to follow him and disappeared inside. Cairenn glanced over her shoulder at the surrounding mist, which seemed to grow thicker, before moving forward. The bronze bosses felt rough to her touch as she pushed them aside to enter. Then she became Calgaich's shadow as he felt his way within a passageway. The flagstones were cold against her bare feet. An indescribable odor drifted about them like the dank breath of an ancient tomb. Then this icy miasma settled about them as though welcoming them into the barrow. Welcoming them in to what? Cairenn thought. The aura was that of stale blood; lichened stone, damp with the moisture of many centuries; and above all, the odor of ancient evil from deep within the bowels of the earth itself.

Calgaich paused. "Lugh of the Shining Spear," he murmured again. Cold sweat dewed his forehead and trickled down his sides. He must move on. There was no other recourse. It was more than his fear of the unknown that he must overcome. He could not show fear in front of this slave woman. That was beneath the dignity of any warrior of the Novantae.

Calgaich moved on through the clammy darkness, probing the shadows with the tip of his spear. Now and again the metal chimed musically as it struck stone.

Calgaich squeezed past a pillar that divided the passageway in two. He moved on with the woman holding onto the tail of his tunic like a little child following its mother. He stopped. "This is like entering the pit of hell itself. We need light." He fumbled at his waist and passed a sealed bladder back to Cairenn. She untied the bladder and took the firestones and some dry tinder from within it. Then she crouched on the cold, flagged floor and struck the firestones together until they shed sparks into the tinder. There was a faint glowing amidst the tinder, like a ruby on black velvet as the flame caught quickly. She snatched up the tinder and blew sharply on it until it was fully afire.

They stood at the entrance to a wide circular room. The roof was just inches above Calgaich's head. Dried reeds and twigs lay to one side. He motioned toward them. Cairenn placed the burning tinder among the reeds and fanned them into flame and warmth. A fitful flame rose.

Calgaich sucked in his breath as the light grew. This *was* the Holy of Holies. The room was very large and roughly circular in shape. Rough-hewn pillars held up the wide stone slabs that formed the subroof on which lay the heaped earth that shaped the mound over the barrow. Beyond the circular room were dark cells, or galleries, from within which came the slow sound of dripping water. The walls were veined with dampness and textured with lichens. The shadows of Calgaich and Cairenn leaped and postured on the damp walls as they moved about.

There was a low stone table or altar at the far end of the room. A ring of white stone was set into the flagstones before the altar. Several exquisitely shaped, fine-grained greenstone axe heads lay within the ring of white stone, mingled with two finely figured bronze axe heads, which had evidently been deliberately broken in half.

Calgaich moved cautiously toward the altar. A cup beautifully shaped from amber was on the altar. The inside seemed to be coated with a dark material like pitch.

A cold feeling crept through Calgaich, for he knew what the substance was, perhaps the blood of a deer or a black cock, or possibly that of another sacrifice—a human—a slave or a condemned criminal. A slave woman? Calgaich did not look back at the lovely face of Cairenn. He hoped she would not notice the amber cup.

Cairenn fed the growing fire from a large pile of branches and pieces of log that lay to one side of the chamber. Steam arose from the damp wood and from the heavy woolen cloak to mist within the chamber. She watched Calgaich as he poked about with the tip of his ever-ready spear. He used it almost as if it were an extension of his arms.

Calgaich leaned his spear against a pillar and then rummaged about within a pile of something heaped behind the pillar. "By Lugh!" he called out. "He has answered my prayers!" His hands had closed on the hilt of a sheathed sword. He held it out to the light. The sheath was of finely-worked and figured bronze and the drag of it was shaped like a serpent's head with its mouth wide open to show its fangs. Its hilt was beautifully fashioned of ivory and wood with a pommel and guard of enameled bronze.

Calgaich stepped back and withdrew the iron-bladed sword from the scabbard with a crisp hissing of the metal. The long, leaf-shaped blade of polished gray iron reflected the dancing firelight like the sun shining on swiftly running water, so that the blade seemed like a tongue of flame itself.

There was a look of sheer ecstasy in Calgaich's eyes. Cairenn watched fascinated as he swung the heavy, balanced blade in slashes, thrusts, parries, crosscuts and a curious weaving pattern that was so swift in its execution she could have sworn she saw the reflection of the blade tip still hanging in the smoky air even after it had passed on.

The sweat of exertion broke out on Calgaich's face and flew from it with his rapid movements. It was almost as if he were repeating his recent battle with the Picts. Now Cairenn knew why Cuill had once spoken of Calgaich with awe and deep-seated fear. *"Don't you know who he is?"* he had asked with astonishment, when she had inquired about her new master. *Calgaich the Swordsman! One*

*of the wild Novantae from southwestern Caledonia who
have no peers in the red wet work of the blades! Calgaich,
son of Lellan, who is lord of five hundred war spears and
the deadliest of all enemies to the Romans! Calgaich mac
Lellan, grandson of Evicatos the Spearman! Calgaich the
Swordsman!* Cairenn knew now who Calgaich's true gods
were—weapons and red battle!

Calgaich lowered the fine blade and ran a thumb along
both edges. He tested the point, the heft and balance of
the sword. He studied the finely figured metal of the
blade, which had been cunningly inset with fine gold
wire in the symmetrical, intertwined patterns that Celts
loved so well. He snapped the nail of a first finger against
the metal and then quickly raised the blade to his ear
as if he were listening for something within it. He raised
the sword and tapped it against the low stone ceiling so
that it rang musically, then quickly placed it next to his
ear again. A strange and faraway look came over his face.

"Does it speak to you, *fian?*" Cairenn asked in an awed
voice.

He stared at her across the blade. It was almost as
if she were looking at a stranger, so different was his
expression. "Aye, woman," he replied softly. "There is
a spirit guardian within all master blades."

"Who is the spirit guardian of that blade?"

He grinned at her like a hunting wolf. "The wolf howls
within the blade. It is a good omen for Calgaich, for the
wolves are my foster brothers in spirit." He held the awe-
some weapon out toward her. "See here? The mark of a
master smith." He tapped a finger on the blade just beneath the cross guard. She leaned close to it and saw the
punch marks of the smith—an oval stamping of two gaunt
wolves with their forepaws resting against a bell-shaped
stone tower while their heads were held back with open
jaws as though they were howling. Under the stamping
were some cryptic symbols.

She looked up into his shadowed face. "What does it
mean? Who was he?"

"Examine the blade of my war spear," he said quietly.
He looked toward the wall of the chamber but it seemed
to Cairenn that he was looking far beyond the wall of

the barrow at something she could never see and would never understand.

She took the heavy war spear and turned it so that the firelight shone on the base of its blade. The same design she had seen on the sword blade was also punch-marked into the base of the spear blade. A strange feeling ran through her hands. She quickly leaned the spear back against the pillar and returned to sit near the fire.

"The war spear was that of my grandfather—Evicatos," Calgaich quietly explained. "He was the greatest war leader of all Albu in his time. Long ago he led the People of the North—the Novantae, Selgovae, Damnonii, Votadini, the Picts and the Older People—across the Great Wall of the Roman emperor Hadrian. They fought against three Roman legions and were driven back in time, but they almost reached Londinium! Evicatos was an older man then but still a great warrior. My father and my uncle rode with him on that raid. Evicatos left that spear to my father who in turn gave it to me when I left Caledonia to take service with the *fianna*." It was as if he were speaking to himself or to someone unseen beyond the barrow.

"And the sword?" she asked, bringing him back to his story.

He looked down at the fine weapon, a masterpiece of the swordsmith's craft. "A master smith came to the country of the Novantae when Evicatos was first chief of the clan. The fame of Evicatos had spread far and wide even then. This smith asked only to forge weapons for my grandfather. He wanted nothing but his food, a woman to cook for him and to sleep with him, and a place to work. He wanted no payment until he could finish his work. Then he would ask for what he wanted. My grandfather promised him that he could have anything he desired.

"That long winter the smith worked steadily, letting no one see him at his work. Night after night the people saw the flame of his forge within his shelter and heard the ringing of the metal as he worked. At times he would leave the *rath* and vanish into the dense woods to the north where he would be gone for many days. When he would return he told no one of where he had been.

"In the spring his work was done. Both weapons were magnificent. They were masterpieces of the metalsmith's craft. None had ever been seen like them. They would help Evicatos become an even greater warrior than he already was." Calgaich's voice died away.

"What price did he want for his work?" Cairenn asked.

"My grandfather's betrothed. Muirgheal was her name. Muirgheal the Beautiful. That was who he wanted."

It was very quiet. Cairenn dared not speak.

Calgaich looked into the flames. "My grandfather was a man of honor."

"And the smith took his betrothed?"

Calgaich nodded, staring into the flames.

"But how did the sword of Evicatos, if it *is* the same sword, come to be in this evil place so far from your country?"

"It *is* the same sword," Calgaich said harshly. "Although my grandfather kept his word, the smith did not. He stole from the *rath* at night with the woman and the sword. My grandfather's two younger brothers trailed the smith to the north against the wishes of my grandfather. They reached the land of the Picts. Before the snow fell, the younger brother returned with the woman. His brother had paid the death price."

"What happened to the smith?"

"He was never seen again. Some say the Picts slew him. Others say he fled from Albu. Some think he was not a human at all, but rather a demon smith."

Cairenn looked quickly back over her shoulders.

"My grandfather took Muirgheal to wife."

The fire was crackling low. Shadows crept back into the chamber from the galleries where they had been lurking. The slow dripping of the water seeping through the roof of the barrow could be plainly heard.

"She bore my grandfather's first son more than a month early," Calgaich continued quietly.

"Your father?"

Calgaich nodded. He placed the sword on the altar and then stripped off his tunic and trousers. He stood there naked except for a thin breechclout that concealed his strong and full manhood. Her eyes narrowed as she saw the crisscross whitish welts on his back. At one time in his life he had been lashed to within a hair's breadth of death. Calgaich hung his trousers and tunic on the edge of the altar to dry. She could see welts and scars beneath the mat of curling, reddish-golden hair on his chest, and she knew these did not come from the bite of the many-tailed cat. Her eyes widened as she noted the bluish tattooing in a curious interwoven pattern on his chest and upper arms.

"You've never seen the warrior patterns?" he asked with a slow smile. He moved closer to the firelight and tapped the designs with his finger tips. "I received my first solid food from the tip of my father's dirk. When I was two years old, they needle-pricked the warrior patterns on my chest and arms and then rubbed in the blue woad. When I was nine years old, I started my fosterage under my father's younger brother, Bruidge of the Battle-Axe. I started my warrior training then. We threw the *sleg,* the light spear, at first against straw targets daubed in different colors. Our spear teacher was Felim of the Long Arm. There was none better." His voice rose in a chanting lilt and he seemed again to look far beyond the barrow and beyond the mist-shrouded hills and grim, wolf-fanged mountains to his homeland. "We threw the *sleg* with all our young strength at the straw targets as Felim called out their particular colors. To hit the wrong target was shameful. To miss altogether a disgrace! For six years we cubs ran with our own pack, hunting under the guidance of Guidd One-Eye, who was like a wolf himself in the forest. We handled the hounds and rode the shaggy ponies. We learned to handle the light chariots over the roughest ground. We learned swordsmanship and the infighting of the dirk. We hurled the *sleg,* and the heavier *gae,* until we could handle the great *laigen,* the hand lance, until we had no peers in the work! There were none better! And Calgaich mac Lellan was the greatest of them all!"

Cairenn fed the fire. She was used to the boasting of her own Ordovician kinsmen and more so to that of the mad Hibernians. All those of Celtic blood were alike, great boasters and fighters, quarrelsome and touchy. Their honor, such as it was, was not easily satisfied, except by payment of blood.

Calgaich wiped the sweat from his face. The mystical light died in his gray eyes. He stared at her as though suddenly realizing she was there.

"The scars on your chest, *fian?*" she asked. He seemed to want to talk.

"The bite of the blade; the slashing of wolf fangs."

She gathered her courage. "And those on your back?"

His face became set and dark with the congested blood beneath the skin. For a moment she thought he was going to strike her. Her questions had finally proved too many for him. At last he turned away from her and picked up his clothing. He held the clothing out to her. "Dry them, woman!" he ordered harshly. He reached for his spear. "Give me the cloak," he added.

"It is all I have," she protested, pulling it more closely around herself.

"Give it to me!"

She stood up and tried to give him eye for eye, but it was of no use. He reached out and stripped the cloak from her nakedness. He did not even look at her as he flung the cloak about his own shoulders and walked into the passageway that led to the outer world. She heard the dull clashing of the bronze bosses on the hide door as he passed out into the dusk.

She shivered as she passed her tapered hands down her body, feeling her outthrust breasts and her nipples hardened by the cold instead of the heat of passion. Calgaich was a strange man. The thought of him possessing her gave her a curious intermingling of images. She had a delicious scared feeling of having him overpower her to slake his hunger in her young, virginal body, and a wanton desire to throw herself at him so that she, too, might slake the fire she felt deep within her bowels.

Her eyes flicked about the gloomy chamber. Evidently no one had been here for many years. Dust was thick where the water did not drip. Soon ruin would overtake the barrow. The Damnonii or whoever had worshipped here after the time of the Little Dark People would hardly come back now. They had left something behind, however, in addition to the votive offerings of the polished greenstone axe heads and the broken bronze axe heads. They had left behind them a feeling of intense and indescribable evil.

Cairenn gathered up Calgaich's tunic and trousers from the altar and began to dry the garments. It was better to keep busy than to think of past memories, which she had held at bay till now. Of her parents and brother murdered in the bloody raid by the Scotti as they swept down the Ordovician coast. Of her betrothed felled by one of the last flying spears as he bade his men flee before him. And better yet not to dwell on what the future might hold for her beyond the first nights of Calgaich's lust, before he tired of her. She did not dare to look beyond the flickering circle of firelight for fear of what she might see, and yet it was the lurking unseen that put the fear of the unknown, so rank in that place of horror, into the very marrow of her shapely bones.

CHAPTER 3

Calgaich walked across the lichened courtyard flagging toward the nearby hill-slope. The cold rain slanted down in a fine misty drizzle. The fitful wind had died away and the sea boomed faintly in the distance. Calgaich worked his way up the hill-slope to a great outcropping of rock like the dislocated bones of a giant skeleton, until he found a series of shallow caves formed by overhanging slabs of rock. The bottoms of the caves were thickly layered with comparatively dry bracken. He nodded in satisfaction and started back up the hill until he reached the crest.

The wind started in again, switchtailing back and forth as though uncertain about which way to blow. Calgaich stopped short with distended nostrils. The faint, bittersweet smell of woodsmoke came to him on a shifting of the wind. He leaned on his spear and peered into the misty dimness toward the distant hills and the head of the sea loch. There was no sight nor sound of humanity in the great gloomy glen that probed deeply into the hard belly of the looming mountains. He had vague recollections of being somewhere in this area on a raid when he had been very young. Perhaps it had been his first raid, but he wasn't sure. Whoever lived in this area would hardly be out on the prowl on such a foul night, and it was unlikely they would come near the barrow at night in any case, much less in day light.

Calgaich returned down the hill and gathered armloads of the dry bracken, which he carried to the barrow and deposited just within the entrance. Then he returned to the top of the hill. He thrust his head forward to peer and sniff into the dimness like a stalking wolf until he was satisfied that there were no humans about the area. Still, it bothered him that someone dwelt not too far away.

He came softly down the hill and paused near the rock outcropping. Something moved at his feet, and from sheer instinct he stamped his foot on a small creature. He heard the dying squeak of a hare. Something ran over his feet and he struck out with the butt of his spear to pin another hare to the ground. He bent and twisted its neck. A third hare leaped from shelter and sped down the slope. Calgaich whirled and poised the war spear. The hare cut sharply to the left but the tip of the blade spitted it to the ground.

Calgaich grinned in the dimness as he walked to where the spear still quivered through the body of the hare and into the soft turf. "Poor sport for you, my brother," he consoled the spear.

He carried the limp hares into the barrow. The fire had burned down to embers. He looked about for the woman. "There is food here to be cooked," he said to the shadows.

Cairenn came out slowly. Calgaich's face cracked into a grin. She wore his tunic, which reached below her knees. The folds of the material did little justice to her figure.

Calgaich flung down the hares. "Skin and prepare them," he ordered.

"I don't know how," she admitted, looking with distaste at the dead animals at her feet. "I was never a serving wench."

"And highborn, I suppose?" he asked sarcastically.

"Yes, *fian*," she said, raising her eyes to him, remembering a time when she was not a slave.

Calgaich grunted. He knelt beside the fire and drew his dirk. He swiftly skinned and gutted the hares as Cairenn watched. He spitted them on peeled branches and then rigged a forked rest for them over the fire. It was all done in a matter of a few minutes. He looked sideways at her. "Surely you can sit here beside the warmth of the fire and see that the food does not burn, woman. Or is that, too, beyond a lady?"

There was a swift shadow of anger across her face. "In my land my father was the equal of yours and commanded many men; and the bravest warrior among them was my betrothed. I did not bloody my hands with the common table fare, nor tend the fires which cooked it. I gave the orders to the serving wenches who did that work. But there are other things I know." She remembered the warm hearths of her father's *rath,* of long evenings of tales and song, and her anger grew. "My fortune has changed, and I like it not—this dark and silent chamber— *but I have not changed."*

He stood up and wiped his hands on his breechclout. "I will not raise my hand to you this time. Listen to me! We are not in my country of the Novantae. It will take days of living and running like hunted animals, and perhaps some fighting as well, before we can reach it. I can fight for you, but you must run for yourself, and there are other things you must and will do, and one of them is the preparing of the food I will find for us. Is that understood?"

"Yes, *fian."* Her anger was spent. First, they must survive.

"My name is Calgaich," he snapped testily.

"I am a slave," she said bitterly. That, and no more. It was not the first time she had so answered him.

Calgaich made a wide bed of the thick bracken while the tempting odor of the roasting hare flesh filled the barrow. He seemed not to notice Cairenn watching him. She looked down at the hares as she turned them. *One bed,* she thought. He means to have me this night. A fine bridal chamber. She smiled wryly.

Calgaich looked at her curiously as she smiled. She was a strange one, this woman of the Ordovices. He spread his cloak out beside the fire. "The cloak will be fairly dry when it's time to sleep. Still, the good wool is warmed by the heat of the body even when it's wet." He sat down crosslegged in the fashion of the Celts, on the man's side of the fire.

She watched him covertly as they ate, avoiding his curious glances. It was warmer now in the chamber and she was getting deathly weary. It had been a long time since they had left Hibernia.

"What is your home like, Calgaich?" she asked.

"Like any other, woman."

"That's not so. I saw the way you looked when you

tried to pierce the mist with your eyes as we entered that deathtrap of a bay. No man who did not greatly love his home would have sailed so eagerly into the rock jaws of Nodons as you did."

His eyes were like granite chips. It was the same reaction she had gotten from him when she had asked about the lash scars on his back.

Calgaich ignored her and stood up. "Time for bed. I want to leave here before dawn light and get into the hills unseen. There is likely a *rath* not far from here, or at least a small village, and perhaps even a *dun,* a hilltop fort of the Damnonii. I do not want to be caught like a badger in his hole. The hills and the forests are the friends of the hunted man."

Something in the way he said "hunted man" struck home to Cairenn. There was more behind his statement than just the fact that likely the Damnonii and positively the Picts would not be friendly. There was much more than that. It was something that allied itself to the scars on his back and his great hunger to reach his homeland despite all hindrances and dangers.

He picked up the dry cloak and walked to the bed of bracken, where he placed the cloak on the bed and turned to look at her. She rose slowly. The fire had died low again, leaving red, secretive eyes that peered now and again through the thick bed of ashes and were gone almost as quickly as they had come.

"Woman," he said quietly from the shadows.

She walked toward him as though under a spell.

"The tunic," he said patiently.

She stripped it from her body and felt the gooseflesh rise on her skin. He took the tunic from her hands. "Get into the bed," he ordered.

She crawled naked over the cloak and lay down, looking up at him. She was not frightened. She had expected it long before this night.

Calgaich bent over the lovely, naked creature looking up at him. He hesitated and then passed a hand across her thick dark hair, then down along a smooth cheek and thence to her throat to linger there a moment. His hand lightly touched her hardening nipples. Suddenly he bent closer and began to gather her up into his arms. His breath came quickly in his throat. Cairenn began trembling, sure the time had come. For what seemed an eternity he held her, and then his grip slackened.

Calgaich stood up. He looked down at her, and then he lifted a fold of the cloak and flung it over her smooth white body. He turned his back to her and pulled his tunic over his head. He drew on his trousers and swiftly cross-gartered them to his knees. He stood erect and withdrew the magnificent sword from its bronze sheath. Then he walked through the dark passageway while fighting back an almost overpowering woman-hunger within himself. The woman-smell was faint within the tunic but it was surely there.

Cairenn could not hear his soft footsteps within the dark passageway, but she did hear the clashing of the metal bosses on the hide door as he drew it aside. Long minutes passed during which she remembered the touch of his hand on her body, his strength as he had lifted her to him. Remembered her fear that it would surely happen now, and then the strange emptiness when he had pushed her back to the rough bed of bracken covered by his cloak. She waited and listened for his return, unable to quiet the beating of her heart. But he did not come, and finally she fell asleep.

Later, Calgaich came silently into the chamber. He crouched beside the embers of the fire and warmed his hands. He sat down on some of the bracken and rested his back against a pillar. He had his war spear close by his side and the naked sword rested across his thighs. He watched the dark entrance to the passageway for several minutes. At last he turned his head and looked toward where Cairenn slept on the rough bed of bracken. Her dark hair cushioned the pearl of her face. And suddenly he thought of Morar, the Golden One, and his vow to return to his land and claim her as his wife. Morar, for whose honor he had fought and won a bitter victory. But he must not think of her and in so doing take his lust for her out on this *cumal*—who was not worthy of his seed. Ah, but she was beautiful as she lay sleeping. The glow from the dying embers touched the ridges of her cheeks, gave color to her lips.

Sleep had finally come to her when she had given up

wishing for its comfort. She dreamed she was back in her father's *rath* again, clothed in soft woolen tunics brought to her from the northern settlements, her long hair being brushed by a fine gold comb. Suddenly the old images fled and she felt a hand close over her mouth and nose. She opened her eyes and looked up into Calgaich's shadowed face only inches away from hers. "Do not make a sound," he whispered. "Say nothing. Get up."

She stood up when he released her. She wrapped the cloak around her and then realized it was shorter. Calgaich had cut long strips from the bottom of it while she had been sleeping. She knew their purpose. She bound them about her bare feet with the strips of leather he had placed beside them.

Calgaich stood beyond the bed of ashes leaning on his spear. Faint gray light filtered down into the chamber from somewhere up above them. When she was ready, he crooked a finger at her. She followed him along the passageway. He paused at the hide covering the entrance. Gray light showed through where the hide did not quite meet the sides of the doorway. The air that crept through the openings was cold and fresh and it hinted at dampness.

Calgaich looked down at her. "There are men beyond the ring stones," he whispered to her.

"Who are they, *fian?*"

He shrugged. "I don't know."

"Could they be friends?"

He laughed shortly. "Not likely. We'll know soon enough. They must realize we are in here."

Calgaich thrust aside the hide covering and stepped out into the cold gray light of the dawn. Soft glistening snow had fallen during the night. It covered the hills and capped the distant mountains behind the hills. Each of the ring stones had its own grotesque gnome's cap of pure white.

Calgaich walked into the center of the ring of stones as a man moved quickly behind one of them. Dim, cloaked figures stood beyond the stones. There were many of them.

"They are afraid to come within the Holy Ring," Calgaich said over his shoulder in a low voice.

"Thank the gods for that." Cairenn blinked at the early morning light but could see nothing beyond the ring stones.

Calgaich reversed his spear and held it butt-upward in

the sign of peace. "It works both ways," he said quietly. "They won't come within the Holy Ring, but we in turn can't go beyond it."

"Then let us stay here in safety, *fian*," Cairenn pleaded.

He shook his head. "With no food? Melted snow for drinking? Hardly enough fuel left for another cold night? No, woman, we must deal with them. There is no other way."

He walked toward the largest of the ring stones, behind which the stranger stood. He rested the tip of his spear on the flagstones.

"Calgaich mac Lellan," a strangely accented voice spoke from behind the ring stone.

"You know me?" Calgaich asked.

"You're a long way from the country of the Novantae."

"I've just returned here from Eriu."

"A strange place to spend your first night in Albu."

"We had no choice. Our *birlinn* was taken by the sea. Who are you?"

The man moved into the space between two of the stones, but he did not step within the ring. He leaned on his war spear and studied Calgaich.

Cairenn turned her face away to avoid looking at the stranger. She knew now why his tongue sounded so strange. The man's face below the rim of his low-pulled helmet was tattooed like the faces of the fierce Picts she had seen the day before. His broad spear blade was dark with drying blood from tip to socket.

"Aengus of the Broad Spear," Calgaich greeted the Pict. There was no warmth in his tone.

The Pict grinned, revealing uneven yellowed teeth. "Well met, Calgaich. It has been a long time since we fought the Red Crests together."

Calgaich looked at the bloody spear. "That is not Roman blood on your blade."

Aengus shook his head. Then he noticed Cairenn standing in the entrance of the cave. It was as though he were trying to pierce through the cloak to eye each intimate detail of her nakedness. Others of the Picts moved in closer to the ring of stones. Their wolfish gazes studied the woman, the tall warrior and his fine weapons. There were at least a score of them. Beyond them the sky was lightening and across it lay a thick scarf of rising smoke like coarse gray hair lying across faded blue linen.

Calgaich again spoke over his shoulder to Cairenn. "They have probably raided one of the *raths* in the great glen. They must have struck before the dawn and are likely returning to their boats. It is their custom to attack just before the dawn."

"And *yours*, Novantae," Aengus added. He had ears like a hunting wolf.

Beyond the Picts were piles of loot on the fresh snow. Ten or twelve younger women stood herded together, guarded by one of the raiders. Evidently the Picts did not know of Calgaich's attack on the Pictish reiving craft. Perhaps they came from different clans. Yet it was hardly possible that two such raiding bands would be operating so closely together and not know about each other. Calgaich had known Aengus some years before he had left Caledonia. It had been during one of those uneasy alliances when Pict and Celt together had fought the Romans. It was about the only thing that could bring them together for a concerted effort—their intense hatred of the Romans.

"What do you want of us?" Calgaich asked.

Aengus grinned. "Very little, *fian*. Your woman. Your weapons. Your finery, such as it is. Then you'll be free to go."

"And if I don't choose to surrender them?"

Aengus rubbed his bristly jaw. "That would be foolish," he suggested thoughtfully. "There would be red work beyond these stones."

"She is my wife, Aengus." At hearing this, Cairenn moved farther back into the passageway. Her cheeks felt warm.

Aengus spat on the snow. "You lie. The *fianna* do not take wives while in service. We also know of the vow you made when you left Albu for Eriu. The tale of your great love for Morar, daughter of Cuno, known as the Golden One, and your vow to return some day and claim her for your wife, has spread throughout Caledonia. We know of your honor in such matters. Give us the woman, the weapons and the finery. I give you your life for old time's sake, Calgaich. I haven't forgotten your great skill in battle against the Red Crests. Those were great days, eh, *fian?*"

Cairenn heard the words with sudden fear. It would be the easy way out for him.

Calgaich slowly reversed his war spear. The growing light shimmered on the polished blade. "My father commands five hundred war spears, Pict," he reminded Aengus.

"They are not here, Celt."

The rest of the Picts laughed softly—deadly sure of themselves.

Aengus tilted his head to one side. "Your father no longer leads the Novantae. Bruidge of the Battle-Axe is chief now, by right of *tanaise ri.* You are nothing, Calgaich mac Lellan, but a *fian* and an exiled outlaw who can be killed by any man without fear of reprisal or having to pay the *galanas,* the blood debt."

"Do you have a champion, Aengus of the Broad Spear?" Calgaich asked formally. "Or is your mouth sharper than your spear blade! Perhaps *you* will try me? Come, a wager, man against man, blade against blade—spear, sword or dirk. Barehanded if you will. Winner take all—including the head of the loser."

Aengus grinned evilly. "Why should I bother? We have you in a snare, braggart."

"Perhaps you fear to try me."

Aengus flushed. "I am a chief! I can't fight a champion who is less than my rank."

Calgaich threw back his head and laughed boldly. "*Chief?* Chief of yonder score of dirty-faced Picts? My old wounds hurt if I laugh too hard, Pict. Spare me that pain."

"Let me clip this cockerel's wings, Aengus," a hoarse voice called from beyond the ring stones.

Aengus rubbed his tattooed face. He eyed Calgaich craftily. "Girich the Good Striker speaks, Celt. He is my second cousin. Cousin to the chief. Girich is willing to fight you, braggart."

The sky was brighter now. The drifting smoke from the Pict-ravaged *rath* up the glen came slowly toward the barrow. It brought with it the odor of burning wood and thatch, mingled with a haunting thread of an odor, one sweetish and sickly that revealed all too well what had happened at the settlement. Cairenn shivered. She remembered that sickly stench. So it had been when her father's *rath* in Wales had been ravaged by the Scotti and burned to the ground with the dead lying in the huts and on the streets.

Cairenn looked at the savage face of Aengus, wondering how his blue tattooings and hairy body would look pressed against her soft fair skin while his dirty, bloodstained hands defiled her private parts with greedy lust. She knew well enough what would happen to her if Calgaich was defeated. Her only good fortune might be in becoming the personal loot of Aengus, or perhaps of the yet unseen champion, Girich the Good Striker. One man, even a Pict, would be far better than the lust of twenty of them. If they meant to move fast away from this place they might have her, stripped and shivering on the slushy turf, one after the other as long as she could hold out. The thought was too terrible. It might be better to die beneath the claws and fangs of the great wolves who haunted the distant misty hills.

"Will you enter the Holy Ring, Girich?" Aengus asked.

There was a moment of silence and then Girich spoke. "There's evil within the great stones, Cousin. Have the Novantae come out here beyond the stones. I will fight him here."

Calgaich looked back at the woman. "I will have to go beyond the stones, Cairenn."

"They will kill you, *fian!* There are too many of them."

He shook his head. "You don't know these people. They are a poor people in most things except honor. The word of a chief is law. Besides, is it not better for them to have one man killed than many?"

"*You* are only one man, Calgaich."

He smiled confidently. "Do you think they can buy *my* life for the price of one man? Before they send Calgaich mac Lellan West-Over-Seas by the Warrior's Road they will pay my blood debt beforehand."

She knew well enough how it was with him and all his mad breed. Honor to him was as food and drink. It was a madness that was bred into the Celtic bone and flesh along with the warrior training that started with their tattooing at the age of two years.

"Come out here," Aengus called and added, as if in answer to Cairenn, "You will fight only one man, Calgaich." He laughed. "You'll find him quite enough even for you, *fian*."

"How shall we fight each other, Pict?"

"Your name means the Swordsman," Girich replied from behind one of the ring stones. "You've earned it well, Novantae. I am Girich the Good Striker. Leave the great *laigen* with the woman." He laughed. "Soon enough she shall have a better man than you to present with that fine war spear."

Calgaich returned to Cairenn and handed the heavy spear to her. He looked down into her eyes and then impulsively passed his hand alongside her face. He smiled a little as though to encourage her.

"Leave me your dirk, Calgaich," she pleaded.

He smiled again. "To fight with, eh, little one?"

She shook her head. "They will not take me alive."

She thrust the dirk down inside one of her leg wrappings and let the cloak drape over it.

Calgaich walked between two of the ring stones to the open area at the foot of the hill-slope. The Picts ringed the trampled turf, leaning on their broad-bladed spears, wrapped in their tartan cloaks and greasy, red-dyed sheepskins. They waited for the musical clashing of the sword blades.

Calgaich saw his opponent for the first time. Girich stood at the far side of the open space with his bared sword in his right hand. He held a small, blue-painted shield on his left forearm.

"A shield," Calgaich requested.

A Pict handed his shield to Calgaich. Calgaich thrust his left forearm through the loops. He walked closer to Girich. A coldness flowed through Calgaich's body. Girich was to be no mean opponent. *You will fight only one man, Calgaich*, Aengus had promised. *You'll find him quite enough even for you, fian.*

Girich was half a head shorter than Calgaich but half again as thick through the shoulders. His shoulders were slightly stooped from the thick covering of powerful muscles. His arms were bare to the shoulders and were corded with muscles under the dark-reddish hair that cov-

ered his arms. The hands were huge, and almost dispropor-
tionate to the arms. Despite the difference in height between Calgaich and Girich, the Pict had much longer arms.
Girich's face seemed to have been roughly carved from
some dark native stone. His nose had been broken from a
savage blow of the past, so that the nostrils were no more
than mere slits, a fact that Calgaich noted for his own
advantage. The Pict would have trouble breathing fully in
the action of combat. His eyes were a grayish-green but
there was a yellowish cast to them like the yolk of an egg.
The hair that showed beneath the boiled-leather helmet he
wore had been red in his earlier years, but was now
tinged thickly with gray. Girich was not a young man, but
the very fact that he had survived so long as a champion
of his clan indicated to Calgaich that he would not be
easy to slay.

Girich came forward, beating lightly on the metal edging
of his shield with his sword blade to drive away the evil
spirits. He stopped just beyond striking distance and stood
there with his upraised blade as steady as one of the great
ring stones.

Calgaich withdrew his untried sword from the scabbard.
The graying light struck against the figured blade, which
seemed to be like a tongue of cold flame as Calgaich extended it. There was a sharp intake of breath from some
of the Picts as they saw the magnificent weapon. Girich
moved his blade to feel the heft and balance of it. Girich
tapped his sword against that of Calgaich. They circled
slowly on the slippery turf. To slip and fall was to die.
Their eyes were fixed on each other. Suddenly, Girich
closed in with a whirlwind attack to test Calgaich's defense.
Calgaich retreated before the wildly slashing sword to let
the Pict tire himself, knowing the man probably had greater
reserves of brute strength than he himself possessed.

The blades crossed swiftly, reflecting the growing light
like the waters of a fast-running stream. Girich closed in
again and again and then swiftly fell back before Calgaich's
sudden counterattack. Girich crouched with his shield
held up high and cut low at Calgaich's knees. Calgaich
leaped back and raised his shield just in time to fend off a
smashing overhead blow that shook him to his heels.
Girich was far swifter than Calgaich had expected him to

be. Calgaich's left arm still stung from the shield blow as he and Girich circled warily, weaving a pattern of cuts and parries. Calgaich's sword tip moved swiftly in the curious cross pattern Cairenn had seen him use against the Pictish reivers and also on the night he had found the fine sword.

Girich retreated, studying the sword pattern being woven by Calgaich. There was no way he could counter it, so he suddenly bulled into an attack to drive Calgaich back with the impetuosity of it. Girich smashed at Calgaich like a smith hammering at his anvil. Chips flew from Calgaich's shield. The tip of Girich's sword drove through the shield and lightly punctured Calgaich's left forearm. Blood ran down his arm to form a pattern on his hand, dyeing the fingers red. The Picts began to murmur.

Girich's mad rushes drove Calgaich backward, ever backward until the Picts behind him stepped aside. He knew he was but inches away from one of the ring stones. He suddenly closed on the Pict, retreated and then leaped aside. Girich's blade rang like a bell against the ring stone and his arm numbed from the shock of the blow. An instant later Calgaich's sword came down in a powerful overhand stroke that glanced from the Pict's hard leather helmet. Girich blinked his eyes. He was half-stunned, and his arm tingled from the force of his blow against the stone. He swayed on his feet as he turned to shield off a thrust toward his belly. His timing and eye were off. Another blow crashed atop his helmet and drove it lower on his head. Girich staggered sideways. His breathing whistled through his slitted nostrils. He backed between two of the ring stones and then realized with superstitious horror where he was. He staggered back toward Calgaich with shield outthrust and his sword flashing in a wild attack.

Calgaich grinned, but he grinned too fast, for Girich cut hard at his shield and then reversed his blow and came down with a sweeping backhanded stroke that split the shield in two. Girich stepped back to allow Calgaich to get another shield. If that shield was destroyed, Calgaich would be allowed a third one, and if that, too, was demolished, he would have to fight this wild bear of a swordsman with only his sword for defense.

Calgaich swept into the attack. He pressed Girich back

again and again. Their breathing was harsh and fast as they circled, feinting and dodging, thrusting and slashing while moving swiftly around like a pair of deadly whirligigs. He had learned something about Girich. His shoulder muscles were so thick they hindered his being able to raise his arms as high and as quickly as he would have liked. There was something else to Calgaich's advantage— Girich was deathly afraid to step within the ring of stones.

They circled. It was fully light now, and the snow was trampled into mush. Here and there on the surface of it were bright flecks of Calgaich's blood. Girich was becoming craftier as he realized Calgaich would soon weaken with the loss of more blood. Calgaich retreated before the steady attack of the Pict. It was as if Girich were chopping wood, but he always stayed back from that damned overhand stroke to the helmet from which he had been unable to defend himself.

"It grows late, Girich!" Aengus called out. "There are not enough of us to fight off an attack by the Damnonii. They will have seen the smoke by now. The hounds will soon be baying in the hills. Kill this braggart of the Novantae and have done with him!"

Girich did not take his eyes off Calgaich. "Would you like to come out here for a while, Cousin?" he asked.

There was no reply from Aengus.

Girich and Calgaich grinned wearily at each other.

Girich drove a crushing blow at Calgaich's shield and then cut low for the knees. The tip of the sword severed a crossgartering around Calgaich's right leg and the leathern thong fell down about his ankle. It trailed behind him as he beat a feigned retreat toward the ring stones. There was a look of fear and almost of panic on his sweating face.

Girich spat to one side. He sensed victory. He drove in, striking wildly and steadily. There seemed to be no end to his great strength. Suddenly Calgaich sidestepped. His sword came down with powerful force on top of the Pict's helmet. Girich could not stop his headlong rush, which was aided by the blow to his head. He staggered in between two of the great ring stones.

Cairenn stepped back and lowered the tip of the war spear toward Girich's back.

"No!" Calgaich shouted.

Calgaich leaped between two of the stones and smashed his sword down atop Girich's battered helmet. Blood began to trickle down from beneath the helmet and into Girich's eyes. Calgaich worked his way around the Pict so that the light of the rising sun shone against the tattooed face of the Pict. Girich's eyes were dazed with pain. His breathing was harsh and irregular. He turned his head from side to side, seeking an escape from the ring of stones. He forgot that Calgaich was really his opponent and not his own intense superstitious fear of the Holy Ring.

No matter which way the beleaguered Pict turned, a grinning Calgaich was there in front of him, feinting and thrusting with undiminished strength and skill. Girich's face was now a mask of trickled blood forming a grotesque pattern with the blue design of his tattooing.

Calgaich drove Girich back toward the stones to give him a choice—to try to escape while presenting his back to Calgaich, or to wait out the attack and put aside his fear of the ring of stones to save his life.

The Pict made his choice. He ran toward the stones, then whirled to get between two of them to hold off Calgaich's pursuit. As he turned, Calgaich's sword splintered Girich's shield down to the metal boss. Girich lowered his shield arm and sword arm. His recovery was too slow. Half-blinded by blood, with the sun shining full in his face, and deathly afraid of the ring of stones, Girich hardly felt the thrust that penetrated a hand's span into his heart. He was dead before he sprawled on the bloody snow.

Calgaich leaned on his reddened sword. His breathing was harsh and irregular. He looked between the stones at the body of Girich. The Picts were silent.

Aengus walked forward. "Your name is truly given, Calgaich—the Swordsman."

"He was a good opponent," Calgaich admitted. "I've met none better. You'll miss your champion, Aengus."

Aengus shrugged. "I never trusted him," he said in a low voice. "His weapons are yours, Calgaich."

Calgaich shook his head. "Take his weapons back with his body. He was a warrior."

The Picts waited, as if expecting something. Cairenn watched them curiously. Suddenly Calgaich raised his sword for a two-handed downstroke. The sharp iron cut cleanly through the neck of Girich and his head rolled to one side. A great gout of blood poured from the gaping neck hole. Cairenn turned aside and vomited.

Calgaich picked up the head and placed it on top of one of the ring stones so that its sightless eyes looked toward his former companions.

The Picts wrapped Girich's headless body in his cloak and carried it down to the shore of the sea loch. They pulled two long, lean rowing boats from the thicker shelter of the reeds, loaded them with their loot and the women prisoners, then shoved off and thrust out their oars. Aengus called out the stroke as the two boats moved out toward the sea mouth of the loch. In a little while the grinding of the oars between the thole pins died away.

Calgaich held out his left arm to Cairenn. "Bind it," he said. He ignored the look of horror and distaste on her face, pale now from being sick.

Cairenn wiped her mouth and did as she was bidden. She cleaned the blood away first, pleased to see that it was only a slight puncture wound, before binding the arm tightly. She could smell the strong male odor. Neither of them spoke as she worked, nor did she raise her eyes to meet his.

Then Calgaich took his war spear. "Come. There's little time to waste. The Damnonii will be along all too quickly. They'll kill any strangers they find in the glen."

He walked between two of the stones and strode toward the distant smoke pall. The snow-covered hills were bright in the rays of the rising sun.

"But why, Calgaich?" Cairenn asked.

He looked curiously at her.

"The head," she said, not looking at the thing of horror on the stone behind her.

He shrugged. "He was too dangerous an enemy in life to have him haunt me after death." He jerked his head backward. "That way, without a head, his vengeful spirit will not have eyes to see me or ears to hear me."

They walked on.

"Perhaps the Damnonii are already at the *rath*," she warned him.

"We'll have to risk it. We need food and you need clothing. Perhaps the Picts left something behind them other than the dead."

She shivered at the thought. High in the bright sky she could see circling ravens. Ravens soon find the newly dead.

CHAPTER 4

The thick smoke lay close about the smoldering huts. A wraith of it rose slowly high above the ravaged path to stain the blue sky. A miasma composed of the smoke, thick piles of manure, heated stonework and the sweetish, stinking aura of burned flesh poisoned the fresh morning air.

Cairenn stopped at the edge of the *rath*. "No, I cannot go in," she whispered when Calgaich impatiently motioned for her to keep up with him. "It is too soon."

"Too soon?" Calgaich repeated. He hesitated as if about to force her to his will, but finally told her to wait there. She was not sure he had understood.

Cairenn crouched low in the snowy bracken on a hill-slope at the edge of the *rath*, watching Calgaich as he walked slowly about the huts. She could not follow him. She knew what he would find. It was too close to what she had left behind in her father's *rath* as she was dragged away by the Scotti when they were through with their killing and plundering. Perhaps it was well that she had been spared the aftermath of their ravages of her settlement, that her hiding place in the dog's shelter had been found. How would she have buried her dead? Her parents and brother? Her betrothed? And where would she have found the strength to live beyond those terrible hours of labor? Head-bobbing ravens flew reluctantly away from the dead, and then circled close overhead watching the stranger with bright eyes. Tumbled, half-naked bodies lay like heaps of clothing on the trampled area of slush, manure and mud. The stiffening bodies were streaked with dark stripes and clots of coagulating blood. Somewhere beyond the *rath* and up the great dark glen a dog howled mournfully. Cairenn

57

shivered. It *sounded* like a dog, but there was no dog to be seen.

Calgaich lifted a half-burned door flap with the tip of his spear and stepped into the smoky interior of one of the huts that had not fully burned. A sprawled body lay to one side. Calgaich found the clothing of a boy—dirty trousers, red-dyed sheepskin tunic and worn hide buskins. The boy to whom the clothing might have belonged lay naked and dead in his bed of bracken with a small hunting spear driven through his belly, pinning him to the bed.

Calgaich passed from one partially burned hut to another. He constantly watched the mouth of the great glen. It was still dark in shadows. Nothing seemed to move in there. He spread a tanned deer hide on the ground and placed his loot upon it—a dried boar's haunch, some smoked venison, several loaves of fairly fresh bread, the boy's clothing, several greasy bed skins and woolen cloaks and a small dirk about boy's size.

There was still something he badly wanted. He poked about in several of the unburned huts until the muted barking of distant dogs drove him back into the open. In the last hut he had found what he was looking for and grunted in satisfaction as he carried three large earthenware jugs of *usquebaugh* to his plunder. He pulled out one of the wooden stoppers and upended the jug. The strong barley spirits seemed to burn down his gullet and then exploded in a ball of fire within his guts. He drove the stopper back into the bottle and placed it on the hide. He bound the hide about the loot and then slung it over his back.

The sound of the barking dogs was closer now—somewhere close within the mouth of the shadowed glen.

Calgaich strode toward the hill-slope, then stopped short. A tiny girl-child lay sprawled beside a pup. Both of them had been pierced by Pictish blades. Her little dress was kilted high above her plump legs and rounded belly. Calgaich stood there for a moment looking down at her. The child's blue, sightless eyes stared up at him. Her lovely golden hair was trampled into the mire and manure.

The dogs were closer now. Some of them were baying.

Calgaich put down his bundle and spear. He bent upon one knee and wiped as much of the mire and manure from the child's golden hair as he could. He closed the staring

eyes and composed the sprawled limbs. He pulled down
the bloody dress and then covered her face with a square
of woolen cloth that lay close to her. For a moment he
looked down at her, then picked up his bundle and spear
and ran lightly from the *rath*.

"Walk!" he ordered Cairenn.

"It's cold! I'm hungry!" she said defiantly.

"Damn you! There isn't any time. You hear those
hounds? They'll tear us to pieces if they catch up with us."
Calgaich pulled her to her feet. "Look!" he added, pointing
toward the glen with his spear. Beyond the *rath* at the
mouth of the glen men were riding shaggy ponies across
the snow. Ahead of them was a loping crescent of huge
hounds.

She looked down the slope. The ravens had landed boldly right behind Calgaich as he had left the *rath*. They
strutted about on the ground, a distinct jet black contrast
to the white snow and the crimson stains of blood. They
pecked at the bloodstained snow and hopped upon the
chests of the corpses.

"They will pick out the eyes first," Calgaich said quietly.

Cairenn followed him through the wet, clinging brush.
Thorns tore at her cloak and exposed skin. Her face went
taut when Calgaich waded into a rushing burn that plunged
head over heels in a mad race to reach the sea loch far below. Calgaich waded upstream. He did not look back at
her.

Cairenn kilted up the cloak and stepped into the flood.
The icy water flowed about her privates and the lower part
of her belly so that she was almost paralyzed. There was not
a stitch of clothing from beneath her breasts to her cloth-
bound feet. Now and again she would stagger toward the
snow-covered bank of the stream with a look of sheer
agony on her face, hoping that Calgaich would take pity
on her; but he never looked back. If she fell behind, she
wasn't sure but what he would abandon her. She knew
what would happen if those savage hounds caught up with
her.

The harsh baying of the hounds echoed across the great
glen. Once, in a shifting of the morning wind, the sound of
shouting was interwoven with the baying of the hounds;

then the sounds receded, seemingly toward the shore of the sea loch.

The sun was up high when at last Calgaich waded from the icy stream and peered down the long tree-shrouded slopes. Cairenn gratefully followed him from the water. She could no longer feel her legs or feet beneath her. She could not feel her sodden wet clothes as they dropped to cling against her reddened legs and ankles.

"They have followed the shore," he murmured, almost to himself. "They are looking for the Picts. The hounds might still pick up our trail into the hills." He looked around to where Cairenn had slumped onto the ground. "Come, we have no time for rest. *Come now,* woman."

He led the way up a steep and slippery slope until at last the two of them stood on the great ridge that formed the southern side of the glen. Far below them the smoke was raveling off thinly before the brisk morning wind.

Calgaich got off the skyline and opened the bundle of loot. He sat with his back against a tree, idly watching Cairenn as she dressed. Once their eyes met and she looked hastily away from him. It seemed to her that he was always watching her nakedness with a mildly speculative eye. The boy's clothing was filthy and it stank, but it was warm. She did not allow herself to think of what the boy's fate must have been, to remember the circling ravens. For now, finally, she was warm. Perhaps renewed strength would also come to her.

Calgaich drank steadily from one of his treasured jugs. He handed Cairenn a piece of the smoked venison and broke one of the loaves of bread in half with his blood-stained hands. He let her take a pull from the jug. She coughed as the fiery *usquebaugh* burned her throat.

Calgaich grinned. "The very water of life. Like mother's milk." He handed her the boy's dirk and took back his own long-bladed dirk. He formed two packs and handed her the smaller and lighter one. "We'll march all this day to put as much distance between us and the Damnonii as we can. This is their country for several days' more travel. In a few more days after that we should be in my country —*if* you can keep up."

"And if I can't?" she said softly.

He shrugged. "March or die," he replied carelessly.

"Will we be safe in your country?"

"Why do you ask?"

"You didn't leave Albu by choice. You were a hunted man here. When we reach your country will you still be a hunted man, Calgaich?"

He looked beyond the ridge toward the jumbled hills and mountains beyond them. "I don't know," he replied softly. "It has been three years. Once I had many friends and relatives among my own people. Now, I do not know. Those Picts in the reiving ship were waiting for me off the coast. They knew I was returning here from Eriu. They meant to stop me. Someone must have paid them to do that. My father is no longer chief of the clan. My uncle, Bruidge of the Battle-Axe, has taken his place by right of *tanaise ri*."

"Your father's only brother. It was he who fostered you until you were a warrior. Does that mean nothing to him?" Her emerald eyes blazed.

He looked down at her. "The man I killed over a woman was Fergus, *the only son of Bruidge*. He was my first cousin."

She stared at him. "You *killed* him?"

"It was fair combat," he said sharply.

"For a woman?" Cairenn felt her cheeks burn. Was this woman, for whom he had killed, Morar—the Golden One —of whom Aengus, the Pict, had spoken? Was Calgaich as anxious to return to her as he was to find his father? Yet Cairenn dared say no more, and Calgaich ignored her words.

"Bruidge hates me now. He has used the ancient right of *tanaise ri* to usurp my father's chieftainship. When my father dies, I should succeed him, but now I can't because of Bruidge."

"*Tanaise ri?*" she asked curiously.

"An ancient custom whereby a brother's right to the succession of a chief is stronger than that of the chief's son."

"But if your father is still alive?"

Calgaich shrugged. "Then he is still chief."

"Can your uncle make his claim stand, then?"

Calgaich grunted savagely. "He has the men and the position. My father is old and weak, nearly blind, and in the hands of the Romans. His only son is an outlaw. The gods curse Bruidge! He *knew* I was coming home. He set those damned Pictish reivers on his own nephew."

Calgaich set off, plunging downhill through the wet brush. Something powerful had driven him from his beloved Albu; something more powerful had drawn him back to it in the face of almost certain death. Again, Cairenn rose wearily and followed him.

Calgaich pressed on at a steady pace through the empty hills and echoing passes. Now and then the faint howling of a hound, or perhaps a wolf, came to them on the wind. There were no signs of humans in the wilderness through which they passed all that long day. Mist had moved in when the short-lived sun had vanished behind low-hanging clouds. Sometimes, through the forest tangle, the mirror-like surfaces of small mountain lochs or dark tarns might be seen. Many little streams of rushing icy water plunged down the long slopes and through the passes.

Darkness was in the offing. A cold, snow-laden wind was feeling its way through the narrow passes when at last they descended from the heights. Calgaich moved on even more swiftly, heedless of the almost exhausted woman.

"Are you in such a great hurry then, *fian,* to reach your home and perhaps your death!" she cried out in desperation.

He turned his head without interrupting his headlong stride. "The night belongs to the wolves in these mountains," he warned her.

It was enough to spur Cairenn on with the last dregs of her strength until at last they reached the shore of a leaden-colored loch thickly fringed with conifers. There was a drystone ruin on a knoll near the loch. It was a bell-shaped defensive tower surrounded by a quadrangle of smoke-blackened stone buildings. Smoke stains streaked the walls of the tower. The gate of the quadrangle lay flat on the ground.

The light was failing fast when Calgaich dragged away the charred timbers of the tower door. The wind moaned about the gaunt-looking structure. Calgaich stooped to enter the low passageway that led into the interior of the tower. The ancient roof had fallen in long ago and now formed a pile of huge jackstraws. Smoke stained the inner walls. Here and there slitted windows seemed to be looking down on Calgaich and Cairenn like the eye sockets in a skull.

Calgaich stood there looking around. Memories came crowding back to him. He had been a new and untried warrior when his father had led the Novantae on a raid to this remote Roman outpost. They had put the Red Crests to the sword and then had fired the structure.

"You know this place?" Cairenn asked, watching him. He grinned crookedly at her. "I set fire to it."

Calgaich led the way up a steep and narrow winding stairway between the outer and inner walls. At the top was a large room with slitted windows that looked out toward the loch. He grunted in satisfaction and dropped his pack. "There is some wood. Make a fire. I'll get more." He paused in the doorway and looked back at her. "No matter what might happen below, don't leave this room until daylight." He vanished into the stairwell.

Cairenn made the fire in the rude circle of stones set in the middle of the floor. She could hear him moving about in the center of the tower. Once she looked down at him. He was working swiftly, tired as he must be, and now and then he would look back over his shoulder toward the gaping doorway as though expecting someone, or *something*.

Calgaich blocked the tower doorway with timbers. He carried several armloads of wood up into the room and then closed the sagging door. He braced a short length of timber against the door and placed his spear beside it.

He looked about the low-vaulted room. The fire was roaring. Moving firelight was cast on the lichened walls. The smoke was drifting through a hole in the outer wall. He grunted in satisfaction.

The fire died down to a thick bed of embers. Cairenn heated some of the meat. "Where are your brothers the wolves, *fian?*" she asked teasingly.

"Listen," he said.

The eerie howling of a wolf rose from somewhere beyond the far side of the loch.

"They know we are here," Calgaich explained. "One of them followed us the last hour. There will be others. *Many.*"

"I didn't see any wolf."

He looked at her. "Once he was only a spear's cast behind you. Maybe he was waiting for you to drop." He grinned as Cairenn turned away.

They ate well of the food Calgaich had looted from the *rath*. Cairenn washed it down with some of the clear stream water with which Calgaich had refilled the jug of whiskey he had emptied that day. His face was flushed from the spirits but he showed little sign of having drunk that much.

They could hear the rising chorus of the wolves. They were prowling now about the base of the structure. Cairenn surreptitiously watched Calgaich as he tore at the food with his strong white teeth. She could not help but think that here, too, was a wolf, a lean wolf of a man, seemingly as lonely as the howling wolves, and just as deadly.

Calgaich started on the second jug of whiskey. He drew his sword from its sheath and placed it across his lap as he sat cross-legged on the man's side of the fire. He studied the fine weapon. He hefted it, and felt it with his hands. He hummed softly to himself as he did so. *"Na tri dee dana,"* he murmured appreciatively. "By the Three Gods of Skill—Gobniu, Credne and Luchta—this is a weapon fit for a warrior. Aye, a chieftain! A king! A god!" He looked at Cairenn with that faraway gaze of his and she knew he was somewhere else in spirit beyond that room. "It did its red work well this day, eh, woman?"

She nodded, shivering a little as the firelight danced along the fine blade. If the sword had not done its "red work well" she would have become a plaything of those bloody-handed Picts.

Calgaich nipped at the jug constantly while he tirelessly examined the weapon. He was completely absorbed and fascinated by it. He turned it back and forth to let the firelight play upon its polished surface. He tested the keen edges. Now and then he would tap the metal against the stone wall and then would listen to something that only he could hear emanating from within the blade itself. His scarred face grew flushed with the outer heat of the fire and the inner heat of the *usquebaugh*.

Cairenn leaned back against the wall and drew her cloak

about her. "Why did you bring me with you from Eriu, *fian?*" she asked him.

"A gift from a king is not to be scorned."

"I have held you back."

He shook his head.

"Perhaps you would not have had to fight Girich if it had not been for me."

He swung the sword and then eyed her across it. "You think that I fought only for you?"

She blushed. "I did not know." She picked at the handle of her dirk. "You haven't treated me as a *cumal*, Calgaich."

"There has hardly been time, woman."

She looked at the bed she had made against the wall. Surely tonight . . . "Was it because you knew what would happen to me at the court of King Crann?"

He shook his head.

"Are you telling me the truth?" she persisted.

He stopped studying the blade and raised his head. The look on his face frightened her.

"I did not mean that you lied!" she cried.

Calgaich leaned forward. The sweat dripped from his lean face into the embers at the edge of the fire and little spurts of steam arose to becloud him. "Then, what did you mean?" he asked in a low voice.

"They thought I was a witch. You knew that." Her voice was low.

"Well, *are* you?"

It was very quiet in the chamber. Wood snapped in the fire. The wind moaned about the outer walls. A wolf howled.

"They said that eyes such as yours can enthrall a man so that he can't see your true face or body, only that which you want him to see," Calgaich said.

"Do you believe that?" Cairenn's eyes held his gaze.

Finally, he shook his head.

"You don't seem certain."

Calgaich leaned back against the wall and drank deeply from the jug. He wiped his mouth with the back of his hand and eyed her shapely legs, wrapped in the boy's trousers and crossgartered. He raised his eyes to where her sheepskin jacket had swung open. The swelling curves of her breasts, dewed with sweat, now glistened in the firelight. He would not look at her green eyes. Supposing it *was* true?

He felt the good *usquebaugh* working with him. There had hardly been time to bed her. She had a body that could shake a man's reason. The thought of that body ran through his mind in recurring images as he sat across the fire from her. Still, there was his vow. A man's honor must come first, above all else, and to Calgaich the honor of his father must be returned to him—the chieftainship of the clan. If a man were to break his vow, he would destroy his honor, and in so doing would not be able to serve his father. It was a rigid code. Calgaich knew no other.

"Will there be danger in your country?" she asked, breaking his reverie.

"I told you before that I don't know." He eyed her body again. "Not to one such as you. A man would be a fool to use that body of yours and then put you to death."

"There are things worse than death," she reminded him, pulling her sheepskin jacket together.

He passed a caressing hand along the blade of the sword. "Woman's reasoning," he sneered. He looked up at her. "Why are you here but to satisfy a man's hunger—the same as food and drink to him?"

She blushed and looked away from him.

Calgaich looked thoughtfully into the fire. "Babd Catha will soon enough fly over the country of the Novantae," he murmured.

Babd Catha, the fearsome Raven of Battle. Cairenn shivered a little despite the heat. Babd Catha usually appeared before a battle attired in her blood-red cloak, with her eyebrows reddened, and mounted on a chariot drawn by a grotesque horse. To inspire horror, she would then change into the form of a huge raven who would gloat over the bloodshed, inducing panic and weakness among the contending warriors.

Calgaich was still hunkered down by the bed of embers when she went to bed in the shadows. She stripped off her trousers and jacket and then made the ritual right-hand turn to ensure good fortune before she bundled herself into Calgaich's great tartan cloak. Utter weariness overcame her. Her belly was full and it was warm beneath the cloak.

She closed her eyes and soon lost contact with the little world in which Calgaich and herself alone existed.

Once during the night she opened her eyes. The only light came from the butt end of a log, which was a rounded mass of glowing red. Calgaich still sat with his back against the wall, the sword across his lap and the whiskey jug between his legs. His head was back and his mouth was open as he slept the sleep of the drunken. Above the moaning of the bitter night wind she heard the distant howling of the wolves.

She lay there awake thinking of this strange and violent man who could kill so easily and who seemed to have no fear at least of man. Yet he had taken time to cover the face of a little dead child to protect its eyes from the ravens. He was the outlawed son of a chief; a man who had killed his own cousin over a woman. Still, he had decided to return to his own country across a dangerous wintry sea, fighting against a score of Picts who had been sent to stop him. He had fought Girich the Good Striker, a champion of the Picts, and had defeated him so that he and Cairenn could pass freely on their way. He held a helpless slave woman in bondage and yet he had never taken her in bed. The wonder and the strangeness of it all ran through her tired mind as she drifted off to sleep again.

Calgaich awoke in the coldest hour before the dawn. His arm wound had stiffened and his muscles were sore. He winced as he felt about on the floor for the jug of barley spirits. The liquor fumes bedeviled his senses. He placed splinters of wood in the ashes and blew on them until the fire caught hold. He threw the last of the wood onto the rising flames. Then he drank deeply, again and again, until the warmth of the whiskey and the fire crept through his body. As he looked across the leaping flames at the huddled figure of the woman in the bed, the thought of her smooth, white nakedness began to work on him.

"The vow, Calgaich mac Lellan," Calgaich said aloud. "Remember the vow that you made in order to return to Morar."

He closed his eyes. He had vowed not to bed any woman until he could return to his betrothed Morar as a free man. *Any* woman? He knew well enough that when he had been in the whiskey, he *had* bedded women.

"Whores," he muttered. Surely they didn't count. Then there had been the women the drink-maddened *fianna* had raped on several of their wild raids against the enemies of King Crann. Did they matter?

Calgaich shook his head. His long fair hair covered his flushed face. He raised the whiskey jug and drank. It sucked dry. He hurled it across the chamber, where it shattered against the far wall. The woman stirred in her sleep and called out a little.

Calgaich closed his eyes. The vision of her came instantly into focus—her high, proud breasts with their pink buds; her smooth, rounded flanks and the lovely long legs. After all, she was a *cumal,* a chattel, a slave only, and *his* to do with as he liked.

He stood up, throwing a hovering giant shadow on the wall. He wet his dry lips as he peeled off his tunic and trousers and dropped them on the floor. He stripped off his breechclout. He wiped his hands on his muscular thighs. "The gods forgive me," he murmured. He walked to the bed.

Calgaich stripped back the tartan cloak and saw the warm whiteness of her like a luscious seed within a dark pod. He lay down beside her. She moved a little and spoke out sleepily. The next thing she knew she was jolted out of her warm sleep by a cold firm body being thrust hard against hers. She opened her eyes and looked up into his shadowed face. His dry lips bruised her soft lips. His hard hands passed down her shoulders to toy with her full breasts, tarried there awhile and then felt down her belly to the triangular meeting of her lower belly and thighs.

For a moment or two she struggled silently and fearfully, while his hilt-callused hands, now surprisingly gentle, toyed with and caressed her tense body. She relaxed gradually and slowly began to respond to him. She wrapped her arms about his neck and drew him closer to her. She placed her hands alongside his sweating face and tried to look into his eyes in the dimness. Calgaich quickly turned his head aside to avoid her gaze. He was fearful that he might see something in her eyes to prove she was a witch.

The fire gave a last dying flicker, and, as if it were a

signal, Calgaich forced apart her legs and thrust his knees in between them. She raised her legs and spread them as far apart as she could. One of his hands penetrated between her legs and caressed her slowly at first and then faster. She drew him down to her. She winced and cried out a little as he forced her, pushing into her very depths, spreading her wide.

By the gods, she was tight! Calgaich thrust harder. She groaned a little, but it was not a groan of pain. Soon Cairenn began to respond to his steady drive and they worked in perfect rhythm until at last they finally exploded together.

Calgaich rolled from on top of Cairenn. "By the gods!" he cried in wonder. "A virgin!" He dropped his head and passed out into a heavy drunken sleep.

Cairenn slept no more that night. Instead, she lay listening as somewhere in the cold darkness of the predawn in the wind-haunted hills a brother wolf to Calgaich the Swordsman raised its voice in the lonely, eerie howling of its kind.

CHAPTER 5

"Listen!" Calgaich cried out.

Faintly, ever so faintly on the wings of the southwest wind, there came the hollow booming of the sea.

Calgaich had led the way from before the dawn light until the early dusk for four long days, striding on through a lonely, wild-looking country with distant low mountain peaks still capped with snow, which shrank visibly every day in the warming rays of the sun, for spring was just beginning. Tiny flashing rivulets wound their way down the steep slopes, dropping here and there into miniature, tinkling waterfalls or spreading out into shallow, wind-rippled pools on the level areas that glistened like silver shields from the reflected sunlight. They had passed lonely lochs surrounded by thick stands of conifers, some of them hardly a spear's cast across and surely haunted by the dreaded kelpies, or so Cairenn thought, the water spirits who were said to fancy young girls, preferably virgins.

Cairenn had turned her head away from that thought, but something else had been planted within her as well as the strong seed of the fierce and moody man who strode through the heather like an avenging spirit and who had hardly spoken to her or looked directly at her since the day he had forced her. Whatever Calgaich had said to her or done to her in the four long days of their journeying had made little difference to Cairenn. She knew now, in addition to losing her maidenhead to him, that she had fallen in love with him.

The morning sun was bright on the land on the morning of the fifth day's journey. Calgaich raised his head like a questing wolf. "We're not far from the *rath* and fortress of my people, Cairenn. We can't very well enter it bold-faced. I don't know what welcome I'll get. There might be bloodshed. I'll have to find a place of safety for you while I go on. If anything happens to me, you know what will happen to you."

She dropped her pack to the ground and placed her hands at the small of her back. Her back, thighs and private parts had ached dully for four days and not from the traveling alone. Calgaich had been surprisingly gentle with her at the time, but there had been a subdued fierceness, almost a desperation, in the act of consummation.

He looked sideways at her. "Where's your tongue, woman?"

She shrugged. "What difference will it make? If you are slain by your own people, my fate is assured. If not with your Novantae, it will be others who take me. I'm a chattel, Calgaich. Nothing more."

"It was the whiskey, woman."

She looked at him. "I was not thinking about that. But, was that *all* it was? Only the liquor? Wasn't there anything else?"

"You talk like a woman!" he said harshly.

"Calgaich, I *am* a woman." Her voice was soft, her eyes held his.

Calgaich looked away from her. Yes, he knew she was a woman, but his only thought now was his return to his father's land, and to Morar.

"Not far from the *rath* is the steading of my old teacher of the hunting craft. Guidd One-Eye may be the only one among the Novantae I can trust, at least until I see what the situation is. You can stay with Guidd until I meet with my uncle Bruidge."

"And if you don't return from that meeting?"

He shrugged. "You just said you were a chattel. I can leave you with anyone I please."

His words stung her, even though she had said them only moments before. "Like Guidd One-Eye?" she asked bitterly.

Calgaich ignored her anger as his face cracked into a wide grin. "Wait until that horny old bastard sees you!" He slapped a thigh and broke into laughter.

Cairenn turned away from him and picked up her pack. A chilling foreboding crept through her tired mind and body, and she did not want to think about what lay ahead anymore. "Let's see this Guidd One-Eye, Calgaich, if that is to be my fate." She moved a few steps away from him, waiting to resume their journey and again trying not to think about the past she had left behind.

Calgaich led the way toward the sea. There was a springing eagerness in his stride; an inner urgency that drew him toward the great estuary in the distance.

A rushing, whirring sound came to meet them as though a sea storm was gathering its strength to sweep in over the land. The wind was rising. It brought that sound with it, mingled with the calling and crying of great birds, which had a thrilling, drawing quality to it.

Calgaich strode up the inland slope of a steep-sided promontory that protruded out into the sea. The sun was shining on the firth, or great estuary, which thrust itself deep into the land. He stopped on the height of land and looked out over the firth. There was a faraway look of mingled wonder and longing on his face.

The rushing, whirring sound was combined with the musical calling and honking of thousands of wild gray geese who were rising into the clear air with powerful beatings of their strong wings to evade the incoming tide, which was driving them from their feeding grounds on the wide expanse of salty mud flats. The geese rose and fell on the strong sea wind, arranging themselves into V-shaped formations only to break them off and to settle again on the vast, shining expanse of pool-dotted mud and sand. Others of the great birds would rise from the flats to join the wheeling masses above them while crying out and calling to each other. Slowly, skeins of the geese shaped themselves together and began to swing in over the land, rising and falling in their flight toward the north, calling back and forth to each other as though encouraging their mates for the long and tiring flight to their northern nesting places.

Calgaich leaned on his great war spear. His face was uplifted and had an expression of remoteness on it as he stood there spellbound by the vast migration that was taking place. "It is surely spring," he murmured to himself. He seemed to have completely forgotten the tired young woman who sat on the turf beside him.

At last the final formation of geese swung in low over

the heads of Calgaich and Cairenn and flew toward the north to follow the far-distant leading formations, which now looked like tiny scraps of charred wood whirled upward from some great bonfire. In a little while the last formation, too, had passed on into the northern infinity. The sound of the wind and the booming of the surf replaced the noisy confusion of the departed geese. The tide was now moving in swiftly to cover the wide expanse of mud flats.

Calgaich led the way to the east, keeping on the lower ground to avoid the skyline. The shoreline dipped and curved to their right. Several times Calgaich motioned to Cairenn, and she would instantly drop flat on the ground. Calgaich would then belly worm his way up to a crest to scan the surrounding area. Once he called to her and she crawled up beside him. A small fishing craft, dwarfed by the distance, was making its way out into the estuary now that the tide had completed its strong course onto the flats.

Calgaich pointed toward the east to where the land closed in on either side to form the great valley the river had gouged out in the thousands of years it had flowed toward the sea. Calgaich pointed toward the southeast. Something flashed along the shoreline. A moment later there was another flash farther to the west. The flashing was repeated until it was lost around the curving of the coastline to the south.

Calgaich rested his chin on his crossed arms. "The Roman wall extends from the northern sea across the land for eighty miles. It ends over there, around the curve of the coastline, although it's not truly a wall once it passes Luguvalium, a large *rath* they have built south and east of where we are now. From there along the south coast of the firth, there are small forts every Roman mile or so, with signal towers in between them. They cover the river mouth where it can easily be forded, and beyond where small boats can cross the firth. The small forts extend about thirty miles along the coast to watch the wider parts of the firth."

"Against whom?" she asked.

He looked sideways at her and grinned. "To keep out the barbarian Novantae along the firth and the wild Scotti raiders from Eriu who attack the coast to the south."

"Such as those who raided my father's *rath?*" she said softly, looking away from him.

He nodded and pointed toward the great curving of the coast. "Your country is far south of there."

The flashing began again and traveled from the right to the left this time. "They are signaling along the line of fortlets and towers," Calgaich explained. "They have seen someone."

"Us?" she asked in surprise, lowering her head to her arms. The ground was rough and cold beneath her.

He shook his head. "Hardly. Their eyes aren't *that* good, even for the mighty Romans. They've likely just seen that fishing craft making its way to sea. They'll watch it until they're sure it isn't going to land on their side of the firth. As if any Novantae in his right mind would try something like that in broad daylight." Calgaich rolled over onto his back and shielded his eyes against the sun with a forearm. "Times past we used to cross the firth at night and get in between their forts and signal towers to raid inland. Sometimes we would get several days' march to the southeast and behind the wall itself." He grinned. "Once we got deep enough into Roman territory to arouse the Twentieth Legion garrisoned at Camulodunum, well over a hundred miles to the south. It's really something big when they call out a legion to handle it. By the time the Twentieth Valeria Victrix arrived at where we had been raiding, we were already gone like the mist on the moor when the morning sun strikes it. We left a trail of burning villas for miles behind us."

"Don't they man the wall with legions to keep you wild Caledonians out of Britannia?"

Calgaich shook his head. "The wall wasn't intended purely as a defensive measure. No wall could keep *us* in our own country. It is garrisoned by auxiliaries—Asturians, Thracians, Gauls, Belgae, Dacians, Helvetians and Numidians, as well as others from all parts of the empire, who serve the damned Romans. Three legions of Roman soldiers are stationed permanently in Britannia—the Sixth Victrix, the Second Augusta and the Twentieth Valeria Victrix. They are only called up when the frontier boils over too much. As I said, it's unusual when a legion is called out to repel a raid."

She looked at him curiously as he lay so close to her on the hard ground. "You seem to know a lot about the Roman military situation in Britannia."

He looked at her quickly. "They are the enemy! To know one's enemy is to be forewarned!" He stood up and lifted his pack. "Come! We have a long way to go before we reach Guidd's steading."

She stood up and slung her pack over a shoulder. "Calgaich," she said.

He turned. "What is it?"

"You didn't mention that Britons themselves served along the Great Wall."

"They don't. British auxiliaries are like most Roman auxiliaries, they don't serve in their own country. The Romans are too clever to allow anything like that. One British auxiliary serves in the Teuton country east of Gaul." Calgaich's voice died away and the faraway look came in his eyes. He looked at her suddenly. "Why did you ask me that?" he asked her sharply.

"I was just curious, that's all."

Calgaich strode on. "There *are* Britons serving in Britannia, but they pride themselves on being Romans."

"What do you mean?" she persisted.

He looked back at her. "Most of the only true Romans in the three legions of Britannia are the legates, tribunes and many of the centurions. The common legionnaires are mostly descendants of the early Roman legionnaires who served in Britannia hundreds of years ago and married the British women whom they had conquered. Their sons, in turn, joined the legions and themselves married British women, or the daughters of other legionnaires, until the strain of blood in the legionnaires of today is almost pure British. But they call themselves *Romans* and are proud of it!"

"And the leaders of these legions? They are Romans?"

He nodded. "For the most part. Some of them are descendants of Romans who served in Spain, North Africa and other places, but they are still *Romans*." He spat out the word "Roman" as though he had a mouthful of bad meat or fish.

"Is it possible then, that these British Romans *like* being under Roman rule?" she asked.

"They know nothing else. They are too many years away from the old free days of their ancestors. Not even the dimmest memories of those days remain with them, or their fathers and grandfathers. The children are raised either in the *vici*, the settlements behind the forts of the Great Wall, or in the *coloniae* farther south, near the legion garrison towns. The *vici* and the *coloniae* are inhabited for the most part by retired legionnaires and auxiliaries with their wives and families. The children are raised to eat Roman food, speak the Roman language, wear their mode of clothing and to follow their religion and customs. They know nothing else.

"The boys, most of them, are sons of legionnaires or auxiliaries and are expected to enlist themselves when of age. They know they can't become Roman citizens until they have served their time. To be a Roman citizen is considered the greatest of honors for Britons or any other slave peoples. When they retire, they return to the *coloniae*, or the *vici*, marry British girls, who are themselves the daughters of retirees, raise their families, and start the process all over again. This has been going on for three hundred and fifty years."

"No wonder they can't think otherwise. Even as you, Calgaich, can't think any other way than the way you were raised."

He looked around at her quickly. "Do you find anything wrong with that, woman?" he snapped.

"There must be more to life than raiding and fighting," Cairenn said defiantly.

He stopped walking and stared at her as though she were not in her right mind. "There is hunting, woman!"

"I meant much more than that, Calgaich." She, too, stopped walking and met his gaze.

A disquieting feeling possessed him. "Where do you really come from?" he asked.

"From the country of the Ordovices. You know that." She straightened her tired shoulders, proud of her heritage.

He narrowed his eyes as he studied her face. He looked into her eyes as though he were trying to penetrate a screen or veil she might have put up to conceal her true self. A man could lose much looking into those eyes, per-

haps even his soul. Calgaich turned quickly and strode off
toward the forest.

They turned inland and found a secluded glade where
they rested and slept until the sun began to slant to the
west over distant Hibernia. When they arose, Calgaich led
the way through the gathering shadows of the late afternoon. A high, precipitous ridge loomed above them. Calgaich climbed it with an eagerness that belied their long
days of hard marching.

Calgaich stood in the shelter of the trees, leaning on his
spear, looking down into the wide river valley that lay far
below the ridge crest. Cairenn struggled up beside him and
dropped her pack.

Calgaich pointed with his spear. "Rioghaine, the King's
Place, the largest *rath* of the Novantae, which stands on
the shores of the great sea loch. It is my home." There was
a warmth and pride in his voice that Cairenn had not
heard before. She watched him silently as he stared out
over the valley. He was almost home.

Thin skeins of smoke from many cooking fires arose
from the sprawling *rath* across the wide river. The many
wattle-and-daub huts of the settlement looked like vari-
colored toadstools, for while the fresh heather thatch of
some of the huts was the color of honey, other huts were
capped with older thatch, dirty with age and smoke. A
bluish haze of smoke hung over the *rath* and drifted toward a low hill, upon which were two great earth and
timber ramparts that followed the slight contours of the
hill and looked like two huge snakes, one coiled within
the other. Within the irregular oval of the inner rampart
were many huts crowded together. The westward-slanting
sun reflected brightly from the spear blades of warriors
who stood guard along the inner rampart.

The frothing water of the shallow river flowed swiftly
over glistening black stones in its course to the bay opening from the great firth to the south. To the left, screened
by a thick fringe of trees, was a wide and long loch surrounded at a distance by high hills that hung over the
valley and dark waters like brooding giants with shaggy
crests of conifers and thick bracken.

A huge and ungainly structure stood on a naked outcropping of rock just to the south of the *dun*, the ramparted

hill fortress. The central part of the structure was not unlike the drystone tower in which Calgaich and Cairenn had found shelter their second night ashore. This tower, however, was many times larger and in excellent repair. Extensions had been built out from it on two sides and one of the extensions stood right on the edge of a precipice overlooking the river. Smoke rose from the central tower.

Calgaich pointed at the gaunt tower. "The Dun of Evicatos, who was my father's father."

"Whose spear and sword you carry."

He nodded. "They were made in an outbuilding of the *dun*. What do you think of Rioghaine, the King's Place?"

"It is beautiful, Calgaich."

"There was much fighting here in the old days. The Selgovae once claimed this place as their own. The Novantae came by sea from somewhere to the southwest. There were great battles fought here. The river ran red with blood. The smoke of burning huts rose high in the sky." His voice began its singsong chant. He held out his spear and shook it. "In time the Novantae drove the Selgovae to the east. It was not until the time of the Romans that the Novantae and the Selgovae became allies against the Red Crests. The Romans defeated the Selgovae, but never the Novantae! That was long ago, long ago." His voice died away.

The wind shifted and murmured through the trees. It moaned faintly through the river valley. Cairenn shivered a little.

"The Selgovae are our allies again," Calgaich continued. "They've fought beside us many times against the Romans. They are great warriors. My own mother, the gods bless her, and keep her well, was the daughter of a union between a chief's daughter of the Selgovae and a Roman legate." It was as though he were talking to himself. His hands tightened on his spear shaft until the knuckles stood out whitely.

Cairenn looked quickly into his set face. She had thought he was of pure Celtish blood, such as the Selgovae and the Novantae, but for him to be of one-quarter Roman blood—and still have his intense hatred of Romans—was indeed strange.

Calgaich looked down at her. "The Red Crests have been too long in this land. Time and time again the wild waves of warriors from Caledonia have washed against and over their damned wall. There were times when even the Novantae were driven back from this land. The Red Crests established forts and outposts in the lands of the Selgovae and the Novantae, but in time they couldn't stand the constant pressure of the tribesmen and fell back themselves. When I was first a warrior, I fought against them. You saw the fort I set fire to with my own hands. It became a funeral pyre for a *turma* of Roman auxiliary cavalry. Not one of them escaped! Aye, they've been in this land too long, like a festering wound that must be cleansed and healed. Some day, some day . . ." His voice trailed off.

There was intense hatred of the Romans in his words *and yet there was Roman blood in his veins.*

"Come," Calgaich said. "It will soon be dark and the wolves are the owners of the nights in these glens."

The sun was almost gone when Calgaich motioned for Cairenn to drop to the ground. Then he vanished into the bracken and woods as silently as a hunting cat.

A faint whickering sound soon came from the direction where Calgaich had disappeared. A few minutes later the sound came again. Then it was quiet except for the wind soughing through the trees.

Suddenly Calgaich appeared. "Guidd comes," he said. Nothing moved except the leaves of the trees.

Cairenn wet her dry lips and looked uneasily from one side of her to the other. The shadows seemed to have taken on the appearances of strange and grotesque creatures who shifted and changed before her very eyes.

Calgaich glanced toward Cairenn. "The forest is alive," he said mysteriously.

Suddenly she seemed to *feel* a presence. A curious musky odor came on the wind. She turned quickly and could not help but cry out. She backed toward Calgaich and pressed herself against him.

A wolflike shape stood between two of the trees, almost like part of their shadow. Its head was held up high and its mouth gaped widely. Its forepaws were thrust out in front of the body and held a short hunting spear. A picture flashed through Cairenn's mind—the punch marks on Calgaich's spear and sword showed two such figures with their forepaws holding them erect against a bell-shaped tower.

The wolf came closer and Cairenn finally saw a human face under the wolf's-head cap. The man moved so noiselessly it seemed as if he were not a man of flesh and blood at all but some creature of the night conjured up out of the dark forest.

"Guidd, old wolf!" Calgaich called.

"Calgaich! Calgaich! Calgaich!" Guidd cried. There was a catch in his hoarse voice. His brown, seamed face glistened with tears from his one yellowish eye. He drew close to Calgaich and Cairenn. Cairenn stepped hastily aside. Guidd's head hardly reached to Calgaich's chin, but he dealt him such a buffet with his right hand that it sent Calgaich staggering backward. Calgaich returned the blow with such force that Guidd went sprawling backward in the bracken and his wolf's-head cap fell off to reveal his gray poll. His foxlike face split into a wide grin. He got to his feet and flopped the headpiece back into position and Cairenn could see that it was still attached to the pelt, which was over Guidd's shoulders and belted about his waist. He wore wolfskin leggings and a necklace of wolf's claws about his neck.

Guidd studied Cairenn with his one piercing eye. He nodded in appreciation.

"She's not my wife, Guidd. She is a *cumal* only, gifted to me by Crann of the Five Hostages," Calgaich explained hastily.

Cairenn again heard his words with sorrow. Their night together had meant much to her, but for him it had been something whiskey had caused, something to shrug off and forget. She straightened her tired shoulders and forced herself to meet Guidd's stare.

Guidd tilted his grizzled head to one side. His eye flicked over Cairenn from head to foot and then back again, slowly, as if he could see beneath her dusty boy's clothing to her young girl's body. "Are these the wages Crann of the Five Hostages now pays his *fianna* for a little pleasurable red work with spear and sword?" he murmured. He whistled sharply. "It was not so in my time in Eriu when I was outlawed from the Novantae."

"Crann had no she-wolves then," Calgaich said as he again clapped Guidd on his furred shoulder.

Darkness was gathering swiftly. The howling of a wolf came from somewhere in the dark hills.

"Come to my wolf's den," Guidd invited. "Our four-footed brothers gather for the night's hunting, Calgaich." He grinned at Cairenn and his seamed face seemed to change as if by magic into the semblance of an old grizzler of a wolf. She shuddered and looked away. Guidd laughed softly as he led them through the darkening forests.

Guidd reached the landward end of the loch where the river ran shallowly over and between great stones. The woodsman skipped ably from one stone to another and waited for the others on the far side of the river. He grinned as he saw Calgaich pick the woman up under one arm and carry her quickly across.

Guidd led the way into the thick forest to the edge of the loch. There was no sign of a habitation anywhere in sight. Guidd looked back at Calgaich. "Do you remember the way across the *crannog* path?" he asked.

"It has been too many years, old wolf."

There was a small, tree-studded island a good spear's cast from the shore. The bald head of a great rock outcropping showed above the trees. Guidd stepped into the water. He looked back at Calgaich. "Stay close behind me, Calgaich," he warned. "The loch is deep and cold."

Calgaich handed the woodsman his war spear. He got down on his knees and looked over a shoulder at Cairenn. "Mount, little one," he invited. Cairenn hesitated a moment before climbing onto his back. She had not been this close to him, her legs spread around his narrow hips, since that night he had taken her, drunkenly forced himself into her, finally exhausting them both. Calgaich stood up without effort as Cairenn held tightly to him, her arms around his neck, her mouth pressed beside the warm mat of his hair.

Guidd began walking out into the water. Calgaich closed up tight behind him. Guidd made a sharp turn to the left, waded a few paces and then made a sharp turn to the right. He waded on for several spear's lengths and

then angled to his left again, then curved right and walked
straight for a time. Calgaich waded close behind him.

Something made Cairenn turn her head. Her heart sank
and her throat went dry. Two wolves stood on the shore
watching the progress of the three people out into the
loch. "Calgaich," she whispered. He shook his head,
intent only on following Guidd.

Guidd made two more turns, one hard left, then a
sharp right-hand turn, and then he angled in to the shore
of the rocky islet. He stepped out of the water and turned
to watch Calgaich and Cairenn. She looked back over her
shoulder again. The two wolves were wading behind them.
She placed a hand over her eyes.

Calgaich eased Cairenn to the ground. "I would not
have made it without your guidance, Guidd. The years
washed away my memory of the path." He looked at
Cairenn. "Have they *crannogs* in your country?" he asked.

She shook her head. "The wolves!" she cried, trembling.
She could not help herself. They were halfway to the islet.

Guidd laughed. He whistled sharply. The wolves barked.
"They are my brothers, woman," he explained. He looked
at her slyly out of the corner of his eye. "They guarded
us on our way through the forest. They are only coming
home."

Calgaich studied the two huge wolfhounds. "Guidd?"
he asked. "Could one of them be my hound Bron?"

Guidd shook his head. "They are both mine, Calgaich."

"And where is Bron?" Calgaich asked.

Guidd shrugged. "I saw the great hound some time
after you left for Eriu. For a long time I did not see him.
One year the pack came out of the hills in the winter
when food was hard to come by. Your father ordered
me to get rid of them if I could. I had the help of several
other woodsmen. We fought a great battle with the wolves."
He patted the wolf head on top of his own head. "This
is one of them. One of the other woodsmen put his mark
on a great brindle of a wolf and was slain in return."
Guidd greeted the two hounds as they splashed ashore.
He grinned at the frightened look on Cairenn's face as she
moved closer to Calgaich.

"Go on," Calgaich urged.

"The wolf was sore wounded, Calgaich. I could have

killed him, but something held me back. I think he was Bron. I left him there in the dark woods. The next day he was gone. The snow was red with his blood. For a long time I thought he was dead. Then one night the pack came down again from the hills. They howled that night. How they howled!" His one eye glistened. He looked up at the dark hills. "Then I heard one of them barking."

"Bron?"

Guidd shrugged. "Have you ever heard a wolf bark, my brother?"

As though in answer to Guidd's question, a wolf howled in the woods on the far side of the loch.

Guidd handed Calgaich his spear. "Come into my wolf's den," he invited, leading the way into the trees.

Cairenn looked back across the smooth surface of the loch. There was no indication of the underwater rock pathway by which they had reached the island.

"A *crannog*, Cairenn," Calgaich explained. "Only those who live here know the way. To step off the pathway is to sink into the deep water. The *crannog* and his wolfhounds are the two reasons Guidd stays alive while my uncle rules the Novantae, otherwise he would be killed on sight by Bruidge's warriors. If Guidd got his chance, he would kill Bruidge in turn. Guidd was my father's hound. He knows no other master."

Guidd's den was a cave in the side of the naked outcropping of rock. He had enclosed the front of it with a palisade of timbers cleverly concealed by brush and trees. Guidd lighted an oil lamp of Roman fashion and threw wood on the smoldering fireplace in the center of the hard-packed earthen floor. The air of the den was thick and close, and redolent with the mingled odors of smoke, stale sweat, cooked food, damp wool, wet hounds, and the scent of strong *usquebaugh*. A wide, low bed stood beside one wall. It was covered with greasy hides and filthy sheep and wolf skins. The rear of the cave seemed to probe into the very darkness of the pit itself. Cairenn was reminded eerily of the barrow in which she and Calgaich had sought shelter their first night ashore in Albu.

Guidd barred the door after the wolfhounds had entered. He placed his wide-bladed hunting spear close beside the door. "Bruidge of the Battle-Axe has his spies everywhere," he explained over a shoulder. "The hounds will warn us if they come to the loch shore."

"Is it as bad as all that?" Calgaich asked.

Guidd's seamed face was grim. "No one in the clan can say that he is still your friend, Calgaich. No one can talk about you or your father without being heard by Bruidge's spies. He rules this country by fear."

"Is he at Rioghaine now?"

Guidd laughed harshly as he placed a jug of whiskey on the table. "He is almost always there now. He rarely ever leaves the Dun of Evicatos. Bruidge of the Battle-Axe? Call him rather Bruidge of the Bottle. He has hardly left the Dun of Evicatos these past few months nor drawn a sober breath."

Cairenn, forgotten by the two men, set her pack against the cave wall and tiredly slumped onto the earthen floor beside it. The warm, stale air of the chamber made her sleepy. She closed her eyes and half listened as the two men continued talking of the changes that had brought Bruidge to Calgaich's home.

"What have any of the Novantae done to rescue my father?"

Guidd looked quickly sideways at Calgaich. "Rescue?" he asked. "The Novantae can hardly do it alone. Your father is in the prison at Fortress ala Petriana, guarded by the cavalry regiment stationed there—one thousand horsemen of the senior regiment of cavalry in the entire Province of Britain. Ala Petriana is now the largest and strongest fort along the Great Wall of Hadrian. Since your father was taken there, a cohort of the Twentieth Legion was brought up from Camulodunum as personal escort to Quaestor Lucius Sextillius, acting governor of the province, who is supposedly on an inspection tour of the wall."

"That perverted pig?" Calgaich demanded.

Guidd unstoppered the jug and filled two earthenware bowls with the powerful spirits. "Half goat and half man. What is it the Red Crests call such a being?"

"Satyr," Calgaich replied. He reached for one of the bowls. "What's he really doing along the wall?"

Guidd threw some wood on the smoldering fire. "The

rumor is that he is really trying to make a deal with your beloved uncle Bruidge."

Calgaich drank deeply, then slowly lowered the bowl. He wiped his mouth and mustache with the back of a hand. "You lie," he murmured. "Not even Bruidge would do that." His voice died away at the look in Guidd's one eye.

Guidd bent his head a little and looked at Calgaich from under lowered brows. "You call me *liar?*" he challenged.

Cairenn opened her eyes in alarm. The honor of a Celt was a touchy thing. Even Calgaich's long friendship with Guidd could not bridge the insult he had given the woodsman.

Calgaich smiled placatingly. He extended his empty hands. "I was not thinking, old wolf."

Almost imperceptibly, the hackles of the woodsman seemed to lie down. Guidd reached out his hands to those of Calgaich. Calgaich drew him close and hugged him hard. "I should have known better," he murmured.

Guidd turned away and looked at Cairenn, seated against the wall. "There is food to prepare," he said huskily. His one eye glistened brightly.

While Cairenn prepared the meal, the jug passed back and forth between Calgaich and Guidd with great regularity. The woodsman's larder surprised Cairenn. There was freshly caught salmon, firm and pink of flesh. She found a jug of thick, sugary honey for spreading on hard brown-crusted bread. There were chunks of mottled cheese tangy to the taste.

All the time the three of them ate, the contents of the jug were steadily lowered. When the food was finished, Calgaich and Guidd sat crosslegged by the fire while Cairenn cleared away the debris of the meal. Now and again she would glance at the two huge wolfhounds who lay in the shadows near the doorway. Their yellow eyes were like moist jewels reflecting the dancing firelight as they watched Cairenn moving about. When she was finished she returned to her place against the wall.

"Can I safely enter the *dun*, Guidd?" Calgaich asked.

"Does a wolf willingly put his head into a trap?" Guidd asked pointedly.

"What can Bruidge fear from me? One man can't kill him in his own den. He knows the law. If I come to him to offer kinship, he can't wet his hands with my blood."

"Don't rely on that kinship, Calgaich. True, he can't kill you himself, but his personal bodyguard is never far away from him. Bruidge no longer trusts the Novantae. His guards are not of our people. Some of them are 'broken men' from other clans—outlaws who have come here to serve him for pay." Guidd leaned closer to Calgaich. "By the gods of darkness! He even has some Picts and Saxons among his guards!"

"Picts? Saxons? Saxon sea-wolves here in Rioghaine?" Calgaich demanded harshly.

"Aye!" Guidd drank deeply and then hiccupped. "I said he trusted no one. As long as he pays his guards well, they serve him well. Once Bruidge of the Battle-Axe was a man to be reckoned with in battle, but now he is a coward. He fears everything, including his own people, and, mark you, he sees things in the darkness of his own bedchamber and hall *that no one else can see.*" Guidd nodded wisely. "Therefore, he is never alone."

"He sees things only in the haze from the whiskey jug." Calgaich spat contemptuously.

"Perhaps. Still, there are things one alone can see— things meant for one alone." Guidd's whiskey-hoarse voice trailed off meaningfully.

The two wolfhounds raised their heads as the faint howlings of other wolves penetrated into the cave. The night wind moaned through the trees.

"There is a cold stone in the fat belly of Bruidge of the Bottle," Guidd said. "He can't be trusted more than a spear's length away. His fear of something unknown makes him doubly treacherous and dangerous."

"What gives him this great fear?"

Guidd shrugged. "His own people. You, his nephew. The Romans. He wants to secure himself in the chieftainship. That's why he is playing the weakling's game of putting himself into the hands of one enemy to save himself from another."

"You talk in riddles, old hound."

Guidd shook his grizzled head. "There have been

Romans here in Rioghaine. For a time they came disguised. Some of them even pretended to be Greek traders. Others came as healers of the eye sickness. But it takes more than a change of name and clothing to conceal a damned Red Crest from *me*, Calgaich!"

"Romans here?" Calgaich stared in disbelief at the woodsman.

Guidd nodded. "There are two of them here now. They promise Bruidge much. They are soldiers, Calgaich. A tribune and a centurion."

Calgaich emptied his whiskey bowl. He refilled it and then drew Guidd closer by gripping one of his shoulders. "How did my father fall into the hands of the Romans?" he demanded. "Was it really the trickery of Bruidge?"

Guidd winced at the pain of Calgaich's grip. "No one is sure. To accuse Bruidge is to die suddenly. Some who spoke openly about the matter were called up to the *dun*, and they were never seen again." Guidd pried Calgaich's fingers loose. "My shoulder sleeps," he protested.

Calgaich released the woodsman. "Paralus, the Greek trader, told me about this treachery. Are there enough warriors to back me up if I have to drive Bruidge from his damned *dun?*"

Guidd thoughtfully rubbed his bearded jaw. "I don't know. Times have changed. Your father was old and feeble. There were times when he talked of peace between the Novantae and the Romans."

Calgaich shook his head. "I can't believe that."

"It's not a bad thought," Cairenn said out of the shadows.

Guidd turned slowly to look at her. There was astonishment on his seamed face. "She spoke into the conversation of *men!*" he exclaimed.

Calgaich shrugged and sipped at his whiskey bowl. "She's only a *cumal*. She doesn't know any better."

"What is wrong with peace with the Romans?" Cairenn persisted, ignoring the stare of Guidd.

Calgaich glanced at Guidd. "It's her way," he explained, looking back at Cairenn. "There can never be any peace between the Novantae and the Romans."

"There is peace between the Britons and the Romans, *fian.*"

He nodded. "The Britons had little choice. We do."

"The Red Crests create a desolation and call it peace," Guidd growled. "Bruidge may need the help of the Romans to hold his kingship. Always they seek to secure the border. They have never conquered the Novantae by war. Now they try to do it by guile."

"And Bruidge is the means," Calgaich added.

"For Roman pay some men will do anything. Aye! They'd sell their very souls!"

Calgaich looked into the embers of the fire as though he could foresee the future in its strange flickering shapes. "If my father is still alive, he is still the chief of the clan. Nothing but his death can take that right away from him."

Guidd spat into the embers. "An old man, almost blind, who is imprisoned in a Roman fort is less of a chief, even by right, than a brother of his seated in the chief's own *dun*, well protected by a personal bodyguard of Picts and Saxons and with the friendship of the Romans to boot."

"You've forgotten that I am still alive and back in Caledonia."

"I have not forgotten," Guidd replied.

Calgaich placed an arm about the shoulders of the woodsman and drew him close. "I know that, old hound. There are times when I forget myself."

Calgaich stood up and began to pace back and forth. "How is Morar?" he asked.

"As beautiful as ever, maybe more so." Cairenn heard the question and answer with sadness.

"Where is she now?"

Guidd reached for the jug and began to fill his bowl.

"Guidd?" Calgaich asked.

"She and her younger sister Bronwyn have gone to Luguvalium," Guidd answered softly, not looking at Calgaich.

Calgaich stopped his pacing. His face seemed to harden. "What's that you say? Luguvallum? A Roman stronghold? Why?"

Guidd shrugged. "Bruidge got permission from the Romans so that they might go there. You know how Morar likes bright things and the shops they have in the city. She has always wanted to live south of the Great Wall. She has no family except Bronwyn. Bruidge is their guardian."

"Perhaps she went to take care of my father?" Calgaich said, standing before Guidd.

Guidd closed his one eye and looked away from Calgaich before he opened it again. "Perhaps," he agreed.

"But you don't believe that?"

Guidd emptied his whiskey bowl and reached again for the jug.

"Guidd! Damn you!" Calgaich snapped. "There isn't anything going on here that you don't know about! Do you believe that Morar went there to take care of my father?"

"Damn you, Calgaich! *No!*"

Calgaich sat down again. "I had thought she might be here when I returned." He did not notice the great eyes of Cairenn studying him from the shadows. He looked sideways at Guidd. "Are you holding something back from me?"

Guidd held out his hands, palms upwards, and shrugged. "Why should I do that?" he asked guilelessly.

"Look at me, Guidd."

The woodsman reluctantly turned his head. They sat there, a few feet apart, studying each other, eye to eye, and then Guidd slowly looked away.

"Tell me the truth, old hound."

"I will if you keep your hand from your dirk."

"I promise."

"I told you that Quaestor Lucius Sextillius, acting governor of the province, is at Luguvalium, supposedly on an inspection tour of the Great Wall, but the rumors have been that he is trying to make some kind of deal with Bruidge. It is also rumored that if he succeeds in making this deal with Bruidge, he will be recalled to Rome to report firsthand to the Senate and the emperor. So Sextillius, the Perfumed Pig, as even some of his own men call him, wanted hostages to take with him to Rome as proof of the good will of Bruidge."

It was very quiet in the cave. The night wind moaned faintly through the trees outside it. Guidd nervously cleared his throat.

"Morar and Bronwyn?" Calgaich asked incredulously. "Morar and Bronwyn?" He jumped to his feet. *"Morar and Bronwyn?"* he shouted.

Guidd leaned over backwards and scuttled away from Calgaich on his hands and knees. He looked back over a shoulder. "Keep your damned hands off that dirk!" he yelled. "I had nothing to do with it!"

The dirk shone softly in the light of the oil lamp as Calgaich drew it. His eyes were wide in his head. His breathing came fast and shallow. He raised the dirk as though to strike, and stood there transfixed, so great was his cold rage.

"There's a way out the back, woman," Guidd hissed as he passed Cairenn.

Cairenn stood up to meet Calgaich as he followed Guidd. "Calgaich," she said quietly.

He looked at her for a long moment, as if he did not recognize her. Then he slowly lowered his dirk. He looked about at the entrance of the cave and the wall, as if he were in a strange place. Guidd watched him warily from the hidden back entrance. "Come back, Guidd. My rage was not for you," Calgaich said at last.

The woodsman came back into the light but stood a few paces behind Cairenn. "Sheath the dirk," he requested nervously. "There is more to tell."

Calgaich thrust the dirk into its sheath. "Go on," he said coldly.

Guidd swallowed hard. "Some say Morar is to be betrothed to Lucius Sextillius. There! I've said it! The gods know I would have been the last to tell you, Calgaich."

Cairenn watched from the shadows as Calgaich shook his head. At last he seemed to understand. "It's better that you did." He reached for his cloak and threw it about his shoulders. He stabbed home the pin of the *fibula* to hold the cloak about his throat. He reached for his war spear and then shook his head. It would be of little use in close combat within the *dun* if Bruidge betrayed traditional hospitality by setting his mercenaries on Calgaich. Instead, he picked up his sheathed sword and attached the scabbard to his belt.

Guidd narrowed his one eye. "The *sword*, my brother."

Calgaich drew the splendid weapon from its sheath and handed it to Guidd. Guidd held the blade so that the light shone on it. The reflection of the light glistened like rippling water on the fine blade. Guidd peered closely at the mark of the master metalsmith and then whistled softly. He looked at Calgaich. "Is it really so?" he asked softly.

Calgaich nodded. "It is so."

"The lost Sword of Evicatos," Guidd murmured in awe. "How did you come by it?"

Calgaich reached for the sword and sheathed it. "I prayed to Lugh of the Shining Spear," he replied simply. "Will you guide me to the shore?"

"The wolves haunt the night along this loch, as you well know. It would be better if you took my *curragh* to the other end of the loch and then walked to the *dun* from there. Even so, the wolves may greet you at the shore. Better still, stay here tonight and we'll go together tomorrow. You may need someone to guard your back."

Calgaich shook his head. "You have no blood ties with Bruidge. His hospitality won't extend to you. You know they would kill you on sight."

"I could take a few of them with me, Calgaich!" Guidd boasted.

Calgaich extended a hand and gripped Guidd by the shoulder. "I can't afford to lose you now, Guidd. You may be the only friend I have left among the Novantae. Not much, of course, but still a friend." Calgaich grinned.

Guidd led the way past the woman. She looked up into Calgaich's face as he passed her but there was no sign of recognition on it. "The woman is yours if I do not return, Guidd," Calgaich said.

There was a sharp, stifled cry from Cairenn.

Calgaich turned to silence her. "It is the only way, woman. Or would you rather be given over to Bruidge and his hired killers?" He disappeared into the darkness of the cave.

Guidd removed loose brush from the opening at the end of the natural tunnel. They both stood up among the trees. The moon was rising. Guidd dragged a small wicker-

and-hide boat from under the bracken. He slid the *curragh* into the water.

Calgaich got into the small craft. He paddled it out beyond the shore. He looked back. "I'll return," he promised.

There was no reply from Guidd. He watched Calgaich for a little while. He shook his head. Then he returned inside the tunnel and pulled the brush back about the opening.

Guidd walked catlike back into the cave where the woman was feeding the fire. He reached for the jug. She jumped a little at his appearance. She warmed her hands at the fire and watched the woodsman sideways.

"If he does not return, little hare," Guidd said slowly with a slanted grin, "what shall become of you, eh?"

She held out a small foot to warm it at the fire.

Guidd eyed her up and down. He liked what he saw. "Perhaps I have let him walk into a trap," he suggested slyly.

She glanced at him quickly. He was startled at the look on her lovely face, for it had turned into a mask of hate. She dropped her hand to her dirk. "If you have, old wolf," she grated between fixed teeth, "you have opened the door to your own sudden death."

Guidd stared unbelievingly at her and then he began to laugh. He rocked his gray poll from side to side while tears streamed from his lone eye. He slapped his hands on his thighs. "By the gods!" he exploded. "I believe you mean it, little hare!"

She walked to the great war spear of Calgaich and passed a hand down the smoothly worn shaft. "Try me, just try me, Guidd One-Eye," she suggested in a broken voice.

The fire crackled lower and lower. Now and then Guidd nipped at the jug. Cairenn huddled under a skin on the low, filthy bed, unable to sleep. She could not drive from her mind Calgaich's cold, harsh words as he had left her behind with no farewell or caress, just the statement that if he did not return, she became Guidd's property, his *cumal*. Thoughts of her love for Calgaich intertwined with her fear of Guidd and the night beyond. She cried silently so Guidd would not hear.

The wind moaned hollowly about the cave. Once the faint howling of a wolf came to them on the wind, but it seemed far away, from the other end of the loch. There seemed to be evil afoot, both of wolf and of man, that moonlit night in the country of the Novantae.

CHAPTER 6

The moon was still behind the hills to the east when Calgaich grounded the *curragh* on the shore. He dragged the skin boat up into the brush.

A wolf howled in the distance. Another wolf called in brotherly greeting; it was much closer, between Calgaich and the path he must take to reach the higher ground below the *rath* and the *dun*. The area was covered thickly with a large copse of close-set birch trees.

Something moved in the thick bracken. Calgaich leaped backward and whipped out his sword with his right hand and his dirk with his left. A dark, lean shape suddenly cleared the bracken and launched itself at Calgaich. Calgaich jumped to one side and glanced quickly over his left shoulder. Another wolf was moving swiftly toward him. He met the attack of the first of the wolves with a sideways slashing of his sword that struck between the beast's open jaws and severed the top of the skull from the lower jaw. The corpse struck against him and hurled him backwards against a birch tree as the second wolf missed its charge and hurtled past him. The bloody sword struck like a woodsman's axe just behind the wolf's head to sever the spinal column. Blood sprayed back against Calgaich as the writhing beast struck against his legs. Its powerful jaws snapped futilely for the last time.

Calgaich whirled. Three more wolves were plunging through the brush toward him. The first of the snarling trio rose on its hind legs. Calgaich's sword caught it across the throat; his dirk sank to the hilt in its belly. The snarling beast rolled over and over, thrashing its legs in its death agony.

The two remaining wolves broke their charges, one to either hand of Calgaich, and then swung about, returning

94

to the attack; but this time they stalked in rather than charged. Somewhere in the woods a pack of wolves howled in unison. Calgaich backed slowly between the trees toward the bank of the loch. One of the stalking wolves cut in between Calgaich and the *curragh*. A dark shape detached itself from the shadows behind Calgaich and launched its attack. The wolf struck hard at his sword arm, but its jaws became entangled in the thick wool of his cloak. Calgaich's forearm was so numbed from the powerful closure of the jaws that he dropped his sword.

Calgaich whirled to meet a second charge from the wolf. He flung out his left arm to raise the entangling cloak between himself and the animal, while he shifted his dirk to his right hand. He drove the dirk up full to the hilt into the belly of the wolf. It fell sideways and wrenched the dirk from Calgaich's hand.

He staggered toward the water. Suddenly a wolf landed on his back and he went down. He rolled over and gripped the throat of the wolf. The wolf's hind claws raked at Calgaich's belly and thighs in an effort to disembowel him, but again the thick woolen cloak muffled the attack.

Calgaich and the wolf fought it out on the rough shingle of the loch shore, and strangely enough they were left alone in their death struggle while a furor of the snarling beasts broke out just within the shelter of the birches. The smell of hot blood came to Calgaich on the wind from within the birch copse. He forced the wolf's head down into the water, and held the powerful beast there with straining muscles until at last the wolf lay still.

Calgaich stood up. His body trembled from exertion. He could feel the blood running down his legs from where the claws of the wolf had raked through his trousers. He dropped his cloak to free himself for swimming out into the loch.

Another huge wolf stood just within the edge of the birches. Its breathing was harsh and irregular. Slowly, ever so slowly, Calgaich bent his knees so that he could feel about on the shingle for his dirk. He did not take his eyes from the great beast. The wolf did not move. Calgaich found his dirk, then extended it toward the wolf to meet a possible charge, while he moved about slowly until one of his feet trod on his sword. He closed his hand on the hilt, and straightened up with ready weapons to face the last and obviously the greatest of the wolves.

Calgaich smiled crookedly. "So, they've fled and left their champion," he said softly. It was a veritable king of wolves. "Come on, brother," he hissed between set teeth.

The wolf moved just a little. Its yellow eyes seemed to glow in the darkness.

An eerie feeling crept over Calgaich and chilled his sweating body. Maybe it wasn't a wolf—at least a flesh and blood creature—but rather something of the nether world.

The wolf moved a little closer. He nodded his head up and down and whined softly like a hound. He came closer and then dropped to his belly to creep closer and ever closer to Calgaich.

Calgaich stared incredulously at the beast. He dropped his weapons. He held out his bloodied hands. The beast came to him quickly, whimpering deep within his throat. "Bron," Calgaich murmured. He dropped to his knees and drew the huge wolfhound close to him. He pressed his head against that of the hound. "Bron, my own wolfhound." Bron pressed hard against his master.

Little wonder the last of the wolf pack had left Calgaich alone to strangle the wolf that had trapped him at the water's edge. Bron seemed to have come out of nowhere to fight savagely against some of the pack to save his master. Where the hound had come from and how he had timed the rescue were beyond Calgaich's understanding.

Calgaich stood up and looked down at Bron. A strange thought crept through his mind. If there had ever been a one-man hound among the Novantae, it had been Bron, but where had the hound been in the years Calgaich served in Eriu?

The answer came on the night wind. A wolf howled from deep within the forest. Bron raised his bloodied muzzle and howled out a response.

Something Guidd had said came back to Calgaich, "I saw Bron some time after you had left for Eriu. For a long time I did not see him. One year the wolf pack came out of the hills in the winter when food was hard to come by. Your father ordered me to get rid of them. I had the help of several other woodsmen. We fought a great battle with the wolves.

"One of the other woodsmen put his mark on a great brindle of a wolf and was slain in return. The wolf was sore wounded. I could have killed him, but something held me back. I think he was Bron. I left him there in the dark woods. The next day he was gone. The snow was red with wolf blood. For a long time I thought he was dead. Then one night the pack came down again from the hills. They howled that night. How they howled! Then I heard one of them barking."

"Bron," Calgaich said.

The hound barked sharply in response.

Calgaich ran his hands over the thickly pelted body and felt the ridged marks of old scars.

Calgaich wiped his weapons on the pelt of one of the dead wolves, then sheathed the blades and swung his cloak about his shoulders. He walked along the shingle and then turned to look toward Bron.

Bron stood there as though carved from wood. A wolf howled from within the forest. The howling seemed to have an almost plaintive quality about it. Perhaps she was Bron's mate.

Calgaich turned and entered the birch copse. He did not look back at Bron. In a little while Bron padded up silently beside him.

Calgaich paused at the edge of the forest. No lights could be seen in the *rath*, in the great *dun* on the hill, nor about the gaunt stone Dun of Evicatos. Night was the time of the wolf and the evil ones. No one ventured out of the settlement or the *dun* until the first light of dawn.

Calgaich looked up at the tower that had been his home for most of his life, save for the years of fosterage with his uncle Bruidge. During that time he had lived farther along the coast of the firth. When Bruidge had succeeded Lellan as chief of the Novantae, he had taken over the Dun of Evicatos as his rightful habitation.

"Rightful?" Calgaich questioned the night.

He looked down at Bron. Bruidge and his men would kill the hound on sight. They would know that Bron had outlawed himself by running with the wolf pack when Calgaich had left for Eriu. "Stay," he ordered the beast.

Bron looked up toward the dark *dun* and growled deep in his throat. Calgaich raised his left arm and pointed into the forest in the general direction of Guidd's *crannog.* "Guidd," Calgaich said. "Guidd, Guidd." Maybe he would remember that Guidd had spared his life the day of the great wolf hunting.

Calgaich did not look back as he climbed the steep slope toward the *dun,* but when he paused outside its door and looked down the slope, Bron was gone. He drew his dirk and hammered the knob of it hard against the rough-hewn planking of the door.

"Who is there?" a suspicious voice called out.

There could be no going back now. "Open the door to Calgaich, the son of Lellan!" Calgaich shouted.

He heard rapid footsteps within the passageway. It was quiet again. He still had time to retreat to the forest.

Minutes passed slowly.

There came the sound of bars being removed inside the doorway. The door grated open on rusty hinges. In the flickering light of a rush torch a man in a bronze helmet and a battered Roman corselet eyed Calgaich suspiciously.

"Are you truly the son of Lellan?" the guard asked.

"Look at me!" Calgaich snapped.

"I did not know him, or you either."

Calgaich leaned close and held the guard eye to eye. "You know me now! Show me the way to my uncle, Bruidge of the Battle-Axe. It has been a long time since we met."

The guard closed the door behind Calgaich, then barred and chained it. "The chief is in the great hall, Calgaich mac Lellan," the guard said. "Follow me."

They passed through the narrow drystone passage. Calgaich had an uneasy feeling between his shoulder blades. The timbered ceiling had been pierced by a number of "murder" holes through which a spear blade could be suddenly thrust into the back of an unwelcome visitor. Calgaich's sharp hearing picked up the sound of weight being shifted about on the floor above the ceiling.

He and the guard walked into the antechamber of the main hall of the *dun,* a circular area that had once been roofed, a little over the height of a tall man, but in the time of Evicatos the roof had been raised much higher.

Above it was another circular space sectioned off into
bedchambers. Now the great hall was a curious affair that
filled the entire southwest side of the *dun* interior. It had
been extended beyond the enormously thick double walls
of the tower to form a rectangular chamber that overhung
a sheer drop of several hundred feet to the roaring river
far below.

It had been Evicatos who had originated the idea of extending the tower, but it had been his elder son Lellan
who had finished it, as it now stood, in honor of the Selgovae woman he had brought home as his wife. Calgaich's
mother had borne the proud Roman name of Lydia, for
she had been the daughter of a chieftain's daughter of the
proud and ancient tribe of Selgovae, who had married a
Roman tribune. Lydia had spent most of her early life
living among the Romans in Britannia and had never become quite used to the rude and violent ways of the Novantae. She had given birth to her only child in the great
dun, he who was to be Calgaich, son of Lellan.

The guard rapped on the inner door. The door was
flung open by a spearman in leathern tunic who studied
Calgaich with a pair of cold, pale blue eyes. Calgaich
pushed past him to enter the great hall of the *dun*.

A thick reek of pungent smoke hung in the hall. Two
large fireplaces stood at each side of the hall on the huge
flagstones that floored it. A servant slowly turned a spit
upon which was thrust the carcass of a large boar. The
mingled aromas of woodsmoke, dried bracken and rushes,
stale food, unwashed humans and dogs, sweat soaked
wool and greasy sheepskins, coupled with the smell of
oiled leather and of the slops of strong drink, settled itself comfortably about Calgaich with the feeling of an old
familiar cloak. It was almost as if he had never been
away.

Torches hung in wall brackets and many Roman oil
lamps hung by chains from the thick, smoke-blackened
rafters. Hides and pelts that were fastened on the walls
moved restlessly in the rising heat from the fires and in
the cold drafts that forced their way in between the cracks
in the drystone walls. The firelight reflected dully from
tarnished shields, battered and still bloodstained weapons
and helmets, and other grim trophies of Novantae battles

with Selgovae, Damnonii, Hibernian sea raiders, Picts and Romans.

Dried rushes and bracken, strewn with large bones cracked by the teeth of hounds, rustled and crackled beneath Calgaich's feet as he walked toward the dais that extended the full width of the hall. A massive table, roughly hewn from timbers, stood on the dais. Nine men were seated about it. At the center with his back toward the wall, sat the man whom Calgaich had come from Eriu to beard in his own den—Bruidge of the Battle-Axe—blood uncle to Calgaich and father of Fergus, whom Calgaich had slain, and for whose death he had been outlawed from the tribe. Three great hounds rose to their feet and stood close to Bruidge as Calgaich approached. Their cold yellow eyes studied him. One of them growled deep in his throat.

In days long past, Bruidge of the Battle-Axe had well earned his name in heroic battles, when he had wielded the fearsome weapon that now hung on the wall close behind his chair. The axe was a crescent of weighty iron, fitted to an oaken shaft as thick as a sapling which was bound about with bronze rings. That axe had been the cause of sudden and bloody death to many enemies of the Novantae. Perhaps the unusual weapon was a clue to the dark soul of Bruidge, for it was not a true Celtic weapon, and it required an unusual mind and body to wield it.

Two men stood on either side of Bruidge. They wore wolfskin cloaks and horned helmets from beneath which depended braided hair as yellow as fresh straw. Their pale blue eyes stared rather stupidly at Calgaich. Saxons in the great hall of Evicatos and Lellan! The thought was that of Calgaich. It was an indication of the situation at Rioghaine since he had been outlawed and his father had been turned over to the Romans.

Calgaich glanced right and left along the table. The immobile tattooed faces of several Picts looked back at him. Most likely they were welcome guests of Bruidge, but in the time of Evicatos or Lellan, the heads of the Picts would have been raised above the battlements of the *dun* with spear shafts for necks.

There were also a number of Celts seated at the table, but none of them were familiar to Calgaich. Probably they were broken men, and not of the Novantae, but rather tribeless warriors or those outlawed from their own tribes. At the far end of the table, in semidarkness, sat two men wrapped in rusty-colored cloaks. Their hair was cut short and their faces were cleanshaven in contrast to the other guests who were long haired and mustachioed. There was something about those two men that sent a chill of warning through Calgaich.

Two gillies staggered past Calgaich carrying a huge wooden trencher upon which rested the roasted carcass of a boar. The beast's ugly, grinning visage still sported its long curved tusks. They placed the trencher in front of Bruidge.

Bruidge leaned forward a little and peered through the steam and smoke which arose from the boar carcass. "My brother's son is either the bravest man in Albu or the biggest fool to come here," he rumbled. "You boldly enter my hall with a blood price on your head. Any man here can kill you, Calgaich, and will not be held to pay the *galanas*."

Time had not dealt kindly with Bruidge. Too much strong drink had ravaged his face. His eyes seemed to protrude from their sockets and there was a glassy look in them. His hair and long mustache were striped with gray like a badger's pelt. His once strong features had lost the sharp, alert look of the warrior and hunter.

"Welcome to your old home, then, Calgaich mac Lellan," Bruidge said heartily, his tone changing. He raised his big silver-mounted drinking horn. "I but jested. Come! All of you. Do honor here to the son of my brother. Bring drink for my foster son and nephew."

A gillie came swiftly from the shadows and filled a drinking horn from a huge bronze-bound heather-beer vat. He handed it to Calgaich and left as swiftly as he had appeared, with a rearward glance of mingled awe and fear.

"Sit and drink, Calgaich!" Bruidge roared. "Do not fear that the good heather beer is poisoned, nephew. Poisoning is a dirty Roman trick we barbarians have not yet accepted as a means of warfare." He glanced toward the two cloaked men at the end of the table.

And treachery is an ancient Celtic trick, thought Calgaich. Even so, it was hardly likely Bruidge would attempt to poison his own nephew in front of strangers.

"What has brought you home to Eriu?" Bruidge asked as he lowered his drinking horn and wiped his dripping mustache both ways.

"You know why I have thrust my head into this *dun*, Uncle," Calgaich replied curtly. "My father is in the hands of the Romans—if he is still alive."

Bruidge's yellowed eyes flicked again toward the two men seated at the end of the table, then he looked back at Calgaich. "My brother is still alive, Calgaich, although his sight is almost gone."

"And his health, my uncle? How is that?"

"He was not in good health when he left here."

"It is better for a man to die in his own country among his own people than in the hands of the Romans."

"The Romans do not think so."

"Is he a hostage then?"

"The Romans are skilled in medicine. They know much about the eye sickness our people suffer from. Some say it is caused by marsh gases. I myself think . . ." His voice died away as he saw the look on Calgaich's face.

"It is also said that my betrothed, Morar, and her sister, Bronwyn, are in the hands of the Romans at Lugu-valium," Calgaich continued.

His uncle shifted uneasily in his seat and studied his huge, veined hands.

"Is the answer in the palms of your hands, my Uncle?" Calgaich demanded.

Bruidge raised his head. "You always did have the bite of a sword's edge in your voice, Nephew. But I will not have it so in my hall."

"In my *father*'s hall, Uncle," Calgaich corrected.

Bruidge smiled faintly. "Times have changed since you fled from Albu, murderer. The blood of my only son still seems to be on your hands, or is that an illusion?"

Calgaich held up his hands. "Wolves tried to stop me from coming here to this den of human wolves."

"You left here. There was no one here who could stand behind your father to lead the Novantae, and to take his place when he was too old and weak to maintain his position. He could no longer lead the war spears."

"If that's so, then he would be of little value to the Romans as a hostage," Calgaich said pointedly.

Bruidge flushed. He drank deeply. He was being bearded in his own den by this upstart of a nephew.

"The food grows cold," a Pict complained.

Bruidge nodded, then he looked at Calgaich. "You know that our hospitality is such that we ask nothing of a man's purpose in being here until he has eaten and drunk his fill. Will you accept that ancient rule, Calgaich?"

Calgaich nodded. He strode to the table and walked behind it, passing behind the cold-eyed Picts and Celts who sat at that end of the table. He kicked back a chair at the left side of his uncle and then drew his dirk, which was still faintly filmed with wolf blood. He leaned across to the wooden trencher and began to hack away at the right thigh of the roasted boar.

An uneasy hush fell over the hall.

"That is the portion of the best man present," one of the Picts coldly reminded Calgaich.

Calgaich looked steadily at him. "Well?" he asked icily.

The Pict half rose from his chair and placed his hand on the hilt of his dirk. "Braggart," he sneered.

Calgaich raised his head a little. "In Eriu the champion's portion is the *whole* boar."

"You are not in Eriu now!" one of the Celts shouted angrily.

"Do you challenge me?" Calgaich demanded.

Bruidge slapped his huge hand on the table. "Enough!" he roared. "Eat and drink! Take whatever portion each of you want, and be damned to you!"

Even Calgaich was momentarily taken aback by the sound of his uncle's stentorian voice. Memories of his fosterage came back to him. Bruidge was not to be trifled with when his ire was up. Maybe it had been the *usquebaugh* Calgaich had drunk with Guidd that had made him speak so foolishly amidst these strong, fierce and prideful men, whose honor, such as it was, was easily touched.

There was little speech as they ate, but all eyes were surreptitiously studying Calgaich. They knew of this wild *fian* by hearsay, and knew he was not to be trifled with, at least in fair combat.

At last Bruidge shoved back his food with his greasy hands, belched and loosened his belt from across his bulging belly. He looked sideways at Calgaich.

Calgaich pushed back the remnants of the boar's haunch. He emptied his drinking horn and had it refilled. "What do these Romans do here in the hall of my grandfather?" he asked Bruidge.

The crop-haired men at the far end of the table looked up from their food. One of them slowly placed his knife on the table and bent his head a little to look at Calgaich from under lowered brows.

"They talk of trade and perhaps an alliance," Bruidge replied bluntly.

Calgaich narrowed his eyes. "Trade? An alliance? Their trading is only a means to worm their way into our country. An alliance can only be dominated by them. They accept no one on an equal basis. You must be joking, Uncle!"

Bruidge leaned back in his chair. "Why not?" he asked thoughtfully. "We Novantae gain nothing by battering our heads against the Great Wall and the shields of the Roman legions. The Romans themselves lose too many men by raiding into our country." He could not help grinning at the thought. "In peace, however, there can be mutual benefit."

Benefit only for Bruidge of the Bottle, Calgaich thought.

Bruidge stared into the leaping flames of one of the fireplaces. "There will come a time," Bruidge continued, "perhaps not during my lifetime, when Caledonia will be one people—the Old People, Novantae, Selgovae, Votadini, Damnonii, Picts, perhaps the Saxon newcomers, and aye, even the Romans. The blood of these strong people will be mixed into one great people. The Caledonians!"

"I no longer hear Bruidge of the Battle-Axe," Calgaich sneered. The mixture of heather beer and *usquebaugh* was making him bold, and perhaps a little careless. "When the *cran tara*, the call to rally for battle against the enemy, went through the hills of Albu to unite the tribesmen in battle against the Red Crests, it was always Bruidge, with singing battle-axe, who fought next to my father. Bruidge of the Battle-Axe! Rather say Bruidge of the Bottle! Where has your fighting spirit gone, my Uncle?"

There was a deathly silence in the hall broken only by the crackling of the flaming logs. Several times the drink-reddened eyes of Bruidge tried to meet the eyes of Calgaich in defiance, but failed. His hands, at one time more used to the worn shaft of his famed battle-axe, opened and closed about his drinking horn.

One of the Picts stood up and rested his knuckles on the table top as he leaned toward Calgaich. "You talk like a fighting man and a champion at the table of your uncle," he insinuated. "In my country you would be stripped naked and flogged to the door, to be driven bleeding into the hills, food for the wolves, for such talk at the table of a chieftain."

Calgaich looked casually at the Pict. "Who talks?" he asked coldly, standing up.

"Maelchon, the Pict," the tattooed man replied.

Calgaich smiled a little. "But you are *not* in your country now, Maelchon, the Pict. Aye, this is the table of a chieftain, but not that of the man who now sits at the head of it. He is a man who has sold his own brother to the Romans so that he himself might sit there. Look you, Pict! In my grandfather's and father's time, your tattooed face would be grinning sightlessly atop a spearshaft set on the battlements. My uncle fouls his own nest by having such filth as you in this hall!"

Maelchon dropped his hand to the hilt of his sword and partially drew his weapon.

Bruidge smashed a massive fist down hard on the table. Plates and drinking horns near him rose into the air and clattered down again. "Silence!" he roared. "Cenwulf! Ottar! Finn! Lulach! Finglas! Cathal! Stay between these two fighting cocks! I'll have none of the red work in my hall this night."

Two Saxons moved quickly in behind the angry Pict. Maelchon slammed his sword back into its sheath and dropped back into his chair. He reached for his drinking horn, but his angry eyes never left the flushed face of the man who had bridled him. He would remember Calgaich mac Lellan. There would come a time when the insult would be paid off by the point of his sword or dirk.

Bruidge leaned toward his nephew. "Look you, Calgaich," he emphasized in a hard, low voice. "This is now *my* hall. It matters little what you say. *I* lead the war spears of the Novantae now. These men seated at my table are my friends and sword brothers. You are alone here. Were it not for the great love I bear your father, I could have had you killed this very night when you arrived at the stinking hut of that swine, Guidd One-Eye. I wanted to see you, Calgaich, to patch up any differences between us. But you came here to beard me in my own hall.

"Now, sit down, and listen well to me, for I won't repeat myself. There was no *galanas* paid by your father to allow you to return here. Therefore the blood price is still on your head, *outlaw*. But murder and hospitality must not lodge together under a chieftain's roof. Now, I give you peace and a guarantee of safety as long as you remain here. You must do the same for me, Nephew."

The old, hard, biting edge had come back to the voice of Bruidge of the Battle-Axe, as Calgaich well remembered it. Bruidge meant what he said. There would be no gain in Calgaich striving against the swift torrent of his uncle's wrath. How had Bruidge known that Calgaich had been in Guidd's dwelling that night? Was it possible that Guidd had somehow betrayed Calgaich? *Bruidge of the Battle-Axe has his spies everywhere,* Guidd had warned Calgaich. Perhaps Bruidge's men had already taken the woodsman and Cairenn into captivity, or perhaps he had slain them. Maybe Bruidge was merely playing the drunkard with Calgaich before giving the killing signal to his mercenary wolves.

Calgaich smiled winningly. "I apologize, Uncle. It was the drink speaking. I had no right to beard you at your own table. I am alone in this country. It was not an easy thing to do to return here with a price on my head, half expecting a spear blade in my back rather than the good beer and meat you've served me here."

Bruidge waggled his big head up and down, looking blearily at Calgaich, his words once again slurred. "By the gods, my boy," he reasoned plaintively, with the self-pity of the drunken, "why should I want to kill you? My son Fergus is long gone. More bloodshed would not bring him back. That blood debt was paid more than a year ago." His voice trailed off as he realized the slip of the tongue he had made.

Calgaich stared at Bruidge. The liquor haze began to clear from Calgaich's mind. "The blood debt was paid more than a year ago," he repeated his uncle's words. *"What is that you say?"*

Bruidge hiccupped. "I meant I had forgotten that the debt was not paid," he lied.

"You lie in your teeth!" Calgaich snarled. He stood up and shoved back his seat.

"Take care, Nephew! I will not forgive you again!"

"Who paid the blood debt?" Calgaich demanded. "Who paid the *galanas,* my Uncle?"

Maelchon, the Pict, leaped to his feet. He brushed back the two startled Saxons and rounded the table toward Calgaich. "I warned you once," he growled.

Calgaich whirled. "So you did, Pict! Well, one of you tattooed swine is the same as another! A reiving vessel of Picts tried to ambush me off the coast and I met them alone on their own deck and slew half a dozen of them!"

"You lie!" the Pict yelled.

Calgaich grinned wolfishly. "And I met more of your tattooed brethren on land, the war band of Aengus of the Broad Spear. I fought their champion, Girich the Good Striker. He died under my sword."

Maelchon stopped short. "Man for man we Picts can drive you Novantae from your own dunghills where you crow like fighting men!"

Calgaich shrugged. "So? I give honor to Girich, one of your own people who did not drive Calgaich mac Lellan from his own dunghill."

Maelchon stared stupidly at Calgaich. "It was not Aengus of the Broad Spear who was paid to meet your *birlinn* off the coast."

Calgaich glanced at his uncle. "So? Then who *was* sent to meet my *birlinn?*"

"Silence!" Bruidge shouted. He stood up and reached for his battle-axe.

A broad-shouldered, red-headed Celt stood up and placed his hand on the hilt of his sword. "He has to die, Bruidge," he said. "He knows too much now."

"Aye," another Celt agreed. "Finglas is right. Your

hold on the Novantae is not secure enough yet. If the tribe learns that the *galanas* was paid more than a year ago and that you sent those Picts to ambush Calgaich at sea, there will be red work within this very hall."

"I give the orders here!" Bruidge cried.

The Saxons looked at Calgaich like hungry wolves eyeing helpless prey.

It was very quiet. Calgaich walked slowly toward the end of the table and stood with his back to a wall. He heard a door bar fall into its supports on the other side of the entryway.

"Lay down your weapons, outlaw," Maelchon demanded.

"Come and take them, Pict," Calgaich invited.

Maelchon looked at Bruidge.

Bruidge wiped his mustache both ways. He opened and closed his hands. He coughed and spat on the floor. "Murder and hospitality cannot lodge under a chieftain's roof," he repeated stupidly.

"Then leave," Maelchon suggested harshly. "What you can't see can then be no concern of yours."

"Yes, Uncle," Calgaich agreed sweetly. "Take your orders from yonder tattooed Pict in your own hall, as you call it. I see now who holds you on the chieftain's seat. Leave the hall, but if it is *I* who comes to tell you of the results here you had better have your battle-axe at hand."

Bruidge looked at his mercenaries. He nodded.

One of the Celts laughed and drew his sword. "Lulach mac Ronan of the Damnonii will try you, Novantae."

"One man only," Bruidge warned the others.

Lulach walked toward Calgaich. He rested his blade tip on the floor. His eyes held those of Calgaich. "One man against another, Calgaich mac Lellan. Surely this is not murder under the roof of a chieftain?"

Calgaich shrugged. "One at a time or all together," he boasted loudly. "It is all the same to me."

"Then draw!" Lulach snapped.

Calgaich drew his sword. The firelight danced along the blade. Bruidge straightened up in his seat. "By the gods," he murmured. He shook his head in puzzlement. He knew not of the magnificent Sword of Evicatos other than the description of it he had heard many times from his father.

Lulach tested Calgaich's sword by tapping the sword with his blade. The metal rang musically. They circled in the pool of bright firelight, their feet crackling among the rushes. Lulach rushed in to carry the fight. Calgaich stepped aside and hammered down Lulach's eager blade, and he leaped back to meet the next flashing attack. Again and again Lulach came on. He was unable to strike one telling blow at the smiling man who so easily fended him off without once attempting a counterstroke.

"Stand still, you leaping hare!" Lulach roared.

"Like this?" Calgaich asked. He planted his feet wide apart and waited for the attack.

Lulach grinned crookedly. He began to flail at Calgaich's sword like a smith at his anvil, but Calgaich did not move his feet. He merely swayed his body from side to side, forward and backward, always out of reach of the Damnonii's sword. All the while his own sword met every cut and thrust of the Celt's with astonishing ease.

Lulach stepped back at last. Sweat streamed down his flushed face. His chest rose and fell with the rapidity of his breathing.

"I don't want to kill you, Lulach," Calgaich warned the Damnonii.

"Damn you! You haven't touched me once!"

Calgaich knew the man's honor was touched. Lulach would rather die than admit he was being mastered. Calgaich stepped back and raised his sword. "Once more," he said quietly. "This sword knows only how to kill."

Lulach rushed in to the attack. The end came so swiftly that Lulach died with a yell of expected triumph on his lips.

Calgaich leaned on his sword. "I didn't want to kill him." It was as if he were speaking only to himself.

Finglas looked at Bruidge. "Lulach was blood kin to me," he said.

Bruidge looked at the corpse. "Would you join him there on the rushes?" he asked. There was almost a note of pride in his voice. After all, he himself had taught Calgaich the fundamentals of swordsmanship, but nothing like this exhibition of pure skill and sudden death.

Finglas was a fencer, a deft craftsman with none of the hurly-burly and rushing attack of Lulach. The blades met and rang together, parted, weaved in and out in swift and deadly patterns. Again and again the two opponents circled, feeling each other out, both of them wary and cautious. Finglas became eager. He knew he could not kill this man by fencing with him and yet he was sure he was the master. He struck hard but Calgaich was not there. He struck hard and sure again, but once more Calgaich was not there. Finglas retreated and then charged in again to meet the hypnotizing effect and deadly flickering of Calgaich's sword point. Finglas missed a stroke. The keen tip of Calgaich's sword slid in easily under Finglas's left ribs, was withdrawn and then drove in over the Celt's blade to sink a hand's span into his jugular. Finglas fell backward over the body of Lulach.

"Who is next?" Calgaich challenged. It was madness. The sweat streamed from his scarred face. "You? Maelchon, the Pict?" He laughed. *"An Fear Mor!* The Big Man!" It was not a compliment.

The two crop-haired Romans at the end of the table had stood up, drinking horns in hand, to watch the combating.

"Will you join the sallow skins, these stiffening corpses on the rushes, Pict?" Calgaich demanded.

"Two dead! That is enough!" Bruidge cried. "Your honor has been upheld!"

"Come on, all of you!" the madman with the bloody sword challenged them. "Come to the raven's feast! Or have you all lost your way in the haze from the drinking horns?"

It was Cathal, of the Selgovae, who could not stand the whiplash of scorn in Calgaich's voice. He rushed at Calgaich. They met between the two fireplaces with a hell's hammering of sword blades. Behind them stood Maelchon and Finn, one of the broken men who served Bruidge. The Saxons still stood with their backs against the wall in the shadows.

Calgaich played with Cathal. He was tired of killing, and he realized that it had been the liquor that had made him act so madly. A hard, twisting thrust disarmed the cursing Celt, and the sword pommel was driven up under his chin. He was unconscious before he hit the rushes.

Calgaich stepped back warily. He watched Maelchon and Finn. They, too, were wary now. Their fiery sense of honor had been replaced by a temporary caution of this mad swordsman.

"By Zeus!" one of the Romans vowed. "Never have I seen such swordplay, even in the Flavian Amphitheatre!"

Bruidge nodded as he lifted his drinking horn. "He is the greatest of them all, Ulpius Claudius," he admitted. He seemed to have no concern about the two dead Celts lying on the floor. Bruidge then looked at the two Saxons. He pointed to Lulach and Finglas. "Get rid of them," he ordered.

The Roman shook his head. "By all the gods! What a sensation he would be at the Games in Rome! It might help to get me a passage home from this accursed island."

Maelchon and Finn glanced sideways at Bruidge. Bruidge studied his nephew. After all, Calgaich had challenged everyone in the hall. "I don't want him killed," he said at last. "He is my nephew. Blood him a little. No more, mind you!"

Maelchon and Finn moved toward Calgaich, warily and with intense respect for his flashing, bloodied blade. They tried to play with Calgaich, staying back, attacking from opposite sides, forcing Calgaich ever backward. Calgaich moved swiftly. His blade tip slit Finn's sword arm. Maelchon staggered back from a flat-bladed blow atop his head. Blood ran down his tattooed face as he fought to keep his senses. Now it was Calgaich who was playing with them, weaving in and out, attacking, retreating, striking enough to wound lightly, but not to kill.

Ulpius Claudius looked at his companion. "You think you could best him, Decrius Montanas?" he asked slyly.

Montanas scowled a little. He placed his hand on the hilt of a short, wide-bladed Roman *gladius* that hung at his right side. "I'd like to try, Tribune," he replied.

The tribune shook his head. "You'd die out there on the rushes, Centurion."

"I am the best swordsman in the Twentieth Legion," the Roman boasted.

Ulpius nodded. "In the front line of battle, behind your shield, Montanas, I've never seen a better man, but this is something else—single combat such as neither of us has ever seen anywhere in the Roman world."

Maelchon was driven down on one knee. Calgaich could

have killed him but instead he whirled to meet Finn's slowing attack. He drove the Celt back toward the great table until Finn's heels struck the edge of the raised dais, and he fell backward. His sword clattered from his hand.

Calgaich whirled. Maelchon charged. Calgaich sidestepped, thrust hard, disarmed the sweating Pict, and then shouldered him aside so that he sat down and planted his rump in the thick bed of embers in one of the fireplaces. He shrieked in agony.

Bruidge looked beyond Calgaich. He nodded to Cenwulf, the Saxon who stood by the door. Cenwulf nodded in return. He withdrew a throwing axe, a well-balanced *francesca*, from beneath his wolfskin coat. He hefted it from one hand to the other and then cast it overhand with a sharp, sideways turn of the wrist. The keen blade flashed in the firelight, but it was the butt end of the shaft that struck Calgaich behind the left ear and felled him, semiconscious, to the rushes. His bloody sword flew from his hand. He tried to force himself up onto his feet with his hands placed flat on the floor. Maelchon and Finn drew their dirks and moved in for the kill.

Bruidge rose from his chair with surprising quickness for one of his bulk. "Step back, damn you!" he roared at Maelchon and Finn. "Kill him face to face if you can and not like butchers slaughtering a hog! That is, if you are men enough!"

Bruidge lumbered toward Calgaich. He raised a foot and kicked Calgaich alongside the head to drop him unconscious on the rushes. "I have long owed you that, Nephew," he said. He turned. "Cenwulf! Ottar! Ulf! Bruni! Get rid of those two carrion lying there! Into the river with them!"

Ulpius Claudius came forward into the firelight. He hooked a foot under Calgaich's body and flipped him over onto his back. He peered at the scarred features. "By Mithras!" he said wonderingly. "Who *is* this man? I have seen him somewhere before."

"You know who he is. He bragged about it loudly enough. Calgaich mac Lellan, he cries, as though he were a god and the son of a god," Bruidge snarled.

Ulpius shook his head. "That I know. But who else has he been in his life?"

Bruidge was puzzled. "He has just returned from his exile in Hibernia. He served as a mercenary for King Crann of the Five Hostages."

The centurion Decrius Montanas came forward, and looked down at Calgaich. He nodded. "I remember him now, Tribune. He was in a legion auxiliary. The Auxiliary Ulpia Torquata—the Double Battalion of Britons. They were stationed along the Rhine among the Teutons."

Bruidge nodded. "Oh, that! He was a youngster then during the time when we Novantae had a temporary peace with you Romans. His mother was the daughter of a Roman tribune and a chieftain's daughter of the Selgovae." Bruidge raised his eyes and seemed to look beyond the smoky hall into the past. "Lydia," he murmured. He passed a hand across his eyes.

"Bruidge?" The tribune looked at him curiously.

Bruidge seemed startled out of his reverie. "Calgaich enlisted in the Ulpia Torquata through the persuasion of his Roman grandfather. It was felt that it would show good will upon the part of the Novantae and the Selgovae. The boy did not want to go, but he knew it would be for the best." His voice died away.

"Go on, Bruidge," the tribune urged.

"Look at his back, Ulpius."

The centurion took the collar of the faded tunic in his hands and ripped the material down the back. Ulpius whistled softly as he saw the crisscross marks of the cat on Calgaich's back.

"He was stationed in the country of the Teutons," Bruidge explained. "Word came to him that his mother was very ill. He requested a furlough. He was refused. He deserted and somehow made his way across the channel to Britannia. He traveled to the north right through Roman Britannia and almost reached here before he was caught. They took him back. He escaped from them and returned here. A few years later he murdered my only son over a woman. She was Morar, daughter of Cuno."

Calgaich stirred. Bruidge beckoned to his Saxons. "Bind and gag him," he ordered. "Lock him up! Mind, I want no harm to come to him here!"

"I remember the story now," Ulpius said. "I was serving in Gaul at the time. The Ulpia Torquata was stationed along the Rhine. There were no better fighters. By Mithras, they were almost of legion quality!"

Bruidge walked back to his chair and raised his drinking horn. "What would you Romans do with such a man if he were in your hands?"

"If he had been a deserter once, he would have been flogged and never again allowed to serve on combat duty. He would have served as a clerk, or perhaps a cook, or in the transport, but never as a fighting man."

"Calgaich?" Even Bruidge could smile at that thought.

"But a second desertion? Once in Gaul we hung twelve such deserters noosed to a ship's cable, strung between two large trees, which was then drawn up tightly by a capstan. It was quite a sight. They were Britons, by the way." He did not notice the cold sideways look of hate cast at him by Bruidge.

"So he would be executed," Bruidge mused.

"Yes. That is Roman law. However . . ."

"Go on," Bruidge urged.

"Who was his Roman grandfather? You said he was a tribune. Was he a man of consequence? Is he still alive?"

"His grandfather was Tribune *Legatus Legionis* Rufus Arrius Niger of the Twentieth Legion. He returned to Rome some years ago."

Ulpius whistled between his teeth. "Old Give Me Another! By the gods! He is now a Roman senator!"

"Would that save Calgaich from execution?"

"From execution, probably. But not from other punishment."

Bruidge studied the Roman. "Such as?"

Ulpius looked sideways at Bruidge. "The scum of the legions are sometimes sentenced to the Games in Rome rather than to execution. Most of them are splendid fighters, despite their bad records, and they give the crowds their money's worth. Sometimes, they may win their freedom by how well they perform." Ulpius reached for Calgaich's sword.

"Don't touch it!" Bruidge warned.

Ulpius straightened up. "Why?"

Bruidge took a brand from the fire and knelt on the rushes. He examined the mark of the master swordsmith. Bruidge drew back in awe. "By Lugh," he murmured. "It can't be, and yet it is—the Sword of Evicatos—my own father." A look of superstitious fear came over his face.

Ulpius also knelt down and eyed the sword. "I have never seen such a magnificent weapon."

Bruidge stood up. He backed away from the sword. He shook his head as though he did not believe what he had seen. He returned to his seat and drained his drinking horn.

Ulpius looked curiously at Bruidge. There was a madness, he thought, in these strange, barbaric people of the north, who fought like the furies in battle and yet could be disarmed spiritually by their superstitions, and the fear of their dark and mysterious gods.

"Will you tell me of the sword, Bruidge?" the tribune asked.

Bruidge drank deeply. He stared into the liquor slops on the table as though he could read the future in them. At last he looked up at the tribune. "Listen well," he said in a low, troubled voice. "I'll tell you about that accursed sword. It was to be the Sword of Evicatos, my father. It was to be the mate to the great *laigen*, the hand lance, made by the same metalsmith who made that sword." Bruidge told the tale between great gulps from his drinking horn, until at last his voice died away and he stared moodily into a dying fire.

Ulpius studied the half-drunken chieftain. "You actually believe that this sword is the Sword of Evicatos? Who was that metalsmith?"

"Who really knows?" Bruidge shook his head. "He vanished into the north and took that sword with him."

"I think you know who he truly was," Ulpius suggested.

Bruidge wiped the sweat from his face. "There are gods that sometimes walk the earth, Roman, and they are not always benevolent gods. *Aes dana*, men of skill among my people, hold high status, a special place between the peasants and the warrior class. Workers in metal are viewed with awe. Our great god, Lugh of the Shining Spear, is a god of many skills—a wright, champion, harper, hero, poet, sorcerer, leech and *a craftsman in metal*. There is Gobniu the Smith. He is one of the Three Gods of Skill—*na tri de dana*—Gobniu, Credne and Luchta."

"We have our Mercury," the Roman said.

Bruidge nodded and looked sideways at the tribune. "Does he sometimes visit the earth in the guise of a human?"

Ulpius shrugged. "So it is said."

Bruidge passed a hand across his eyes. "The man you saw here this night, he who is called Calgaich the Swordsman, is the true son of my elder brother Lellan. The strange smith who made both the Sword and the Spear of Evicatos, my father, had come from nowhere to Rioghaine. No one knew him; no one had ever seen him before. No one knows what happened to him in the land of the Picts."

"You say that your brother Lellan was born early?"

"Ahead of his time by several months, in the dead of winter, during one of the worst storms known in the history of the Novantae."

"*Was* his father Evicatos?" the Roman asked quietly.

Bruidge looked quickly about himself. "I didn't say that!"

"If this fairy tale is true," Montanas said, "then Calgaich the Swordsman is a strange breed indeed—one half of him being Celt, one quarter Roman and one quarter god or demon."

"Whatever he is, Decrius Montanas, it would be a great waste to hang him as he deserves. He could be a featured attraction in the amphitheatre, and after all, that is one of the reasons we are in this damned fog-ridden land—to find more of these wild barbarians for arena fodder." The tribune spoke in a low voice so that the brooding Bruidge could not hear him. Bruidge had no great love for the Romans.

"Remember that his grandfather is a Roman senator, Tribune," the centurion reminded Ulpius.

Ulpius shrugged. "Even a Roman senator can't save a man who has been condemned for deserting the Eagles."

Bruidge emptied his drinking horn. The faces of the two whispering Romans seemed to swim in and out of his blurred vision. He did not trust Romans and especially this smooth-faced fox of a tribune. "I don't want Calgaich's blood on my hands," he warned.

"That can be taken care of in the arena," Ulpius said.

Bruidge smiled slightly. "I'd like to see that," he murmured. He looked suddenly at Ulpius. "I want him out of here tonight. I do not want the Novantae to know he has been here."

"What of the woodsman, Guidd, and the woman Calgaich brought with him?"

"I don't care, just so they are gone from this place. Do what you will with them. How soon will you leave for Luguvalium?"

"Our business here is now concluded. But Bruidge, what of Lellan and the two sisters, Morar and Bronwyn?"

Bruidge shrugged. "Take them to Rome with you."

"Lellan is old and feeble in health."

Bruidge's hooded eyes held those of the tribune. "Perhaps he will die in captivity. The prison in which you hold him is damp and cold."

"Then it doesn't matter to you?"

"Do not kill him, Tribune, or, by the gods, I'll come to Rome and hunt you down. You understand?"

"I understand. My beloved uncle, Quaestor Lucius Sextillius, has taken quite a fancy to your two golden-haired women. The rumor in Luguvalium is that he wants to take Morar for his wife. How does that set with you, Bruidge?"

Bruidge smiled a little. "It is all right. But he may regret taking her into his bed, Ulpius."

"What do you mean?"

Bruidge waved a hand. "Just an idle thought."

"She could do you a great deal of good in Rome."

Bruidge shrugged. "More likely she could do herself a great deal of good in Rome."

"He talks in riddles," Decrius growled to Ulpius.

Bruidge heard like a wolf. "You will see, Centurion. I do not talk in riddles." He buried his red nose in his drinking horn. Thanks to the gods, he thought, Morar will be leaving Britannia. God help Quaestor Lucius Sextillius!

"This woman of Calgaich's," Ulpius said. "Is she another of these golden-haired barbarians?"

Bruidge looked at the Celt, Fidach. "You saw her," he said.

Fidach nodded. "She is dark of hair and fair of skin. She was dressed in men's clothing."

"But beautiful?" Ulpius queried.

"Yes. If Morar has the light and beauty of a sunlit day, this other woman has the soft, dark beauty of night."

Ulpius wet his sensuous lips, and drank a little. "Take her, Ulpius, if you want her," Bruidge suggested.

Ulpius stood up. "My thanks to you, Bruidge. Montanas will take Calgaich to my escort, which waits two days' ride east of here. I'll need a few men to help him."

"I can handle him alone, Tribune," Montanas insisted.

The tribune shook his head. "We can't risk losing such a captive."

Bruidge looked about the hall. "None of you shall speak of what happened here this night. If one word gets out, I'll personally cut out the tongue of every one of you."

Ulpius fastened his cloak about his throat. "I can understand now why you took over the chieftainship of the Novantae."

"Because of the fact that my brother and I might not have the same father?" Bruidge shook his head. "The right of *tanaise ri* is mine by ancient custom, and the line of the mother is as strong, and sometimes stronger than that of the father among our people. But that is not why I took the chieftainship. Lellan could no longer lead the war spears. That is what is important. *He* can't and *I* can."

Ulpius and Montanas walked toward the door. Ulpius turned. He could not help himself. "But what of the son, Calgaich, Bruidge? Could *he* not lead the war spears?"

The blood rushed into Bruidge's face. "Roman!" he cried. "Leave my hall and take that damned, accursed sword with you!"

"Pick it up, Montanas," Ulpius ordered. "That's an order, Centurion."

Montanas picked up the weapon and hastily sheathed it in its bronze scabbard. He mumbled a prayer to Mithras as he followed the tribune from the hall. Something the drunken Bruidge had said came back to haunt the centurion at that moment. *There are gods that sometimes walk the earth, Roman, and they are not always benevolent gods.*

From somewhere beyond the *dun,* hidden in the dark shroud of the nearby forest, a wolfhound raised its voice in plaintive howling. Bron was still waiting for Calgaich.

Decrius Montanas rode from Rioghaine that night after moonset. Behind him Calgaich rode between two of Bruidge's mercenaries. His ankles were tied together by a rope which passed beneath the belly of the horse. A stick had been thrust between his elbows and behind his back and his wrists had been tied together by a rope that passed across his middle. Now and again Montanas would look back at Calgaich, but when their eyes met it was usually the centurion who looked away first.

In the post-moon darkness a shadowy figure moved swiftly on the trail behind the mounted party. Bron was following his master.

CHAPTER 7

The firelight flickered against the crumbling courtyard walls of the long-abandoned Roman outpost fortlet and reflected from the light body armor of the hard-bitten Asturians who formed the *turma,* or thirty-man unit of auxiliary cavalry, temporarily commanded by the Centurion Decrius Montanas. The Asturians were nervous. The fortlet was hardly defensible, and it was a distant thirty-five Roman miles to the northwest of the great Fort ala Petriana and also Luguvalium. If the unpredictable Novantae attacked, there would be no help from the cavalry garrison at Fort ala Petriana.

The Asturians off duty stood about the cooking fires in the courtyard. Now and again one of them would glance toward the old guard room where Calgaich lay chained to the wall by his wrists.

Some of the older men who had served along the Wall of Hadrian knew of Calgaich the Swordsman. He was renowned among the auxiliaries for his courage and great fighting skill. They knew he had deserted the Eagles, not once, but twice, and that he had been given the lash for that first offense. The second time he had vanished into the north country, and rumor had said he was fighting as a mercenary for a Hibernian king. They were sure now that he was being taken to Fort ala Petriana to be executed.

Thank the gods that Tribune Ulpius Claudius had not ordered the *turma* to escort him deep into the wild, isolated country of the barbarian Novantae. The tribune had been either a fool or a man of great courage to go there accompanied only by the centurion Decrius Montanas, even though the chieftain of the Novantae had granted them safe conduct. The Novantae could not be trusted beyond a

120

spear's cast. The doubled sentries on the walls of the outpost peered into the dark and windy night, envisioning
those hairy barbarians behind every tree and bush. They
knew well enough of their silent approach, their swift and
furious charge out of nowhere, and their deadly killing
skill.

Lutorius, the broken-nosed *calo*, or body servant and
cook, of Decrius Montanas, nodded to the sentry at the
entrance to the guardroom. "Food for the wolf," he said
out of the side of his mouth.

The guard grinned. "Watch out he does not bite, *calo*."

Calgaich looked up as the *calo* entered the guardroom
through the doorless entrance. It was obvious that he was
not of Spanish blood like the Asturians of the *turma*, and
he did not wear their uniform.

The *calo* grinned at Calgaich. "Does a captured wolf eat
Roman rations?" he asked in mongrel Gaelic.

Calgaich nodded. "I've eaten such rations before, *calo*,"
he replied quietly in Latin. "I once served with the Ulpia
Torquata, the Double Battalion of Britons."

Lutorius spat to one side. "Auxiliaries," he sneered. "*I
was a legionnaire!*"

Calgaich studied his broken nose and his drink-puffed
features. "What legion kicked you out for drunkenness?"

The servant flushed. "I served ten years in the old Twentieth," he replied bitterly. "Ten years in the Drunken
Lions, and in the first cohort at that. It wasn't really much
of a drunk that cost me my retirement. I had spent only
two days in the Crown of Bacchus with an imported Syrian
whore who could teach even a legionnaire new tricks, by
Zeus!"

"Was that *all* that happened?"

"Well, there was also a little matter of my refusing to
pay my bill," the servant admitted. "There was a fight
about that, of which I remember little, except that the
saloon keeper got a broken head. Then the legion guard
was called out. That's when the fighting really got started.
I laid two of them out with a chair and was throttling
another when some bastard broke a chair over *my* head."

"He broke your beak?"

The man grinned. "Hellsfire no! I got that from Old
Give Me Another in my early days in the legion. I was

with the old Fifteenth Legion then, the Apollinaria, and a helluva fine unit, Caledonian! That was in Cappadocia." He looked down at Calgaich's food bowl. "Eat, Caledonian! I swiped some of the pig meat from the tribune's personal stores and put it in that soup. If he ever found out he'd kick my rosy ass all around the courtyard."

Calgaich tasted the food. "Thanks. Where is the tribune now?"

"Who knows? Back in the wilderness somewhere. One of the barbarians who helped bring you here said the tribune was looking for a woman. A foreigner, he said." Lutorius laughed. "The man is mad. The stews of Luguvalium are full of some of the finest spintrians in whoredom! I should know!"

"What else do you know about this woman?"

Lutorius shrugged. "The barbarian said she had come with you from Hibernia. That's all."

"How do they call you?"

"Lutorius." He grinned. "That was my beloved mother's idea of a fine name for a son, but the boys in the old first cohort used to call me Bottle Emptier. That was an honor in the Twientieth, I tell you!"

Calgaich dipped a thick crust of bread into the soup. "You say you were in the Fifteenth Apollinaria serving in Cappadocia? It's unusual for a legionnaire to serve in any legion other than that in which he first enlisted, isn't it?"

Lutorius squatted on his heels. "I was born and raised here in Britannia, in the old *colonia* at Camulodunum, the permanent station of the Twentieth Legion. Like all boys raised in the *coloniae* and the *vici*, I was expected to enlist. My old man was promoted to centurion and sent to the Fifteenth in Cappadocia after they had gotten the shit kicked out of them in battle there. When I was fifteen years old, I ran away from home. I worked as a hand on a Greek trading ship and got to the Mediterranean. In time I located my father's cohort. Both of us lied about my age, and I enlisted. My father died in battle and I was wounded. The tribune found out how old I really was. They gave me a discharge, and I came back to Britannia. My dear old mother had died from too much drink. I couldn't make it in civilian life, so I reenlisted in the Twentieth. Believe it or not, I wasn't back in the ranks one month when the same tribune who had commanded the Fifteenth in Cappadocia showed up at Camulodunum to take command of the Twentieth."

"Old Give Me Another?"

Lutorius looked quickly at Calgaich. "You know him?"

"You said it was he who broke your beak, Lutorius."

"So it was! Tribune *Legatus Legionis* Rufus Arrius Niger. Old Give Me Another!" He shook his grizzled head in appreciation. "Now, there was a *soldier's* soldier! The high-class perfumed pimps they have serving as officers in the legions these days couldn't hold that old man's piss pot! He was as tough as shield leather. A man who had followed the Eagles all his life. Fought his way up from centurion *decimus hastatus posterior* of the tenth cohort, up to senior centurion of the Fifteenth Legion—centurion *primus pilus prior* of the first cohort. Why, many's the time, even when he was a tribune in the old Twentieth, he'd come into the ranks and do a day's march with us against you wild barbarians—twenty-four miles in eight hours, neither more nor less, head and spear up, shield on your back, cuirass collar open one hand's breadth. That's how the legions conquered the known world!" He cocked his head to one side. "You know how the old man got to be called Old Give Me Another?"

Calgaich nodded. "From the Legion Apollonaria, in Cappadocia. After he had broken a cudgel on a coward's back, he'd roar out in that damned bull's voice of his: 'By Mithras! Give me another!' "

Lutorius stared at Calgaich. "Now how in hell's name did you know *that,* barbarian?"

Calgaich shrugged. "I heard the story when I was in the Ulpia Torquata."

Lutorius nodded. "And you must know that the old man did not break my beak for cowardice, Calgaich."

"I didn't think so."

Lutorius passed a greasy hand across his eyes. "It was for disobeying orders. It was in the battle where my father was killed. My cohort was cut off. Old Give Me Another was cut off with us. There was no chance of escape for him, because his leg was broken. He ordered the rest of us to fight our way back to the legion so that at least a few of us could be saved. I refused to go. I stayed with him, stood over him, and fought off the enemy until the legion advanced to save us." His voice died away and he stared unseeingly at the damp wall of the room behind Calgaich as though he could again see the dust, the heat and the broken, bleeding bodies of the dead and wounded.

"Go on," Calgaich urged. He could not help but like the man.

Lutorius came to with a start. He grinned a little. "Well, the rest of the story is short enough. When we got back to the legion, Niger had a couple of men hold him up off his broken leg, and then he beat the shit out of me."

"For saving his life?"

The *calo* shook his head. "For disobeying orders. Seems like I had set a bad example." He grinned. "Then the crazy bastard recommended me for the *corona civica,* a chaplet of gold oak leaves, for saving a comrade's life in battle."

"Did you get it?"

Lutorius stood up and took the food bowl. "No, because I had disobeyed other orders in the same battle."

Calgaich looked past Lutorius and through the open doorway. The Spaniards were seeking shelter in the ruins against the misty drizzle that had begun. Several of them, wrapped in their reddish-brown cloaks and with covers over the yellow plumes of their helmets, paced the sagging guardwalks along the walls.

"You've got no chance to escape, Calgaich," Lutorius said quietly. "You'd be dead before you reached the wall. Those Asturians out there know what would happen to them if they let you escape. That bastard Montanas would have their hides flayed off."

The *calo* walked to the door. "I'll get you a blanket for the night, barbarian."

"Do you know where Old Give Me Another is now?" Calgaich asked.

Lutorius nodded. "The old bastard finally got out of uniform and made it back to Rome. Some say he became a senator. Some months ago I heard he was in Britannia."

"Where?"

"Down in the southeast. He was inspecting the forts of the Saxon shore. He's probably heading back for Rome about now. Ah, Rome! The center of the world!"

"I thought you were a Briton."

"I am, but that doesn't stop me from admiring Rome. I was there on my return from Cappadocia. That's the city of cities, I tell you, Caledonian. By Zeus—the whores, the gambling dens, the chariot races in the Circus Maximus, the Games in the Flavian Amphitheatre, are enough to make a man die happy, dead drunk in a whore's bed, instead of passing away his life in this miserable, fog-ridden suburb of hell they call Britannia." He studied Calgaich. "Say, how is it you speak such good Latin?"

Calgaich shrugged. "Learned it from my mother."

"She was Roman?" Lutorius asked incredulously.

"No. Her mother was of the Selgovae. Her father was a Roman."

"In the legion? Maybe I knew him."

Calgaich nodded. "You knew him all right, *calo*. He broke your nose over twenty years ago in Cappadocia." He grinned widely.

The food bowl shattered on the floor. "Name of Light!" Lutorius cried. "Not Old Give Me Another!" He looked quickly about himself. "You won't tell anything I told you?"

Calgaich shook his head. "I never knew him, except by reputation."

Lutorius studied Calgaich. "Some of the Asturians say you're being taken back to Luguvalium to be executed for deserting the Eagles."

Calgaich shrugged. "Either that, or to Rome for the Games."

"Which means the same thing, eh, barbarian?"

"I'd rather die in the arena with a sword in my hand than hang."

Lutorius rubbed his whiskered chin. "I'll be right back," he said. He vanished into the misty drizzle outside.

The *calo* seemed sympathetic, Calgaich thought, but he had never let himself get close enough for Calgaich to grab him. Besides, Lutorius was right—those Asturian cavalrymen knew what would happen to them if they let Calgaich escape. The time was not now. Still, Calgaich felt that he might have found an ally in Lutorius. Could the man be trusted? On the other hand, Calgaich had no one else to help him.

Lutorius reappeared in the open doorway, wrapped in

an old legion cloak. He looked back over his shoulder. "If I'm caught, that damned Montanas will have the skin off my back." He turned back to Calgaich and tossed him a blanket. "We'll have to sit here in the darkness." Lutorius came closer to Calgaich and handed him a wine bottle. "Here! Drink! This is like stale camel piss, but it will help keep off the chill."

Calgaich drank deeply. "More like boar piss, *calo*, but it will do." He handed Lutorius the bottle. "What kind of a man is this Tribune Ulpius Claudius?"

Lutorius took his turn at the bottle. He looked quickly over his shoulder. "Ambitious. Hard. A good soldier. Nephew to Quaestor Lucius Sextillius. Neither one of them can be trusted a spear's length away."

"Sextillius? The one they call the Perfumed Pig?"

Lutorius spewed out a mouthful of the wine. He slapped a thigh. "You've got it, barbarian. But, as you love your dark and mysterious gods, don't ever call him that within his hearing."

They passed the bottle back and forth. Lutorius became more expansive. He had not noticed that the wine in the bottle was not appreciably lower every time Calgaich passed the bottle back to him. "Damned if I don't like you, barbarian. I wouldn't trust you out on those damned misty moors of yours, especially when you couldn't be seen, but here, nice and cozy with you chained to the wall, I like you."

Calgaich studied the broken nose and sodden face of the ex-legionnaire. "A man can lead a good life north of the wall," he suggested quietly. "There is good beer and whiskey. There is fine hunting and fishing. There are strong Caledonian women, with ice on the outside and hellsfire on the inside once they get you into the bed straw. By your gods, Lutorius, your Syrian spintrian was but an amateur compared to them."

Lutorius grinned. "Let be, barbarian. I know what you're thinking. Sure, sure, I could help you to escape and hie myself to the north with you to find one of them ice-on-the-outside and hellsfire-on-the-inside women of yours only to end up with my head hanging from someone's horse bridle. By Mithras! When I first joined the Twentieth, we did some hard fighting north of the wall. Captured some of your tall, yellow-haired women we did, like those two Quaestor Sextillius is keeping in his *mansio* quarters at Fort ala Petriana. One of those we captured was the wife of a chief of the Votadini. Our centurion laid her the hard way, she being trussed up, spread-eagled on the ground, and naked as a newborn babe in front of the whole damned cohort. That night she went quietly with him to his tent. But he made one mistake. He left his sword and dagger near her. In the morning she was gone and so was his head. They say she took the bloody head back to her husband and then cut her own throat with the centurion's knife. You think I want a she-devil like *that* in the bed straw?"

Lutorius nipped at the bottle. "Now, if you were to talk of something more negotiable, like gold. A man could pay his passage to Rome with something like that."

Calgaich reached for the bottle. "I have nothing with me," he admitted, "but to the north, in my country, I can lay hands on such things."

"You lie like a Greek," Lutorius declared. "Montanas told the decurion of the Asturians that you had been a *fian* in Hibernia: a mercenary with no lands and no possessions. Besides, it is said that you are an outlaw among your own people. Well, Caledonian, you haven't even got your weapons now." He reached for the bottle. "They say your grandfather is a very wealthy man," he added thoughtfully.

"So I, too, have heard."

"Supposing I were to get word to him, that is, if he hasn't left Britannia?"

Calgaich shrugged. "I'm not sure that would do any good. You know him and the laws of Rome. No man deserts the Eagles and goes unpunished. I deserted them twice."

"There is something about you that reminds me of him. Honor was his god."

"All the more reason he'd give you nothing, Bottle Emptier."

"*Honos et Virtus.* Prestige and Valor. The gods of the legion. They also say that the old man reached the Father degree of Mithraism, which rates honor above all else, even life."

"Which means that there is absolutely no hope that he'd want to do anything for me."

Lutorius stood up and placed the bottle beside Calgaich. "I'd better get out of here lest that crocodile Montanas find me in here." He walked to the door and turned. "Niger is still your grandfather, barbarian."

"No man deserts the Eagles and goes unpunished, Roman."

"The knee is nearer than the shin," Lutorius said cryptically, disappearing into the misty drizzle.

Calgaich tested the rusty wrist chains that held him to the wall. One of the rings set into the wall to hold the chains was a little loose. He emptied the wine bottle and then smashed it under the blanket to muffle the noise. He selected one of the larger pieces of hard pottery and began to pick away at the crumbling mortar that held the ring into the wall.

A faint hint of graying light was in the east. The moors beyond the fortlet were thickly swathed in mist. The decurion walked about in the quarters, kicking his Asturians to their feet. Six of them double-timed to the wall ladders to stand the dawn watch beside their comrades of the last watch. This was the time of day—when a man's spirits were at their lowest ebb—that the wild northmen preferred to attack. The barbarians could move through that mist as though they were a part of it.

Decrius Montanas fingered his vine staff, the legion baton of office, and watched Lutorius kindling a fire. "Drunk again last night, eh, Bottle Emptier?" he asked.

Lutorius shrugged. He did not expect the solid stroke of the vine staff to his ribs that struck him sideways onto the flagstones. He looked up into the hard, set face of the centurion.

"Well?" Montanas asked. "Have you nothing to say, *calo?*"

Lutorius stolidly shook his head as he got to his feet.

The centurion smiled. It was a mechanical smile, produced only by the facial muscles. His eyes were cold, like chips of basalt. "Is that how they answered questions in the Twentieth, you pig-shit, you!" he snapped.

"No, sir," Lutorius mumbled.

The centurion reached out and gathered the loose folds

of Lutorius's cloak, drawing him close. "Bastard son of a diseased spintrian," he grated between his teeth, "take care I do not have your back laid open with the cat before this little pleasure trip is over." He shoved Lutorius against the wall. He rested his hand on the hilt of the sword at his right side. "Go ahead, *calo*," he murmured coldly. "I'll give you the first blow."

Lutorius shook his head. There was no escaping this madman of a centurion. How he had lived through as many battles as he had without getting a legionnaire's spear or sword in his back during the press of combat was beyond Lutorius.

The wind shifted and one of the Asturians leaned over the crumbling wall. Sound carried well through the mist. He heard the chink of a horse's bridle. A man coughed somewhere out there in the drifting wool.

The decurion scaled the ladder at a beckoning signal from the Asturian. "What is it?" he whispered.

"Horses. Men. Five or six of them."

The decurion leaned over the low wall on the courtyard side and pointed out positions to his men.

A harsh voice hailed the fortlet. It was Tribune Ulpius Claudius. A small party of horsemen appeared before the gate. One of them held a rope in his hand. The other end was noosed about the neck of a man on foot. The prisoner's wrists had been bound together across his lean belly. A broken spear shaft had been thrust across his back through the crooks of his elbows. His face was masked with dried blood and his torn leathern tunic was darkly stained with it.

Ulpius dismounted stiffly and limped over to Montanas. "That barbarian swine helped the woman escape," he explained with bitterness, "and he killed my best horse. Have him strung up for flogging! I'll have the hide and flesh from his bones!"

Calgaich heard the voices in the courtyard. He tested the ring bolt set in the wall. It came loose and he jerked it free, catching the rusted chains so that they did not clatter on the flagstones. There was only one exit from the room, through the open doorway that led to the courtyard. Calgaich catfooted to the narrow slit window beside the door. He muffled the chains inside his cloak.

Two of the Asturians untied the prisoner, then lashed his wrists together. They threaded the end of the rope through a ring inset on the wall above the prisoner's head and drew it up tight.

"Lutorius!" the tribune snapped. "Where is that damned wine bibber?"

Lutorius came forward and saluted Ulpius. "Here, Tribune."

"Make a cat. I want you to start work on his back. The gods know you've had enough experience in the business."

Lutorius grinned crookedly. "Both in the giving and the receiving, sir."

Lutorius found some extra bridle reins and tied the ends together about a piece of branch. He slit the free ends and bound sharp-edged stones to them in lieu of the usual leaden pellets. He strode to the prisoner and ripped the leathern tunic off his back.

Calgaich narrowed his eyes. There was something familiar about the prisoner.

Lutorius threaded the short lengths of leather between his fingers. He looked at the tribune. Ulpius nodded.

Lutorius spread his stocky, hairy legs and expertly eyed the prisoner's back. He idly swung the lash back and forth and then suddenly, with a solid slashing stroke, he set to work. He struck from right to left and then from left to right, but he was not putting his full weight and strength as yet into the cruel task. Each stroke of the cat drew a sharp, grunting ejaculation from the prisoner. The blood began to run down his back.

"Caledonian swine!" the tribune cried. "Scream, pig! Beg for mercy! Hell and furies, Lutorius! Lay it on, damn you! I want to see the color of his bones. Kill my best horse, you barbarian dog! You'll pay for that! Make him feel that he is dying, Lutorius."

There was little chance that Calgaich could get out of the guardroom and behind the Asturians to reach the gate. The wall guards could see every movement within the courtyard. Calgaich needed a weapon; anything with which to strike at least a blow or two to win his way out into the concealing mist.

Lutorius stopped his work. His breathing was harsh between his teeth. He looked at the tribune. The tribune jerked his head at Decrius Montanas. The centurion walked to the prisoner and drew back his grizzled head to look into the bloodstained face. The prisoner opened one eye to look at the centurion through his mask of blood. He spat full into the centurion's face.

"Guidd!" Calgaich cried.

Calgaich dropped his cloak and ran through the doorway, freeing his chains to their full length. He crashed between two of the Asturians to send them sprawling, then he swung out his right arm. The chain whipped out to strike Ulpius Claudius across the chest. The chain thudded against the Roman's bronze corselet and drove him backward. Calgaich hit Lutorius with a fist and flattened him on the ground. Decrius Montanas freed his sword. He jumped aside, with his feet planted wide apart, to await Calgaich's charge. Calgaich swung his left arm outward. The chain whipped around the centurion's neck and Calgaich jerked back on it with all his strength to dump Decrius on the ground.

The decurion darted in, striking with his long-bladed *spatha*, the auxiliary cavalry sword. A chain whipped around his sword wrist and then it was jerked backward and upward. The sword flew through the air to strike against the wall. The next sweep of chain caught the decurion across his privates and he doubled over in agony. The rest of the Asturians had drawn their swords. They danced about in futility, not daring to close with the mad barbarian.

"Tullus!" the tribune shrieked. "Drop me this madman!"

One of the Spaniards on the wall reached inside his cloak. He withdrew his sling and looped a leaden ball in it. He eyed Calgaich, waiting for him to get away from the wall so that he could get a clean shot at him.

A semicircular ring of cavalrymen had formed around Calgaich, just beyond reach of the whistling chains. He knew there was no chance to break through that metal-tipped ring. He lowered the chains to the ground.

Guidd turned his head. "Escape, if you can, Calgaich."

"No chance, old wolf. We can only die together."

It was quiet now in the courtyard. The cold dawn wind whispered through the mist.

Tullus came softly down a ladder, out of sight of Calgaich. Now and then feet grated on the ground as the Asturians waited their chance. They had Calgaich cold, but none of them wanted to die with him.

"I want him alive," the tribune ordered. He looked at Calgaich. "Stop fighting. Tullus can break your thick Caledonian skull from forty feet away. Come! Surrender, and I'll stop the punishment of the one-eyed man."

Calgaich laughed. "I'd sooner trust a hungry wolf, Roman."

"By the Lord of Light," Ulpius vowed.

Calgaich studied the tribune. There was a slight scar between the man's dark eyebrows, the sign of the Raven degree of the cult of Mithras. Lutorius caught Calgaich's eye. The *calo* nodded.

"Give me a sword, Roman," Calgaich urged. "Come! Try Calgaich mac Lellan! The winner takes all."

Montanas came forward. His hard eyes never left the scarred face of Calgaich. "Let me try him, Tribune," he requested. "I'll fight him for you."

"I can do my own fighting, Centurion." Ulpius shook his head. "No. We have need of this madman elsewhere."

Calgaich held up his arms. "By the Lord of Light," he reminded the tribune.

Guidd fell heavily to the ground as he was cut loose. Calgaich cradled the woodsman in his arms. "Steady, old wolf," he murmured. "By Lugh of the Shining Spear, that perfumed Roman pig will pay the full blood price for this."

Calgaich saw the greaved legs of the tribune close beside him. He looked up into the eyes of the Roman.

"Look you, Calgaich mac Lellan," the tribune said. "Only by the grace of the gods are you two still alive. The grace of the gods and that of Ulpius Claudius. Why your uncle let you live back in that filthy hall of his is beyond my understanding. How you got past his Pictish allies off the coast is also beyond understanding. You seem to be a man who laughs in the face of death, barbarian. But, now you are again in *Roman* hands. The arm of Rome is long and strong, and *no* one escapes its punishment. Remember, too, your father is in Roman hands, and that bloody, worthless thing in your arms is also our prisoner. I have sworn by the Lord of Light that you will not die, at least not while in my custody. I want no more attempts to escape. If you do try again, the life of that man lying there is at once forfeit, and should you succeed, the life of your father is then forfeit. Do I make myself clear?"

Calgaich nodded. He stood up. "The woman, Tribune. Where is she?"

Ulpius shrugged. "Somewhere in the hills. Pericol! She fought like a man! She drove a great war spear clean through one of the Saxons who had come to take her, and sorely wounded Maelchon, the Pict."

Calgaich could not help but grin.

Ulpius nodded. "I *knew* that would please you. Your one-eyed hound there killed another Saxon in the escape. We pursued them into the hills. We rounded them up. One-Eye there fought so that the woman might escape. By Zeus! He killed my Spanish mount! For that alone I should have him flogged to death." His voice rose high and then broke.

"By the Lord of Light, Tribune," Calgaich again reminded Ulpius.

Ulpius became calm, although at times there was almost an hysterical quality about the man. "Lutorius!" he shouted. "Bring salve and bandages for this one-eyed man."

The sun was tipping the hills to the east of the fortlet when the small command got ready to leave for the ride south. Calgaich and Guidd had been mounted on transport mules, with their ankles tied together by ropes that passed under the bellies of the beasts.

Ulpius fastened his cloak about his throat. "By the way," he asked Calgaich, "how did you get free this morning?"

Lutorius looked up from where he was loading one of the pack animals. He didn't know how Calgaich had done it, but he felt sure that somehow he had unintentionally helped the barbarian.

In one sentence Calgaich could have placed Lutorius's back under the lash. He did not trust the man, but a poor friend among the Romans was better than none at all. "There were some sharp stones in the guardroom," Calgaich replied. "I dug out the wall ring to free myself."

Ulpius studied Calgaich. "I saw no sharp stones in there."

Calgaich smiled. "There was only one, Tribune."

They rode from the fortlet. The mist was being swallowed up by the rising sun. From somewhere within the mist there came the plaintive howling of an animal, followed by a series of sharp barkings.

Montanas looked back over his shoulder. "I've never heard a wolf howl during the daytime in this accursed country," he observed.

Ulpius shrugged. "Everything is backward here."

Guidd looked sideways at Calgaich. He shaped the name "Bron" with his lips. Calgaich nodded.

When the cavalcade vanished over the first of a series of ridges, a great brindle wolfhound rose from a hollow beyond the fortlet and trotted steadily along the rough track on the trail of the Romans and their prisoners.

When Bron had disappeared over the first ridge, a lone rider appeared in the north. Clad in a boy's rough skins, with her long, dark hair piled up underneath a disreputable leathern cap, and with a great war spear slung across her back, Cairenn the Ordovician *cumal* rode south on the track of the Romans and Calgaich mac Lellan. Bron was her only escort. Cairenn had made her choice. There was no past to return to, only the hope that the future would reunite her with Calgaich. Nothing existed—Morar, the Romans, Bruidge—beyond that wish and her fear of the enveloping night.

CHAPTER 8

The Wall of Hadrian was across the river extending to the east where it vanished into the distance. The cavalcade approached the bridge, which spanned the river in a series of graceful timber arches. Ulpius Claudius dropped back from the head of the band of cavalrymen and prisoners. "See the long arm of Rome, barbarian?" he asked Calgaich with deep satisfaction. "The Wall of Hadrian! It has stood there for two hundred and fifty years. It spans eighty miles from the Northern Sea to this point. Seventeen forts, eighty castles—one every mile—and one hundred and sixty signal towers. A masterpiece of engineering. There is nothing else like it in the world."

"Why, Roman?" Calgaich asked dryly. "Why is it here?"

"What do you mean?"

"If there is no other wall like it in your empire, there must have been a great need for it here alone."

Ulpius was puzzled. "It has kept your people in check, Caledonian."

Calgaich smiled crookedly. "We have been across your wall many times. My grandfather, Evicatos the Spearman, led the tribes almost to Londinium in his time."

Ulpius laughed. "And where is he now?"

"There will be others."

The Roman shook his head. "The wall still stands. Your people are still beyond it. It has served its purpose well. It is a tribute to the power of Rome."

Calgaich spat to one side. "It seems to me, Roman, that all Rome itself is a fortress, beyond whose wall are we barbarians, in the hundreds of thousands. How much longer can your empire stand against them?"

"It is her destiny to rule the world. If by any chance

135

you barbarians should succeed in overrunning the empire, and the very thought is utterly ridiculous, the lights will go out all over·the world, and it will revert to barbarism. Can't you fools see the great wisdom of Rome? Her magnificent cities? Her unconquerable legions? Her roads, bridges, aqueducts and fortresses? Her trade? The Roman Peace that has brought happiness to all peoples? What have you barbarians to offer that can replace the great gifts Rome has given the world?"

Calgaich looked over his shoulder toward the distant purple hills. "The freedom with which every man is born," he answered softly. "We don't need your wisdom, your cities and all else you offer in the guise of gifts. What good are they to a man if he knows that the heel of Rome can rest on his neck for the span of his life and that of his children?"

"Many peoples have accepted that heel. It can be a benevolent heel, barbarian."

Calgaich shook his head. "You'd never understand, Roman. Your great civilization is really nothing but an enslavement. You create a desolation in the world and call it peace."

"Many of your own Britons have accepted our ways, and, I might add, with more alacrity than many other peoples."

"You're not speaking of the Caledonians, Tribune," Calgaich challenged swiftly.

"The only reason you Caledonians have survived thus far is because you have the longest legs, the better to run from the Roman legions."

"Some day, Roman, you and I will see between us who has the longest legs for running."

"It might be interesting," Ulpius admitted. "However, it can hardly come to pass. Rome is unconquerable, barbarian. Your fate is cast."

Calgaich shrugged. "My own grandfather once said that Rome was a prisoner of her own ambition, that she had conquered the world, and in so doing, had woven a tight net of barbarians about herself. It was only a matter of time, he said, before that net would close in and strangle her to death."

Ulpius laughed. "Your grandfather? Evicatos the Spearman? What could an illiterate barbarian know about such things?"

"I was not speaking of Evicatos, Roman. I meant my *Roman* grandfather—Rufus Arrius Niger—once tribune *legatus legionis*, and now a senator of Rome. Even now he is said to be inspecting the forts of the Saxon shore. Why? Could it be that Rome is deeply concerned about the Saxon wind that is blowing stronger every day against the southeast coast of Britannia?"

The tribune spat at Calgaich's feet and spurred his horse toward the head of the cavalcade. Already the advance riders were trotting their horses across the bridge. The low thunder of hooves echoed along the river valley. A trumpet sounded from the fort. A detail of auxiliaries trotted out of the guardhouse that stood at the far end of the bridge.

Guidd spoke to Calgaich out of the side of his mouth. "What was it you said to him that angered him so, Calgaich? I haven't mastered much of their twisted Latin tongue."

"He seemed to think that Rome will stand forever against us barbarians."

Guidd growled. "They are afraid. They walk about as though they still owned the world, *but they are afraid.* When you were in Eriu, Calgaich, and after your father had been turned over to the Romans, I came here to Luguvalium and this fort to see what could be done to rescue him."

Calgaich looked quickly at the woodsman. *"Alone,* old hound?"

Guidd nodded. "No one would come with me. Your uncle had outlawed me. Many of the Novantae were afraid to be seen with me. So I came alone." Guidd's voice died away. "He was my master," he added simply.

"Why do you think the Romans are afraid, Guidd?"

"Look at the gates of the fort. They have been narrowed by half. It is so the length of the Great Wall."

"The better for defense."

Guidd nodded. "I walked the streets of Luguvalium disguised as a trapper of wolves, to sell my pelts. The town had changed much. Many of the houses had been torn down to repair and heighten the Great Wall. Only their foundations showed, with weeds sprouting between the flagstones. The faces of the people showed fear. Remember, Calgaich, that it was only seventeen years ago that your grandfather led the Novantae, the Selgovae, the Damnonii and many Picts across the Great Wall almost as far south as Londinium."

Calgaich nodded. "Those were great days. I can remember when the Novantae war spears came back, all of you loaded with fine loot."

Guidd laughed. "By Lugh! We got further south than any other Caledonians ever had. I still swear I could smell the privies of Londinium on the breeze the day before we fell back, laden with loot and women prisoners, rather than to try the massed might of two legions and their auxiliaries."

There was much food for thought in these matters. A thread of thought, a dark and twisted one, meandered through the fabric of Calgaich's thoughts. The tribune Ulpius Claudius had not been in the country of the Novantae to pick berries. What was it Guidd had said about Bruidge? *That's why he is playing the weakling's game of putting himself into the hands of one enemy to save himself from another.* The Romans were afraid of the Novantae, the only border tribe that had steadfastly resisted Roman domination, and had never accepted any of their overtures of friendship, that is, up until now. Bruidge had put himself into the debt of the Romans, whom he hated as much as any other of the Novantae, in order to secure the chieftainship for himself.

"The Romans are afraid of us," Guidd said.

Calgaich nodded. "Right now they are winning the dice game."

"They fear you, Calgaich."

"One man? What can I do now to overthrow their empire?"

"You are the grandson of Evicatos, and the son of Lellan."

"And the grandson of a Roman," Calgaich added dryly.

"Even so, Calgaich, you must return to our country some day."

"We are being taken to Rome, old wolf."

"You will return," Guidd insisted. "It is in the stars. You must return!"

They crossed the bridge and passed the great Fort ala Petriana, watched curiously by the sentries on the walls. They crossed through open fields to a large *mansio*, or villa, that had a fine view of the fort and of the town of Luguvalium, sprawling along the other side of the river. The villa was large, and had recently been modified, so that it was more of an outlying bastion of the fort, rather than the quarters for visiting dignitaries for whose use it had originally been built. Additional walls had been constructed to bring the villa closer to the protection of the fort and to provide for the small garrison who guarded the villa.

A cold wind came up as the sun set. The gate of the villa was swung open to admit the cavalcade. Calgaich and Guidd were then unbound and lowered to the ground from their horses, hardly able to stand or walk.

Ulpius dismounted. He eyed his two prisoners. "This *mansio* is the temporary headquarters of Quaestor Lucius Sextillius, acting governor of this province. I warn you that he is a harder man to deal with than I. You will be confined here until he decides your fate." He looked directly at Calgaich. "Remember that the hangman's noose is being woven for you. A second desertion, such as you committed, makes such punishment mandatory. Perhaps the quaestor will make different provisions. I will recommend that you be taken to Rome for the Games."

"Has your recommendation any weight with him?"

"Some," Ulpius admitted. "You see, he is my uncle."

They watched the tribune walk toward the largest of the buildings within the walled enclosure. "You know what that means, Calgaich," Guidd said in a low voice. "It's to be Rome for you, under the personal escort of that perfumed bastard of a Roman."

"It's a long way to Rome," Calgaich said cryptically.

"Move, damn you!" Montanas barked.

Ulpius had stopped just outside the entrance to the largest building of the villa complex. He was talking with a cloaked person near the villa. The sun was almost gone and the gloaming was filling the courtyard with shadows, but there was a streak of gold about the head of the person talking with the tribune. Her musical laughter carried to Calgaich. She flung back her head and the hood of her cloak fell back letting fall a cascade of golden hair. Likely a whore, Calgaich thought, for he knew Roman whores traditionally wore dark clothing and dyed their hair saffron in color. The woman turned to look toward Calgaich.

Calgaich stared at the woman. He took a few faltering steps toward her on his numbed legs but could not continue. He did not want to fall. A great longing filled him. "Morar! Morar!" he cried in anguish.

The woman looked at Calgaich for a few seconds, until Ulpius moved between them; then she turned quickly and entered the building. Ulpius smiled knowingly at Calgaich as he followed her in.

A sandaled foot struck Calgaich just over the kidneys. Numbing pain shot through his body as he went down on the graveled ground.

"When I give an order, pig-shit," Decrius said in a low hard voice, "you'll obey, or I'll have your hide in bloody strips."

The killing urge swept through Calgaich. Guidd helped him to his feet. "For the love of the gods," he hissed, "take what he gives out, and bide your time."

"Lock these Caledonian cattle up!" Montanas barked at the decurion. "Separate them!"

"There is only one available cell, Centurion."

"Then find another! I don't care what it is!"

A spear butt struck Calgaich between the shoulder blades. He stumbled toward a row of outbuildings. He was driven into a room and the heavy door was slammed shut behind him.

He looked about him. In the dimness he saw great jars and containers lining the walls. There were trusses of hay and straw piled against an end wall. A faint ray of dying light shone through a small barred window.

Calgaich paced back and forth. He was sure the woman he had just seen was Morar. No hair dyed yellow could have that golden sheen. Even though her dark cloak had effectively concealed her body, he could still see it well enough in his mind's eye. The thought of her and that lush body had tortured him many a night during his exile.

Even at fourteen, when Calgaich first met her, Morar had the mark of the woman, rather than the girl. Her parents had been long dead, and she was the ward of Bruidge of the Battle-Axe, who had let her do what she willed, perhaps too much so. There were times when the other girls said dark things about Morar. It was rumored that one of her uncles had been a Druid of the highest rank. It was said that he had been able to travel into the life-after-death, and to return to the land of the living at will. He had taught her much. Calgaich had never believed such rot, because to look at Morar was to see the light of life and the sun rather than the dark and bloody mysteries of the eerie Druids.

Morar and Calgaich had become betrothed just before he traveled south to enlist in the Ulpia Torquata, the Double Battalion of Britons. While stationed with his battalion along the Rhine, the news came to him that his mother was dying. He asked permission to see her and was refused by a brutal centurion. There was no holding him then. He made his way to the channel, where he stole a small *birlinn*. He crossed the channel and then made his way north by night. An Asturian cavalry *turma* caught him ten miles north of the Great Wall. He was brought back for the vicious and brutal flogging prescribed by legion law. After that experience he was more determined than ever. He killed his guard and escaped again. He reached Rioghaine only to find that his mother had died that same day.

There followed weeks of mourning for Calgaich. He spent much time hunting with Guidd One-Eye, living with him in his *crannog*. One day when the rains were in their third day, Calgaich unexpectedly returned to the Dun of Evicatos. He took a torch from near the entrance and went from room to room looking for someone to drink with while he silently mourned his loss. He would never forget what happened next as long as he lived.

Two rooms beyond the great hall, in the last bed-chamber, he came upon Morar and Fergus alone together. Morar was stripped to the skin and lying on a low bed little-used except by the servants. Fergus, half-dressed, stood over her. Morar screamed as the rusted hinges of the door announced Calgaich's entrance and she saw him.

"Calgaich, I have been raped," she cried. Her sobs filled the room as Fergus caught up his tunic and fled. Calgaich rushed to Morar's side and took her in his arms. Her hair was a mass of tangled gold; her eyes were wild. He could still remember the touch of her soft skin, her breasts wet with her tears of pain and relief that he had found her and saved her from more of Fergus's assaults. He tried to quiet her.

"Hush, Morar, there is no need to talk." He called a servant in to bathe her. Then he left, promising to return after avenging her terrible ravishment. An hour later Calgaich found his cousin, Fergus, in one of the guard huts. He called to him to come out for fair combat or he would fire the thatched roof. Fergus appeared, babbling things Calgaich was too crazed to hear. The weapons were drawn. Fergus was no match for the sword of Calgaich. He died within minutes, but not before he managed to leave his mark on the face of his killer. Calgaich's anger subsided almost instantly as he stood over the body, and he knew there was no going back to Morar at that time. Once again he became an outlaw and fled from the country to Eriu. There he joined the *fianna* of King Crann and plotted his return to his home and to Morar.

Calgaich's foot struck something partially buried in the thick layer of floor straw. He bent to pick up a heavy jar, stoppered by a wooden bung. He pulled the bung free. The heady, fruity odor of strong spirits rose to tingle within his nostrils. He grinned widely. "Lugh is still with me," he whispered to the night.

The first drink seemed to hit him like a leaden ball hurled by one of the famed Balearic slingers. He coughed and tears came into his eyes. He drank deeply again. "*Sa ha!*" he cried. "I have found a true friend in this Roman hellhole!"

He pulled several trusses of straw together to fashion a bed, and he lay down on it with the jug resting on his chest. From time to time he nipped at the spirits, but the wanted drunkenness did not come. Raindrops began to patter on the roof.

Dim pictures flowed through his mind. He could see the Ordovician woman as though she were standing there naked, her skin a pristine whiteness. The lovely, beautifully molded breasts with their pink buds, outthrust from the rough bite of the cold sea wind, while she stood on the deck of the doomed *birlinn*. He saw her, too as she stood in the dimness of the barrow, that place of evil and indescribable horror, after she had given him her concealing cloak at his demand. His body shook as he remembered every detail of the time he had violated her maidenhood. He could still see her great emerald eyes looking up into his lust-twisted face as he had forced her. He recalled the velvety smoothness of her buttocks and the inner parts of her thighs, the soft fullness of her lips and the lush swelling of her breasts beneath his calloused hands.

Sleep came at last. Sleep came, but not rest, for Morar, the Golden One, came to him through the whiskey haze. It was not the first time she had done so in his dreams. He had often seen her so while in Eriu, and always after battle, when the liquor was strong in him. Morar had always appeared naked, as she had been when he had surprised Fergus in his attempted rape. Still, when she had come to him in his dreams, there was little enough of her body to be seen, for she clothed herself in her thigh-length golden hair, shot with glintings of light like honey suspended in the pouring. She usually appeared through a swirling mist like those that hung over the marshes in the damp nights of fall and spring. She could be seen and yet she could not be seen, at least not as he *wanted* to see her, and whenever Calgaich would reach out to her with his bloodstained hands, toward that living flesh of purity beyond purity and longing beyond longing, she would vanish with an enigmatic smile, gently mocking, that promised so much and yet gave nothing.

This time she came to Calgaich robed and cloaked and sweetly fragrant. He reached out for her, knowing well enough that his hands would only pass through air. He grasped her by the shoulders and drew her down to him. She twisted loose and drew back. Her hooded cloak came loose and released a flood of her golden hair. The cloak dropped to the floor. Calgaich got unsteadily to his feet and reached for her again. He gripped the loose fabric of her woolen gown, and stripped it from her to throw it aside. She retreated back against the piled-up trusses of straw and hay.

Calgaich followed her and closed with her body. She struggled to get around him but he thrust his aching loins hard against her softness. He bent to kiss her, and her hair fell across his face. She twisted her head to one side and raised a small, hard knee to his groin. He grunted in pain and staggered back.

She tried for the door, but Calgaich thrust a leg out and she fell over it into the damp straw of the floor. He straddled her and ripped her undergown free from her squirming body. He stood up and dragged her naked to her feet, then he lowered her onto the bed of straw. "Morar! Morar!" he cried.

"Calgaich!" she said his name just before he closed his mouth on hers. He raised his head and tore loose his belt. "They'll hear you!" she cried.

He stood up, and as she tried to get to her feet he struck her once, to drive her back onto the straw pallet. He stripped off his clothing and dropped on top of her. He had been waiting a long time for this night to come. She struggled hard. Once she bit into his lower lip and blood dripped from his chin to stain her breasts. He pressed his lips against hers and passed his hands down her breasts to her belly. He wedged his knees in between her thighs and pried her legs apart. For a moment or two she continued to struggle as he strove to penetrate her passageway. She became rigid as he succeeded in entering her, and as he probed deeper she clasped her arms about his neck and spread her legs as far apart as she could.

She cried out sharply, just once, as he forced her to his fullest extent. Slowly at first, and then faster, she began to move with him. She was awkward and not quite in rhythm until she got the feeling of the act and then she began to respond in a pleasurable manner. At last she pressed her mouth against his, loosely and yet with passion as they flowed together.

Later they lay quietly side by side, fully sated. The rain pattered on the roof. Footsteps approached outside. Calgaich sat up quickly. The footsteps receded in the distance.

"Calgaich," she said quietly.

He looked down at her. Something in her voice made him spread the golden hair from off her face. It was not Morar, the Golden One. He was horrified.

"Bronwyn," he cried.

"Let me up," she pleaded. "It's cold and damp in here now that the heat has passed from both of us." She reached for her undergown, thrown to the floor beside the straw pallet.

Calgaich pressed his hands flat on the straw and forced his body upward away from her soft form. "Bronwyn!" he said again thickly.

"You knew all along," she accused him.

He stood up and stared down at her in the dim light. Even during the act he had thought that this woman seemed smaller in all respects than what he had anticipated Morar would have been like. But this had not been enough to stop him. Had he known? His mind was not clear.

As Bronwyn stood up, something metallic struck the jug of *usquebaugh*. She quickly bent to pick up her small dirk.

"Did you have that dirk with you all that time?" Calgaich asked her.

She nodded without looking at him as she pulled on her ripped undergown and attempted to fasten it around her.

"You should have used it, Bronwyn! I had no right to force you." Calgaich flushed as he remembered his strength of a few minutes ago.

"I know," she agreed quietly.

He took her by the shoulders and drew her close. "But why? What were you doing here? Why didn't you tell me who you were? You could have cried out and brought the guards running."

"Would it have made a difference to know it was not Morar, but Bronwyn? You were lost in a whiskey haze."

He shook his head in bewilderment. "You were no bigger than a hare when last I saw you at the *dun*."

"That was more than three years ago. I was only fourteen then. You never did pay much attention to me, Calgaich." She raised her eyes to meet his gaze.

"It seems as though I have now," he said ruefully, brushing some straw from her cloak.

"It doesn't matter, Calgaich."

"But it does! I was betrothed to Morar! Now I have raped her little sister. How can it not matter?"

She put on her cloak. "You had better not tell Morar," she warned him. "There is no need for her to know."

He walked before her to the door and opened it. The rain was slanting down from a dark sky. The large courtyard was empty. A faint yellow light showed from the small guardhouse near the gate.

She turned to face him as she was about to leave. "Are you sure you didn't know it was I, instead of Morar?" she asked softly.

He shook his head. "I swear!" He came closer to her. "Are you betrothed?"

She shook her head, and some of her golden hair fell free of the hood.

"The men of Rioghaine are either blind or complete fools, then."

"It isn't that," she said bitterly.

He stared at her dim, beautiful face. "What do you mean?"

"There is not time to talk about it now, Calgaich. I took my life, or my soft hide, at least, in my own hands by coming to you tonight."

"How did you get past the guard?" Questions were beginning to form in Calgaich's mind, out of the haze of the whiskey and spent passion.

Bronwyn smiled a little wickedly, reminding Calgaich of the mischievous child she had once been. "He is a stupid Asturian who likes the golden women of the north, or so he said when I brought him some of the quaestor's Falernian wine. He didn't know I had laced it with plenty of poppy seed. His dirty hands were rougher than yours, Calgaich, but he didn't get too far before the wine put him to sleep."

He took her by the shoulders. "Where did you learn such a trick, Bronwyn?"

She laughed softly up at him. "From Morar. Morar knows many tricks with men." Her voice died away as she saw the hard look on his face, and his hands gripped her shoulders harder.

"With *men?* What do you mean?" Calgaich demanded.

"I spoke in jest," she replied quickly. "Here, you've little time to lose. Take my dirk. The guards are in the guardhouse, sheltering from the rain. You can go over the wall. The rain and mist will hide you so that you can get across the bridge and beyond the Great Wall."

He took her dirk. "Does Morar know that you are here?"

Bronwyn shook her head.

"Why didn't she come herself?"

His words seemed to hurt Bronwyn and she looked away from him. "Morar has changed much since you left for Eriu, Calgaich. She says and does strange things. Even now, as we talk here, she is drinking wine with Ulpius and his greasy pig of an uncle, Lucius. I only wish Bruidge had not sent me along with Morar."

Calgaich was lost in his own thoughts and did not hear the last. "Where is my father?"

"He's imprisoned in a building in the next courtyard, the one whose gate faces the fort. You can't get to him, Calgaich. Besides, even if you could, he's too weak to travel. Some say he is slowly dying because of the quaestor's wishes."

Again he gripped her by the shoulders and studied her face. "What do you mean?"

"Poison, Calgaich."

"Where is this drugged Asturian?" He looked beyond her to the courtyard.

"In the stables." She wrinkled her nose as the memory of the Asturian's rough hands came back to her.

"His weapons are with him? His cloak and helmet?"

"Yes." She narrowed her eyes. "Calgaich? You can't hope to rescue your father." Her voice pleaded with him.

"I was planning to do that anyway. The Romans gave me passage here. You've freed me."

"But not to be caught again. I wanted you to flee. You're mad!"

"Perhaps," he admitted. "But a son can't let his father die in the filth of a Roman prison."

"But it is said he hasn't long to live."

"Then he must die in his own country." Calgaich picked up the whiskey jug and drank deeply, then wiped his mouth with the back of his hand. "Can you reach your quarters safely?" he asked. She should not have to die for freeing him—or worse, have to submit to the drunken advances of guardsmen.

"Let me go with you," she cried, placing a small hand on his arm.

He shook his head, passion again rising at her touch. "Can you get into your quarters?" he repeated.

"Easily enough. The others will be drunk by now." She turned away from him, sick with having to return to the Roman rooms.

"Morar, too?" he asked quietly.

"I don't know. I do not understand Morar anymore."

"Where is Guidd?" Calgaich asked.

"In a room at the stables." Bronwyn pointed to the dark, past the guardhouse.

He opened the heavy door. "Go back to your quarters, quickly." He looked down at her as she passed close in front of him. "I am sorry I forced you, Bronwyn."

She paused and looked up at him. Then she smiled a little. "No harm was done."

"You little witch! You could have told me who you were."

Bronwyn was silent for a few seconds; then she said, "But maybe I didn't want to stop you."

He narrowed his eyes and put a hand on her shoulder. Tendrils of her golden hair touched his hand. "So the struggle you put up was just an act."

"The struggle, perhaps. But not later." She drew away from him. "It was to happen to me soon anyway. I wanted you to be the first." Her voice was bitter. She was no longer a girl. "And now I must return." She faced him once more. "You can think any way you like, Calgaich. I shall always have tonight. And aren't we lovers now?" With that, she disappeared quickly into the misty drizzle, leaving Calgaich puzzled and open-mouthed. Perhaps he should have taken her along. He did not like to think of what she was returning to in the fort beyond, in the care of the Perfumed Pig. But it was too late for regrets.

Calgaich eased open the door of the stable and found the drugged Asturian guard sprawled in the straw. Calgaich relieved him of his sword and short spear, then stripped off his helmet and cloak. The guard started to arise. His own sheathed sword came down on his skull.

Calgaich catfooted to a barred door. "Guidd?" he whispered.

"Calgaich? Is that you?" Guidd replied.

Calgaich opened the door and thrust the spear into the woodsman's hands. "Follow me. My father is imprisoned here. We're going to free him."

Calgaich donned the Asturian's helmet and swung his cloak about his shoulders. Guidd found a worn saddle blanket which he draped about his head and body and tied with a bridle rein.

Like two drifting shadows they crossed the misty courtyard. The gateway between the two courtyards of the villa was open. They passed into the darkness of the second courtyard. Calgaich drew Guidd into the shelter of the wall. "Go now, if you want to," he whispered. "They'll never catch you on a night like this."

Guidd shook his head. He raised the spear. "I am still your father's hound, Calgaich. Lead the way, my brother!"

CHAPTER 9

Calgaich and Guidd stood in the shadows and watched the lone legionnaire who stood guard outside a long building with barred windows. The Roman stood under the low, overhanging eaves behind a thin curtain of water running in leaden-colored streams from the tile roof. The structure had been built using the rear wall of the courtyard as one side. To the left, across the puddled courtyard, was another such edifice, in which small windows glowed with dim yellow light. The faint sound of voices came from within it. At one end of it was the outer gateway facing the south wall of the fort across a narrow field. Another guard stood there, huddled in his cloak against the chill drizzle of the rain.

"I'll take one of them and you take the other, Calgaich," Guidd whispered.

Calgaich shook his head. "We can't risk an outcry. If we can get my father and then win free of the fort, we'll be on foot, so it will have to be done by stealth." He pointed to the lighted building. "See who is in there."

The woodsman vanished into the dimness as silently as a hunting cat. In a few minutes he came back. "It's a barracks, Calgaich. There are some legionnaires in there, but mostly auxiliaries, Asturians from the looks of them. There's a dice game going on and the wine bottles are passing back and forth merrily. The guard at the gate is an Asturian."

"Did you see their commander?"

Guidd shook his head. "But I know who he is. It's that bastard Montanas. The stable guard told me when he warned me not to try to escape. I pray to the gods that he tries to stop us."

150

"I pray to the gods that he doesn't find out, at least until my father is safely out of this place and across the border. Then, old wolf, you'll have to reach that damned centurion before I do, for I'll not leave much of him for anyone else." Calgaich drew Guidd close to him. "Watch the gate guard. See that he doesn't come toward the building where I'm going."

Calgaich swathed the cloak about himself and waited until Guidd had returned toward the gate. Then he walked quickly across the courtyard to where the legionnaire stood guard.

"The centurion sent me to check the prisoner," Calgaich said.

"Why? He's all right. I looked in on him an hour ago. He was sleeping like a babe."

"I've got my orders, *caligatus.*"

"Damn you! Be careful how you address a legionnaire of the first cohort of the Twentieth Valeria Victrix! Listen, auxiliary, we regulars of the legion take no nicknames from you! *Caligatus?* I'll plant *my caligae* against your Asturian rump!"

Calgaich almost grinned. The slang name for legionnaires among themselves was *caligati,* the "booted ones," and they jealously guarded their name for themselves.

"Pass on, Asturian rump of a goat!" the Roman snapped. He spat at Calgaich's heels as Calgaich passed him.

Calgaich unbarred the door. He glanced back over his shoulder as he did so. The legionnaire had turned to the deep shadows under the eaves. He couldn't see the doorway from where he was standing.

Calgaich eased into a long hallway. A lamp flickered in a small room where a legionnaire was sleeping on a cot. His spear and shield leaned against the wall. He never knew what hit him. Calgaich gagged, blindfolded and then bound him. He took his cloak and helmet.

Calgaich padded down the hall. The door on the end room was barred. He gently lifted the bar from its sockets. The door swung back by itself. Faint yellow lamplight appeared. An old, white-haired man sat on a cot. "What do you want, Roman?" he asked. "Have you come to kill me at last?"

"Father," Calgaich said. He hardly recognized him, so

aged had he become in the past three years. He was not the tall, strong man Calgaich had known.

The dim eyes stared. "I hear the voice of my only son, Calgaich," Lellan murmured.

"Yes, Father."

"The gods are playing tricks on an old man. My son, Calgaich, has gone West-Over-Seas, by the Warrior's Road to *Tir na n'Og*. Soon I hope to join him."

Calgaich approached the old man and took his hands, no longer hilt-calloused, but thin and almost ascetic. It was his eyes that wounded Calgaich like a spear. They were wide, filmed with white, and did not blink.

"Do you trick me, Roman? Did I not hear the ghostly voice of my son?"

Calgaich gathered the old, broken man into his arms. Hot tears ran down his face.

"Is it really you, Calgaich?" Lellan sighed.

"Yes, Father. I've come to take you home."

"The Romans have freed me at last?"

"No, Father, it is *I* who will free you."

"You have brought the war spears of the Novantae to fight beside you?" Lellan asked in an eager voice. Now his voice sounded much younger, almost like that of Calgaich himself.

"No. I came here alone. Guidd waits outside to help us."

"There are many Romans guarding this place."

"Trust in the help of Lugh, Father."

"Can we reach our own country?"

Calgaich hesitated. Could he take this broken old man from the heart of a Roman stronghold and through the night to escape from the Asturians who would likely be baying at their heels? Calgaich and Guidd could make it alone. But he had to try to get his father to safety, too. That or die in the attempt.

"No, it is hopeless, Calgaich. To attempt to free me would cost you your lives. The odds are too great against you. But you're young and strong. Go now! Swiftly! Take the chieftainship from my brother Bruidge. It is yours."

Calgaich placed the guard's cloak about Lellan's shoulders and put the helmet on his head. He tucked the thin white hair up under the helmet and then drew the hood of the cloak over the helmet.

"You are still chieftain," Calgaich murmured.

Calgaich led the old man into the hall and along it to the outer door. He got the shield and spear of the guard and hung the shield on Lellan's back. "Father," he said, "you must walk straight as a legionnaire behind me to the gate. You must stay silent. Let me do the talking."

"But if we are found out?"

"Do we Novantae fear death, Father?" Calgaich asked fiercely.

The rain was slashing down. Calgaich eased through the partially opened door. "Wait here," he whispered.

The guard under the eaves was dozing as he leaned on his spear. The hilt of the Asturian sword struck him on the nape of his neck just under the rim of the helmet. Calgaich caught him before he hit the ground. Calgaich relieved him of his spear and his short sword. He dragged the unconscious man into the building and to the cell where Lellan had been imprisoned. He dumped the Roman into the cell and then closed and barred the door.

"Ready, Father?" Calgaich asked.

Lellan nodded. "Lead on, my Son."

Calgaich placed an arm about Lellan's stooped shoulders and drew the old man close for a moment. "Follow me," he said. "Hold onto my cloak for guidance."

Guidd One-Eye stood in the shadows of the barracks, behind a buttress, within a few feet of the Asturian gate guard who stood huddled within the deep doorway of the barracks, out of the rain but unable to see anyone approaching his post. Guidd turned as he heard footsteps on the flagstones. He saw the dim figures approaching the gate. He moved like a hunting cat through the leaden-colored rain and shadows and hooked an arm about the throat of an Asturian guard. He drew it tight. In a moment he eased the unconscious guard to the flagstones.

Lellan staggered weakly and lost his grip on Calgaich's cloak. He went down on one knee. Guidd ran toward him.

"Get the gate open, Guidd!" Calgaich snapped. "Hurry!"

Calgaich turned to help his father to his feet. Guidd started to lift the bar from the gate sockets, but it was too heavy for him. It slid sideways and the butt of it struck the flagstones. Guidd tried to lean it against the wall but it got away from him and fell hard against the end door of the barracks. Guidd dragged back one of the heavy half-doors of the gate. The wind swept rain through the opening.

Calgaich tried to run while leading his father, but Lellan could not keep up with him.

Suddenly the door of the barracks was flung open and a flood of yellow lamplight shone through the driving rain. A man came through the doorway and stumbled over the unconscious Asturian.

"Pericol! What the hell is going on?" Centurion Decrius Montanas shouted.

Calgaich shoved Lellan through the gateway into the hands of Guidd, then whirled to face the cursing centurion. Calgaich held the long cavalry sword in his right hand and the short-bladed legionnaire's *gladius* in his left hand.

"The guard!" Montanas roared. He whipped out his *gladius* and plunged toward Calgaich with short, stiff-legged steps.

Calgaich thrust his sword toward the face of the centurion. Decrius slashed his *gladius* sideways and struck the sword to one side. The shock of the blow made Calgaich's sword arm tingle. He retreated to block the gateway so that Guidd and Lellan could escape.

Legionnaires and auxiliaries plunged two by two through the open doorway of the barracks. Two of them held flaring torches. Montanas ran at Calgaich but he could not get in a slashing attack because of the narrowness of the gateway, which was blocked by Calgaich. Calgaich's sword seemed to leap out and the point drove into the unprotected right forearm of the centurion, who dropped his sword and staggered sideways.

The nailed sandals of the Romans thudded against the flagstones as they rushed Calgaich. He slipped back and to one side and caught the first of them who came through the gateway with a stroke across the nape of the neck.

Calgaich ran from the gateway. A legionnaire rushed up the stairway to the walk just behind the ramparted wall and thrust his torch up high with his left hand. He poised his *pilum,* the short and deadly Roman spear, and cast it downward beyond Calgaich. Lellan shuddered as the spear point caught him low in the back.

A group of Romans burst through the gateway and charged the three Novantae. Guidd drew back his right arm and cast his spear. It struck an auxiliary in the throat. Calgaich charged and plunged his sword into the chest of a legionnaire and followed through with a chopping stroke across his throat with the *gladius*. A sword glanced from Calgaich's helmet and drove him down on one knee.

Lellan turned slowly and saw his son go down. He knew his own time had come. He swung the heavy Roman shield to his left arm and couched the spear under his right. He charged the nearest Roman as though he were again a young warrior leading his famed Novantae spearmen against the hated Red Crests.

Guidd snatched up the *gladius* Calgaich had dropped and followed his chief. More Romans and auxiliaries had come through the gateway. More torches flared along the rampart above the gate. A trumpet blared from Fort ala Petriana after an alert guard had seen the torches and had heard the combating at the villa.

"Get you gone, Calgaich!" Lellan shouted. "I'm done! Let me die on my feet like a warrior!"

The melee became wilder. A sword knocked Calgaich's helmet from his head. A spear tip stuck lightly in his left shoulder and he felt the hot blood run down his breast.

"*Abu! Abu!* To victory! To victory!" Lellan cried in a voice of amazing strength.

Calgaich was cut off from his father. Three Romans closed in on him, chins tucked behind their shields, short-bladed *gladii* feeling for his life's blood. It was the end. He knew it now. There could be no escape. He saw the grimacing face of the cursing centurion as he charged toward the fray.

Suddenly a huge, brindled shape came out of the shadows and launched itself at one of the Romans. The weight of the great wolfhound drove the Roman onto his back and his jugular was severed by a powerful snap of the hound's jaws.

"Bron!" Calgaich yelled as he struck down an Asturian. Decrius Montanas went down with the snarling Bron on top of him. The centurion rolled over onto his belly to protect his vulnerable throat from the slashing fangs.

Lellan had gone down under the sword blows of three Romans. Guidd had his back against a tree and was defending himself against two Asturians. Calgaich was fighting to reach the side of his fallen father.

The sound of many tramping feet came from the direction of the fort. A trumpet blew through the windy darkness. The other gate of the villa was thrown open as Ulpius Claudius appeared leading a group of legionnaires.

Bron dropped back to stand beside Calgaich for the fight to the death. Sword blades rang against each other. Men shouted. Torches flared in the rising wind.

A horseman appeared out of the darkness beyond the road. The torchlight glistened wetly on the blade of a great war spear just before it drove past Calgaich and sank into the chest of a Roman. The horse brushed against Calgaich. He looked sideways into the face of the rider. "Cairenn!" he shouted. The horse knocked Romans and Asturians aside. The war spear struck into the throat of an Asturian and was withdrawn, dripping blood.

The Romans and Asturians fell back before the fury of Cairenn's attack. Lellan lay alone on the muddy ground, slashed and stabbed by dozens of sword strokes.

Calgaich whirled. He dropped one of Guidd's opponents and the other one fled before the fury of the Celt.

Cairenn turned her horse. "Run, Calgaich!" she shouted. "I can't drive them back much longer!"

"My father!" he yelled back.

"He's dead!" Cairenn screamed.

"Run, Calgaich!" Guidd shouted.

Battle madness was still within Calgaich. He felt no pain and no fatigue.

The crumpled body of Lellan was red with blood. His clothing was saturated with it. Only his face had been untouched, and the long white hair was still unstained.

Cairenn swung the horse toward Calgaich. "Run, *fian!*" she cried.

Calgaich took ten long strides. The upswung *spatha* flashed in the torchlight, glistening with blood, to come down in a solid sure stroke that cut the head of Lellan clean from the trunk. Calgaich snatched up the head by its long white hair, and as Cairenn rode past him he dropped the *spatha* and reached up with his right hand to grip the pommel of the saddle. He swung up behind Cairenn. She spurred the horse into the shadows, passing Guidd, who gripped one of her legs and ran lightly alongside the horse. Bron loped swiftly after them.

Calgaich turned and held up the severed head. His eyes were alight with the battle fire. He raised his voice in a rhythmic chanting:

"A head I carry, close to my heart,
Head of Lellan, generous leader of the war spears,
And on his white breast, a black carrion crow.
A head I carry . . .
Alive he was a refuge for the oppressed,
A head I carry . . .
Whose war-bands patrolled vast territories,
The head of much sung Lellan, whose fame is far-
    scattered.
A head I hold which once sustained me . . .
My arm is numb, my body trembles,
My heart breaks;
This head I cherish, formerly cherished me."

"Do not try for the bridge little hare!" Guidd cried. "Ride to the east and behind the Great Wall! Somewhere there may be a place where we can cross it this dark night!"

The rain slashed down in a cold torrent and extinguished the torches. Ahead of the escaping trio and the great wolfhound was the clinging darkness of the rolling moors.

CHAPTER 10

It was as it had been before, Cairenn thought wearily, as she urged her horse up a long slope wreathed in mist. The mist obscured the hills and streams so that even the directions became confused. Calgaich and she were running again. She reined in the blowing horse, then turned in the saddle and looked behind. Bron raised his head and looked curiously at her. He had been given orders to stay with her when Calgaich and Guidd had vanished into the mist at dawn light. Somewhere behind them and close at hand, there had been other horsemen.

The rounded object in the torn piece of cloak had been hung from the saddle, and during the long night's ride it had bumped against Cairenn's right knee with the rhythm of the horse's stride. She reached down and pushed it farther forward. The mental picture of Calgaich's flashing sword blade as it had descended and the sight of the head rolling on the blood-soaked turf had stayed with Cairenn all that night.

Bron turned quickly, his hackles rising. He growled deep within his throat, then padded off into the mist. Cairenn was alone again. Somewhere behind her and to the north was the Great Wall. They had covered many miles during the night, riding and walking to the east.

Her horse turned his head and whinnied. Cairenn drew her dirk. There was no place to go. She could not run. The horse was worn out.

A plover complained querulously as it was disturbed.

A faint wind began to blow along the rolling moors.

"You're looking in the wrong direction, little hare," Guidd said from just behind Cairenn.

Cairenn was startled. She turned the horse around.

"Damn you!" she cried. "Must you sneak up behind me like a hunting wolf? I would rather be alone than followed by the likes of you."

Guidd looked surprised. "Why, I *am* a hunting wolf."

Calgaich joined them, grinning. "He believes it," he said to Cairenn, calming her horse as it shied away from their sudden appearance.

The wind shifted. A faint and rhythmic thudding sound was borne on it. The chink of metal striking stone, now and again, wove a counter melody into the thudding sound.

"What's that?" Cairenn asked as the horse moved restlessly about.

Calgaich turned. "The wall," he replied quietly. "That's probably a dawn patrol walking between the mile forts."

"So close to us?" she asked.

"The mist carries the sound. It is about half a mile from us. We're safe enough as long as the mist holds. Still, we can't get over the wall today. We'll have to hide on this side of it until nightfall, and then risk it. I had hoped we could reach this point before daylight. Every minute we have to spend on this side of the wall is dangerous."

Guidd leaned against the horse. "It's a good thing those Asturians who were following us got lost in the mist."

"Did they see you?" Cairenn asked anxiously.

Guidd and Calgaich looked blankly at her.

"I should have known better," she admitted.

Guidd grinned. "They're past us by now, heading east."

"But there will be others," Calgaich warned.

They moved to the east, with Guidd prowling through the mist ahead of them. They stopped at last in a deep hollow thick with bog myrtle. Calgaich and Guidd again vanished into the mist.

Soon, they came back as silently as disembodied spirits. "All clear," Calgaich announced. "If anything happens, and we have to run again, we'll split up. Remember, Cairenn, run that way, *away* from the wall." He pointed to the south. "Soon they will start using hounds and trackers to find us. If you are alone, follow a stream, and wade in it to throw the hounds off the scent. Then turn north once you've eluded them."

"And what of you?" she asked.

Calgaich looked at Guidd. Their faces were grim. "We won't be taken alive this time," he replied quietly. He looked at the bundle that hung from the saddle. "It might have been better, at that, if I had died back there beside my father with half a dozen dead Romans at my feet."

"You talk like a fool!" Cairenn said. She almost winced in anticipation of an expected blow. Her courage returned as Calgaich stood there silent. "Your father died to pass the chieftainship on to you. He knew he would not live much longer in a Roman prison. You are his only son. Is the son not worthy of the father's sacrifice?"

"She talks like a female Druid," Guidd growled.

Somewhere within the dense bog thicket a snipe drummed steadily.

"Do they come?" she asked. Her face was taut and pale.

Guidd shook his head. "The snipe drums only because he thinks all is well."

Cairenn placed a hand on Calgaich's arm. "If it had been you lying in the filth of a Roman prison, half-blind and dying from poison bit by bit, would you not have wanted to die as he did, with the wind on his face, fighting his enemies?"

Calgaich did not reply as he shook off her hand. He unsaddled the horse and placed the bundled head to one side. He led the blown animal to the very edge of the bog. He jerked his head at Guidd. The woodsman came to stand beside Calgaich. Calgaich stroked the horse's nose to quieten it, then suddenly jerked the head up and sideways. The slashing stroke of the keen-edged dirk came so swiftly across his throat the horse hardly felt it. Cairenn looked away as a dreadful bubbling sound escaped from the severed throat artery. Calgaich and Guidd threw their weight against the side of the horse so that he fell into the quagmire.

Guidd took the bloody dirk from Calgaich's hand and skinned back the hide on the flank. He placed a square of the horsehide on the bank of the quagmire and then expertly cut long, thick strips of meat from the flank of the horse. By the time he was through, the horse had half sunk into the mire. Calgaich hurled the saddle as far as he could into the bog.

Guidd worked quickly. He broke open a half-rotten log

and made a small fire of the dry inner wood. The thin smoke drifted up into the concealing mist. The meat was only partially roasted when he put out the embers. The woodsman handed Cairenn one of the roasted strips of meat. Calgaich and Guidd squatted on the wet ground and ate.

"This is barbarianism!" Cairenn cried, holding the meat at arm's length.

Calgaich shrugged. "We *are* barbarians, at least according to the civilized Romans."

Guidd grinned. "Would you rather starve as being civilized, or eat as a barbarian?" he asked. He chuckled.

Bron growled a little as he worried at his raw meat. He looked sideways at Cairenn with his yellow eyes.

"He's got his eye on your meat," Calgaich warned her.

By the time Carienn was through eating, the saddle had disappeared into the bog and the horse was half-submerged. Guidd eradicated all traces of the fire and bundled the remainder of the meat within the square of horsehide.

Calgaich found a hollow, well shielded by trees where leaves had drifted thickly. He beckoned to Cairenn. "Sleep here," he said. "We'll sleep separately, for fear of surprise. Bron will guard us. Are you all right?"

She nodded, looking up into his scarred face. "What will you do with the head?" she asked quietly.

He looked toward the north. "Take it back to Rioghaine if I can. I will not leave it here on this side of the wall."

Cairenn did not always understand Calgaich's passion for warring, but she did respect his love for his father. She knew he was doing what he must do. It was a question of honor. Finally he turned back to her.

"Sleep, little hare," he told her. He waited while she lay down on her cloak among the leaves. She wished he would lie down with her and keep her warm. He hesitated for just a moment and then moved away to sleep alone. Several times during the night Cairenn was aware of the great wolfhound, Bron, coming to sniff at her makeshift bed. Mostly, she slept.

The mist burned off with the rising of the watery-looking sun. Cairenn awoke once. There was no sign of Calgaich, Guidd or Bron. She raised her head as she heard the sound of men's voices coming faintly to her on the wind from the north. Metal thudded against stone. She got up on her knees.

"They are working on the wall, little hare," Guidd said.

She turned quickly. The woodsman lay on his belly beside a pool of rainwater. He scooped the clear water up into his mouth. He looked sideways at her. "They are *always* working on the wall," he added.

She turned to look north again. The sounds continued. Now and then she thought she heard the sound of men's voices. Once a dog barked. When she turned around, Guidd had vanished. The bog and thicket were silent under the rising sun. The horse had sunk out of sight.

When dusk came at last, they moved out of the bog. The mist had moved in again with the departure of the sun. They did not see the wall through the mist and darkness until they were almost upon it. It seemed to tower above them, about the height of three tall men.

Cairenn slowly put out a hand to touch the famed Wall of Hadrian. Although it had been there for almost two hundred and fifty years, and had been made of native stone, and much of it by native labor, there seemed to be an alien quality about it, at least to Cairenn. She knew the Caledonians hated it almost as though it were a living thing.

Calgaich had chosen this crossing point well. Here the Great Wall plunged into a deep, narrow valley, then spanned a shallow stream on bridge piers. Near the edge of the stream was a mile castle, and on the far side of the valley a signal tower stood on the heights.

Guidd pointed out the thick brush that had been allowed to encroach on the wall. He pointed upward to where part of the rampart had been allowed to fall off. "The Red Crests are getting careless," he whispered. "See here?" He thrust his fingers deep into the joints of some of the tiers of stone to indicate where the mortar had fallen out and had not been replaced.

Calgaich drew Cairenn close. "There are small castles every mile, and in between each of them are several signal towers. I am sure a signal has been passed along the wall by this time, from west to east, warning the garrisons that we escaped and are headed this way. They will likely double the watch, at least for part of the distance east from Luguvalium and Fort ala Petriana. We're going to try to get in between two of the wall posts. We'll have to move fast. If we're seen, we must scatter, and hope that some of us, at least, can escape. Do you understand?" His arms tightened around her.

She nodded. "I do not want to be taken alive, Calgaich."

Guidd had uncoiled a rough but serviceable rope he had fashioned from strips of his blanket and part of Calgaich's cloak. He fastened one end of it to his belt and then worked his way up the side of the wall by thrusting his fingers and toes into the crevices where the mortar had worked loose. A few moments later the end of the rope dropped beside Calgaich. Calgaich fastened the rope around the chest and forelegs of Bron. He jerked twice on the rope and then lifted the heavy hound up as far as he could. As soon as Guidd had taken up the slack in the rope Calgaich climbed up the wall to help Guidd haul up the hound.

Cairenn was alone. She looked up. Bron was just disappearing from her sight. Not a sound came from above her. She looked back over her shoulder. What if they did not help her up the wall? What if something happened to them up there?

Minutes drifted past. The rope dropped beside Cairenn. Calgaich came easily down the rope. "They are safe on the other side," he whispered. He slung his war spear across his back. "Can you climb it?" he asked.

"I can try," she said, looking up at the wall.

"I'll help you." He grasped her by the waist and lifted her as high as he could. She gripped the rope and began to climb while thrusting her toes into the deep cracks. Once she slipped, but she felt one of his hands against the small of her back. She knew he was climbing the wall just below and to the right of her.

Calgaich climbed above her once he knew she might make it. He lay flat across the rampart and reached down for her, drawing her up beside him to the rough stone track that lay between the two ramparts.

To the west the faint, square yellow eyes of unblinking light showed the small windows of the mile castle. The smell of food cooking came to Calgaich and Cairenn on the night wind.

Her breathing was harsh and thick in her throat. Her muscles trembled from exertion. She lay flat on the track and covered her eyes with a hand.

"It's a longer drop on the outer side," he whispered into her ear. "The wall here is built on a steep slope."

"I can't make it, Calgaich." It felt like the end to her.

"By the gods! You'll *have* to make it! I won't leave here without you!"

The rampart door at the mile castle tower was flung open. A flood of yellow, smoky light poured out onto the track. Dark-cloaked figures showed against the light. A man's hoarse voice sounded, giving orders. The voice echoed along the wall. The door was slammed shut. Shortly thereafter came the metallic, thudding sound of nail-studded sandals on the flagstones of the track.

Calgaich cursed. "The watch!"

A moment later the sound of men's voices, mingled with the thudding of feet, came from the east.

"We're between the pincers," Calgaich said.

There was no time for a safe and easy descent from the wall. Calgaich worked swiftly. He tied the rope to the outer rampart and turned to Cairenn. "Over with you," he ordered. His voice was harsh, a command.

She climbed over the rampart and gripped the rope. Her arm muscles still trembled from the strain of climbing up the other side. "I know I can't make it, Calgaich," she whispered tensely.

He pushed down on her head. "Damn you! Try! Slide to the end of the rope and then drop!"

Cairenn slid down the rough rope. Her hands were abraded and her knees bumped against the rough surface of the wall. Once she spun about and struck the back of her head against the stone. She prayed silently to her gods and then the rope slid through her sweating grasp and she dropped down into the darkness and the unknown.

Calgaich peered over the wall. He heard her strike far below. He knew she would not cry out. She had the guts of a warrior in the body of a beautiful woman, but it would never do to let her know. This was a *man's* world.

It was pitch dark at the bottom of the wall. Calgaich wanted to drop his spear over the side, but was afraid it might strike Cairenn or Guidd. He cursed softly as he slung it over his back. He threw a long leg over the rampart.

A man shouted hoarsely from the east. Nailed sandals rang against the flagstones as the watch began to turn toward Calgaich. The same sound was echoed from the west as the other watch patrol began to run.

"Lugh of the Shining Spear," Calgaich prayed. He slid down the rope. He felt his legs dangling in air and then he let go. By the luck of the gods he landed on his feet with a jolt that carried all the way up his spine.

"Over here, Calgaich!" Guidd called out.

Calgaich whirled. "Get the hell out of here! Get the woman away from this damned wall!"

A torch was cast from the ramparts. It fell through the swirling mist while trailing a shower of sparks. Dark-helmeted heads showed above the rampart. Something flashed dully in the light from the torch. A *pilum* point struck in the soft ground right beside Calgaich.

More torches were cast over the wall. An archer leaned over the rampart and drew a nocked arrow back so that the feathers touched the point of his jaw. The polished arrow flashed through the air and plucked at Calgaich's tunic. Calgaich ran, darting from side to side like a hare fleeing a hunter. Then he disappeared into the thick mist. Those damned archers, possibly Syrians or Numidians, were the best in the auxiliaries, and they rarely missed at such a short range. If it hadn't been for the mist they would have hit him.

Armor and weapons clashed as an auxiliary slid down the rope. A man cursed in some unknown tongue. He hadn't known the rope only reached partway to the ground. Calgaich grinned.

Calgaich glanced backward. Far to his right, to the east, he could see signal torches flaring up. He looked to his left. Signal torches were flaring at the mile castle. In a matter of minutes the signals would be traveling east and west along the wall for many miles.

The wind shifted. Somewhere along the wall a dog bayed; shortly thereafter the sound was repeated further along the wall. The outer gates of the mile castles would be opening soon to emit mounted auxiliaries and hounds.

They would converge diagonally toward the fugitives beyond the wall.

Guidd and Cairenn waited in the thick oak woods. "Are we safe now, Guidd?" she asked, gasping.

He looked down at her. "We're never safe around the wall. There is nothing we can do now but run, and run. Are you ill?"

She shook her head. "Only tired."

"A woman can't be weak in this country," he said sarcastically.

"I'm not here by choice, woodsman!" she said bitterly.

Calgaich came noiselessly through the misty woods. The dogs bayed incessantly behind him. Far across the moors, echoes of the baying seemed to come to life, but the tone was different. Bron raised his head and looked to the north. The wolves of the moors were calling back to their half-tamed kin.

Calgaich looked down at Cairenn where she rested on the damp ground. He handed Guidd his war spear. "Lead on," he said quietly. He picked Cairenn up and swung her across his broad shoulders.

Guidd led the way through the woods to the banks of a rushing stream. He stepped into the shallow icy water and began to wade upstream, followed by Calgaich and Bron. Cairenn slid an arm about Calgaich's neck. He turned his head to look at her. She smiled a little.

They pressed on, hour after hour, while the sound of the pursuing hounds became fainter and fainter and then died away altogether.

Cairenn awoke in a swirling opaqueness. She lay on a bed of dry bracken, sheltered in a cave. She was covered by her own sheepskin tunic and the remains of the Asturian cloak Calgaich had been wearing. There was no sign of Calgaich and Guidd, and for one awful moment she thought she had been abandoned. She couldn't blame them. She was holding them back, and their lives were at stake.

The sun was high, slowly burning away the ground mist, when Bron came silently through the woods and lay down just outside the cave to study Cairenn with his cold yellow eyes. She shivered a little and drew the rough cloak up about her as she sat up with her back against the back wall of the cave. She smiled gingerly at the wolfhound. There was no response from him. Tentatively she extended a small hand toward the great beast. He raised his head as though to respond, then turned it to look back into the woods.

Calgaich and Guidd came silently out of the forest. Calgaich shook his head. "Nothing, by the gods," he said wearily. "Not a steading, or a hut to beg, borrow or to steal a crust of bread. Not a cow, sheep, or even a dog loose on these damned empty moors. There is something wrong here."

Guidd nodded as he squatted beside the wolfhound. He rubbed his grizzled jaw. Once he looked up sideways at Calgaich. "I do not like to think about it," he murmured.

There was something chilling in the air besides the mist. Cairenn looked beyond them through the thinning mist and into the silent, dripping forest. "Where are we?" she asked nervously.

There was no reply.

"Fian?" Cairenn asked.

Calgaich looked back over his shoulder. It was as though they were again back at the eerie barrow on the shores of the sea loch in the distant land of the Damnonii. *Something* was putting fear into him. He had been unafraid to enter the *mansio* prison to rescue his father, he had not seemed afraid when he had scaled the Great Wall within shouting distance of the mile castle garrison. But now fear itself seemed to have alighted on his back.

"What is it, Calgaich? The auxiliaries?" she asked.

Calgaich shook his head. He wet his lips. When he looked directly at her, she seemed to sense something lurking behind his troubled gray eyes.

Guidd shifted about. His eye flicked nervously back and forth. Bron became uneasy. He, too, sensed that something was wrong with those surrounding woods, and that something was haunting his master.

"Medionemeton," Calgaich murmured at last.

"I don't understand," Cairenn said.

Calgaich stood up. His strong hands tightened on his spear shaft, but he knew full well that no weapon devised by man or used by a great warrior would prevail against that which haunted the great oak woods. "A sacred grove," he explained quietly. "A grove of great oaks, greater than any Guidd and I have ever seen. Do you know the meaning of this place?"

She nodded. "A place of worship for the Druids."

"The name Druid itself means 'knowledge of the oak,'" Calgaich explained.

"I know," she said quickly.

He looked closely at her. His suspicion of her since he had taken her from Eriu returned full force to him. Quickly he looked away from those huge emerald-hued eyes. He felt he could never penetrate that magic screen to see who and what she really was.

"There are no birds within the wood," Guidd said quietly. "There is not a hare or a deer. Not a mouse or a cricket. Not a bird flies over it. Beyond this place the sun shines fully, like the face of Lugh of the Shining Spear. There is not a trace of mist on the moors just beyond this place. The sun shines strongly in the sky, but the bright light does not penetrate these woods."

Calgaich nodded. "The Druids have the power to do many strange things. *They* can drive a man to madness with their incantations. *They* can bring down a shower of fire on their enemies. *They* can raise a mist to bring the darkness of night over the land at high noon."

"*They,* Calgaich?" she asked.

"Men of the Oak," he murmured.

A faint hum sounded through the dense grove of mighty oaks. It was a mysterious sound, as though the words of Calgaich had awakened sleeping spirits.

Cairenn stood up. "But most of the Druids were stamped out many years ago by the Romans. The legions followed the Druids to their holy island of Mona off the west coast of my country and wiped them out. They cut down the sacred grove of oaks. They put out the sacred oak log fire. They slew the priests. That was hundreds of years ago, Calgaich. There is nothing to fear from them now."

He turned on her savagely. "I fear nothing, woman!"

"Nothing you can *see,* Calgaich mac Lellan."

Calgaich gave no sign that he had heard her. He looked down at Guidd. "We've got to get some game, old hound."

"Not in here, Calgaich. There is nothing."

"Then we'll go beyond the woods."

Guidd looked up at him. "Can we find our way out of this mist?"

"We can try."

Guidd stood up. "If we do reach the open country," he added, "we'll be exposed to the Red Crests and their damned hounds."

"It's a risk," Calgaich admitted.

"We'll need Bron."

"Stay here," Calgaich ordered Cairenn.

"And if you don't come back?" she asked again. She felt she was always asking that question.

Calgaich did not answer. He whistled at Bron and strode off through the misted woods, followed by Guidd. In a little while the woods were silent again.

In the middle of the afternoon Cairenn awoke from a fitful sleep. A strange, sweetish, rotten odor seemed to have crept into the cave. She sat up and looked about. There were no flowers within the forest. The sickening odor was unrecognizable. She thrust her nose into the rough fabric of the Asturian cloak. It smelled of woodsmoke and perspiration, but it was not as bad as the other repugnant odor she had noticed.

After a while Cairenn was thirsty. She threw aside the cloak, stepped out of the cave and promptly fell over a rounded object swathed in a piece of cloak. The aura of rotting flesh arose from the bundle. The head of Lellan. She ran, stricken with panic, into the misty forest.

She found a small tarn of clear water and dropped onto her belly to drink from it. Something glistened brightly through the clear water. She thrust a hand into the pool to retrieve a beautifully worked enameled arm torque. It was a small masterpiece of the metalsmith's craft. Cairenn stood up and fitted it about her left arm. A strange cold and tingling feeling seemed to come from the bright metal, but perhaps it came from the chill of the water.

Cairenn looked about her. She narrowed her eyes. Which way had she come? Each of the dim vistas between the huge oaks seemed exactly the same. She studied the soft, damp ground to see if she could discern her footprints, but could not see them. She looked about again. An eerie feeling came over her. The forest was so quiet it seemed unnatural.

Cairenn began to walk in the direction from which she thought she had come. In a little while she knew it was not the right route. She paused, hesitated, looked about and then strode off in another direction. The result was the same—everything looked exactly alike.

She walked back toward the tarn, but could not find it. Faint panic began to work in the back of her mind.

Now and again she would turn her head quickly as though someone, or *something*, was behind her, and although she never saw anything, she was quite sure that whatever it was had moved quickly, just beyond the corner of her eye.

There is something wrong here, Calgaich had said.

She was utterly lost. It was as though she had somehow wandered off the earth into some unknown and alien land, in which she was doomed to wander throughout eternity.

She stopped walking at last, and stood resting with her back against a great oak. She sensed, rather than saw or heard, the movement in the dense shadows. Terror crept through her and then was succeeded by sheer panic. She started to run.

Suddenly the huge wolfhound appeared in front of her, watching her with unblinking yellow eyes that seemed to glow in the dark like foxfire.

The wolfhound turned and began to walk through the forest. Cairenn hesitated; then he turned and looked back at her as though waiting for her to follow. She wasn't sure it was Bron, but she had no choice. She followed him through the darkness.

A concealed fire cast a faint glow of light against the rear of the cave. Calgaich strode toward Cairenn as she started to run toward the fire. She ran into his strong arms and clung to him while the tears ran from her eyes and sobs racked her body.

"There is good pig meat," Calgaich said kindly, leading her to the fire. Cairenn dropped to the ground, exhausted.

Guidd squatted by the fire roasting the meat. "What did you find in the forest, woman?"

"Nothing." Cairenn said, her voice husky.

"Fear and panic," the woodsman murmured. "Even the hound has enough sense not to wander off alone in there."

They ate swiftly and without speaking. Now and then either Guidd or Calgaich would look sideways at the silent woman. Cairenn forced herself to swallow the food. They finished eating. Guidd kicked dirt over the fire. The woods were as dark as pitch. Only a few of the larger embers still glowed through the thick bed of ashes, like secretive red eyes, winking open and shutting quickly.

Suddenly Calgaich laughed.

Cairenn stared at him as she wiped the grease from her mouth. "What is it, *fian?*" she queried.

"In Eriu a champion is entitled to a *whole* pig. A leg for a king. A haunch for a queen. A boar's head for a champion charioteer."

"And a whole pig for a fighting champion," Guidd echoed.

"Here I sit in these damned woods, with a woman, a hound and a one-eyed woodsman, grateful for the tough meat of a thin sow." Calgaich laughed again. He slapped his hands on his thighs.

"How many whole pigs were your lot in Eriu, *fian?*" she asked.

He waved a greasy hand.

"Many, Calgaich?" she persisted.

He nodded. He seemed to look beyond the cave into the dark forest and the not too distant past. "It was not a bad life," he said absentmindedly.

"Fighting, drinking, raping and killing."

Calgaich looked curiously at her. "What else is there in life?"

"A home and a family. A woman by the hearthside and little ones to greet you on your return from the hunt." She met his gaze with her clear emerald eyes. Calgaich did not look away.

"Listen to her!" Guidd exclaimed.

"Faugh!" Calgaich said. He suddenly leaned toward her as an ember flared up. The firelight reflected from the golden arm torque Cairenn had found in the tarn. "What is this?" he demanded.

She shrugged. "I found it in the forest in a tarn."

He drew back his hand as though he had touched fire.

"For the love of the dark gods!" he exclaimed. "Cast it back into the forest!"

"But it's so beautiful!" she touched the torque as if to share its beauty.

He stood up and dragged her to her feet. He untwisted the torque from her arm and ran with it into the darkness. He hurled it as far as he could and then ran back to the cave.

"What's wrong with you?" she cried angrily.

He drew her close and shook her gently. "It had to be an offering to the oaks! It belonged to *them!* Don't you understand?"

She looked quickly behind her then turned to look up into his shadowed face. "Is that why I was lost?" she whispered.

He released her and rubbed his hands hard against his soiled tunic. "Never touch anything like that in the sacred groves. Even now, with the torque cast back into the woods, perhaps a curse has already been put on us."

Guidd nodded solemnly. "There will be a moon later on. We can then find our way out of this accursed place. It's too dark now. Even Bron could not guide us from the forest."

A keening wind suddenly swept through the forest. The branches of the huge oaks thrashed wildly. The night seemed to come alive with something that was more than just manifestations of nature.

It seemed hours before the first fitful light of the gibbous moon shone through the trees. Calgaich and Guidd slept. Cairenn awoke at the sound of the wind. She looked out into the forest. The wind had swept away most of the mist. The forest had long moonlit vistas between the boles of the immense oaks.

A faint sound came from the distance. Cairenn turned her head and the sound came again. She hoped it was her imagination. She stood up, dropped the cloak with which she had been covered and stepped to the mouth of the cave. Bron raised his head.

Something moved within the forest. Cairenn saw, or *thought* she saw, a line of black-cloaked figures moving slowly through the clearing mist. Two of the figures carried great curved trumpets which glistened as though made of gold. A low chanting sound came to her.

Cairenn tried to speak. The words would not come. She moved backwards into the cave. "Calgaich," she husked at last.

Calgaich's head snapped up. His hands dropped instinctively to his war spear. "What is it? The Romans?"

Cairenn pointed toward the file of cloaked figures.

Calgaich stood up slowly. Fear was etched on his face. "The gods protect us," he whispered hoarsely. "It is them . . ."

"The Druids?"

He nodded. "If you value our lives, woman, do not move or make a sound." He reached down and clamped a big hand over Guidd's mouth. Guidd's one eye opened. "The Men of the Oak," Calgaich whispered to him. Guidd nodded.

The long file of cloaked figures disappeared into the forest. The night was deathly quiet again.

"Can we leave now?" Cairenn asked. "The moon is up."

Calgaich shook his head. "Not until they have done whatever it is they have come to do. Not until they leave this most accursed of all places!"

So they waited. Now and again, they could hear faint chanting mingled with the eerie blowing of the golden trumpets, and other sounds which they could not identify. None of them spoke. Their useless weapons lay to one side. The wolfhound was behind Calgaich, and only his great eyes moved now and then.

The mysterious night and the eerie sounds from within the huge sacred grove of oaks eroded what little courage they had kept in store.

CHAPTER 11

The cloaked figures returned within a spear's cast of the three crouching people in the cave. Not a sound came from the Druids as they moved through the moonlight like disembodied spirits. A deathly stillness hung over the oak forest. As the Druids vanished from sight, so, too, did the moon, as low, drifting clouds passed over the forest. The night became as dark as the pit itself.

"We'll have to wait until dawn light," Calgaich said at last. "Let's hope the Romans have not reached this place."

None of them could sleep. They sat in the cave, side by side in the thick darkness. The odor of the decaying head of Lellan sickened Cairenn, but it did not seem to bother Calgaich and Guidd.

Slowly, almost imperceptibly, they could distinguish the separate tops of the great oaks, rather than the dark and forbidding masses of them.

With the first light of dawn, Calgaich led the way, with Bron pacing at his side. Calgaich held his war spear in his right hand, while the head of Lellan was tucked beneath his left arm. Cairenn followed Calgaich, with Guidd bringing up the rear. Instead of leaving the forest by the way they had entered it, Calgaich seemed to be penetrating deeper into it, going in the direction from which they had heard the trumpeting and chanting of the night before.

"This is not the right way, Calgaich," Cairenn said boldly.

He turned to look at her. "We've lost too much time. If we go back the way we came we'd risk running into those damned Romans."

"Isn't there the risk of something worse up ahead?"

"She might be right at that," Guidd agreed.

174

Calgaich continued on. "Go back if you like!" he snapped over his shoulder.

They followed him on through the grove. Not a leaf stirred. Nothing moved. Not a bird twittered. There was nothing in the forest but utter stillness, as though they walked through a long abandoned tomb. Calgaich stopped short and thrust his spear forward. Bron slunk behind his master.

A large, circular open hollow was ahead of them. In the center of the hollow there was a pool, so still and dark that it seemed like molten lead had been poured into it, to harden with a gray-silver surface as smooth as polished metal.

"Look!" Cairenn cried suddenly.

An immense oak, a giant among its kind, stood beyond the far end of the pool. Torques and fibulas of gold and of enameled bronze hung from the branches, mingled with thick growths of mistletoe. Miniature spears, swords and other weapons were mingled with toylike tools of many kinds. In front of the oak a tree trunk had been set into the ground. Its top had been skillfully carved into the likeness of a three-faced head, with flowing mustaches and long hair once painted yellow. One of the countenances stared impassively back at the intruders, while the other two profiles stared toward the empty glades in front of them. Great cracks had appeared in the carvings, and rot had set in deeply, so ancient were they in origin. Dark stains showed on the trunk below the carved faces.

"The Holy of Holies," Calgaich muttered tensely.

"Let's flee!" Cairenn cried, pulling at his arm.

Calgaich nodded, but he could not move. His legs seemed too weak to carry him away from there.

"For the love of the gods, Calgaich," Guidd said hoarsely, "there is nothing but evil for us here in this accursed place!"

"Aye," Calgaich agreed, but he could not move his legs. It was as though a creeping paralysis had set into them. Sweat broke from his face. "I can't move," he whispered.

"Call to your gods! Pray to them!" Cairenn cried.

Something from somewhere within the dark reaches of his fertile imagination, the gift or the curse of many of those who were of Celtic blood, held Calgaich fast there, staring toward the rotting, blood-smeared idol.

Slowly, ever so slowly, like an old man, or a cripple who is again learning to walk, Calgaich moved toward the idol and the monarch oak. He forced the butt of his spear against the soft ground as an aid to his snaillike progress. Cairenn and Guidd stared after him in superstitious awe.

Calgaich looked beyond the great oak. He saw what looked like a large, lidless coffin made of sheets of stone. It was filled to the brim with water. Calgaich shook his head, trying to clear the spell from his mind. He tried to tear his intent gaze away from the coffin, but it was to no avail. Foot by foot he approached the coffin until he stood looking down into the clear water.

Calgaich tried to raise his head. He could not do it. His heart beat erratically. The icy sweat streamed down his face and body. Something was holding him rooted there as if he were made of stone. Something . . .

Guidd turned quickly. The faint sound of baying hounds carried to the glade. "Calgaich!" he shouted. "The Romans!"

Calgaich paid no attention. He peered closely down into the water and found himself staring into a pair of incredibly large light-gray eyes that returned his stare. He tried to turn his head but found it impossible.

"Calgaich!" Cairenn cried. "The hounds are closing in on the forest! Why do you stay?"

The nostrils of the strange-looking face were just above the water level, and they moved slightly as if the creature, or whatever it was, were breathing. Again Calgaich tried to break the hold of those eerie-looking eyes but it was no use. A message seemed to come to him. Calgaich dropped his spear and pushed his hands into the icy water to touch a large, flat stone that rested on top of the creature. Whether he wanted to or not, Calgaich knew he was being mentally forced to lift the stone from the water.

Calgaich gripped the edges of the stone and lifted it. Beneath it was the white body of a naked man, who was still looking up into Calgaich's eyes. Calgaich dropped the heavy stone on the ground. The being sat up. Water flowed from his long silvery hair and his blue-white features. The great eyes stared without blinking at Calgaich. Calgaich reached out and touched the icy flesh, and then helped the creature from the coffin.

Calgaich stepped back. The fear of death swept over him.

Guidd ran forward. "Calgaich! It is an evil spirit! Strike it or run! The Romans are within the forest! There is not much time!"

The creature waved a hand toward Calgaich's eyes. Calgaich suddenly seemed released from the iron spell that had bound him to do the creature's bidding.

"Lugh of the Shining Spear," he gasped. "Who or *what* are you?"

"Say not what, but rather who," the being replied. "I am only a man, such as yourself." He looked beyond Calgaich and past Cairenn and Guidd. "Romans," he added quietly. "They will find this holy place at last." He looked sideways at Calgaich. "I must have clothing."

"We haven't any time left," Calgaich said. Now that he was released from the spell he was again himself, the man of war and action. He picked up his spear. "Whoever you are, or whatever you are, you must take care of yourself. I don't know how you came to be in that coffin with that stone on your chest but you're free from it now. Look out for yourself!"

The man shook his head. "You can't escape. The Romans have surrounded this grove. There are hundreds of them out there now."

"How can you know that?" Calgaich demanded suspiciously.

The man waved a hand. "I *know*. If they find me here, they will kill me at once."

"You're a Druid?"

The man nodded. He did not seem afraid, although he faced instant death if the Romans caught him. "Do not let them kill me. I can be of great service to you. I owe you a debt."

"You owe me nothing." Calgaich turned. "Cairenn!" he called.

Calgaich stripped off his shortened cloak. Cairenn came to him and he tore off her clothing. She stood there shivering in her nakedness as he tossed the trousers and the sheepskin tunic to the Druid. Then he draped the cloak about Cairenn.

"Quickly!" he commanded the Druid.

Calgaich picked up Cairenn and thrust her up into the lower branches of the great oak. "Be absolutely still," he told her. She disappeared into the leafy maze. Calgaich pointed to another tree as he looked at the Druid.

The Druid shook his head. "It's of no use. The hounds will smell me out."

"By the gods, priest! If you had not cast a spell on me, we might have escaped."

The Druid looked through the mystic grove as though he could see something the others could not. "You could not have escaped them."

Calgaich jerked his head toward Guidd and Bron. "The three of us will die here, rather than be taken captive by the Red Crests."

The Druid smiled a little. "Why?"

Calgaich looked at him curiously. "We will not be dragged back to Luguvalium with ropes about our necks like slaves."

The hounds were crying in full voice now. Men called to each other from around the huge grove. The Druid was right then, the Romans had surrounded the grove.

"Will you fight beside us?" Calgaich asked.

"Fighting is not for Druids."

Calgaich spat. "Spoken like a priest!"

"We fight other ways, *fian*."

"How do you know that I am a *fian*?" Calgaich asked suspiciously.

The Druid shrugged. "It's obvious, isn't it?"

Guidd came to Calgaich, carrying the bundled head. He held it out to Calgaich. "What of this?" he asked. "Can we let the Romans desecrate it?"

The Druid wrinkled his fine nose. "Cast it into the sacred pool," he suggested. "This is the Holy of Holies. The head of Lellan, chief of the Novantae, should not be allowed to become a plaything of the heathen Romans."

Calgaich closed his eyes, prayed, then cast the head into the sacred pool. The ripples flowed concentrically to the edge of the water and lapped quietly there. In a little while the pool was again like a sheet of polished metal.

Calgaich looked at the priest. "What have you done that you should have been so cruelly punished?" he asked.

"Punished? Don't be a fool! I was there of my own free will."

"You're mad. All Druids are mad. This grove seems to be madness itself!"

Guidd nodded. "How did he know that was the head of Lellan?"

"Well?" Calgaich asked the priest.

The Druid smiled a little. "There are many things we know, Calgaich mac Lellan. There is not time to tell you of them now, with the Romans baying at your heels and mine." His clear gray eyes once again held those of Calgaich so that Calgaich could not look away. "I willed you to help me. Now we are trapped. We can gain nothing by fighting to the death. Let them take us. You may think there is no hope to survive the fate they have in mind for you, but I say this to you—you have saved my life. I will not forget that. Somehow, somewhere, I will repay you. But now you can't fight those Red Crests and win a victory. This place is doomed now that they have found it. We too are doomed if you stand and fight."

The will to fight to the death suddenly left Calgaich. He dropped his war spear. His mouth was set like a wolf trap, but his face was calm as he stood beside the strange and confident Druid, with Guidd and Bron, waiting for the approaching Romans.

They could be seen now, moving slowly and cautiously through the forest. They were Asturian cavalrymen, with a handful of black Numidian archers among them. Here and there strode a few hard-core Roman legionnaires, as superstitious of the place as any Asturian or Numidian, but bound by the iron discipline of the legions not to show fear in the face of an enemy.

"How did your friends escape last night through the cordon of Romans, Druid?" Calgaich asked out of the side of his mouth.

"We Druids can create mists. We can baffle and confuse the eye and the mind. That is why we still survive despite the efforts of the Romans to stamp us out completely."

"Why can't you baffle and confuse these Romans?"

"This is not the time, Calgaich."

"You'll need a name, priest."

"I can't tell them my true name. It would be the end of me." He glanced sideways at Calgaich and grinned. "Give me a name, Calgaich."

Calgaich smiled crookedly. "Fomoire."

"Excellent! Fomoire—Misfortune!"

"You were misfortune enough to us," Calgaich murmured. He looked at the great oak. "The gods help her."

Fomoire shrugged. "Her lot is women's lot. Their future can be read easily in the flame of a candle."

"And ours?"

"The web of man's destiny is skillfully spun. No man can discern the pattern. Perhaps it's just as well. There are some things we should not see, or else we'd go mad at the thought of them."

Several of the Numidians paused just beyond the sacred clearing to nock cane arrows to their bowstrings. Calgaich picked up his spear and raised it, butt uppermost. Fomoire and Guidd held out their empty hands.

"Throw down that spear, Calgaich mac Lellan," a familiar voice ordered from behind an oak tree. Tribune Ulpius Claudius stepped out into view. He had his right hand resting on the hilt of his sword.

Calgaich threw down the spear. He held out his empty hands. Bron stood silently beside him.

Ulpius Claudius strode forward into the clearing, with a confident air, although his eyes darted sideways, as though looking for something evil or dangerous. "By the Lord Mithras," he exclaimed, "this is a foul place!"

"You should feel at home here, Tribune," Calgaich suggested dryly.

The tribune reddened. "The only thing that saves you from being strung from that great oak is the fact that my uncle, Quaestor Lucius Sextillius, has specifically ordered that you be brought back to Luguvalium. Do you know how many men you barbarians killed or wounded there?"

"Hopefully, a great many."

The tribune's hand tightened on the hilt of his gladius. He eyed Fomoire. "Who is this mangy-looking creature?"

The Druid bowed his head and smiled. "Men call me Fomoire, that is to say, in your language, Tribune—Misfortune. A healer of the eye sickness. A leech. A juggler. A teller of tales. A worker of simple conjuring tricks. I have some knowledge of the telling of fortunes. A singer of songs. A bard of some skill."

Ulpius threw his cloak back from his shoulders and rested his hands on his hips. "All of these things? I'll warrant you're no more than a beggar. Sing me a verse, bard, to test your skill."

Fomoire bowed again and waved his slender, graceful hands.

> "The girls of Spain were honey sweet,
> And the golden girls of Gaul,
> And the Thracian maids were soft as birds
> To hold the heart in thrall."

"You'll have to do better than that," Ulpius said.

Fomoire narrowed his eyes. "There is a better one."

Ulpius smiled unpleasantly. "There had *better* be. Any tosspot, in any wine shop throughout the Empire, can sing at least a dozen verses of 'The Girl I Kissed at Clusium.' "

Calgaich had been surveying the situation while Fomoire engaged the tribune in talk. He could see more Romans in the oak grove. Their horses were restless, jerking back on their reins, and whinnying incessantly. The hounds were cowed. They stood behind their handlers, with their ears laid back. The grove was lighter now with the rising of the sun. There wasn't a chance for a hare to slip through that blade-tipped ring of fighting men. Why was the tribune playing with Fomoire? Did he suspect that the Druid was someone other than whom he was portraying?

Decrius Montanas met Calgaich eye to eye. The two tough fighting men studied each other. Calgaich knew that if it wasn't for the tribune, Montanas would kill him on the spot.

"Sing, lark," Ulpius commanded.

It would be the acid test for Fomoire. If he failed, instant death for him would be the result of his failure. "There is a woman," he began quietly, "who has powers to steal the heart and soul from any man. She is a golden woman, Tribune. She is a barbarian woman of the wild north country. I will dedicate this composition to her. It will be heard for the first time here in this most ancient of all oak groves."

Ulpius looked startled. He narrowed his eyes.

Fomoire waved his hands.

> "With golden hair, eye-blinding,
> Blue-irised, tempting eyes,
> Cheeks blood-tinged like foxglove,
> Like to the flash of snow,
> The flash of her teeth's treasury,
> Between crimson lips' treasure."

Ulpius cut his hand sideways. "Enough, damn you! You know of her?"

"Morar, the Golden One? I have heard of her great unearthly beauty, Tribune. Does it trouble you so much?"

Calgaich looked sideways at the calm Druid. Fomoire met his glance. There was a warning in his eyes. Ulpius evidently was enamored of Morar. What kind of game was this mad Druid playing with the tribune?

Ulpius looked about him, anything to escape the calm, deep-seeing eyes of Fomoire. He beckoned to a Numidian archer. He pointed at the great sacred oak. "Shoot me down one of those baubles," he ordered. "I want a memento of the grove of hell before it is burned to the ground."

Calgaich closed his eyes. He prayed to Lugh, asking him to save the woman from harm.

The grinning Numidian nocked an arrow. He raised his bow, and almost without effort loosed the arrow at the biggest of the ornaments dangling from the oak—a gorgeous arm torque of soft, reddish Hibernian gold, skillfully decorated with a red and white enamel design. The arrow struck and severed the golden chain from which the torque hung. The torque dropped to the turf, as the arrow continued on and struck into the trunk of the oak. A startled cry rang out from the leafy cover.

Ulpius picked up the torque. "Name of Light!" he shouted. "Who or what is *that?*"

The archer nocked another arrow. His action was stayed by an outflung arm of the tribune.

The leaves rustled and a slight figure dropped to the

turf. Ulpius strode forward. "So! Another one! Who are you!" he demanded. He gripped Cairenn by the shoulder and as he did so she twisted away, and the cloak dropped from her naked body to the ground. The sunlight coming through the leafy branches shone on her pure white skin, her full, pink-budded breasts and her long, shapely legs.

Ulpius stared unbelievingly. "*Roma Dea!* What is this? A dryad?"

"She's mine," Calgaich said. He picked up the cloak and draped it about Cairenn's shoulders. Cairenn looked up, and saw in his eyes his concern for her.

"You own nothing! You have no rights!" the Roman snapped.

"Nevertheless, Tribune, she *is* mine. She is a *cumal.*"

"A slave?"

"That is what a Roman would call her."

Ulpius glared at Calgaich. "But for my uncle, barbarian, you'd die in these blood-stinking woods, and this woman would be thrown to my Numidians for bed sport!"

Fomoire came forward. "It would be a great waste, Tribune, to throw this tidbit to the Numidians. Your uncle, the quaestor, might appreciate such a gift. It might ensure you a passage to Rome, as you so much desire."

Ulpius studied the Druid. "You know too much," he insinuated quietly. "Who *are* you?"

"Fomoire! A healer of the eye sickness. A leech. A juggler. A teller of tales. A worker of simple conjuring tricks. I have some slight knowledge of the telling of fortunes. A singer of songs. A bard of some skill."

Ulpius looked into the clear, seemingly guileless eyes, then turned abruptly away, as if he were not quite sure of what he saw. "Get these barbarians out of here, Montanas. Fire these damned woods if they're not too wet. There is an evil here that must be cleansed with purifying fire." He twisted the golden torque about his left arm and shouted for his horse.

"Your woman is safe, at least for the time being, Calgaich," Fomoire said.

"If he ever sees through you . . ."

Fomoire shrugged. "Man's time on earth is short. There are greater things in the hereafter." He watched the tribune mount his horse. Then sun glinted from his gold arm torque. "He took an offering from the Sacred Oak," he murmured, almost as though to himself. "Such a man is accursed from now on."

Calgaich spat to one side. "I cursed him long ago, priest."

Fomoire looked quickly at Calgaich. "Be careful! The centurion might hear you!"

"Nothing, not the vengeance of your Druid brotherhood for despoiling this sacred grove of yours, or all the power of mighty Caesar's legions, *shall keep that Roman dog from death at my hands!*"

Fomoire looked quickly at Calgaich. This time it was Fomoire who felt uneasy at what he saw in the hard eyes of Calgaich mac Lellan.

CHAPTER 12

Quaestor Lucius Sextillius sat in judgment on the four bedraggled prisoners and the huge wolfhound who stood before him in the audience chamber of the *mansio*. The Roman was bald as a grape. His pure white woolen toga contrasted with his round, olive-hued visage, which seemed to exude a faint greasiness. His plump wet lips were pursed as he studied the barbarians.

Tribune Ulpius Claudius leaned against a pillar to one side of the chamber, while Centurion Decrius Montanas was in charge of a guard behind the prisoners.

The faint musky odor of perfume, mingled with a sour odor of perspiration, drifted from the quaestor. He constantly moved back and forth on his seat. There was something reptilian about the Roman, and yet something gross, as though a serpent and a sow had mated to bring forth into the civilized light of Rome the not-quite-human creature known as Lucius Sextillius.

"The law of Rome is such that you should be executed forthwith, Calgaich mac Lellan," the quaestor explained. "Not only for your second desertion from the Eagles, but also for your efforts to free a political prisoner, one Lellan, former chief of the barbarian Novantae. We add to those charges the murdering and wounding of soldiers of the Empire. What have you to say for yourself?"

Calgaich shrugged. "What does it matter *what* I say, Quaestor? You Romans claim to rule the known world. You make the laws. All men must obey them, whether they are Romans or barbarians. We who are not Romans, and who do not have the rights and privileges of being Roman citizens, are still bound by the laws of Rome."

"You have the impertinence to object? You must know

185

that it is the mission of Rome to civilize and rule the world."

"A mission set by you Romans, Quaestor. Did you Romans ever think to ask any Egyptian, Thracian, Dacian, Briton or any other barbarian if he *wanted* to be ruled by Rome?"

Sextillius leaned back in his seat and studied Calgaich. His gaze rested on Calgaich's broad shoulders and muscular arms and then drifted furtively down to Calgaich's loins. "Your people are war mad and quick to battle, Calgaich," he accused.

"Like Romans, Quaestor," Calgaich countered.

"But it is our mission!"

"To my people, you are invaders. This is *our* country. We do not want you here, Roman."

Sextillius glanced at Ulpius Claudius, as if to say, "What can you do with this barbarian?" Ulpius shrugged. The quaestor leaned forward. "Don't you understand, Calgaich, that if we Romans leave Britannia, your country is doomed?"

Calgaich smiled a little. "Perhaps Rome itself is doomed."

Lucius Sextillius threw up his hands in despair.

The tribune looked at his uncle. "As I told you, Quaestor, the barbarian is hopeless. Death itself could not convince him of your argument. However, there is not a warrior and swordsman in Britannia today who can match his skill."

"Except yourself, Nephew?" Sextillius asked slyly.

"I was speaking only of the barbarians. I could easily master him with the *gladius*."

"Try me, Roman!" Calgaich challenged.

"I'll champion Rome against this barbarian!" Montanas cried.

Ulpius shook his head angrily at the eager centurion. He looked at Calgaich. "Do not try my patience again, barbarian."

"You have not accepted my challenge!"

Fomoire spoke sideways to Calgaich, but his lips did not move. "For the love of the gods, Calgaich, hold that serpent's tongue of yours," the Druid hissed.

Lucius Sextillius had not missed the byplay between

Calgaich and Fomoire. There was an alien strangeness about this Fomoire, the quaestor thought. His eyes drifted past the one-eyed man and studied the dark-haired woman. They were a strangely assorted quartet, these barbarians.

Lucius looked at the tribune. "You say this is the woman who wore men's clothing and charged into battle wielding the great war spear of Calgaich the night he escaped from here?"

"That is true, Quaestor. The bitch killed two of my men."

The quaestor eyed Cairenn. *"Her?* She killed two Roman soldiers?" He beckoned to Cairenn. "Come forward, little one."

Cairenn walked forward. She was still draped in the cut-off Asturian cloak. She stood there, with head upraised, giving the Roman eye for eye. She would not allow this pig of a Roman to see her fear. Too much had happened since the time she had been dragged from her father's *rath.* She had changed. She was stronger now.

Sextillius leaned back in his seat. "Strip," he ordered her, his plump mouth moving back and forth.

Cairenn slowly dropped the cloak to the floor and stood there, cold and beautiful. She told herself that she disrobed for Calgaich only. This might be the last time he saw her thus. She turned her emerald eyes to him in a long look before again turning back to Sextillius.

"Turn," Sextillius ordered. She turned. He nodded, pleased. "Face me, woman," he ordered. "Do not look at the barbarian." He inclined his head toward her with an ingratiating smile. "Tell me, woman, can you bathe and massage a Roman quaestor with any skill at all?"

"I can drown one with great skill," Cairenn answered coldly.

Sextillius stared at her. He broke into a false, cackling sort of laughter. "They say these barbarian women are ice on the outside and hellsfire within." He looked at Calgaich. "This one, perchance, Caledonian, is she perhaps the *other* way around?"

Calgaich knew that if Cairenn went into the service of the quaestor she'd be forced into forms of utter depravity by this porker of a Roman. He had heard the low-voiced chatter of some of the Roman legionnaires while waiting in his cell to be taken before Sextillius. "Man, boy, woman, sheep, goat or camel," one of them had related, "our beloved quaestor is equally at home with any of them in his bed. By Mithras, he could make a male spintrian blush!"

"You didn't answer the quaestor," Ulpius snapped.

Calgaich looked casually at the angry tribune and smiled a little. "Are you so angry, Tribune, because you want this barbarian *cumal* for yourself? Or is it that you are interested only in the golden-haired barbarian women?"

Lucius Sextillius looked quickly at Ulpius. "What is this he says, Ulpius?"

Fomoire came close to Calgaich. "Do you love this *cumal?*" he whispered.

"The gods forbid! I am still betrothed to Morar."

"But you don't want her in the playpen of this foul Roman?"

Cairenn had turned to look at Calgaich. Her face was impassive, but her great emerald eyes held his.

Calgaich shook his head. "No, Fomoire."

"Then leave this to me."

Cairenn heard Fomoire's words to Calgaich. Somehow she trusted this strange man. Her people had not been afraid of the Druids. Only the Romans feared their powers.

Lucius eyed Cairenn again. "Cover yourself," he ordered. "They'll have to scour you with brick dust and water before you can serve me."

"I will never serve you," Cairenn thought. She felt the gaze of the assembled men on her as she bent to retrieve the ragged Asturian cloak. Calgaich moved toward her as if to help cover her lovely nakedness.

"Stay where you are," Sextillius ordered him. "Slaves need no help. They are for the sport of others." His eyes wandered to Fomoire. "You," he said. "I am told you are a bard."

Fomoire bowed his head a little and held out his slim hands. "With certain skill, Your Honor."

"What else can you do?"

Fomoire smiled knowingly. "I have little skill in bed, with woman, boy or man, quaestor."

Sextillius stared wide-eyed, then he broke into his shrill,

cackling laughter. "Amuse me, bard. It is said you are a conjurer. Show me."

"May I approach?" Fomoire requested. "I am harmless."

Lucius waved a plump hand.

Fomoire walked forward, while gesturing with his fine hands. In each palm were three pebbles. "Quaestor," he murmured, "can you blow a strong breath on my two hands and blow two pebbles from each of them, leaving but one pebble on each palm?"

"No man can do that, trickster."

"*I* can."

"Do so then!"

The Druid bent back each forefinger to hold the center pebble in each hand tightly to the palm. He then blew hard on each palm and the four pebbles pattered onto the mosaic floor.

Sextillius stared, and then he roared with shrill laughter. "Well done! Well done! But you must do better than that to earn your way to Rome."

"*Rome*, Quaestor?" Fomoire's eyes widened.

Sextillius shrugged. He rubbed his hands together. He looked at Calgaich. "To have Calgaich mac Lellan, the son of a Caledonian chieftain in hand, a man who is considered to be the best swordsman in this accursed fogbound island, and perhaps in the world, is reason enough for me to end my tour of duty here. Then, too, I have many other barbarians being collected all over Britannia, to be taken to Rome for the Games." He looked at Bron. "As well as a shipment of such great beasts, who fight to the death in the arena." He smiled at Fomoire. "Then, why not take you too, trickster?" The quaestor studied the Druid. Then he looked quickly away as though he did not like what he saw.

"He'll have to do more than simple conjuring tricks, Uncle," Ulpius put in.

The quaestor nodded. "That is true." He smiled winningly at Fomoire. "Otherwise, trickster, you will be taken from here and put to death." His voice had changed from one of simulated warmth to a graveyard iciness.

Fomoire seemed nonplussed. He eyed Ulpius Claudius. "This is a brave soldier of Rome. He has said he could match the skill of our great swordsman Calgaich, with the famed short sword of the Roman legions."

"There is none better in the use of the *gladius,* trickster," Lucius admitted.

"You will want to save our Calgaich, for the amusement of the crowds at the Games in Rome. But will the tribune face me with the *gladius* in his hand?"

Lucius stared at Fomoire. "Are you jesting? Are you mad? Or perhaps you are somewhat skilled in the use of the *gladius?* I do not want an exhibition of swordplay here, which would certainly result in your sudden death."

Ulpius held up a hand to Montanas. "Give this fool your *gladius,* Centurion."

Fomoire shook his head. "I need no weapon against you except a finger."

"He'll split you like a goose," the quaestor warned.

"Let me but place a finger tip on his wrist," Fomoire requested, "then he may draw, *if he can,* and kill me on this spot."

It was very quiet in the audience chamber. A drapery moved in a draft. Leather creaked as some of the soldiers moved to get a better view of the anticipated slaughter. A large drapery hung from ceiling to floor on the wall behind the chair of the quaestor. It seemed to Calgaich that someone was behind it, looking through a parting in the material, but he could not see who it was.

The tribune stood in front of the Druid. "The man is mad. Look at his eyes, Uncle. See how they stare at me? There is a well of madness within each of them." His voice trailed off.

"Are you afraid, Tribune?" Fomoire asked. "See? I am unarmed."

"Let him try, Ulpius," Lucius suggested. "But don't kill him if he fails. Wound him a little, perhaps, a very little, so that he may learn the error of his ways."

Ulpius dropped his hand to the hilt of his sword.

"Wait," Fomoire warned. "You are not to draw before the placing of my finger, Tribune."

Ulpius nodded. Fomoire extended his forefinger, looking at the same time into the tribune's eyes. The Druid placed the tip of his finger in the center of Ulpius's right wrist.

He held the Roman's eyes with his. "Draw and slay, Tribune," he suggested softly. *"If you can . . ."*

"This is murder!" Cairenn cried.

Ulpius gripped the hilt of the *gladius*. The muscles of his bare arm stood up and his knuckles whitened. He could not draw the weapon.

The quaestor stood up for a better view. "Draw, Ulpius!" he cried.

The tribune's face worked. His chest rose and fell. His right arm shivered with the strain put upon it, *but he could not draw!* There was really nothing holding him from drawing; nothing, that is, except the tip of a slim forefinger pressing against his wrist, and something in the eyes of the prisoner that made it impossible for him to draw his *gladius*.

Sweat broke from Ulpius's working face. It ran down from his temples to his cheeks and then glistened on his bronze *cuirass*. It was obvious that he was now in bone-shaking pain, for his body shivered like a sapling in a driving spring storm. He tried to speak, but words did not come to his writhing lips.

"Ye gods!" Sextillius cried. "Never have I seen the like! Even the Egyptians can do nothing like this!"

Fomoire smiled, but he did not take his eyes or forefinger away from the Roman. "Now, Tribune," he suggested cheerfully, "I will take away my poor finger, but you must not, you will not, draw your *gladius* until commanded to do so by the golden-haired woman who stands behind that drapery." Fomoire looked away from the tribune as he stepped back, withdrawing his forefinger from Ulpius's wrist at the same time.

Suddenly Ulpius found his voice. He cursed violently as he tried to draw his sword. If ever hell and murder had been etched on the face of a man, they now contorted the features of Ulpius Claudius.

A golden-haired woman stepped from behind the draperies. "Morar! Morar!" Calgaich cried. He started forward and then stopped because of the warning glance she gave him.

She was dressed in a *stola* as white and soft as that of Sextillius. It fell from beneath her full breasts in gentle folds, drifting over her rounded hips to her sandaled feet.

Her long golden hair was curled and dressed in an elaborate fashion and fastened high on her head with a gold band. She seemed already to be a Roman woman. Calgaich's loins ached for her, and anger rose in him that she should see him as a prisoner of the pig, Sextillius, rather than the proud champion he had been when they were betrothed.

Cairenn, too, was awed by Morar's incredible golden beauty, but she felt sadness, also. Here was the woman Calgaich truly loved. Cairenn still held her head high, the rough cloak around her shoulders, but her heart was heavy.

Morar moved gracefully to stand beside Sextillius's chair. She did not look at Calgaich again, as if to say to him, "Beware. Now is not the time for our reunion."

"Lucius," Morar said in her musical voice, "shall I test the word of this trickster?"

Lucius smiled. He saw nothing else but this exquisite creature in front of him, holding him by her great blue eyes even as Fomoire had held the tribune in subjection. "Please do, Morar," he replied.

Morar turned and extended a slim and lovely hand. "Draw, Tribune!" she cried.

Ulpius at last ripped the *gladius* from its sheath, raised the sword, and ran toward Fomoire with murder in his blazing eyes.

"Ulpius!" Lucius shouted. "Do not kill him, you fool!"

Calgaich moved forward and thrust out a foot. Ulpius fell headlong, sliding over the smooth mosaic floor until his head struck the wall and he lay still. He raised his head painfully and looked at Morar, then he dropped back to the floor. A thin trickle of blood wormed its way across the bright tiles.

Morar laughed like a pleased child. Her laughter rang throughout the gloomy audience chamber and brought a pleased look to Lucius.

Calgaich studied Morar. There was something different about her. She was still golden of hue, but there seemed to be a dark aura about her that puzzled and repelled him. *Morar has changed much since you left for Eriu, Calgaich,* Bronwyn had told him. *She says and does strange things. Even now, as we talk here, she is drinking wine with Ulpius and his greasy pig of an uncle, Lucius.* And where was Bronwyn now? What else had Morar taught her gentle sister? Morar was his betrothed, but it was Bronwyn who had risked her life and honor to come to him.

Morar walked to the quaestor, and every man in the room had his eyes on her swaying hips as she did so. What is more, Calgaich thought, she *knows* they are watching her.

"What do you intend to do with these people, Lucius?" Morar asked.

The quaestor seemed to brighten like a good little boy under the radiance of the woman. "The trickster has earned a place in my entourage. He goes to Rome. Calgaich also goes, of course, with his hound, to test their survival in the Games. The one-eyed man will provide fodder for the arena."

"And the dark-haired woman?" Morar queried. She turned and gestured toward Cairenn. For a moment the two women stood locked in a strange communion, Morar golden-haired like the sun and Cairenn dark and lovely as the night. Sextillius, with his enormous depraved appetites, wanted them both.

"Well, I had thought—that is she's a slave, so they say, to that barbarian there, who has no rights, no rights to her at all, Morar, so I thought . . ."

She smiled. "You thought you'd give her to me as a serving maid for an early betrothal gift. Isn't that it, Lucius, dear?" As Morar leaned over Sextillius, her white *stola* fell away from her full breasts. Her arm rested lightly on the back of his chair.

Calgaich stared at her. It tore through him to see Morar playing up to Sextillius to get her way. He took a step forward, but again Morar sent him a warning glance. Fomoire, too, glanced sideways at him. "No, Calgaich," he whispered. "It is better this way."

"What the hell is she up to now?" Calgaich asked, anger in his voice.

"Who knows? But at least the slave woman will live." It was true. Morar had saved Cairenn from the certain fate of Sextillius's bed—at least for a time. But he loathed the wiles she used to get her way.

Lucius Sextillius pursed his lips. He had to treat this golden woman with great care. She was the ward of a powerful barbarian chieftain, and it would never do to

rile the wild Novantae beyond their usual waspishness.
Then, too, there was her virgin sister, almost as beautiful
as Morar. Lucius had designs on both of them. Two such
sisters in his bed at the same time! The gods *could* be
kind at times.

"Well, Lucius?" Morar asked. Her great blue eyes
seemed to hint of something he had not dared to hope.

Ulpius sat up. He rested his back against the wall, while
he dabbled rather foolishly at the blood trickling down
from his scalp.

Morar glanced at Calgaich. She knew she had him puzzled, but that had never been difficult to do with that great
lout of a swordsman. The slave woman meant something
to him. Morar was sure of that. Cairenn might be a useful
weapon in Morar's reconquest of Calgaich.

Lucius sat back in his seat and waved a grandiloquent
hand. "She is yours, my dear." He smiled at her. "You see?
Anything you desire is yours. You need but ask me."

"Stand fast," Fomoire whispered to Calgaich. "I can
sense that great rage of yours. Stand fast, Calgaich."

Cairenn felt great relief at escaping the pig Sextillius and
his loathsome bed, but she did not understand why Morar
had rescued her. Was it a gesture of kindness from one
woman, who had been given as a hostage by her uncle
Bruidge, to another woman, who had been dragged from
her chieftain father's *rath* and presented to Calgaich as a
lowly servant? Somehow Cairenn knew there was another,
darker reason. She thought Morar the most beautiful
woman she had ever seen, but she did not trust her.

"Ulpius," Lucius said, "my work here is done. I am
returning to Rome to give a personal report on conditions
here in the north. I will leave in two days for Dubris to
take ship for Gaul. It is my wish that these prisoners,
along with the others that have been gathered here in the
north, travel with us. Enroute to Dubris we will pick up
any other consignments of prisoners and animals destined
for the Games in Rome."

"A triumphal entry, my Uncle?" Ulpius asked tartly.

Lucius nodded. He had not missed the acid tone in the
tribune's voice. "I plan to sponsor several days of games
in the Flavian Amphitheatre with a motif of these northern
barbarians and their savage hounds."

Ulpius knew his uncle had greater plans than a triumphal entry into Rome. Lucius wanted publicity, of the sort that could be gained by pleasing the mob in the arena. He wanted it to be known that he, Quaestor Lucius Sextillius, acting governor of the province of Britannia, was the unquestioned authority on conditions along the Wall of Hadrian. There was no doubt but that he would also claim credit for dealing with Bruidge, the chieftain of the wild, unconquered Novantae, and for gaining Morar and Bronwyn as hostages, as well as garnering the barbarian prisoners.

"You understand, Nephew?" Lucius asked. There was a silky tone in his voice. Despite the soft, porcine appearance of Lucius, he possessed a backbone of iron in matters of political importance.

The tribune nodded. "Who shall command the escort, Uncle?"

Lucius twiddled his porky little fingers. He held up a hand and studied a ring. "Decrius Montanas should be more than capable of that, Nephew."

Ulpius scowled. "I had thought . . ."

Lucius waved a hand. "I think your work here is more important than a simple matter of escorting these barbarians to Rome." He looked directly at Ulpius.

"Well, I had thought that my mother, your dear sister, would like to see me, my Uncle," Ulpius insinuated.

The quaestor flushed. "My beloved sister Tonia," he said coldly. "All right, damn you, Ulpius! You shall command the escort."

Their eyes met like fencing blades. Antonia, the elder sister of Lucius and the mother of Ulpius, her only child, was a political power in Rome, behind her bumbling senator of a husband. It was the Lady Antonia who had seen to it that Lucius had received his appointment as quaestor in Britannia and that Ulpius had been appointed tribune, despite his youth and lack of experience, to accompany his uncle to the wild northern frontier where reputations were easily made and more easily broken. Lucius would do well to see that he returned to Rome.

"The audience is over," Lucius announced. He placed his two hands on the sides of his chair and heaved himself up like a fat sow getting out of a mudhole. He held out his arm to Morar.

She ignored him and spoke softly to Ulpius. "Have the slave woman taken to my chambers. First see that she is washed and given proper clothing. Do not harm her." She glanced once back at Calgaich, but her eyes betrayed no emotion.

Calgaich knew it would be foolish for her to respond to him. He had to believe this was the reason for her cold manner. She had spared Cairenn, and she must have done this for him. He felt sick as he watched her take Sextillius's arm and walk gracefully from the chamber.

Guards moved forward to lead the prisoners out. Cairenn managed a tremulous smile as she passed Calgaich to be taken to the woman he loved. The fates were strange that she should become servant to Morar. There had been a mysterious feeling passing among the three of them— Cairenn, Morar and Calgaich—and only time would unravel their destinies. For now, she was safe.

Calgaich, Fomoire, and Guidd One-Eye were marched out into the star-sparkling darkness. Once again the heavy storeroom door slammed shut behind Calgaich, but this time he had companions to share his imprisonment— Fomoire, the Druid, Guidd One-Eye, and great Bron, the wolfhound.

CHAPTER 13

The moon shed a soft ray of light through the barred window of the storeroom to illuminate Fomoire's pensive face. "Sixteen years, a long sixteen years in training, to fail at the first of the final tests. Sixteen years as a Listener and an Ovate to reach the first of the Bardic tests, then to fail. Can you understand that, my warrior friend?"

Calgaich was poking about behind the straw bales while Guidd searched among the great container jars. "No," Calgaich replied shortly. He looked at Guidd. "Any luck, old wolf?"

Guidd shook his head. "The only spirits around here must be in the head of that damned priest there."

Fomoire smiled. "Let me look," he suggested. He stood up from the bale upon which he had been lying and reached down behind it, then he turned with a big jug in his hand. He pulled out the stopper. "Wine," he said. "Falernian, at that."

"How long have you known it was there?" Calgaich asked suspiciously.

"Since we were thrown in here."

"Damn you! That was hours ago!"

Fomoire smiled. "I thought we might use it to bribe our guard."

Guidd shook his head. "Fat chance, priest. Those are not Asturians out there. They are legionnaires."

Fomoire shrugged. "Then we might as well drink this before they find it."

They sat down in the straw with their backs against the bales. Bron come out of the shadows and lay down beside Calgaich. The wine jug made the rounds.

Calgaich scratched behind Bron's ears. "I thought most of you priests had been stamped out by the Red Crests."

"We were too strong for them. We lived as ordinary people, such as yourselves—hunters, herdsmen and craftsmen."

Guidd eyed Fomoire's slim, tapered hands. "I'll be damned if you did."

"I was a leech, a healer of the eye sickness, a teller of tales, or whatever else I could do rather than break my damned back working for a living."

"Your friends could not have thought too much of you to let you drown slowly in that stone coffin," Calgaich commented dryly.

Guidd grinned. "That is true! What great sin did you commit for such a punishment?"

Fomoire drank from the jug. "I was not being punished, my illiterate friends. I was there of my own free will."

"What does illiterate mean?" Guidd asked suspiciously.

"That you can't read or write," Calgaich told him.

"*You* can," Guidd said.

"But there is no written language among your people," the Druid commented.

"He was speaking of Latin," Calgaich said.

Fomoire eyed Calgaich with new respect.

"His grandfather was a Roman," Guidd explained. He drank deeply from the jug and then wiped his mouth. He looked slyly sideways at Calgaich.

Fomoire stared at Calgaich. "Is that true?"

Guidd spat. "Tribune *Legatus Legionis* Rufus Arrius Niger of the Twentieth Legion. He was Calgaich's mother's father."

"And she?" Fomoire asked.

Calgaich looked at him. "Her mother was a chieftain's daughter of the Selgovae."

"Then you are one-quarter Roman blood."

Calgaich nodded. "You figure well," he agreed dryly.

"Calgaich mac Lellan, the greatest swordsman in all Britannia, is part Roman." Fomoire shook his white-haired head.

"I don't talk much about it, priest," Calgaich warned.

"Where is your grandfather now?" Fomoire asked.

Calgaich shrugged. "He is a senator. I've heard he was recently inspecting the forts of the Saxon Shore and is soon to return to Rome, to make his report personally to the emperor." He did not want to discuss the subject further. It was something of which he was not proud. "I said at the time I found you that you were mad. Why were you there in that stone coffin, Fomoire? To be there of your own free will must surely mean that you are mad."

"Because of ambition, friend."

Calgaich laughed. "Ambition? To lie naked in icy water with a great stone upon your chest to hold you fast? A great ambition, friend!"

"For sixteen years I trained for the third degree, that of Bard. As a lad I learned of the thirteen secret societies of my brotherhood—the Society of Beavers, and those of the Mice, Wolves, Rabbits, Wild Cats, the Owls and all the others. It took extraordinary skill and immense patience to learn by ear the long-versed poetic tales of the gods, of law and astronomy, of music and many other things. That took twelve years, and for three years after that I studied and learned omens and magic."

"Such as you exhibited to the Perfumed Pig?"

Fomoire smiled. He waved a deprecating hand. "I can teach those simple tricks to even Guidd here, wild and clumsy as he is."

Guidd lowered the jug and glowered, one-eyed, at the Druid. "Take care, priest!" he snapped.

"I jest, good woodsman! To continue—I studied medicine and learned the crafts of the leech and the healer. I could have remained as a Listener, or even an Ovate, but I was not satisfied. I wanted to be the truest of all Druids —a Bard. You found me undergoing the first of the tests for the Bardic Degree."

The jug went the rounds. The measured trampling of nailed sandals sounded from the courtyard. Tribune Ulpius Claudius was taking no chances with his prisoners.

"My brother Druids brought me to the sacred grove," Fomoire continued. "They placed me naked in the icy water, with just my nostrils above the water level so that I might breathe. The stone was placed upon my chest. It was impossible for me to remove it by myself. The head priest whispered a subject into my ear before I was placed in the water. The test was to compose a poem of great length, in the most difficult of bardic metres, on that subject. My brothers would have returned just at dawn. I would have been taken from the water to be given a harp. I would then have had to compose a melody on the harp to accompany my poem . . ." His voice died away and he reached for the jug.

Calgaich leaned forward. "But you cast a spell on me to make me release you from that coffin."

Fomoire lowered the jug. "I could not compose that poem. I knew I could not compose a melody to go with it. I was sure that if I was taken from the water I would have failed that most fearful of tests."

"At dawn?" Calgaich asked. "I saw no Druids in the sacred grove."

"They must have known the Romans were coming."

"How could they have known that?" Guidd asked.

"They have ways, woodsman. If the Romans had found me in that coffin they would have driven a pilum point through my heart and left me there."

"Perhaps that would have been better than that which you now face," Calgaich suggested.

There was a lurking fear in Fomoire's clear gray eyes. "I dare not return to my brotherhood. If they ever found out I left that coffin by the help of anyone other than the brotherhood . . ." He reached for the wine jug. He drank deeply. He smiled a little. "Besides, I have always wanted to see Rome."

"You have no choice," Calgaich said. He leaned back against the wall and looked beyond his two friends. "Can you foretell the future in the lees from that wine jug, Druid? What lies in store for us, eh?"

"I don't know."

"You have the gift of second sight."

"Within reason. I know this much—nothing can prevent us from being taken to Rome."

Calgaich nodded. "I felt as much. There they will feed you on dainties and you'll be allowed to live in luxury while entertaining the Roman two-legged swine. For myself, Guidd and Bron here, there is only one ending— death in the arena. They shall not find us an easy mark, Fomoire."

"Only the gods know that, Calgaich." Fomoire looked sideways at Calgaich. "This golden woman, this Morar, has great ambition. She plans to go far. Lucius Sextillius might find that he has taken an adder to his bosom."

"For the love of the gods, priest!" Guidd cried.

Calgaich clapped a hand on Guidd's back. "It's all right, old hound. The mad priest is probably right."

"Then you've put her out of your mind?" Guidd asked.

Calgaich shook his head. "I didn't say that."

"She had a hold on you," Fomoire said. "There is something I sense in her. She is old, and wise, in a sense, far beyond her years. There is evil within her. A lovely chalice to hold such deadly poison. We saw how she worked that fool of a quaestor. She has him and the tribune wrapped around her little finger."

"Be careful," Guidd warned Fomoire.

Calgaich suddenly smashed a fist into his other palm. "By the gods! I must have been blind. She was with Fergus all along. Was I so blind with hate that I couldn't see that?"

Fomoire looked questioningly at Guidd.

"Morar was Calgaich's betrothed," Guidd explained. "She did not expect him to come to Rioghaine, after he had deserted his auxiliary unit and had been captured. She thought that would be the end of him. He returned unexpectedly and he found her with his cousin Fergus, the only son of Bruidge, uncle to Calgaich."

"She lay naked in a bedchamber. Fergus was half-dressed. When I burst in on them she cried rape. Fergus fled to a guard's hut. There was only one solution." Calgaich slowly touched the scar on his face as he remembered that awful scene of Morar crying, and then the bloody battle that followed.

"And for her false accusation, you killed your cousin Fergus. Did he not try to tell you otherwise?" Fomoire asked.

"I was in a rage. I went to the guard hut and called him out. He came saying things I would not listen to. Finally he took up his sword like a man."

"And died, falsely accused."

"Yes, he died. Unjustly." Calgaich sat silent as the jug passed around again. Then he said, "I wonder now if the only reason she became betrothed to me was because I was the son of Lellan and next in line for the chieftainship of the Novantae."

Guidd nodded wisely. "I think you are one of the few Novantae who did not think that, Calgaich." Guidd moved a little farther away from Calgaich, still not sure of his loyalty to his love for Morar.

"Then, why didn't you tell me? It would have saved my cousin from an untimely death?" Calgaich demanded.

Guidd laughed bitterly. "I'm not *that* big a fool! No one could talk to you about Morar in those days, or he'd risk a blade in his guts."

"And my Uncle Bruidge, is that why he turned on my father? Did he know Fergus was innocent?" Questions were coming quickly to Calgaich's mind.

Guidd shrugged. "He might have guessed. But he didn't know for sure. Fergus was his only son, and his death alone was enough to make Bruidge crazed for revenge."

"*I* had been like a son to him. He was my tutor in the ways of the sword." Calgaich was now beginning to understand the horrible chain of events that had been set in motion by Morar's accusation. He had had to flee his country and had not been there to defend his father from Bruidge's thirst for power and revenge. He felt sick.

"Morar played you for a fool. You must beware of her," Fomoire said from the shadows. He passed Calgaich the jug. "This Ordovician woman, the *cumal,* does she mean much to you?"

Calgaich shrugged, still lost in memories of past treachery. "She's a chattel, no more."

Guidd winked at the Druid.

"Morar doesn't think so," Fomoire asserted. "Why else would she have saved the *cumal* from the bed sty of that rutting pig of a quaestor?"

"But *why* did she rescue the *cumal?* And what will happen to the woman now that she is in Morar's service?" Guidd asked. "No good can come of Morar owning the Ordovician woman. What were Morar's reasons, Calgaich?"

Calgaich had no answer. It had bothered him at the time to see Cairenn led away to Morar's quarters. Now that he knew of Morar's evil ways, he was sure that Morar had a dark reason for her intervention. But he kept his fears to himself; he did not like to admit in front of his companions that Cairenn meant anything to him at all. He no longer felt so sure of his emotions. Could any woman be trusted? He tried to put these thoughts out of his mind. "Pass me the jug again," he said to Guidd. It would be a long night.

CHAPTER 14

The long column of prisoners was headed by the entourage of Quaestor Lucius Sextillius as it traveled slowly and steadily southward toward the channel that separated Britannia from Gaul. The quaestor, his women and his servants rode comfortably in horse litters and in curtained wagons, with a suitable distance between them and the prisoners, due to the growing stench of the unwashed Celts, Picts, and a group of condemned criminals and deserters from the legions or their auxiliaries—Asturians, Dacians, a Thracian or two, and one lone Syrian. The prized wolfhounds had it better than the human prisoners, for they rode in barred carts at the rear of the column, the better to preserve their strength and ferocity for the arena.

Tribune Ulpius Claudius commanded the entire column and its escort of Dacian horsemen. Centurion Decrius Montanas was in charge of the prisoners, whom he ruled with a brutal, heavy-handed authority that was held in check only by the constant supervision of the tribune. It was not a question of humanity with the tribune: he knew his ticket to Rome, as well as his future there, depended on his uncle, Quaestor Lucius Sextillius, who wanted those prisoners in fairly reasonable shape when he arrived in Rome.

The captives had been fitted with iron collars attached to chains, which passed back along each file of the column of fours. In addition, chains had been fitted about the waist of each man and then attached to the next man, so that each quartet was bound together laterally, as well as longitudinally. Thus the column moved as one man, a long and snakelike line of silent, trudging men.

On each side of the prisoners rode Dacian auxiliaries,

while two sets of fours followed the rear of the column. Centurion Decrius Montanas and one of the decurions of the Dacian cavalry led the column. The leading quartet of prisoners was composed of those considered most dangerous—Calgaich, Guidd, Fomoire and Niall, a lean Selgovae with a shock of red hair, who thought he was a cousin of Calgaich's, from his mother's side of the family. On dry days the dust from the horses' hoofs swirled about the prisoners and whitened their faces and clothing while it furred their nostrils and parched their throats. On wet days thick mud splashed back from the hoofs, and always the heavy droppings of the two stallions splashed up to cover the legs of the prisoners. Montanas had said, when the lead quartet had been selected personally by him, "You shall act as the shield of the prisoners behind you." His hard face had smiled, but his eyes had not.

The farther south the column traveled the more obvious was the undercurrent of fear of the Roman Britons. The gateways of the towns through which they passed had been narrowed and the walls had been built higher, just as Guidd had described concerning Luguvalium and the Wall of Hadrian. Many once-prosperous farm villas were now dark and empty.

Fomoire knew the country well. He had often traveled the same roads and visited the same towns in his guise as a leech, seeking knowledge of the Roman Britons for his secret brotherhood. "There are many fewer people here now, Calgaich, than in years past," he had said one day as their column trudged through the midlands of Britannia. "Once this road and others were crowded with traveling merchants and the thriving business of the province. Now those who have not fled to the south, or out of Britannia altogether, shelter themselves behind the town walls. Even the Roman soldiers seem fearful of the future."

"Britons, serving the damned red-crested Roman bastards! I'd like to show them a thing or two about love of the country that gave them birth!" Calgaich had snapped.

"When, and how?" Fomoire had queried quietly.

"If I survive Rome, priest. All I have to do is to get back to Albu, drive my drunken uncle from the chieftainship of the clan and organize the Novantae. Then the cran tara will be carried through the hills and glens to

raise the people against the Red Crests. I'd even consider
fighting beside the damned Picts."

"And the Saxons and Jutes as well?"

"I'd use them and then turn on them after they had
served my purpose."

"The trustworthiness of the Caledonians."

"They'd do the same to us."

"Truly spoken. Even now it is said in many places that
Rome struggles more and more each year to keep the raiding barbarians from entering the Empire. Once I heard a
rumor that she eventually plans to withdraw her three
legions from Britannia to defend her other borders. You
know what will happen then."

Calgaich had nodded. "All the more easy for us. Still,
I'll not count on it, Fomoire."

Days later Fomoire and Calgaich had taken up the same
discussion again. It was always the Druid who instigated
these talks. "You are a warrior and a leader, Calgaich.
None of us here can know our fate in Rome, or even if
we'll ever get there. But if by any chance the opportunity
comes for you to escape and return here to Britannia, let
me stand by your side when we drive these accursed
Romans into the sea."

Guidd laughed dryly. "We'll likely need every man we
can get. Even you, priest."

"There is much we can teach each other, much we can
learn from the Romans. Remember, they have ruled the
known world for many centuries, and not by the fortunes
of the gods. When in Rome, I hope to gain the confidence
of Lucius Sextillius. I think he means to use my poor abil-
ities to help him advance his career. He seeks publicity
and fame. In so doing, he must be seen in many places—
the homes and palaces of the great and powerful. I mean
to be near him when he does so. There is much I can
learn."

"While I rot in prison, awaiting the day I will be called
out and given the tools of my trade, either to live for a
short time or die suddenly."

"You shall not die that way. I *know*. . . ."

Calgaich laughed. "It is said you Druids can forecast the
future by staring entranced into the steaming guts of a

freshly slain man. Let's hope you do not have to read my future in such a way."

Calgaich became pensive. During the march, he had kept quiet counsel to himself, but the hidden spark of his burning vengeance still flickered deep within his soul. Even if he paid for his wonted vengeance with his life, the risk would be worth the gamble. The sweetness of the revenge would overcome the bitterness of death, and, after all, was not *Tir na n'Og* the Beautiful Land of Youth, where there was no pain, disease or death?

Now and again he also thought of Bronwyn, who was riding ahead of the column in the entourage of the Perfumed Pig. He had always thought of her as a mere, undeveloped child, that is, until the night she had come to him at the *mansio*. The memory of her lush young body often returned to him, to the exclusion of the golden beauty of Morar and the dark lunar beauty of Cairenn.

"Bronwyn," Calgaich said aloud one day, when the going was particularly grim.

"The young slim one?" Fomoire asked, overhearing him. "I thought it was Morar who had snared you in a net of her golden hair."

"Perhaps I have been blind," Calgaich mused.

"Listen to him," Guidd jeered.

"She was only a child when you left Albu," Fomoire said. "How could you have known she'd have changed that much?"

Calgaich shrugged. "I should have known. She came to me the night Guidd and I escaped from the villa. Without her help I could not have freed Guidd and my father. She wanted to go with me, but I refused. Her safety would have kept me from my task. I sent her back to her quarters. She, too, like Cairenn, is at Morar's mercy."

His voice died away for a time. He began again, "She came to me in the flesh, as Morar had so often come to me in the spirit after battle in Eriu."

"Tell me of this," Fomoire requested. "When and how did she come?"

"It was always after battle. When the blood was still drying on the blades and the cries of the badly wounded sounded through the darkness until we put them out of their misery. I would help to finish the bloody work, and then I'd fling myself down on the bare earth to sleep. It was always then that she'd come to me, across the heaps of bloody dead, like a spirit from the shades. My spear brothers never saw her, of course. It was only I who saw her—warm, soft, perfumed, and taunting me with that mysterious half-smile of hers. It was almost as if the mingled odors of the fresh blood and the foul air that leak from the bodies of the swollen dead had drawn her to the scene."

Fomoire nodded. "I thought so."

"You know of these things?"

"I do."

"How can a man be blinded by such utter foolishness in such a beautiful form as Morar?"

Fomoire waved a hand. "She has the power to blind a man until she is through using him."

"But she can't blind *you*, eh, priest?"

"No, but sometimes I think she *knows* who I really am."

"How can she know that?"

"How has she risen from a stinking *dun* beside a lowly *rath* in Caledonia, now to be borne in a fine horse litter to the channel and thence to Gaul, and eventually to Rome itself? How could she cross the Hibernian Sea to Eriu to find you after bloody battle and to tempt you with that never obtainable and magnificent body of hers? She *was* drawn by blood and terror! That is what gives her spiritual strength to do such things. She will let nothing stand in her way until she has reached the pinnacle of the living. Nothing can stop her! *Nothing*, I tell you!" His voice rose in pitch, so much that Decrius Montanas rested his hand on the cantle of his saddle to look back at the plodding prisoners.

"Watch yourself!" Calgaich hissed out of the side of his mouth.

The centurion turned his head to look forward, then slowly, looked back again and his hard eyes met Calgaich's.

"If you think she knows who and what you are, Fomoire," Calgaich suggested, "why has she not turned you in?"

"Because she fears me, Calgaich. Perhaps in her devious, twisted mind she thinks I might be of some use to her in

Rome. Who knows? But, *fian,* fear that woman more than the sight of a legion cohort charging you with bared *gladii!"*

It rained the two days the column waited in the filthy slave pens on the outskirts of Londinium while Lucius pampered Morar and Bronwyn in the shops and homes of the important. Then the column had been driven out onto the highway by the whips of the Dacians.

Now the column was trudging through the mud of a neglected road. The leading prisoners were so covered with mud and manure that they were not distinguishable one from the other except by height. They trudged on and on, soaked to the skin, with bared heads bent and eyes almost closed.

"How much farther is it?" Niall, the Selgovae, asked.

"Dubris is ahead," Fomoire croaked. "You'll soon smell the sea."

The salt smell of the channel came to them on the wind from the south and east. Already the entourage of the quaestor had increased their speed in anticipation of the warm and comfortable quarters due an official of his standing at Dubris. The carts and horse litters vanished into the mist.

"What happens when we get there, Fomoire?" Niall asked.

"We take ship across the channel to Gesoriacum in Gaul."

"And then?"

"We march south through Gaul to Massalia, a port on the Mediterranean. From there we take ship for Portus Ostiensis, the port of Rome, which is about eight days sail from Massalia."

"How far is Massalia from the channel?"

Fomoire stumbled in his stride. He was a man of great spiritual strength, but he lacked the toughness and endurance of the warriors, huntsmen and herders who made up the bulk of the prisoners. Calgaich caught him up under one arm and Guidd the other.

"Fomoire?" Niall asked.

"Perhaps six hundred Roman miles."

"On foot?" Niall asked incredulously.

Calgaich grinned through the mud plastering his face. "How else?" he asked.

"We'll never make it, Novantae," Niall said gloomily.

"You'll have to make it, Selgovae!" Calgaich snapped. "March, or die in the dust of a Gaulish highway with an auxiliary's dagger drawn across your throat. *I* will make it!"

They passed slowly through the narrow, busy streets of Dubris. Rome's great strength still gave a feeling of some security to the people. Many Roman warships were stationed along the coast, which was protected by forts of the Litus Saxonicum, the Saxon Shore. The ships were not the huge biremes and triremes of the calmer Mediterranean, Adriatic and Ionian Seas, but rather lighter galleys used to fight the Saxon vessels in the stormy Northern Sea. Even so, it was rumored that the Saxon wind was blowing ever stronger each year against the low coast of southeastern Britannia, while the Caledonian wind was blowing ever stronger from the north.

"The Romans try to hold back the Saxons and Jutes," Fomoire told the others, "by building their great forts at Branodunum, Gariannonum, Othona, Regulbium, Rutupiae and here at Dubris. These are great forts, but I believe they are doomed, in time, for the Saxon wind will one day prevail here."

Calgaich spat. "Those Saxon bastards might eventually defeat these Romans, but they will not conquer Albu!"

"Perhaps. Perhaps. But if the Saxons do not conquer all of Britannia, there will be other conquerors, worse tyrants than even the Romans."

Calgaich looked at the priest with scorn. "First we shall deal with the Romans and then we shall deal with the others."

The street became wider. The traffic was heavy despite the increasing rain. As the head of the column of prisoners reached a small square, the door of a wineship was flung open with a crash and a man seemed to hop out into the streaming gutter like a great and ungainly frog. He struck hard in the swift-flowing rainwater and then shook his head as he tried to get up by planting both hands in the water to force himself up on to his feet. The wineshop door slammed shut behind him.

Decrius Montanas fought with his rearing horse, which had been frightened by the sudden appearance of the man in the gutter. "By the gods!" he shouted, as the man turned his head sideways to look up at him. "Lutorius!"

Calgaich saw the familiar drink-sodden face, with its badly broken nose, and the chin gall, the thickened line of paler skin along the lower jaw and chin which could only be made by many years of wearing the chin strap of a Roman legionnaire's helmet. "Run, Bottle Emptier!" he roared.

Lutorius got clumsily to his feet. He knew damned well what his fate would be if Montanas got hold of him. He turned and ran awkwardly like a circus bear toward the nearest side street.

"After him, damn you!" Montanas shouted at the Dacians nearest him.

Four Dacians wheeled their mounts away from the prisoner column and galloped after the *calo*. Lutorius had almost made it to safety when he slipped in a pile of fresh manure and fell headlong again into the streaming gutter. He tried to rise. A cavalryman brought the butt of his short spear down hard alongside Lutorius's head. Blood spurted. Lutorius staggered gamely to his feet. He reached up and dragged the cursing Dacian from his saddle. He ripped the long-bladed cavalry *spatha* from its sheath and tore the shield from the Dacian's back. He then jumped back into the junction of two walls to face the three remaining Dacians who had dismounted and were moving in on foot.

All traffic had stopped. The Dacians swung their wet cloaks back over their shoulders to free their arms for swordplay. Their *spathae* seemed to hiss as they were whipped from their scabbards.

Montanas reined in his horse in the middle of the street. "Throw down the sword, Lutorius," he commanded.

Lutorius spat to one side. "Let your damned auxiliaries face a lone legionnaire!" he roared. "I'm Lutorius, the Bottle Emptier, a man who served more than half a score of years in the legions. Come on, you damned Dacian swine!"

Montanas nodded to the Dacians. "I want that drunken bastard alive! I want the skin flayed off his back for a purse!"

The cavalrymen closed in. Lutorius held his shield up close to his square chin and tight against his left breast and side. He held his sword low, at an angle for thrusting, as with a *gladius.*

"He hasn't a chance," Fomoire murmured.

"Watch him," Calgaich suggested with professional interest. "Drunk or sober, I think he can handle those three."

The rain slashed down. The street was very quiet except for the blowing of the horses and the occasional chink of a bit.

"*Impetus gladiorum!*" Lutorius shouted, as he gave himself his own commands. It was the famed legion "Onset with swords." He drove forward, taking three hasty strokes against his shield. His *spatha* darted out like the tongue of an adder. A Dacian cursed as blood flowed from his sword arm. He dropped back out of the fight. Lutorius swung up his shield to protect his head and then cut low at the legs of the two remaining Dacians to slow their attack.

A *spatha* skinned the *calo*'s forehead. Blood flowed down his face, partially blinding him, but Lutorius was in his element, like a butcher cutting beef.

"Go to it, Bottle Emptier!" a man shouted from the door of the wineshop from which the *calo* had been evicted.

"*Euge! Euge!*" yelled a carter, giving Lutorius the victory cry of the arena.

One of the Dacians went down from a flat-bladed blow on top of his helmet that snapped off a third of the *calo*'s *spatha.* The other Dacian limped back, cursing hotly as he gripped his slashed shoulder.

Four more Dacians dismounted and drew their swords. They advanced on the *calo.* A fighting, cursing fury met them and drove them back across the square. Lutorius yelled, half-mad with Chios wine and his aroused blood lust.

"He is *fey,*" Guidd murmured. "He feels nothing. No fatigue, wounds or pain."

"He'll die soon enough," Niall prophesied.

"Tullus!" the centurion snapped.

The Balearic slinger came forward.

"Drop him," the centurion ordered. "But, *alive!* If you kill him, I'll have your hide."

Tullus reached into his pouch. He selected a heavy lead ball. He placed it in the loop of the sling and walked forward slowly. Lutorius was fighting like a whirligig, spinning about on a heel, striking out, then dropping to one knee to drive his blade upward, followed by a leap to his feet and a short and furious charge. Tullus whirled his sling, almost casually, and with seemingly little effort. The missile hit the *calo* just behind the left ear. He dropped into the gutter. His sword clattered on the cobblestones. The blood flowed from his face and tinted the rainwater pink.

They dragged Lutorius to the feet of the dismounted centurion, who kicked him viciously in the ribs and spat in his bloody face. He beckoned to a carter. "Haul this carrion to the slave pens in your cart," the centurion ordered.

The column of prisoners resumed their slow march toward the waterfront. Soon they had reached the misty quays where the galleys loading for Gaul lay ranked side by side in the harbor.

It was Fomoire who brought Lutorius back to the land of the living. The Druid worked with skillful hands at the base of the *calo's* skull. In a little while Lutorius opened one bleary eye. "Who's paying for the next round?" he asked thickly. "Heads or ships, barbarians? Toss the coin! Best out of three!"

"Well met, Bottle Emptier," Calgaich greeted dryly. "Your timing, as usual, was excellent. How did you happen to get thrown out of that wineshop at the exact instant Montanas was passing by?"

Lutorius sat up. He hiccupped. "It takes some skill, barbarian," he admitted.

"Who won the fight?" he asked.

"You were winning, *calo*. It was Tullus who struck you with a leaden thunderbolt."

"By the gods of the legions," the old soldier growled. "Had I my old *Hispanicus gladius,* my helmet and my legion shield I would have wiped out the lot of them."

He looked about at the silent, mud-plastered prisoners. "Where is this sad-looking lot bound, barbarian?"

"To Rome, *calo*. At least *we* are."

Lutorius placed his back against the wall of the shed. "Well, from the looks of things, it seems as though I might be going with you to the end of the road, wherever that might be."

"The arena," Guidd said quietly.

Lutorius shrugged. "So be it. That'll take a couple of months or so. Meanwhile I'm still alive, still half drunk and in fairly bad company, so I'll make the best of it."

Calgaich squatted in front of the *calo*. "What were you doing here in Dubris?"

"I came here hoping to catch Old Give Me Another, before he took ship for Gaul. I got lost in a wine haze for a day or two. Happened to pick a whore's purse when she passed out next to me in bed. That kept me going for another few days." He grinned. "I did see the old man riding through the streets on his way to the ship. Before his aide kicked my rosy ass into the gutter, I managed to blurt out that you were a prisoner of the quaestor Lucius Sextillius at Luguvalium and that he meant you no good. I also said I thought you were headed for the Games at Rome."

"And?" Calgaich asked.

Lutorius shrugged. "He looked down that long beak of his like a vulture eyeing a juicy, rotting corpse, and said, 'No one deserts the Eagles! *No one!*' He hasn't changed a bit, Caledonian. Old Give Me Another! Tribune *Legatus Legionis* Arrius Niger! Now, *there* is a soldier's soldier!"

"Did he recognize you?"

"Look at me, friend. My own dear mother, the gods rest her drunken soul, wouldn't recognize me if she came from the shades looking for me to make me pay back the money I owed her when she died."

"So you got nothing." Calgaich grinned. "I thought as much."

"Well, I only wanted to pay my passage to Rome and get on the welfare rolls as an old soldier covered with honorable scars. They say half the city is on the free bread and meat rolls. Ah, Rome! The center of the world! The city of cities! A man can fall out of one wineshop and stagger into the one right next door without missing a round. And the whores! They say a man can die happy with them and never wear them out!"

"They may yet hang you at the quays," Calgaich suggested speculatively.

Lutorius shook his grizzled poll. "I doubt it. They've been gathering prisoners from all over Britannia for the great Games to be held there early this summer. Deserters like you and me, barbarian. Picts, Silurians, Saxons, Jutes, Britons and Caledonians, as well as condemned criminals, prisoners of war, and deserters from the legions and auxiliaries. They've been shipping them out by the hundreds. They take them in chained droves clear through Gaul to Massalia, for shipment to Portus Ostiensis.

"No, Calgaich, they won't hang me. I've been a soldier too long, and I'm too skilled with the tools of my trade to escape fighting in the arena. Well, it's either that, a rope around my neck, or maybe slow death in the galleys, or, worse than that, in the salt or sulphur mines. A soldier ought to die standing with his weapons in his hands, eh, barbarian?"

Calgaich nodded. "Or a warrior," he added absentmindedly. "With the wind in his face and his enemies in front of him." He stood up and walked to the open end of the shed to look toward the misty quays.

"What's wrong with him?" Lutorius asked.

"You can't cage an eagle, or a wolf," Guldd replied. "They don't live long behind bars."

The salt tang of the sea came to Calgaich through the cold drizzle. Faintly above the busy hum of life in the port city, he heard the crying of the harbor gulls and the distant sea wash of the channel.

CHAPTER 15

The first part of the long journey to Rome had seemed interminable, but as the prisoners drew closer to Massalia, the days moved on with incredible speed. The entourage of Quaestor Lucius Sextillius and the long column of prisoners had taken ship across the channel to Gesoriacum in Gaul. Day after day, the convoys of prisoners moved southward. Additional prisoners were added to the column. There were Gauls, Helvetians from the towering Alpine areas east of Gaul. Groups of stolid, blue-eyed yellow-haired giants from the dark forests of Germania formed segments of the convoys. Near the end of the journey to Massalia the prisoners were joined by dark-faced and dark-haired men from Iberia. The universal coating of yellow dust made them almost indistinguishable from each other except for the larger size of the northerners.

The prisoners had two things in common—the thick layer of dust and the resigned look in their eyes. They knew their destiny. If it was not to be bloody death in the Flavian Amphitheatre or the Circus Maximus of Rome, it would be their end when they either broke their backs or burst their hearts tugging at a galley oar. Still, it could be worse, for some of them might be condemned to the salt mines, where their fingers and toes would rot off as they slowly went mad with fatigue and pain; or perhaps the horrible sulphur mines of Sicily, which were a living death.

The tang of the sea came to them as they approached Massalia, an ancient Phoenician port situated on the Gulf of Lions. The dusty column of prisoners tramped through the cobbled streets of the ancient Phoenician port city to the harbor where they were confined in open pens, customarily used for livestock. The reek of stale wine, olive oil, fresh manure, green hides and rotting wheat hung over the quays and rose from the holds of the round-bottomed, high-sided, clumsy merchant ships. There was constant activity along the waterfront. Lines of loaded and empty carts passed each other, rumbling over the greasy cobblestones. The cries of the stevedores and seamen mingled with the creaking of the blocks and tackles of the ships as they were being loaded or unloaded. Above all other noises there was the persistent crying of the harbor gulls as they hovered over the dirty water of the harbor.

Fomoire leaned on the fence surrounding the cattle pens and looked out at the harbor. "*Mare Nostrum,* Our Sea, the arrogant Romans call it. The old name was *Mare Internum,* the Inland Sea, but in more modern times the name was changed to *Mediterranean,* the Middle of the Earth, and so it truly is. The commerce of the known world is centered in this sea—from Africa, the Middle East, Greece, Gaul and Iberia. And in the epicenter of this central sea of the world is Rome. Everything and everyone seems to be drawn to Rome from all parts of the Empire, and even beyond the Empire. Great are the Seven Wonders of the World, and of them, Rome is assuredly the greatest."

Calgaich looked up at Fomoire from where he sat on some filthy straw. "What are these Seven Wonders?" he asked.

"The rainbow, the echo, the cuckoo, the negro, the volcano, the sirocco and Rome."

Lutorius laughed. "Don't forget the *Book of Elephantis,* weasel! By the gods, I'd rather have that scroll to read than any damned Wonders of the World!"

Fomoire shrugged. "The encyclopedia of pornography. They say Quaestor Lucius Sextillius has a copy."

Lutorius picked at his yellowed teeth with a dirty fingernail. "You're damned right he has! Many's the time I saw him reading it when I served temporarily as a *calo* in his villa at Luguvalium. He'd pore over it and then hurry off to his bedchamber with a boy, a whore, or a goat, with his instructions fresh in his damned bald head. Try as I would to peek over his shoulder, I could never get a real crack at it."

"If you could read, *calo,*" put in a bearded seaman of the Veneti, from the channel coast of northern Gaul.

"Shit!" Lutorius cried. "Who said anything about reading? I was looking at the pictures!"

The Venetus stood up with a jangling of his rusty chains and looked at the long lines of merchant ships moored to the quays. "What a row of tubs," he sneered. "These piss pots would sink on a calm day off Gesoriacum. These damned Romans never did understand the sea. No wonder they're having such a hell of a time keeping those Saxons and Jutes from landing in Britannia."

"But *you* understand the sea, eh, Venetus?" Calgaich asked, suddenly taking interest.

"My father was a whale and my mother was a dolphin. I was born at sea, with rope yarn for hair, and tar for blood. I was teethed on a marlinespike, and had flippers for hands and feet until I was three years old. I shit sea shells and piss salt water. Anything else you want to know?"

"By the gods, a human dolphin!" Lutorius cried. "How do they call you, Venetus?"

"Cunori, son of Struan. And you, *calo?*"

"Lutorius, son of Bacchus!" The *calo* thrust out a hand and gripped that of the Venetus. "How did they happen to gather you in this cargo for death?"

"My little fishing craft met up with a fat Roman merchant ship in the channel. It was foggy. They didn't see us until we were alongside them and over their railing with our knives in our teeth. Then we found out what her cargo was."

"And?" Calgaich asked. "What was it?"

Cunori shrugged. "A battalion of Batavian auxiliaries bound for Portus Adurna. It was a good fight while it lasted." Cunori looked at the ships again. "I had hoped to slip away before we got this far south."

"You'd never make it back to the channel, Cunori," Guidd put in. "Gaul swarms with auxiliaries."

Cunori looked about as though someone might be listening. "I didn't figure on going north by *land*. I thought that when we neared here, I'd slip away and steal a small craft to sail back to my own country."

"How?" Lutorius asked sarcastically. "Up the rivers?"

"I'm not joking."

Calgaich looked quickly at the seaman. "You never meant to return by land, eh, Cunori?"

The Venetus shook his head and jerked a thumb back over his shoulder. "South first, then west, then north," he said mysteriously.

"Beyond the Pillars of Hercules," Foimoire suggested.

The Venetus nodded.

It was very quiet among the group of prisoners about the seaman. Those closest to him looked at each other secretively out of the corners of their eyes. Some of them looked back over their shoulders toward the Gaulish auxiliaries standing guard at the gate of the enclosure.

"It is said that few men have been beyond the Pillars of Hercules," Lexus, a giant Gaul, murmured.

"*Ne plus ultra,*" Chilo, a slim Greek tutor put in. "No more beyond. It is said that the Phoenicians, the world's greatest seamen, saw such a message carved on the rocks at the Pillars of Hercules, and dared not go beyond them."

"There have been many ships that have sailed out into the great sea to the west," Fomoire added.

"And many of them did not come back," the Greek argued.

Lutorius spat. "Shit! I passed that way when I was just a stripling. I was on a Greek ship loaded with tin. It was rough, and I was damned sick most of the way, but we made it."

Cunori nodded. "I too have made that passage, *both* ways."

"Then you must know the way." Calgaich leaned closer to the Venetus. "Cunori, if you had such a craft, would you really go?"

"Try me," the seaman suggested quietly. "It's better to die in the clean sea with the fresh salt breeze against your face than to die like a slaughtered hog in the arena to amuse these damned Romans."

"Aye!" Lexus, the Gaul, cried.

Guidd nodded quickly. His one eye glistened.

"We'd need someone to read the stars," Cunori added. "We couldn't hug the coast, for fear the Roman naval galleys in the ports of Iberia might be alerted."

"You talk like fools," Lutorius asserted. "Here we are

in chains, under heavy guard, and you talk of stealing a ship and escaping to sea, as if there were nothing to it."

"*I* can read the stars," Fomoire said quietly.

Suddenly the gates crashed open, and a file of Gauls marched into the pen. Decrius Montanas followed them, holding a perfumed handkerchief to his nose. "Up on your feet, you dogs!" he shouted. "We've arranged passage on a first-class ship for some of you! The naval trireme *Neptunus*. Pride of the South Mediterranean Squadron! Up, up, I say, so that I may reward the best of you with this great prize!"

"That's one I'd like to take along with us," Cunori said out of the side of his mouth. "We could hang him up by his prick to the yardarm for luck and hope it held together until we rounded the Iberian Peninsula into the great sea."

The centurion planted his hands on his hips and eyed the sullen prisoners. "Calgaich, the Great Swordsman; Guidd, the One-Eyed Rat; Fomoire, the Unhuman; Chilo, who raped his master's young daughter; Lexus, the Bull in Human Form; and the rest of you whispering dogs in that far corner there! I need a score of you, for a healthy voyage at sea! I assure you, my friends, that it will do you a world of good between here and Portus Ostiensis!"

The selected score of captives were marched along the stone quays and halted beside the *Neptunus*. The strong odor of vinegar and hot tar, mingled with a clinging smell of incense, drifted from the moored ship. A thin wraith of bluish smoke arose from the altar set on the foredeck.

"She's getting ready for sea," Cunori observed. "They've made an offering to the gods." He looked at a Gaulish stevedore who lounged against a pile of bales which were to be loaded onto the trireme. "Is she a fever ship, mate?"

The Gaul nodded. "They've been burning pitch and sprinkling vinegar inside of her for a week to kill the fever within her rotten guts. She came in over a week past with half her rowers dead or dying from fever. She's a hoodoo ship."

"Where's she bound?"

"Ostia. There's a rumor she's going to be blessed there, to kill the evil within her. Some British official has commandeered her to carry him and his women and slaves to Ostia. She's to leave on the afternoon tide."

"Wash the filth off that vermin before you bring them aboard my ship, Centurion!" the Greek captain of the *Neptunus* shouted at Decrius Montanas.

Grinning seamen hauled up buckets of filthy water and sloshed them over the prisoners. They held their noses as they approached to wash them down. Calgaich wiped the harbor filth from his face and squeezed the dirty water from his long hair.

A train of carts and horse litters rumbled and clattered along the quay to shipside. The drenched prisoners stood watching as the litters stopped. Curtains parted on one of the first, and Calgaich caught his breath as Morar extended a slim foot and ankle toward the ground. His eyes met hers for an instant before she looked away.

"By Zeus," a seaman whispered. "Look at *her!*"

Calgaich made an effort to harden his heart against her incredible beauty.

Quaestor Lucius Sextillius got down from his horse litter. He held his sharp little nose between a thumb and forefinger. "Pericol!" he exclaimed. "The stench is overpowering!"

"His loincloth must have shifted when he got down," Lutorius said to Calgaich out of the side of his mouth.

Tribune Ulpius Claudius dismounted from his horse and hurried to help Morar get down from her litter. "They're used to it, Uncle!" he called back over a shoulder. "Have you ever been in the huts and halls of these northern barbarians? By Mithras, your eyes smart and your stomach turns over at the stench of them. They have no knowledge at all of the baths."

Lucius Sextillius eyed the prisoners. "Will any harm come to them aboard the ship, Centurion? I want them in good enough condition so that they make a good showing in the Games."

Decrius Montanas saluted the quaestor. "They have just covered about a thousand miles, mostly on foot, sir. Those who are still alive have proven their ability to withstand hardships. After a few days aboard the trireme at the oars, they should be in even better condition."

Morar leaned on the arm of the tribune. Her great blue

eyes again roamed about over the dripping prisoners. They came to rest for a matter of seconds on Calgaich, who again gave no sign of recognition. There was a puzzled expression on her lovely face as she looked away from him. Then Quaestor Lucius Sextillius and his entourage began to mount the gangplank to board the ship.

The house slaves and servants of the quaestor began to unload the luggage carts. Cairenn descended from one of the carts. She was dressed in a soft *stola,* and her dark hair was caught up in a silver band. She looked from one prisoner to another as she worked to unload the baskets on her cart. The men were dirty almost beyond recognition, but she knew Calgaich immediately. She hesitated in her task and looked fully into his eyes. She would know him anywhere despite his present condition and appearance. It was strange to see him without his weapons—the great war spear and magnificent sword of his grandfather, Evicatos the Spearman. Much had changed in Calgaich except the fierce light in his eyes. Nothing but death could ever dim that light. She walked toward the trireme, past the waiting prisoners. "Calgaich," she called softly, but Calgaich had turned away. He wanted no one, least of all Cairenn, to see him as he was.

One of the male servants trudged toward the gangplank. He carried a great war spear over one shoulder and had a scabbarded sword in his hands.

"At least your weapons are still within reach, Calgaich," Guidd whispered out of the side of his mouth.

"If I had my hands on them . . ." the warrior murmured.

Cairenn had taken her basket aboard the trireme and returned for another. Calgaich could sense that her eyes never left him as she passed, but he did not look at her again. She carried the last basket to the vessel where Morar stood waiting, having watched Cairenn as she passed the prisoners. She called for Cairenn to hurry and pointed for her to go below.

More carts were unloaded, and another group of horse litters drew up to the ship. Again the seamen stopped their work as another blonde woman descended from the litter. Bronwyn! Calgaich's heart cried out. She looked pale and weak, although still beautiful. A guard rushed forward to escort her on board. She, too, looked for Calgaich in the crowd of prisoners as she passed the men still strung together by the chains around their waists. When she saw him, she tried to catch his eye, but he did not look at her. Disappointed, she went up the plank and joined Morar at the railing of the trireme. There the two sisters stood together like two shining suns, although Calgaich now knew that only one had a heart of gold.

The trireme was a large vessel. She was about two hundred feet long and was manned by one hundred and eighty oarsmen, a crew of twenty seamen, and an afterguard of thirty marines. An altar smoked on the foredeck.

The prisoners were led aboard in single file to one of the hatchways that led down into the depths of the hold. The stench within the cavernous hold thickened the deeper one descended into it. Even the strong acrid odor of the vinegar and the tang of the burning pitch had failed to overcome the sickening miasma compounded of stinking bilge water, human waste, and rotting food that had dropped from the rowers' benches into the bilges. There was also the faint and persistent odor of death itself. The ship seemed to be a floating charnel house.

Calgaich, Lutorius, Fomoire, Guidd and Loarn, of the Brigantes, were chained to one of the long oars and seated on benches that descended one below the other and side by side, to the inner bulkhead of the ship. There the oar protruded into the water, so that each man sat to accommodate the angle of the oar as it was being worked. The rest of the prisoners were assigned where there were other vacancies. The galley slaves were asleep, or lying on the deck between the benches. None of them raised their heads to look at the newcomers. It was not a life they were leading, merely an existence. The day would come when they would finally fail at the oar or perhaps drop dead. The end was always the same. The chains were struck loose, and the body was dropped over the side, while one of the relief oarsmen was immediately chained to the same oar, still warm from the sweat of the man who had just died. No one on the deck would even bother to look aft to watch the body sink into the sea.

A burly Numidian slave drove home the last of the heavy staples into the end of the chain that fastened Calgaich to the great oar. There was no recognition of his fellow men in his dull stare. He was like a machine. Once Calgaich looked up into the man's dark eyes. It was like looking into a black, bottomless tarn of stagnant water. There was no spirit within the twin pools.

Calgaich rested his head on the thick handle of the oar. Something hard poked him in the side. It was the vine staff of Centurion Decrius Montanas. Calgaich looked up into the flat, basilisk stare of the centurion. The *hortator*, or rowing master, stood beside the centurion. "These are the dogs to watch, Perus," Decrius instructed the round-headed Sicilian. "Understand, the quaestor wants no harm to come to them, but see to it that they work themselves to the fullest."

The Sicilian's face was a set, emotionless mask. "It makes no difference to me, Centurion, as to *who* they are. Once they are chained to that oar, they are *mine*. They are not men, but merely rowing machines. They obey the commands. They row. They work to their fullest at all times, for if one oar in a bank begins to fail, the whole bank is thrown out, thus breaking the rhythm. If that happens, it is my responsibility, not theirs. You understand?"

Montanas nodded. "It is understood." He smiled thinly at Calgaich; it was a smile of the facial muscles only. "Well, barbarian, I promised you a sea voyage for your health. Four hundred miles of it, at say, fifty miles per day. Eight to ten days at sea. Of course, you'll have to row to enjoy this cruise, and to *live*. You understand?"

Calgaich nodded.

The centurion's vine staff lashed out like the tongue of a striking asp to strike Calgaich alongside the head. "Say 'yes, sir,' barbarian, or I'll arrange it so that you can row all the way to Ostia with a cracked skull!"

Calgaich turned his head a little. He looked full into the eyes of Decrius. "Yes, sir," he responded mechanically.

For a moment the centurion held the gaze of Calgaich, looking for subtlety or guile, but it was as if he were looking into a painted face, or a mask, revealing nothing of the barbarian's true feelings.

Lutorius looked back over his shoulder as the centurion and the rowing master strode along the walkway between the rowing benches. "You're learning to act like a legionnaire, barbarian. Always hide your feelings. To show them is to get into trouble. But wait for your chance. When I was a recruit in Cappadocia, serving in the old Fifteenth Apollinaria, there was a junior centurion, a real sonofabitch, in the last maniple of the tenth cohort, and there ain't no lower rank than that in a legion. Me, being a kid recruit, I was the bottom man in the whole damned legion! My old man, at that time, was in the third cohort, and he had had a few run-ins with this particular junior centurion, about the way he was handling his men. Well, naturally, this junior centurion couldn't get back at my old man or he'd have gotten his balls kicked in. So, guess who he took it out on?"

Calgaich shrugged. "I haven't the slightest idea, *calo*."

Lutorius grinned. "Me, of course. There wasn't any way of getting back at him, outside of being in the heat of battle when a lot of such matters are paid off."

"How did you finally get him, Bottle Emptier?" Guidd asked.

Lutorius looked surprised. "Did I say it was me?"

Guidd smiled. "Go on, O King of Liars."

"It seems as though we were bivouacked in an area where those damned Cappadocians would creep into our camps at night and slit a few throats just for the hell of it. One night this particular centurion was asleep in his tent, with his back sticking out against the leather. I happened to be on guard that night. I caught and killed a native who sneaked into the camp. It was then a simple matter to thrust the native's knife into the hump sticking out of the side of the centurion's tent. After that, I roused the rest of the guard and showed them the native I had killed. They found the centurion dead in the morning."

"And you got away with it," Fomoire suggested.

Lutorius nodded. "They granted me the native's knife as a reward and kept me drunk for weeks in honor of my valiant deed. I hocked it in Rome and it kept me drunk until I left the city to return to Britannia. So, you see, barbarian, *wait your chance*."

Guidd looked sideways at Calgaich. "We have need of you, Calgaich. If we're to survive to reach Rome and live through the Games, we must have a leader," Guidd said.

Calgaich shrugged. "To lead where and to what end?" he asked dully.

"Have you already forgotten our plan?" Cunori whispered.

Niall looked at Calgaich and nodded fiercely. Chilo, the Greek tutor, and Lexus, the giant Gaul, were on the benches behind Calgaich and his four rowing mates. Calgaich looked back at them. He caught the same message from their eyes. There was no hopeless resignation in the dark eyes of the Greek and the blue eyes of the Gaul.

"You see what I mean, Calgaich?" Guidd asked out of the side of his mouth.

Calgaich laughed suddenly. "By the gods! What have I done to deserve such a ragtag bunch of followers?" He rolled his eyes upwards. "Lugh of the Shining Spear," he prayed, "be with me in any attempt I might make to escape, for I will fear those who are standing behind me almost as much as the Romans before me!"

Guidd grinned. "The wolf is not yet dead, Bottle Emptier. He rested a little while, with good cause, but he will rise to do battle against the Red Crests when the time comes."

CHAPTER 16

The storm struck the *Neptunus* a week after she had left Massalia. The howling wind came from the south across the Tyrrhenian Sea and seemed to funnel its greatest strength between the Isle of Corsica and the coast of Italy to the east.

The interior of the laboring vessel was a living hell for the toiling oarsmen. They swung the heavy, lead-weighted oars in unison with the resonant clack-clack-clack of the *hortator*'s hammer on the sounding board, which was placed at the after end of the long and narrow walkway that passed between the banks of oarsmen. The clumsy vessel rolled wildly and pitched like a bucking horse, so that at times the oar blades fanned the air before they were plunged deep beneath the waves. Water spurted in through the oar ports and drained down from the deck above through the gratings.

The trireme creaked and groaned in the powerful liquid grip of the seas. The deepening bilge water sloshed back and forth in rhythm with the pitching and rolling of the vessel, and the stench that arose from the bilges filled the nostrils of the laboring galley slaves. Their sobbing cries never ceased, "*Hoooo, yahhh! Hoooo, yahhh! Hoooo, yahhh!*"

Every now and then an oar loom would snap and the lashing end of it would smash back under the extended arms of the oarsmen to crush in their chests and ribs. Whenever this happened, the bank of rowers behind the broken oar would have the injured oarsmen hurled back against their oar, thus breaking the discipline of their own stroking. Crewmen rushed to the broken oar and cut loose the injured, the dying and the dead. The broken oar was shoved through the oar port and the injured slaves

227

who could not be placed at another oar were dropped into the bilges where they soon drowned in the stinking water.

A grandfather wave swept the trireme from stem to stern and carried most of the seamen with it, and injured Aulus, the Greek sailing master. The laboring ship swung broadside to the wind and began to wallow, taking green water over her sides, which soon swept the decks clear of men and fittings.

Tribune Ulpius Claudius came down into the hold of the ship. "She'll soon sink in these seas, *hortator!*" he shouted against the creaking din of the hold. "Can you take command, Perus?"

Perus shook his shaven head. The steady, inexorable clacking of his hammer went on. "I can't leave my post, Tribune, or we'll lose complete control of the ship!"

"You fool! If no one can take charge of the ship, there'll be no need for your damned oars!"

Twenty years of Roman naval discipline showed on the set face of the Sicilian. He would drown at his sounding board before he would leave it. "I am no seaman, Tribune," he said. "I am the *hortator* and no more."

"This might be our chance, Cunori!" Calgaich gasped out.

Cunori looked startled. "We can't get free of the chains, Calgaich."

"They'll cut you loose quickly enough when you volunteer to save their damned ship for them. They need seamen. Let no one get ahead of us in this matter."

"Tribune!" Cunori shouted above the din. "I am a seaman, and once master of my own ship in the channel!"

Ulpius pointed at the Numidian slave. "Cut him loose!" he commanded.

"I'll need seamen!" Cunori added.

"Take whom you will!" the tribune cried, "only save this ship!"

The full force of the wind caught at the captives when they reached the deck. The *artemon,* or foresail, streamed in shreds. Both triangular topsails were gone, blown out from their bolt ropes. The square mainsail was bellied out, as taut as a sheet of painted tin.

Cunori made his way aft to the steering position, and

shoved aside the marine who had taken over when the helmsman had been washed overboard. "Relay my commands to the *hortator*, Chilo!" he shouted at the Greek tutor. "Lutorius, get any spare sails up on deck! Can any of you steer this tub? You, Loarn? Good! Take over. Don't let her broach to once we bring her around into the wind! Chilo! Have that baldheaded Sicilian *hortator* bring her head into the wind! Calgaich! Get down that mainsail! Guidd! Go below and check for any major leaks! Niall! Get below with some men and bring up any spare oars you can find. Get moving, damn you, or you'll sink in this stormy chamberpot the Romans call a sea!"

It was touch and go as the experienced Venetus fought with all his skill to gain control of the clumsy trireme. The straining oars slowly brought the vessel around to head into the wind so that she began taking green water over her bow instead of her weather side.

Niall and his helpers hauled half a dozen oars up onto the deck and under Cunori's instructions lashed them together. Cunori swiftly fashioned a sea anchor by using a spare topsail, which he attached to the bundle of oars. The sea anchor was dropped over the plunging bow and immediately streamed out to help hold the vessel's head into the wind.

Guidd came up on deck. "The ram has partly broken loose, Cunori!" he yelled above the howling of the wind and the crash of the boarding seas. "A plank has split on the larboard bow and she's taking green water into the forehold!"

Cunori looked at Calgaich. "Can you stop the leak, *fian?*" he asked.

Calgaich shrugged. "I can try," he said. He turned. "Lexus! Give me a hand!"

The huge Gaul followed Calgaich to the bows. They stood knee-deep in the water while Lexus held onto Calgaich as he leaned over the larboard side. The bronze ram's head had turned a little to the starboard side after the fastenings had loosened, and in so doing had sprung a larboard plank. Lexus drew Calgaich back. Calgaich looked into his streaming face. "It's bad, Gaul," he said. "If we don't cover it, we'll go down like a stone within the hour."

The men worked quickly under Calgaich's directions. They used a spare sail and fastened ropes to the four corners. Lexus held onto Calgaich as he let himself down on the precarious footing of the ram. The trireme seemed to be plunging deeper, what with the extra weight of the water rising within her hull. Every third wave swept over Calgaich's head as he worked, and had it not been for the strength of Lexus, Calgaich would have been swept away from the ship and lost in the spray and spume astern.

Calgaich looped the ropes on the bottom of the spare sail under the ram as the trireme rose sluggishly to meet the cresting seas. The lower ropes were drawn back on the starboard side and under the hull while the upper ropes were drawn back on the larboard side so that the sail crept slowly over the gap between the planks.

Calgaich grinned up into the bearded face of the Gaul. "It might work," he shouted. The next wave struck him on the back. He lost his footing on the ram. The surging of the vessel threw Lexus to one side. He lost his grip on Calgaich. Calgaich plunged under the surface of the water. He rose to the surface, gasping for air. He was swept aft next to the side of the trireme and the ranks of steadily dipping oars. He caught at the last oar and slid down toward the blade. The oar just ahead of it swung back and hit him on the back of the head. He seemed to be looking into a dim haze as his senses reeled. His grip weakened.

Cairenn had been watching in terror from the small window of her cabin. She could remain still no longer. Quickly she came out and stripped her clothing off as Lexus screamed at her to return to safety. She ignored him and snatched up a line that was fastened to a cleat. Cairenn dived cleanly over the side into a great wave, then surfaced and began swimming strongly toward Calgaich. The seamen watched in wonder as she passed a line about his chest and fastened it. She gestured wildly for someone to pull him in just as he lost his grip on the oar. The last thing he remembered was looking into a great pair of emerald-hued eyes just before he drifted astern.

Quickly the men worked to pull him over the rail and then sent the line out into the roaring sea for Cairenn to wind about her waist. Gasping, she was pulled over the side to where Calgaich lay. As soon as she caught her breath, she moved to his side, but Lexus pushed her away. "Go back to your cabin, woman. He has no more need of you." She gave Calgaich one last glance before pulling her clothes around her and leaving him to the mercy of the guards. It was enough for now that he was alive.

"He'll live," the quiet voice said from out of a dense fog. Calgaich opened his eyes to look into those of Fomoire. He was lying on the deck of the trireme. "I didn't know they had sea nymphs watching out for me in these enemy waters," he murmured. He grinned.

Fomoire stood up and held onto a stay to steady himself. "It was the Ordovician woman, *fian*. Your *cumal*."

Calgaich nodded. He closed his eyes again. He felt ashamed that he had not thought about Cairenn for a long time.

The *Neptunus* was riding easier under the skilled hands of Cunori. The wind seemed to have lost some of its power. Calgaich sat up. Tribune Ulpius Claudius stood beside Cunori. A file of tough-looking Roman marines were watching the captives who had saved the ship under the orders of Cunori. Centurion Montanas stood with folded arms, looking down at Calgaich.

"You saved my ship, Venetus. For that I owe you much," Aulus said to Cunori.

"My freedom, and that of my mates?" Cunori smiled.

The Greek shook his head. "Yours, possibly, at least in the future, but not theirs."

"You'll need them to handle the ship until she reaches Ostia, master."

The Greek nodded. "That's fair enough. I am sorry that I can't help them any more than that. At least they'll be off the oars."

"With one exception," Ulpius put in.

They dragged Calgaich to his feet and hustled him below. The oarsmen on his bench did not stop rowing while the chains were again made fast to the bench and the oar. Calgaich placed his hands on the oar. He listened for a few seconds to the clacking of the *hortator*'s hammer. Then he began to pull in rhythm with the others. "*Hoooo, yahhh! Hoooo, yahhh! Hoooo, yahhh!"* The sobbing breath was wrenched from his throat as he swung the heavy oar.

The prisoners stood chained on the deck of the *Neptunus* as a bireme towed her into the harbor at Ostia. Even Calgaich was awed at the sight of the great port city of fifty thousand inhabitants, which was situated at the mouth of the Tiber River. The bright sun shone on the white red-roofed buildings that spread up the slopes behind the harbor. It reflected from the blue waters of the sea. Everywhere there were ships and smaller water craft. There were naval biremes and triremes, as well as smaller, single-banked galleys, and sturdy, round-hulled merchant ships. A huge grain ship, in from Egypt, was all of one hundred and eighty feet long.

Lutorius pointed out the small island, surmounted by a tower, that lay off the twin harbor moles. "Manmade, Calgaich. Nobody builds like the Romans. If they need water and there is no river or lake, they bring it to the city on aqueducts. If there are no roads, they build them. Here they needed an island, so they built it. They steeped great stones in cement and dumped them into the sea until they had an island. They couldn't get ships up the Tiber, so they built a city. There wasn't much of a harbor here, so they made one. That was in the time of Claudius. The harbor was exposed too much to the open sea, so they built two great moles on either hand. Some say they are over two thousand feet long.

"The new harbor brought great prosperity to the city of Rome. Ostia is called the 'lung' of Rome. Ships come here from all over the known world, laden with cargoes of many kinds. That big merchantman you see there is probably loaded with Gaulish wheat. Those two smaller ones may be loaded with sand from Egypt."

"For building purposes, *calo?*"

Lutorius shook his head. "For the arena, barbarian."

"Don't they have enough sand in Rome?"

"They do, but it's not as absorbent as that from Egypt."

The sluggish *Neptunus* was eased between the ends of the huge curved moles and into the outer harbor. Slowly she moved into one of the inner harbors and was moored to a stone quay. The thick and acrid stench of animal droppings drifted on the fresh wind. The sound of animals could be heard.

"That's where they unload the animals for the Games," Lutorius explained. "Elephants, lions, leopards, wild boars, crocodiles, wolves, wild dogs and bears come in by the shiploads."

"And men," Calgaich added quietly.

Lutorius looked into Calgaich's eyes. "There is always the chance that a man might please the mob and be given his freedom."

"How much of a chance, *calo?* You're a gambler. Tell me."

There was no answer from Lutorius.

Cunori came to them after the ship was moored. "I'll not be going with you," he said quietly. "I've saved my own life. The Romans seem to be short of good seamen. It seems as though I'm more valuable here than I would be in the arena."

Fomoire approached the Venetus. "Will you stay in this area?" he asked in a low voice.

"I think so. There is always work to be done on these Roman tubs, setting up their rigging, mending sails, or caring for the small private vessels of the influential people of Ostia and Rome. Look, there is one such vessel there, so the Greek told me. It is owned by a senator who loves the sea; a strange feeling for a Roman."

The small craft was strange looking, at least for a Roman port. She was low in the water and very long for her beam. She had a single mast set amidships and a small cabin at her stern. She had a beautiful sheer line along which was a row of oar ports to be used from the deck.

Calgaich narrowed his eyes. She had some resemblance to a *birlinn* such as he had often sailed himself at home in Albu.

"No Roman ever built that craft," Guidd said.

"She's Greek-built," the sailing master of the trireme put in from behind them. "I ordered her built for a senator two years ago. She's called the *Lydia* and belongs to Rufus Arrius Niger."

Calgaich showed no emotion on his face.

"He needs a skipper for her," Aulus added. "Not long ago, before the senator left here for Britannia, he asked me to look around for a good man. A northern barbarian seaman, he insisted." Aulus placed a hand on Cunori's shoulder. "You saved my ship, Venetus. As a seafaring man, you'll know what that means to me. I'll put in a good word to the senator for you, if you like."

Cunori looked strangely at Calgaich. There was something going on about which he was not aware. Calgaich nodded slightly.

"Well, Venetus?" the Greek asked.

Cunori nodded. "I'd like that."

The Greek smiled. "Consider it done." He walked aft to bid goodbye to Quaestor Lucius Sextillius.

"Well?" Cunori asked Calgaich.

Guidd looked about quickly. "Rufus Arrius Niger is grandfather to Calgaich, on his mother's side."

Cunori's face fell for an instant, as though he had been betrayed. He smiled quickly. "You jest, eh, wolf?"

Calgaich shook his head. "My Roman blood means nothing to me, Cunori. If I could drain it from my veins I'd gladly do so."

"Yes," Cunori murmured, "I believe you would."

"That craft," Niall, the Selgovae, put in. "Could she outrun any Roman ship in these waters?"

Cunori eyed the vessel judiciously. "Aye, she could, with some changes in her rigging and perhaps another sail or two. If the mast were stepped farther forward, say, and given some rake, it might give her a few extra knots."

"Beyond the Pillars of Hercules," Calgaich murmured.

"Perhaps in time," Fomoire said.

Calgaich gripped Cunori's hand just before the prisoners were marched off the ship and into the tender care of a *turma* of wild-looking Mauretanian auxiliary cavalry. Calgaich looked back once as they were marched off along the quay. Morar stood at the end of the quay, with Bronwyn close beside her. The sun shone on their golden hair. Morar was looking entranced toward the city. She did not see Calgaich. He turned his head, unaware that Cairenn had been watching him from behind Morar and Bronwyn. It was the first time that Cairenn had seen Calgaich since she had rescued him, and until now she had not known if he were alive or dead after his ordeal with the god of the sea.

Decrius Montanas met the group of captives from the trireme at the foot of the mole. One side of the road was lined for a long distance by files of prisoners chained together. Calgaich and his mates were chained to the end of the column. A whip cracked. The long column began to march to the east, on the last leg of the prisoners' march to Rome and the arena.

The hot sun beat down upon the land. Often the prisoners were pushed off the road by long lines of wagons and carts. The road followed the course of the yellow Tiber, and now and then the river itself could be seen, beyond the convolutions of the ground, with the sun bright upon the water.

The entourage of Quaestor Lucius Sextillius passed the column of prisoners. Calgaich looked up. Cairenn was riding in the last cart. Their eyes met as she passed. Calgaich strained to tell her with his eyes what his lips could not. His throat grew thick with emotion. She held out a slim hand toward him and had it slapped down by one of the servants. Calgaich watched the cart until it was out of sight. The gods be with her, he thought.

Guidd looked sideways at Calgaich. "She saved your life at sea. If she had hesitated an instant you would have been gone."

Calgaich nodded. "I know."

"She should have been a man. By the gods, how she fought with the Spear of Evicatos at the *mansio* at Luguvalium! I could not believe it. Aye, she has the heart and soul of a man!"

"No," Calgaich said quietly. "She has the heart and soul of a woman. I thank the gods for that, old hound."

"Fortunate for you, Calgaich, to be loved by two such women."

"Cairenn? Morar? Morar loves no one but herself." Calgaich spat.

"I was thinking rather of Bronwyn."

Fomoire shook his head. "Unfortunate, the man who is loved by two such women."

"Listen to him!" Lutorius jeered.

Guidd shrugged. "Among our people a man can have more than one wife."

Fomoire looked at him. "Does that solve the problem, woodsman?"

Guidd laughed. "Not for *me*, priest! I want nothing to do with them. The woods and hills are my women."

Lutorius grinned. "How does one go about that?" he asked curiously.

"Your mind is always at waist level, *calo*," Calgaich put in.

"What else is there in life?"

The prisoners could sense Rome, long before they neared the outskirts of the great city. Weary and dispirited as they were, they could raise their heads to see the late-afternoon sun shining on the marble of the buildings covering the fabled Seven Hills. The traffic became much heavier along the Ostian Road. Carts and drays, litters and chariots poured to and from the city. Little or no attention was paid to the column of trudging prisoners by passersby.

"We'll be just a commodity in Rome," Lutorius explained, "like olives, corn, wine, hides or salt. Products for the blood market of the Flavian Amphitheatre or the Circus Maximus. This damned city, with all her beauty and pomp, thrives like a vampire on the blood of men and wild animals. Still, if a man shows up well in the arena, he might be given his freedom and possibly allowed to fight as a freedman gladiator."

"And die anyway," Chilo grunted.

"Sure! Sure! But a top-ranked gladiator gets the pick of the best foods, wines and women."

"The pick of the whores, you mean," Chilo said.

Lutorius leered. "You may be learned in the matter of letters and books, Greek, but you know nothing of the patrician women in Rome. Some of the best of them, in the highest of places, are not against having a hairy, big-balled gladiator in bed with them."

"From what I've heard, patrician women consider it fashionable to be unfaithful to their husbands," Fomoire added. "It is truly said—this is the city of blood and whores."

The column turned off the road, within a mile of the Ostian Gate, and plodded across the dusty fields toward the Tiber.

"What the hell is this?" Lexus demanded.

Lutorius shrugged. "You saw the Perfumed Pig breaking his rounded little ass to get into the city ahead of us, didn't you? By now he's soaking in the baths, with his women safely tucked away in his villa. Tonight he'll probably dine like a Persian king, perhaps have a virgin boy for dessert, then get a good night's sleep. But he'll be up at dawn, be dressed in his official toga, and then ride out here to meet us, so that he can return into the city by morning light, leading us like a conqueror, so that all Rome may see his triumph."

"But, we haven't had water or food," the Gaul complained.

Lutorius jerked a thumb toward the yellow-hued river. "There's your water. You might find your food there, too, if you're unlucky enough," he said mysteriously. He grinned.

The *calo* was right. The prisoners rushed toward the river when they were unchained from each other. Some of them stopped short as they saw the polluted waters. The great Cloaca Maxima of Rome, the main sewer, and many other sewers of the city emptied their wastes into the river to be carried down to the Tyrrhenian Sea.

Calgaich turned away from the water. He looked into the masklike face of Decrius Montanas. What the centurion saw on Calgaich's face, however, was a mask similar to his own, showing no emotions, although he knew his prisoner was just as thirsty as those others who now lay belly-flat beside the polluted river, drinking in the fouled waters as though they came from a clear mountain stream.

While Decrius Montanas rode into the city, the prisoners sat on the dusty ground, surrounded by the hardfaced Mauretanians. After dark a cart came out with water, wine and food for the escort. They built fires on the higher part of the bank, so that they might see the prisoners better. They began to cook their food. The firelight reflected from the many eyes of the captives as they watched the cavalrymen eat and drink.

Calgaich lay on the ground. He watched the Mauretanians. "A handful of Novantae, armed only with dirks, could creep up on them in the darkness, and wipe out every damned one of them," he murmured.

"In Caledonia, or Britannia," a young Pict said out of the darkness. "I know . . ."

"You're young to have had such an experience," Calgaich suggested. "It has been many years since the Picts have raided south of the Great Wall."

"But, *you* have, eh, Novantae?"

Calgaich nodded. "A few times."

The Pict looked about himself. "Such modesty!"

Guidd, Lutorius, Fomoire and Niall eyed the young cockerel. He was treading on dangerous ground.

"How are you called?" Calgaich asked politely.

"Girich, son of Aengus, Novantae. And you?"

Calgaich narrowed his eyes. "Calgaich, son of Lellan."

"Not Calgaich the Swordsman?" The Pict grinned. "How did they get *you* into the net?"

Calgaich shrugged. "We had a little disagreement."

"Girich?" Guidd asked. "That's a familiar name to me."

The Pict nodded. "I was fostered by my uncle of that name. Girich the Good Striker, as he is known throughout my country."

"And your father is Aengus of the Broad Spear?" Guidd persisted.

"That is so. The most famous of the war chiefs in my country." The Pict spat dryly to one side, and wiped his mouth with the back of a hand. He eyed Calgaich. "It is too bad that you can't ever test your blade against that of my uncle. I am afraid you'd lose your famed reputation, Novantae."

A picture formed slowly within the haze of Calgaich's memory—an area of trampled snow, with gaunt ring stones standing sentinel about it, and the sudden down-flashing of the magnificent Sword of Evicatos as it sheared the head of Girich the Good Striker clean from its body. He saw again the head, resting on one of the bloodstained ring stones, with its sightless eyes looking toward the distant, misty hills.

"Is that not so, Novantae?" the cocky Pict asked.

"He fought well, and he died well," Calgaich murmured, as though to himself. "What more can a warrior ask at the end?"

The Pict looked about himself. "What the hell is the matter with him?" he demanded. "What is this talk of fighting and death?" He stood up and looked down at Calgaich. "Are you saying that you killed my uncle?"

Calgaich looked up. "It was a fair fight, young one. He championed your father. He lost."

The blood rushed into Girich's tattooed face. "By the gods! You lie, Novantae!"

Instinctively the prisoners around the two men moved quickly out of the way, leaving Calgaich seated on the ground at the feet of the tall young Pict.

"Did you say I lied, Pict?" Calgaich asked softly.

"You heard me, Novantae!"

"There are others here who can verify what I have said."

"Were *they* there? No! I can see it in your face! It's only *your* word!"

"And you insist that I lie?"

"Why is Calgaich so calm?" Niall whispered to Guidd.

Guidd shrugged. "I don't know. At any other time, or place, that loud-mouthed Pict would be lying dead on the ground by now with a broken back."

Girich reached out with a foot. He poked it against Calgaich's side. "I say again, you lie."

Calgaich got up slowly. His chains jangled together as he did so. He smiled a little. Suddenly his big hands shot out to grip the Pict by the front of his ragged tunic. He jerked Girich close to himself and stared into his eyes. "You damned young fool," he hissed. "Do you want to make a spectacle of yourself in front of those grinning Mauretanians? They'd like that. No, young Girich, this is not the time or the place for us to settle any differences we may have." He shoved the Pict backward and then crouched a little with his hands outheld. "It was a fair fight. He fought well. He died well. That is the truth. If you deny that again, then you must attack, and I'll kill you."

For a moment Girich hesitated. By the gods, he wanted to attack, but there was something in the cold gray eyes of the Novantae that held him back. He looked away, turned to look at Calgaich again, then walked off. The jingling of his chains died in the distance.

CHAPTER 17

Lutorius's forecasting of Quaestor Lucius Sextillius's re-appearance early in the morning, ready for his self-planned "triumphal" entry into Rome, had been right in every respect save one—he had *not* tucked all of his women safely away in his villa on the Viminal Hill. For in the morning, as the quaestor came forth carried on a litter of polished wood and ivory, he was followed by a second litter bearing Morar. She looked like a queen of the Britons, so splendid and regal did she appear.

Fomoire scratched within his ragged tunic. "I knew it," he murmured to Calgaich. "She'd never miss such an opportunity to make herself known in Rome the first day she is here. By all the gods, she's gulled that stupid quaestor into letting her come along with him. Who'd look at the Perfumed Pig, when there's that splendid woman riding in the litter behind his?"

The prisoners were kicked to their feet and rechained together into their column. They shuffled and jingled back toward the road, with the cracking reports of the whips just behind them. The long, dusty column fell in behind the two litters and entered the cavernous mouth of the Ostian Gate.

The litters had passed on just ahead of the prisoners into the narrow street beyond the gate castle. "Look at the little prick," Lutorius growled. He jerked his head toward the quaestor. "You'd think he rated a triumph, such as the oldtime generals were granted by the Senate."

"How did they rate such an honor?" Fomoire asked.

"I don't know all the conditions, but they had to be commander-in-chief of a victorious force, the enemy must have been decisively defeated, and Roman casualties must

241

have been slight. At least five thousand of the enemy must have been killed."

"You're jesting," Fomoire suggested.

"Look at the Perfumed Pig! Don't you think he rates that?" Lutorius grinned.

Burly servants of the quaestor walked ahead of the two litters, motioning with their staves toward the people who filled the narrow street. "Stand aside! Stand aside!" they cried loudly. "Make way for the Honorable Quaestor of Britannia! Make way for Quaestor Lucius Sextillius! Clear the way there! The famed quaestor has just returned from Britannia with slaves for the arena! Make way! Make way!"

The streets were filled with people who were pushing their way through the crowds or standing in front of the many small shops that formed the lower floors of towering buildings, some of which were six and seven stories high. The mingled odors of cooking food, cheap wine, human wastes and stale perspiration hung between the tall-fronted structures. Bluish smoke arose from cooking braziers and from the street corner altars. Artisans hammered and sawed in their cubicles of shops. The constant tinkling of metalsmith's hammers mingled with the loud and constant hum of human voices. The people parted just in front of the flourished staves of the servants and then flowed back together again just as soon as the column passed.

Little attention was paid to the prisoners or to the quaestor for that matter, but the crowd did not ignore Morar. The eyes of the Roman men and women followed her as she sat boldly erect in her litter, which was borne by eight brawny Nubian slaves. Her golden hair and great blue eyes were a startling contrast to the black-skinned Nubians and the dark-haired and dark-eyed Roman women of the streets.

"Flava Coma! Flava Coma!" some of the grinning street women called after Morar.

Morar looked proudly back at the women, who obviously must be admiring her golden hair. Quaestor Sextillius turned his bald head sharply to one side or the other and stared imperiously at the shouting women.

"Flava Coma?" Calgaich queried. "Yellow Hair? What's irritating the Perfumed Pig about that, Lutorius?"

Lutorius grinned. "It means 'Yellow Hair,' sure enough, but it has another meaning here in Rome. The whores usually dye their hair yellow, and to yell *'Flava Coma'* at a respectable woman is to insult her."

"They *dare* to do this in the presence of the 'Great One' up there?" Calgaich grinned back at Lutorius.

"The Roman mob can't be handled by *anyone*. The mob can say and do damned well anything they like and get away with it, for the most part."

"Does Sextillius have money, *calo?*" Calgaich asked.

Lutorius nodded. "A great deal. The family money is said to be controlled by the quaestor's elder sister, the Lady Antonia. She is the mother of that pouter pigeon Tribune Ulpius Claudius. She financed the senatorship of her husband Mucius Claudius, a spineless jellyfish, so that she could get herself a mouthpiece in the Senate. It was she who got Ulpius Claudius his appointment as tribune, on the long chance that he could work his way up to tribune *legatus legionis*." Lutorius chuckled. "That stupid sonofabitch couldn't handle a *decuria* of Greek auxiliaries in a wineshop brawl."

"What's so political about such a position?"

Lutorius glanced sideways at Calgaich. "Are you jesting? How do you think your own grandfather got to be a senator? To be promoted to the rank of tribune *legatus legionis* automatically carries with it a seat in the Senate."

"It's beginning to make sense now," Fomoire put in.

Calgaich looked at the Druid. "What do you mean?"

"Simply this: Antonia already has control of one seat in the Senate—her husband's. She had her son appointed tribune on the frontier, with the idea that he might be able to work his way up to the rank of tribune *legatus legionis*, and then he could retire from the legion as a senator. That, in time, would give her two seats in the Senate. By backing Sextillius in his pursuit of political power, she might in time get him a seat in the Senate as well. Thus, if the dice fell right, she'd have control of three seats in the Senate."

Calgaich nodded. "It makes sense."

"There's one catch however," Lutorius said. He jerked a thumb toward Morar, resplendent in her glittering litter.

"Sister Tonia will find *her* between herself and the Perfumed Pig."

As the prisoners progressed toward the center of the city, it became noticeable that the people in the streets were not standing about the shops, or idling on the street corners. They were moving in the same direction as the column. The street ahead of the litters was filled wall to wall with pushing, jostling people. Each side street contributed more people until, as far as the eye could see ahead, the street was a solid mass of bobbing heads.

"What's the great attraction?" Guidd asked Lutorius.

"You'll see soon enough, woodsman."

Then, as the street curved more to the north and east, it became wider, and in the distance a colossal structure many stories high. The fitful morning wind was moving the vast parti-colored awning that covered the immense opening in the top of the structure, so that it almost looked like a gigantic galley under sail.

Calgaich stared at it in astonishment. "What is it, Lutorius?"

"The Flavian Amphitheatre," Lutorius replied.

The amphitheatre loomed up before the prisoners, towering high above them and the masses of people who struggled toward the wooden palisade that encircled the structure. They were pouring into the many entryways— a constant stream of sweating, cursing, hurrying humans, eager for the bloody attractions that drew them there.

The column of prisoners was forced to a stop. There was no way the servants of the quaestor could force their path through the mass of crowded humanity. Lucius stood up on his swaying litter, a ridiculous-looking figure, despite his snow-white toga and the cosmetics on his face, with his naked head, rounded paunch and short, pudgy legs. He frantically waved his stubby little arms.

"Look at the clown on the litter!" a man called out.

"Look at the golden whore on the other one!" a woman cried.

"Why, damn you all!" Lucius shouted hysterically. "I'll have you in the arena yourselves!"

"Go fornicate with yourself, baldy!" a grinning boy shouted.

"Get him!" Lucius commanded his servants.

"Up your ass, pervert!" the boy yelled. He vanished into the surging crowd.

The crowd swayed against the quaestor's litter and he fell headfirst from it in among the people. His short, chubby legs stuck up over him. A dirty hand reached over the heads of the people closest to the quaestor and gave him a firm, hard goosing. The people nearby roared with laughter.

"You see what I mean?" Lutorius said to Calgaich.

Centurion Decrius Montanas instructed some of the guards to stand by Morar and then worked his way toward the screaming quaestor. Sextillius was out of sight now, somewhere beneath the trampling feet of the crowd.

A sound suddenly overwhelmed everyone. It was a sustained roaring, almost like the howling of a pack of wolves in the snow-covered forests of Caledonia, Calgaich thought. He looked toward the amphitheatre, the source of the sound.

"The roar of the crowd," Lutorius murmured.

They were chanting something. Calgaich could not, at first, make out the words. The roaring sound came again. *"Verbera!* Strike! *Iugula!* Slay!"

Calgaich looked at Lutorius. "Are they fighting in the arena already?" he asked in amazement.

Lutorius nodded. "The games start at dawn and usually end about dusk, although I have been in there when the games went on into the torchlit night."

The roaring sound welled up from within the great bowl and burst forth over the surrounding area. *"Habet! Habet! Habet!* That's got him! That's got him! That's got him!"

"Some poor bastard has gotten it, barbarian," Lutorius explained.

"Hoc habet! Hoc habet! Hoc habet! Now he's got it! Now he's got it! Now he's got it!"

The savage roaring sickened Calgaich. He turned his head and looked into the eyes of the men standing behind him. Their eyes were on the colossal amphitheatre. There was no light in them, merely a hopelessness that sickened Calgaich almost as much as the bloodthirsty mob.

The crowds hurrying toward the entryways had begun to thin out. Decrius Montanas upended the quaestor and stood him on his feet. His toga was covered with street filth. The cosmetics on his face had begun to run with the heat and flow of perspiration.

"You are all right now, sir," Montanas said.

The quaestor slapped the centurion across his face. "You privy maggot!" he screamed. "You pig-shit! You after-birth of a whore's mistake! Where were you when that mob attacked me!" His face was contorted and spittle flew from his mouth.

Red plumes and spear blades suddenly showed above the heads of the people. The crowd parted to let a tall man in armor pass through. He came to a halt before the quaestor and eyed the disheveled appearance of the little man. "You're late in coming, Lucius Sextillius," he said in a cold, hard tone.

Lucius smiled weakly. "Aemilius Valens! How good to see you, Procurator."

The procurator was a handsome man with blond hair and eyes that were almost a golden color. His lips were thin, and curled slightly, as he looked at the pompous little quaestor.

"Aemilius Valens, cousin and favorite of the emperor Valentinian and procurator of the Games," Lutorius murmured out of the side of his mouth. "It's said that he's a stud of the first order, and that most of the women of Rome would give one of their tits to be able to sleep with him."

"Before or after?" Calgaich asked. He grinned.

"They say he's got a cock as long as his forearm."

"He wouldn't get far with a twig like that in my country, *calo*."

Lutorius grinned back at Calgaich.

"The quaestor is afraid of him," Fomoire whispered. "He looks like he's going to wet a leg any moment now."

"Why am I late, Procurator?" Lucius asked nervously. "I don't understand."

The procurator gestured toward the prisoners. "I need this arena fodder for this afternoon."

"But Aemilius Valens, they are *mine!* I have brought many of them from Britannia, and others from Gaul. It was my intention, that is, I had planned . . ." His voice died away as he saw the hard look in the procurator's eyes.

"These prisoners are the property of the emperor. I had intended to give them a few week's training before turning them into the arena, but we ran out of arena fodder a few weeks back. No new shipments of any amount have come in. Oh, a few Scythians, some Thracians, a handful of mangy Greeks, and a dozen or so Illyrians. Most of them died this morning, without giving any kind of a show. That mob in there is restless, Quaestor, and I have no intention of letting them get out of hand." The procurator was speaking to the quaestor, but his eyes were on Morar. "*Roma Dea,*" he murmured. Where did you find this golden goddess, Lucius?"

The quaestor smiled. He knew the character and sexual voraciousness of the procurator. Besides, he was only interested in women. He was no connoisseur of the many varieties of sex acts, and probably had *never* read that classic, the *Book of Elephantis.*

"My betrothed, Aemilius Valens. Morar, daughter of Cuno, and a hostage from the wild northern Novantae."

But Valens was not listening. He approached Morar. "Welcome then, to the Imperial City, Goddess!" he cried.

Morar smiled and extended her hand to the procurator.

"It is said that there are many goddesses of love— Venus and the others—aye, but in my rather short experience as a soldier in Britannia, I had not learned that the wild Britons had a living goddess of love in their midst— a veritable living legend."

"Listen to him," Fomoire whispered.

"We are anxious to get home to my villa, Aemilius Valens," Lucius put in. "It is hot. We've had trouble. The sun will soon burn the pale white northern skin of my betrothed."

Valens cut him short with an imperious wave of a hand. "You're right, Lucius! But you should have had an awning over her litter. To expose such a pale-skinned, golden treasure to our cruel Roman sun was carelessness indeed."

"Then with your leave we'll be on our way."

Valens stepped back and looked down the long line of prisoners. "What have we here!"

Decrius Montanas came forward and saluted. "Most of them are Britons or Gauls, sir. The wild fighting men of the north."

"Good! They always fight well, no matter the odds. Losers always, but, as a rule, fighters to the end."

The procurator eyed the first rank of prisoners. He studied Calgaich. "This one," he said over his shoulder to the centurion. "What is he?"

"Calgaich mac Lellan, sir. A chieftain's son of the Caledonian Novantae, a tribe that has never been subjugated."

"Is that so? Then what is he doing here?" Valens smiled a little at his own joke. "I'll take him, of course." He raised his head and looked along the long line.

"But, Your Honor," the centurion began, instantly stopped by a stern look from Valens.

"How many prisoners do you have here, Centurion?" the procurator asked.

"About two hundred and fifty, sir."

"I'll take them all."

"But, Procurator," Lucius faltered.

Valens turned. He smiled a little, but it was not a very friendly smile. "Well, Lucius Sextillius?"

"I personally selected some of the prisoners myself. For the Games, which I hope to sponsor within the next few months. I had thought that they would make a good showing for me."

Valens was amused. "In your quest for political fame?"

"Well, one knows how it is here in Rome."

The procurator shook his head. "No, Quaestor. These are prisoners of the state."

"But they are not prepared for the arena!"

Valens came closer to Lucius. "Damn you, Sextillius! I don't give a fig for your opinions on the matter. You hear that mob in there!" He gestured toward the amphitheatre. The roaring sound was rising again, an eerie, spine-chilling massing of voices. "They want blood! And *every* day! It is my job to supply that blood!"

"The chief vampire," Fomoire whispered to Calgaich.

Aemilius Valens turned. "I have no more time for this bickering! Damn you, Centurion! Lead those prisoners out!"

"Procurator!" The melodious voice caused Valens to quickly turn his head toward Morar.

Morar smiled winningly. "Surely you can spare the personal prisoners of my betrothed, Procurator? He has gone to great peril and expenses to bring them here to Rome."

Valens was intrigued by her eyes. He had not experienced, as yet, the spell the Caledonian woman could cast upon men, *all* men. . . . He turned toward Sextillius. "Very well! How many of them do you consider to be your personal property, Quaestor?"

"One hundred?" Lucius asked hopefully.

"Impossible!"

"Perhaps seventy-five?"

Valens shook his head.

"Fifty?"

"That will leave me only two hundred."

"Surely that is enough, Procurator? At least for today?" Morar said softly.

Valens glanced sideways at Morar. He saw the fullness of her magnificent breasts, the rounded thighs beneath the thin, almost transparent material of her gown.

"Fifty, Procurator," Morar said. "His choice."

Valens shrugged. "Very well! But what will you do with them now, Quaestor?"

"They are destined for the Ludus Maximus, the state gladiatorial school."

Valens laughed. "You'd take these wild-eyed, long-bladed swordsmen to the Ludus Maximus? Why? To teach them the arts of the Thracian School, or perhaps the *murmillones?* Surely not! These barbarians can be no match for Roman gladiators and swordsmen, even with their own weapons."

"I'd like to get him out into the heather for a little swordplay and bloodletting," Calgaich murmured.

The procurator turned his head quickly and looked into the cold gray eyes of Calgaich. He opened his mouth to speak.

The roaring of the crowd suddenly raised to a new pitch of hysteria. "Procurator," Morar put in sweetly, "you had better hurry. As you said, the mob wants blood every day; it is your job to supply it."

"Take your pick, Lucius," Valens said.

The quaestor nodded to Montanas, who walked slowly along the line, reaching out to tap the shoulders of those he selected—Calgaich, Guidd, Lutorius, Fomoire, Niall, Lexus, Chilo, Loarn, Girich, Conaid, the Little Hound. There were others—several Saxons; a Jute or two; Garth, a Silurian harper and singer of songs; a trio of Picts of the Niduari, one of the tribes of the "Picts of the North"; two brothers of the border Votadini; and a miscellaneous mixture of border Britons, some of whom had deserted the Roman auxiliaries in Gaul. The fifty selected were unchained from the rest of the column.

The Mauretanians cracked their whips. The prisoners destined for the arena obediently shuffled off across the wide, sun-bright street toward the amphitheatre. Calgaich was the only one of the fifty prisoners still standing in the street who turned his head to watch. He knew the men went to their death. They were not too tired to fight—they had the spirit for battle always—but *they were too tired to win*. Morar had saved him from their fate. Morar, with her golden hair and musical voice, had cajoled Valens into allowing Lucius to keep a few prisoners. Calgaich was grateful for that, for the chance to live a little longer before he was taken to the Games. But his destiny seemed to be determined by Morar once again, and that trick of fate he did not trust at all.

"Put it out of your mind, barbarian," Lutorius advised as the last prisoner disappeared into the amphitheatre. "Just thank your gods it's not you this time."

Calgaich turned and looked at the *calo*. "I can't put it out of my mind. I'll never be able to put it out of my mind."

"Then I am sorry for you, barbarian."

The fifty were marched toward a triumphal arch that dominated the street. Nearby was a cone-shaped fountain, spouting a feathery plume of spray which glistened in the bright sunlight. A man came from the direction of the amphitheatre. He wore a cuirass, which shone in the sunlight. He staggered a little in his walk and then recovered. His face was dripping with sweat that had cut tiny channels through the dust on his face. He walked on toward the fountain and then dropped to his knees beside it to plunge his face and forearms into the water.

"A gladiator," Lutorius informed his mates. "That fountain is the Meta Sudans, where the victorious gladiators wash off after their duels."

"How did it go, Thraxus?" a passerby called.

The gladiator raised his streaming face from the water and nodded. "Victory, of course, or I wouldn't be here. My third."

"But you're bleeding, eh?"

Thraxus stood up and thrust a hand up under his *cuirass.* As he felt about a strange look came over his face.

The passerby came close to the gladiator. "What is wrong?" he asked.

Thraxus walked a few uncertain steps and then fell face down flat on the street. Some latecomers hurrying toward the amphitheatre paused for a few seconds to look at the fallen gladiator. "He's done," one of them said. They hurried on.

The prisoners marched past Thraxus. A thin thread of blood had run from under the dead man. The prisoners' feet passed through it.

"Get the cuirass off of him," a bystander said. "We can turn it in at the Ludus Maximus and they'll pay us for it."

Calgaich looked up at the towering facade of the immense bowl that was the Flavian Amphitheatre. Maybe it was his powerful Celtic imagination, but it seemed to him that the smell of blood and death came from that place of hell.

Calgaich felt his anger, dampened for so many long days, being fanned into flame again. "I'm no damned gladiator!" he snarled. "I'm Calgaich, son of Lellan! Grandson of Evicatos the Spearman! A warrior! A *swordsman!*"

Lutorius shrugged. "It's all the same to these Romans, barbarian. The only difference here is that instead of fighting for pay in Hibernia, or patriotically for your tribe in Caledonia, you'll end up fighting for your life, and nothing else, here in Rome."

"Bring on any Roman!" Calgaich sneered.

"You won't find any of the mob in the arena. You'll likely face professionals, like that poor, stupid bastard lying in the dust back there. He didn't even know he had been mortally wounded. You saw that prick Valens back there, marching those poor bastards into the amphitheatre, right off the street and into the arena, likely without time to get a drink and take a leak before they face sudden death."

Calgaich looked at the prisoners closest to him. "That bastard of a centurion selected us for his own reasons, as well as those of the Perfumed Pig. Good! He picked the best of the lot. In so doing, he's joined us together in a common purpose. And I don't have to remind you what that is. From now on, each one of us will hold that allegiance to this group. To the last man . . ."

"And, if there are none of us left alive?" Chilo asked quietly.

Calgaich smiled wryly. "Then we will have died like men."

CHAPTER 18

The huge double gates of the Ludus Maximus, the great gladiatorial school, swung open at a hail from Centurion Decrius Montanas. The prisoners plodded through the gateway and came to a halt. The heavy gates swung closed again with an echoing crash.

The prisoners stood within an immense rectangular quadrangle, surrounded on three sides by many buildings along the fronts of which were fluted columns supporting the red-tiled roofs of open passageways. At the far end of the quadrangle was a large open area with tiers of seats arranged on each side. The floor of the area was covered with sand. Men, whose figures were small to the eye at that distance, moved about on the sand, exercising, or practicing with weapons.

"That training area back there is about half the size of the arena in the Flavian Amphitheatre," Lutorius whispered. "These buildings are the barracks, a headquarters, mess hall, an armory and a hospital. This is the biggest of the four state-operated schools here in Rome."

Calgaich looked about, noting that the "school" had its own large guard detachment. Some guards were in the gate towers and the arena area. Others were patrolling the wall walks.

The prisoners were lined up just outside the headquarters building. Montanas entered the building and then, within a few minutes, reappeared accompanied by a powerfully built Hercules of a man, who seemed to have been hewn from the solid trunk of a weathered and seasoned oak tree. His large, rounded head was shaven, and seemed to sit directly upon his broad shoulders, so short was his muscular neck. His chest was deep and broad. His bare

253

arms stood out from the sides of his body, so thickly layered were they with corded muscles. The whitish cicatrices of old wounds showed on his face, arms and thick thighs. Across his low, broad forehead were the parallel lines of old helmet welts. Still, with all his weight and build, he moved easily on his feet like a huge hunting cat.

"By the gods," Lutorius muttered. "It's Quintus Gaius, one of the greatest gladiators in the history of Rome. The Oak Tree!"

"You know him?" Calgaich asked.

"Shit yes! He was in my maniple of the Fifteenth Apollinaria in Cappadocia. Many's the time we got drunk together. I heard later he had been condemned to the arena for striking an officer. That was years ago."

"You're sure of this?"

"How can I be mistaken? Have you ever seen such a man?"

Calgaich shook his head.

Montanas looked along the line of prisoners. "You have reached the end of your journey here, barbarians. This hero of all Romans is Quintus Gaius, master of the Ludus Maximus, once the greatest gladiator in the history of the Flavian Amphitheatre. Four times he was offered the *rudis*, the wooden sword of honorable retirement from the arena, after three years of service there, and three times he refused it. He carried the palms of victory fifty-two times in the arena during those years of service. He was finally forced to retire by Aemilius Valens, procurator of the Games, upon the direct order of the emperor Valentinian, so that his skills might be taught to others." Montanas turned toward Quintus. "I leave these prisoners in your tender care, gladiator master. You understand, of course, that these men are destined for the Games, which will be sponsored some time later on this summer by the esteemed Quaestor Lucius Sextillius. It is also to be understood that they will fight in the arena with their own weapons and in their own style."

Quintus Gaius nodded. He looked at the prisoners from under beetling brows. His eyes were seemingly as hard as basalt. "A rare lot, Centurion. But, I've had worse, and I've done well with them in the arena. You say they are to be kept together?"

"I understand they are to fight as a unit, with perhaps one or two exceptions."

"Such as?"

The centurion pointed his vine staff at Calgaich. "That one. The tall Caledonian with the proud look about him."

"So? Why?"

Montanas smiled mechanically. "Know you not who he is, Quintus Gaius?" he exclaimed with exaggeration. "No, you would not, of course! That is Calgaich, son of Lellan, known far and wide in Britannia as Calgaich the Swordsman!"

The gladiator master studied Calgaich and nodded. "He has the look of a warrior about him, Centurion."

"Don't turn your back on him, Quintus. He is an untamed wolf."

"I'll remember that. And the other one?"

Montanas pointed at Fomoire. "The weasel there."

"Why?"

"He is a trickster, a soothsayer, and only the gods know what else. He is not to go into the arena."

Quintus nodded.

"Feed them well. Work them hard. They are in your charge. If anything happens to any of them, particularly the wild swordsman, Calgaich, you'll have to answer to the quaestor."

The faintest trace of a smile crossed the scarred features of the big man. "The Perfumed Pig?"

Montanas turned aside as though he had not heard. "I'm off to the baths, Quintus. I've got a thousand miles of dust in my pores." He raised his vine staff in salute and strode toward the gate.

Quintus watched the centurion go. Slowly, ever so slowly, he turned his head to look at his new charges. He walked to the head of the line. His eyes met those of Calgaich, and the tall Celt did not turn away or lower his gaze. There was no expression on Quintus's scarred face. He stepped sideways, then stopped to look at the drink-ruined visage of Lutorius. He eyed the whitish line of the chin strap gall on the *calo*'s jaws. There was no recognition on his face as he looked at his old legion mate.

Quintus paused in front of Guidd. He suddenly looked sideways at Lutorius. "What legion?" he asked quickly.

Lutorius involuntarily snapped to attention. "Twentieth Valeria Victrix, sir!" he barked.

"Not the Drunken Lions!"

"The same, sir!"

Quintus rubbed his jaw. "You seem familiar, somehow. How did you get your nose ruined, eh? In the Twentieth?"

Lutorius was trapped. "No, sir. That was when I was in the Fifteenth Apollinaria."

"At Salata in Cappadocia?"

Lutorius nodded.

Quintus looked more closely at Lutorius. "By Mars! But it can't be! Wasn't it Old Give Me Another who smashed in your beak after the battle at Carrhae?"

"The same, sir."

"The Bottle Emptier!"

"That is so, master."

For a few seconds Quintus studied Lutorius, and then he passed on to pause in front of Fomoire.

"What does all that mean, *calo?*" Calgaich asked out of the side of his mouth.

"Who knows?"

"You say he was condemned to the arena?"

"So I heard."

"Then how did he get the position he has today?"

Lutorius shrugged. "Only the gods may know."

Quintus studied the Druid. "A trickster, eh, barbarian?"

Fomoire bowed his head. "Men call me Fomoire, Your Honor. A healer of the eye sickness. A leech. A juggler. A teller of tales. A worker of simple conjuring tricks. I have some knowledge of the telling of fortunes. A singer of songs. A bard of some skill." His lilting voice died away as he eyed the gladiator master.

Quintus reached out with his huge right paw. He grasped the front of Fomoire's ragged clothing and twisted it into a knot. Slowly, ever so slowly, he raised the Druid up off the ground and then held him out at arm's length. He shook him a little.

"I am not to harm you in any way, trickster, according to that asshole of a centurion who just left here, but, mind you, *I* am master here. If, by any chance, you try any of your trickery while in my charge, you'll suffer for it in rather unpleasant ways, which will leave no outward marks on your body. But, your soul, if you have one, will be scarred for life. You understand, barbarian?"

Fomoire nodded.

The master set him down on the ground. *"Sir!"* he snapped.

"Yes, sir!" Fomoire barked.

Quintus laughed. "You learn quickly, wild man."

The gladiator master walked slowly down the line, pausing here and there, studying certain of the men, and then he returned in front of the line. He placed his huge hands on his hips.

Quintus raised his chin. "There are rules here. This is the Great School. The best of them all. And the hardest. We are proud of our production for the arena. We have our own prison, suitably equipped with leg irons, shackles, branding irons and whips. We have a solitary confinement cell with a ceiling so low a man can't sit up, and so short he can't stretch out his legs. Twenty-four hours in there and you'll kiss a camel's asshole to get out.

"You will be guarded twenty-four hours a day. You will be locked in your cells each night. The food is good. Meat for killing energy and barley because the rich grain covers the arteries with a layer of fat and so helps to prevent a man from bleeding to death from a wound.

"Once you pass your apprentice training and are ready for the arena, girls are brought in to you once a week. It might not be a bad life for most of you at that, compared to your home life. I don't know what the plans are for you Dirty Fifty, but if any of you survive the arena after the quaestor's games, you might very well get to join the professionals and, if you're a winner, you've got Rome by its hairy ass. Money, food, wine and women; women such as none of you have ever seen before. You understand?"

The long line of prisoners nodded.

"Let me hear from you! Dammit! Show me some spirit! Yell with delight! You've made it to the Great School!"

A ragged cheer went up from the Dirty Fifty. The guards who were watching them from the sidelines and the wall walks broke into wide grins.

Quintus held up a ham of a hand. "One more thing. You must take the oath. Raise your right hands. Repeat after me—I will suffer myself to be whipped with rods, burned with fire, or killed with steel if I disobey while here at the Great School."

The oath was duly repeated by the prisoners. Their voices died away.

Quintus looked along the line. His eyes rested on Lexus, the giant Gaul. "You! Come out here!"

Lexus stepped forward with clanking chains.

Quintus beckoned to a guard. "Strike off his chains, Aelius."

The chains jingled on the hard ground. The guard withdrew.

"Here!" Quintus snapped. He pointed at the ground in front of him.

Lexus walked slowly forward and stood face to face with the huge master.

"Your name?" Quintus asked.

"Lexus."

A block of a fist drove out so fast it caught the Gaul unawares. It struck the point of his jaw and drove him flat on his back. He lay there dazed, looking up at the impassive face of Quintus. A slow trickle of blood leaked from the Gaul's mouth.

Quintus leaned forward. "You forgot *sir*," he reminded Lexus. "Get up!"

Lexus staggered to his feet.

"Your name?" Quintus asked again.

"Lexus, sir."

The fist lashed out and again Lexus lay flat on his back, half-stunned.

"I want you to *snap* that out, Gaul!" Quintus roared. "All of you remember that!" He beckoned to the guards. "Take this stinking rabble to the baths. Burn those clothes. Issue them school garb. Take them to the mess hall and have them fed. Then lock them up." He turned on a heel and strode back to his headquarters.

"Lovely man," Chilo murmured.

Bathed, issued fresh clothing, and, fed to the fullest, the prisoners were marched to the barracks as the sun slanted far to the west. As they entered the long, arcaded passageway in front of the building they could hear the cell doors being slammed shut and barred for the night, as the regular students finished their hard day in the practice arena.

"Two to a cell!" the chief guard Aelius called out. "You'll be crowded for a few days, but after the Games this weekend, there will be plenty of room." He grinned.

Calgaich and Lutorius were paired off for the first cell. The door slammed shut behind them. On each side of the cell was a stone shelf upon which was a straw mattress. There was a niche in the wall over each bed, for whatever personal god the occupant favored. A large earthenware jar served as a chamberpot. A very small, barred window opened on the outer wall.

"By the gods!" Lutorius exclaimed. "Look at the girl's names and addresses! Paetina! Lepida! Antonia! Callina! Eunice! The last occupant must have been a real boar!"

"How long do you suppose those names have been there, *calo?*"

Lutorius shrugged. "There might be one or two of them still around, barbarian."

"Do you think you'll ever get to look them up?"

"I can always hope."

There were crudely drawn pictures of naked women scratched on the plastered walls, with exaggerated breasts and hips. Some literate had scratched prayers to his god into the dirty plaster.

"Look here," Lutorius said.

There were other drawings, this time of gladiators in combat. One of them lay on the ground with his left arm extended, forefinger raised from a clenched fist, in the traditional plea for mercy from the arena mob. The victor stood with poised sword, ready for the death thrust into the throat. Over the victor's head had been written "Astacius, 13 wins," while over the head of the vanquished was the inscription "Baccibus, 7 wins." Below Baccibus was a sign: Θ

Calgaich placed a finger on the circular sign. "What does this mean?"

"*Habet,* barbarian."

"*Habet?*"

Lutorius quickly drew a forefinger across his throat. "Killed," he replied quietly.

Lutorius dropped onto one of the bunks. He laced his fingers together at the nape of his neck and looked up at the cobwebbed plaster of the ceiling.

Calgaich sat down on his bed. The wind had shifted with the coming of the dusk. The faint roaring sound of the wild animals penned up in the menagerie near the Praenestine Gate came to him.

"Strange, isn't it, barbarian," Lutorius mused, "that there must be hundreds of men confined in this barracks and yet not a sound can be heard from them? But listen to those wild animals roaring."

Calgaich shook his head. "It's not strange at all, *calo*. The prisoners here in the Great School know something the wild animals do not know. *They know their destiny....*"

CHAPTER 19

Calgaich opened his eyes. The cell was semidark except for the faint gray opening of the barred window. Calgaich sat up and reached over toward Lutorius. His questing hand touched the rough cover of the straw mattress. It was cold. The *calo* wasn't yet back in his cell. Calgaich turned his head quickly. There was a faint sound of movement outside the cell door. He stood up and reached for the heavy chamberpot.

A week had passed since Calgaich and his comrades had been in the Ludus Maximus. Not once had Quintus Gaius made any indication of recognition toward his old legion mate, Lutorius. Even out on the practice arena, where the instructors had begun to put the Dirty Fifty, as they called them, through their preliminary training, there was no sign of recognition from the gladiator master, who sometimes paced the edges of the arena, watching impassively as the training went on. This night, long after dark, when the prisoners had been locked in their cells, a guard had come for Lutorius. That had been hours past.

A key grated in the cell door lock. Calgaich raised the chamberpot. He trusted no one in this place.

The door swung open on creaking hinges.

"Calgaich?" Lutorius whispered. He hiccupped.

"Who's with you?"

"You'll see."

A huge form had filled the semidarkness behind the *calo*. Lutorius swayed a little as he walked into the cell. Calgaich stepped back against the wall beneath the window. The door was locked from the inside. The sour and fruity odor of wine came to Calgaich.

"It's the Oak Tree," Lutorius whispered.

"Put down the chamberpot, barbarian," the gladiator

master requested. "By the gods, I've been hit with all different kinds of weapons, but never with a chamberpot in the hands of a barbarian. I hope it's not full."

Calgaich lowered the pot to the floor.

"Replace it with this," Lutorius suggested. He passed a wine jug to Calgaich. "It's Cyprian. The best." He chuckled. "The Oak Tree does well for himself, eh, barbarian?"

Calgaich did not question the offer. He took the jug and drank deeply. He lowered the jug and nodded in satisfaction as he wiped his mouth. "Like mother's milk, *calo*."

Lutorius and Quintus sat down on the *calo*'s bunk. "Drink your fill," Quintus invited. He held up another jug. "There is plenty for all of us."

"To follow that which you've already downed, sir?" Calgaich queried.

Quintus waved a ham of a hand. "Forget the sir, at least this night."

"I don't want any of your gentle reminders, master."

Quintus grinned. "Oh, that? I do that to impress newcomers. It's part of the business. It's how I hold my job. If I didn't, the procurator of the Games would soon have me out of here."

Lutorius nodded. "Under that hard outer shell old Quintus here is as soft as butter."

"I can believe that," Calgaich agreed dryly. He drank again. The wine *was* good.

"If it were found out that I had been a comrade of Quintus during my legion service in Cappadocia, and he had gone easy on me here in the school because of that, there would have been trouble."

Quintus drank from his jug and then passed it to Lutorius. "Bottle Emptier has told me you're a grandson of Old Give Me Another. He's such a damned liar, I had to hear it from your own lips, barbarian."

Calgaich nodded. "It is so, Quintus."

Quintus shook his head. "Well, the old bastard must have been quite a stud. Does he know you're his grandson, or are you an unknown product of one of his bastards?"

"He was legally married to my grandmother."

"Good for you! I never knew my own father. Some say he was a satyr who crept up on my mother when she was asleep." Quintus grinned.

"More likely a bull," Lutorius suggested.

"Bottle Emptier tells me your grandfather knows you were captured in Caledonia, and did nothing about it."

Calgaich shrugged. "I was a deserter from the auxiliaries —twice. You know what that means."

Quintus nodded. "Don't tell me about it, friend. That's how I ended up in Rome ten years ago."

"I never could figure you out for being a deserter, Oak Tree," Lutorius said.

"I made the mistake of beating the shit out of a prick of a centurion when he called me a coward to cover up one of his own mistakes. I deserted. I was caught. It's as simple as that."

"*You?* You who had enough decorations to cover the front of your cuirass? You who had the honor of bearing the standard of our cohort? You who had been recommended for the *corona civica?*" Lutorius asked.

Quintus shrugged. "That was what saved me from the lash. I was shipped back to Rome with a load of prisoners for the Games—Cappadocians, Syrians, Cilicians and some other mongrels whose origin I never could remember. Most of them were driven, untrained, into the Games and they died there. I was lucky enough to get sent here to the Great School."

"And you became the premier gladiator of all Rome."

Quintus modestly waved a hand.

"Fifty-two victories," Lutorius added.

"A paid killer," Calgaich put in boldly. The wine was getting to him.

"That's right, barbarian," Quintus agreed. "There was only one way out of the arena and that was the victorious way."

"Yet you refused the wooden sword three times."

"Why not? I was like a king. I became rich with the money and jewels that were showered on me. Women in the stands threw their undergarments to me as I paraded around the arena after a victory. You know what that means, barbarian? I had the best of everything. Everything, I tell you! Instead of retiring after twenty years in the legion, with worn-out teeth from chewing stone-hard legion-ration bread, with aching joints from sleeping on the ground in all kinds of weather, with scars of battle on my chest and the marks of the lash on my back, old long before my time, I instead became the commoner king of Rome! Look at me now! I have my own villa just outside the city. I have ten slaves to do my bidding. I am recognized wherever I go. Here, in the Great School, I am like a minor god. My word is law!"

Calgaich leaned back against the stone wall. "But there is nothing you can do for your old legion comrade there, to save him from the arena?"

"And, even if I could, what would the future hold for him?"

"I could follow in the footsteps of the Oak Tree here, barbarian," Lutorius said. He hiccupped as he reached for the bottle.

"How long do you think you'd last?" Calgaich asked.

"Maybe you think I couldn't win victories in the arena?"

"I didn't say that. But it would only be a matter of time. I've seen some of the other students here, some of them half your age and half again as big as you are. You'd be matched against some of them in time."

"Why, damn you! I can take care of myself! Why, in the old Twentieth, aye, and in the old Fifteenth I was the best in the business. Ask Quintus here! Tell him, Oak Tree!"

"You're getting drunk, Bottle Emptier," Quintus said. He placed an arm about Lutorius's shoulders. "You drunken bastard. Remember the good old days? After Carrhae when we were drunk for three whole days? We were only recruits then."

Calgaich studied the scarred face of the master. The faint grayish light from the window shone on the brutish face, seemingly devoid of all emotion. All the other times Calgaich had heard him speak his voice had the rasp of a hoof file in it. But now, it was different. Quintus seemed genuinely affected by seeing once again his old comrade of the Fifteenth Apollinaria.

"Fifteen years ago." Lutorius hiccupped. He slid sideways from the protection of Quintus's arm and fell onto the floor. Quintus picked him up as though he were a child and placed him on the mattress. He pulled the rough blanket up over him.

Quintus turned and then sat down on the bunk next to Calgaich. "He's one of the best, barbarian."

Calgaich nodded. "I know."

"He might last a few months in the arena."

"Possibly."

"But you, it is said you're a master with your own weapons. Bottle Emptier has told me of that."

"He talks too much, Quintus."

"You know what is in store for you once you and the others are conditioned?"

"The arena, of course."

Quintus leaned back against the wall and drank deeply. "There's more to it than that. The Perfumed Pig is ingratiating himself into the highest places of Rome. You know of his sister?"

"Antonia? The one who stands behind the curtain and manipulates her puppet husband, her son and possibly her brother?"

"You know more than I thought you did."

Calgaich shrugged. "I've heard things."

"Have you heard that Sextillius has offered you and the Dirty Fifty to Aemilius Valens, chief procurator of the Games, for any use he may make of you?"

"Why, Quintus?"

"It's simple enough. Valens ranks as one of the highest in Rome. He has the ear of the emperor. Further, he has slept with Lady Antonia, the dear sister of Lucius Sextillius. But that in itself means little, for Valens is a stud, a human satyr, and he'd screw a female snake if someone held its head. They say he now has his eye on some of the women Lucius brought with him from Britannia."

Calgaich sat up straight.

"You know them, of course?"

What was he driving at? Calgaich had been warned about the devious, plotting Roman character, long before he had left Caledonia for his service with the Ulpia Torquata.

"Bottle Emptier tells me the golden woman, who is betrothed to the Perfumed Pig, was originally your betrothed."

Calgaich raised the wine jug and drank deeply.

"Then it's true?"

"She was," Calgaich admitted.

"But she still means much to you?"

Calgaich shrugged. "I don't know."

"I have seen this golden woman, barbarian."

"She has a sister. You saw her too?"

Quintus nodded. "They say Lucius will marry the one, to get the other." He slanted his eyes sideways to study the dim face of Calgaich. There was no show of emotion upon it. "There are strange things that go on in the villa of the Perfumed Pig. How does this affect you, barbarian?"

Calgaich shrugged, pretending indifference. "Why should it affect me?"

"I think it does, and so does Lutorius."

Calgaich did not speak. He lifted the jug and drank from it. He looked sideways at Quintus. "There was another woman brought here by Sextillius, a dark-haired woman with great eyes like emeralds. Have you seen her?"

Quintus shook his head. "I have not been into the quaestor's villa, other than in the entrance hall. That was where I saw the two golden Britons. I went there at the request of the quaestor, but I did not see him. I spoke instead to that prick, Ulpius Claudius, the nephew of Sextillius."

"I know him well, Quintus." Calgaich's big hands closed tightly.

"The tribune informed me of the contemplated plans for you and your mates. Further, he wants me to arrange what is called a showing, for Valens, here at the school, to take place in several weeks, to exhibit this great skill of yours with your native weapons."

"Like a circus performer."

"More than that; you will be matched with some of the best men we have here."

"To the death?"

"I don't know."

"Why are you telling me this?"

Quintus stood up. "I hate the guts of those people, barbarian. When I stood in the arena dripping blood from many wounds, raising my sword in the victory salute, acknowledging their plaudits as the greatest gladiator of all time, I hated them for turning men such as myself into beasts without feeling, eager only to kill, and kill again. I have not forgotten. I think of it every day and sometimes long into the night, and not even the good Cyprian wine can dull those hated memories. I swore then that somehow I would make fools of them, and get away with it."

"Why are you telling me this? It's a dangerous secret to tell another man."

Quintus laughed harshly. "Who would believe you or that drunken Bottle Emptier there? It would be my word against yours, if they would listen to you. Me! Quintus Gaius, the Oak Tree! The greatest gladiator Rome has ever known! Gladiator master of the Great School! Friend and confidant to the mighty of Rome. They come here to my school and sit in the practice arena for my judgment on the best of the present crop of students, and for tips on the betting in the forthcoming games. Who would they believe, barbarian?"

"You're right, Oak Tree."

Quintus leaned forward. "Further, if I suspect in the slightest that you have carried this tale to other eager ears, you will die very suddenly here in the school, and no one will ever know who was the cause of your death. You understand?"

Calgaich nodded.

"Empty your jug. I can't leave the wine jugs here. Get drunk, but remember, you've a full day ahead of you tomorrow on the practice field, and, by the gods, I will be there as gladiator master to see that you do not shirk!"

Calgaich emptied the jug. He handed both jugs to the master. "Thanks, Quintus," he said.

"It is nothing. Lutorius was my friend, and you are the friend of Lutorius, so that is the same to me. Good night, barbarian."

The door closed behind the gladiator master.

Lutorius opened one eye. "The fates work in mysterious ways, barbarian," he murmured. He laughed softly.

CHAPTER 20

The blazing Roman sun beat down upon the practice arena of the Great School. Although it was long before mid-morning, the students had been out for hours upon the sands, learning and practicing the high art and science of killing other men. The sand burned up through the soles of their sandals, and greedily sucked in the sweat that dripped from their taut faces.

Some of the students lifted and manipulated weights designed by Quintus Gaius himself to develop the particular arm and shoulder muscles necessary for sword fighting. Pairs of wrestlers strove against each other, grunting and panting in the tense struggle. Runners sped around the track that encircled the arena and leaped over hurdles. New students, those eventually to be designated as *tirones,* who had yet to fight their first duel in earnest, practiced with wooden swords. The *tirones* themselves, those who had passed beyond the fundamental wooden sword stage, used blunt, lead-weighted swords twice as heavy as the regulation type to practice cuts and parries against thick wooden poles set upright in the sand.

No student was shirking or laying back. They had the best of reasons. Their only hope of survival was to perfect their skill. The profession they were learning must be a total way of life. Another reason for the practice field dedication was the presence of the trainers and instructors, the muscular hardfaced veterans of the arena who had survived to win the coveted *rudis,* the wooden sword that signified retirement. These scarred worthies paced about the arena, holding long-lashed whips in their hands, the same type that was used in the actual arena to force reluctant combatants to close in against their opponents. They could take a patch of skin as big as a sesterce coin from a man's back, with hardly an effort.

Calgaich finished running around the track. He was naked except for a loincloth. His muscular body streamed with good sweat mingled with the dust. The long weeks in which he had been in the school had served him well. He was back in excellent condition.

Ostorius, a *doctor*, or instructor, in the Thracian School of gladiatorial lore, paced toward Calgaich. "Barbarian! Get cleaned up! No more exercising for you this morning!" He grinned secretively. He studied Calgaich. "They have a treat for you, later on this morning."

"Yes, sir!" Calgaich snapped out.

The instructor eyed the muscular body, with its blue chest tattooing and multiple scars. "You look as though you had been in the arena in Britannia," he suggested.

Calgaich shook his head. "We have no arenas in my country, sir."

"That is not so! I know there are arenas there."

"In Britannia, yes, but in Caledonia there are none."

Ostorius nodded. "I see what you mean. Well, you'll soon get your chance here in Rome, *tiro*."

Calgaich watched the instructor pace off. He picked up a *strigil*, a curved bit of metal, and began to scrape the dust and sweat from his skin.

Lutorius wandered over and sat down on the sand beside Calgaich. He intently examined the heel of one of his calloused soles. "I think I know what that was all about. The Oak Tree tipped me off that Aemilius Valens will be here with a large party of guests, for a private showing, this day."

"And I'm to perform?"

Lutorius nodded.

"Who will I be matched against?"

Lutorius shrugged. "They said some of the best."

"Students, or veterans?"

"Veterans, most likely."

"To the death?"

"I think not. However, they will not let *you* get killed here. You're too valuable a prize for that."

"It's not that which bothers me. I was thinking of the

man who will be matched against me, for I will surely kill *him*."

"Don't be so damned sure of yourself."

Calgaich grinned. "Have you no confidence in me?"

"The most, and you know it, barbarian. But what is bothering you about this match? There is something in your eyes that warns me, Calgaich."

Calgaich looked across the heat-shimmering arena to where slaves were erecting a large, many-colored awning over the podium seats, which were always reserved for the most important spectators. There had been a private showing the past week, in which three students had died on the bloody sand, while the Roman audience had become sick with laughter, watching their unskilled efforts against Togatus, a veteran of twenty-one victories in the arena, who had fought all three of them at once.

"Calgaich?" Lutorius queried.

"I don't like the thought of killing a man who is not an enemy of mine, for no other reason than for the enjoyment of these bloodthirsty leeches of Romans."

Lutorius shrugged. "You'll have to get rid of that feeling in this business. Your opponent will not think that way of you."

"But, if he knows that I am not to be killed?"

Lutorius shook his head. "He won't know that."

"Suppose they pick you to fight me? You know these damned Romans. From what I've seen of them these past months, they'd like nothing better than to set two comrades against each other."

There was a haunted look on the battered features of Lutorius. He looked about himself.

"There is no escape, Lutorius. The only escape from here is into the arena, and the only escape from victories or a quick death. You've said so yourself."

Lutorius shook his head. "The Oak Tree won't allow it."

"Wrong, *calo*. He will do it if he is ordered to do it."

Ostorius cracked his lethal whip. "Bottle Emptier! To practice! Barbarian, to the baths! *Jump,* damn you!"

Lutorius picked up his blunt, lead-weighted sword, and began to hack away at a thick pole, almost as if he were back in the ranks of the Fifteenth Apollinaria or the Twentieth Valeria Victrix.

Later Calgaich came from the baths and walked toward
the headquarters building. The great gates creaked open to
admit a series of litters filled with laughing men and a few
women. Calgaich looked back over his shoulder. The practice arena was empty of students. Slaves were removing
some of the equipment while others raked the arena and
spread fresh sand where needed. Still other slaves were
laying out food and wine on low tables covered with snow-
white cloths.

A woman laughed as the litters passed behind Calgaich.
He did not turn. He had no need to. He knew the flowing,
musical trilling of Morar's voice.

Calgaich was admitted to the chambers of Quintus
Gaius. The gladiator master was seated behind his desk.
A flask of wine and two cups were on the desk. Quintus
was studying a scabbarded sword that lay before him.

Quintus looked up. "You know this sword, barbarian?"

Calgaich nodded. "Yes, sir. It is mine."

"It was sent here by Quaestor Lucius Sextillius for your
use this day."

"I thank him for that, sir," Calgaich said dryly.

Quintus studied the emotionless features of Calgaich,
seeking for guile on the scarred face. "I don't approve of
these long-bladed stickers, barbarian."

"As you wish, master."

Quintus leaned back. "It is said that you're a master
with this weapon."

"I have my native skill, sir."

Quintus nodded. "You will use it this day in the practice arena. I sent for several of your types of shields.
Luckily they had some in the vaults at the Flavian Amphitheatre. They had been there for years, or so they told
me, gathering dust, along with other trophies of war.
Look behind you there."

Calgaich turned. Three lime-whitened wooden shields
rested against the wall. He nodded. "They will do, sir."

"I have had the leather arm-loops replaced in our
armory, and any repairs that were necessary have been
done. You will need a helmet."

"I have never worn one, sir."

"You will this day."

"I do not need it, sir."

"You will wear one. That is final."

Quintus drew the magnificent sword from its scabbard and handed it to Calgaich. "Get the feel of it again."

Their eyes met as Calgaich gripped the familiar hilt. Calgaich smiled. "I would not try it, sir," he said quietly.

"I was not testing you, Calgaich. Even if you killed me, where would you go? You see?" He filled two cups with the wine. He shoved one of the cups closer to Calgaich. "I am anxious to see how you use that toothpick of yours."

"Why are you doing this?"

Quintus shrugged. He downed his wine and quickly refilled his cup. "Aemilius Valens wished it so. His word is law in such matters. He's always anxious to make himself look good." He looked up at Calgaich. "The yellow-haired woman will be in the group. Both Lutorius and you have already told me that she was once your betrothed."

"That is so, master."

"And she is to marry Lucius Sextillius?"

"That is what they say."

"This means nothing to you?"

Calgaich shrugged. "I am a prisoner. A student in the Great School of Rome. Destined for the arena, where death is to be my business." His voice had a mechanical sound to it, as though he had memorized his little speech but cared nothing for the meaning of it. Besides, it was another yellow-haired woman, Bronwyn, who occupied his mind when he allowed himself to remember the past.

"You learn well, barbarian."

Calgaich drank the good Cyprian wine. He shook his head as the gladiator master reached over to fill the cup. "The sun will be too hot this day to have wine drugging me, sir."

Quintus Gaius leaned back in his chair. "I have fought hundreds of men while in the legions and in the arena. I have trained thousands to fight and die in the arena. There are two kinds of men we send there. Those who are eager to go, to gain fame and fortune. Those who are afraid to go and will not fight until forced to do so. You are neither one of these, Calgaich. How do you really think?"

"I am a prisoner," Calgaich parroted. "A student, *tiro,*

in the Great School of Rome. Destined for the arena, where death is to be my business."

Quintus nodded. "I see. So be it." He stood up. "Crates!" he roared.

A gray-haired slave came into the room. "Yes, master?"

"Take this sword, the shields and the helmet to the arena."

Quintus waited until the burdened slave had left the room. "I could not trust you to carry them yourself. Supposing the quaestor Lucius Sextillius, or the golden woman he took from you, might stray a little close to that long-bladed toothpick?" His eyes searched Calgaich's face in vain for any sign of emotion. There was none.

The gladiator master left the room followed by Calgaich. The sun was brilliant in a clear blue sky. The sound of laughter came from beneath the colored awning at the arena podium. Hundreds of students were walking toward the sunlit common seats of the arena. There were to be no classes that afternoon.

Calgaich looked up at those gathered under the awning as he stopped in front of the podium seats. They were all there—Lucius Sextillius, Aemilius Valens and Tribune Ulpius Claudius, as well as Morar, wearing a sky-blue gown of diaphanous material that hardly concealed her full womanhood. She had taken readily to the daring styles of the patrician ladies of Rome.

Calgaich's eyes caught those of Fomoire, who was seated in the last row of seats behind the highborn audience. The Druid had been taken from the school some weeks earlier, to serve in the villa of Lucius Sextillius. There was no expression on his thin, ascetic face. Calgaich wondered idly what his experiences had been.

The seats across from the party of Aemilius Valens were filled with trainers, instructors and students, both *tirones* and *veterani*. Guidd was there with Lutorius, Niall, Chilo, Loarn, Girich and Conaid. Thank the gods that he would not have to fight them, at least. He did not see Lexus, and some of the others, but the seats were filled with hundreds of the school members, and they might be among them. Quintus Gaius had not allowed many of the Dirty Fifty, as he called them, to remain together. It might have been a dangerous policy.

"Gaius!" Valens called out. "We are ready for the performance."

The gladiator master stood in front of the podium. "Your excellencies, I have arranged a match between this barbarian, Calgaich, and several of our school members, as an exhibition of the Britannic style of swordplay, as opposed to our more formal and stylized types of gladiatorial combat."

"With wooden swords?" a young Roman called out. He laughed and looked about himself as though pleased with his witticism.

There was no expression on the scarred face of the gladiator master. "The school members will fight with the regulation weapons of the gladiatorial types of combat. The barbarian will be armed with his own native weapons, long-bladed sword and dagger, shield and helmet."

"How long do you think he'll last against one of our Roman boys?" another viewer called out.

"We'll have to wait and see, sir, won't we?" Quintus replied. "Bastard," he added beneath his breath.

"To the death?" Ulpius Claudius called out.

"These are valuable men, sir," Quintus replied.

A tall, middle-aged woman, sitting between Ulpius and a paunchy little man, leaned forward. "That is not an answer, gladiator master!" Her voice was hard and cold.

Quintus looked at Valens. The procurator nodded. "It will be to the death then, Lady Antonia."

"If this barbarian is as good as he's said to be, it should be no trouble for him!" she called out.

Calgaich looked at Lady Antonia. The words of Lutorius flashed through his mind. *The family money is said to be controlled by the quaestor's elder sister, that is, the Lady Antonia. She is the mother of that pouter pigeon, Tribune Ulpius Claudius. She financed the senatorship of her husband, Mucius Claudius, a spineless jellyfish, so that she could get herself a mouthpiece in the Senate. It was she who got Ulpius Claudius his appointment as tribune, on the long chance that he could work his way up to tribune legatus legionis.* The paunchy little man beside her must be the "spineless jellyfish" to whom Lutorius had referred.

"Don't send any of your *tirones* in against him, Oak Tree!" a man shouted. He was already half-drunk.

Crates brought Calgaich's sword, shield and helmet to him. Calgaich placed the helmet on his head and thrust his left arm through the loops behind the shield. The shield was almost identical in shape and weight with those to which he was accustomed.

"The Oak Tree said you were to drink this, barbarian," Crates said.

He handed Calgaich a cup of dirty-looking water. Calgaich shrugged. He downed the liquid and made a wry face.

"To fall in the arena is to die," Crates said in a low voice. "This is a charm used by charioteers against such a happening. It is the ashes of boar shit mixed with water. It never fails." Crates stepped to one side, still holding Calgaich's scabbarded sword.

"What the hell is holding you back, barbarian?" one of the spectators yelled. "Get on with getting spitted like a goose."

Calgaich looked up at him. "Nothing's holding *me* back, Roman. What's holding *you* back from coming out here to get spitted?"

"Why, damn you!"

The rest of the audience laughed at Calgaich's quick return, surprised at his command of Latin; but Quintus Gaius was not amused. "Watch your tongue," he warned.

"Let him watch his own tongue!"

Quintus raised a big fist.

Calgaich smiled a little. "Not out here, Oak Tree."

Their eyes clashed, and then Quintus almost seemed to smile; a sort of a ghostly thing.

Two men approached the podium. One of them was an instructor, a *doctor retiarius,* or master of the net and trident school of fighting. The man with him was unknown to Calgaich. He was helmetless and carried a net and trident.

"Rodan," Crates said quietly, looking at Calgaich. "A *veteranus retiarius.* Twelve victories. How many victories do you have, barbarian?"

Calgaich shrugged. "I never counted them."

Quintus Gaius drew a line on the smooth sand. Calgaich stood on one side and Rodan on the other. The *retiarius* looked impersonally at Calgaich. He was not a big man, but he was tall and of a wiry build, with the look of speed and agility. He wore no armor.

Quintus held up his arms. "A contest," he called out, "between Rodan, *retiarius*, with twelve victories, and Calgaich, swordsman, and a barbarian. To the death!"

Rodan stepped back from the line and spread his legs apart, balancing easily on the balls of his feet, with his eyes on those of Calgaich. Calgaich reached for his sword. He drew it from the scabbard with a crisp hissing of metal against metal, and then stepped back from the line and raised his shield. He had seen the tactics of the *retiarii* in practice during the weeks he had been at the school. *Retiarii* were usually matched against *secutores*, or gladiators called Gauls, from their type of armor and weaponry. The Gauls were helmeted and wore a light breastplate. They wore a *greave*, or shield of armor, on their left legs, and a metal-linked sleeve on their right arms.

"Three to five on the netter!" one of the spectators called out.

"The barbarian hasn't got a chance," Valens sneered.

"Fifty to one on the netter then!"

There were no takers.

Quintus walked to one side. He folded his arms across his chest, then nodded at two instructors who stood one on each side of the combat area. They both carried whips.

"To the death!" Quintus cried.

Rodan moved forward, waving his trident and heavy net, while he sang the formalized song of the netter:

> "I see not you, I seek a fish.
> Why do you flee from me, O Gaul?"

Calgaich grinned. "Come closer, fisherman, where you can see that I'm no damned Gaul!"

They circled slowly, never taking their eyes off each other. Rodan leaped forward, and flung out his net. The leaden weights that fringed it opened it out into a perfect circle aimed to settle over Calgaich's head. But Calgaich was not there. The net landed on the sand. Calgaich had leaped aside. He closed in. Rodan retreated, running swiftly while he dragged the net behind him. Suddenly he stopped and whirled, casting out the net low and sideways toward Calgaich's legs. Calgaich leaped high over the net and landed lightly on the sand. The trident drove in toward his unprotected throat. His sword flashed in the sunlight, parrying the trident.

Rodan leaped backward and drew his net toward himself. As Calgaich charged, he dropped to one knee and thrust the trident upward toward Calgaich's crotch. Calgaich leaped sideways and slapped the trident aside with his sword.

"Stand still, barbarian!" Rodan snapped.

"Come closer, Roman!"

They circled slowly. The sweat dripped from their faces.

Calgaich began to beat on the edge of his shield with the flat of his sword. He moved in closer, ever closer.

Rodan moved back. He leaped sideways and flung out the net toward Calgaich's face to confuse him and then released it. He crouched low and drove in hard with both hands on the shaft of his trident.

Calgaich thrust out his shield to catch the net. He swept the shield to one side, carrying the loose net with it. One downward sweep of his sword struck the trident between two of the prongs just as Rodan raised it. They stood there poised like statues as the sword and trident rose higher and higher above their heads. They stood face to face, straining against each other. Calgaich raised a knee up into Rodan's crotch. The netter gasped and crouched forward. Calgaich threw him to one side. Rodan then turned away from Calgaich, leaving his back unprotected. Calgaich planted one foot on the trident and the other on the net.

Rodan staggered toward the edge of the combat area. A whip cracked just over his head. He turned to look at Calgaich. There was an agonized look on his face.

The arena was very quiet.

Rodan straightened up. His eyes held those of Calgaich. Death in the arena was always formalized. There could be no fuss to disgust the audience.

Calgaich stepped back and rested the tip of his sword on the sand. Rodan moved forward cautiously, then stopped a few feet short of his weapons. Calgaich carelessly turned his back on the netter.

"You damned fool barbarian!" Lutorius roared. "You had him. He was cold meat! He'll never give you such a chance!"

Calgaich turned. Once again Rodan was armed and moving in for the kill. He felt no gratitude toward Calgaich. The barbarian had made him look bad, almost as though it were beneath his dignity to kill him.

"Don't do that again, barbarian," Quintus Gaius warned.

Rodan had death in his eyes. His burning anger was his undoing. He flung out the net too fast, following it with a driving thrust of the trident. Calgaich swung his sword. The keen edge slashed through the net, cutting it into halves. A return backhand sweep of the sword hit the trident shaft just below its head and cleanly sheared it off. The return stroke caught Rodan across the side of the neck and cut halfway through it. Rodan fell flat on the sand. He struggled convulsively for a few seconds and then lay still.

It had all happened so fast the spectators had been caught unawares.

Calgaich looked lazily about. "Who's next?" he asked carelessly.

A tall, broad-shouldered man had taken a seat in the sunlight beyond the awning. His hair was iron-gray, almost matching the color of his eyes. His nose jetted out from his bronzed face like the ram of a trireme. There was a look of absolute authority about him even as he sat.

Slaves dragged away the body of Rodan. They took away the damaged net and trident, then spread clean sand over the combat area to cover the widening blood stain and raked it smooth.

Crates brought vinegar water out for Calgaich. "The procurator Valens is angered," he whispered. "Rodan was one of his favorites."

"Then he should not have sent him out here."

"He will find it hard to forgive Quintus Gaius for that. He was sure Rodan would defeat you."

A Thracian fighter was next. He wore the peaked Thracian helmet, and his legs were protected by greaves. He carried the small, round Greek shield and was armed with a long scythelike dagger that was about the same length as the famed *Hispanicus gladius* of the legions.

The sweat was running off Calgaich. His tunic was soaked. He placed his sword and shield on the ground and took off his helmet. He stripped the tunic from his body and threw it to one side. The bluish tattoo patterns on his broad chest glistened from sweat.

Lady Antonia gasped a little. Her husband looked quickly at her. Her dark eyes were riveted on the splendid physique of the barbarian. She leaned forward a little. Lucius looked at his sister and then nodded knowingly to her husband.

Calgaich looked toward the podium. His eyes met those of Morar. She was so damned beautiful! She sat amidst the dark-haired, dark-eyed Romans like a lone golden flower amidst a bed of dark evergreens. She smiled slightly at him. How could a woman so beautiful be so evil? Was it truly so?

Calgaich put on his helmet and picked up his sword and shield. The Thracian stood beside Quintus Gaius. He was a younger man than Rodan had been, perhaps not quite as tall, but more more muscular, with a deep chest and broad shoulders.

Quintus drew a line on the sand. He looked toward the podium. "A contest," he called out, "between Scylax, Thracian, with fourteen victories, and Calgaich, swordsman, a barbarian. To the death!"

Calgaich smiled. "You forgot my one victory, gladiator master," he reminded Quintus.

Quintus Gaius turned his head a little. "If you are trying to make a fool of me out here, barbarian, remember that once you are through here, you are back in my charge again."

"If I *live*, master."

"I'll see that you don't, barbarian," Scylax offered.

Their blades touched tentatively as they felt out each other's guard. They circled. Their blades rang musically. Scylax was fast on his feet. He moved in, thrust his shield up under a downcoming stroke of Calgaich's sword and stabbed toward his chest. The tip of his blade slit Calgaich's skin. A slow trickle of bright blood ran down to mingle with the bluish warrior patterns. Scylax leaped backward, grinning at his slight victory. Then Calgaich's blade leaped out like a tongue of flame. The tip of the sword cut a similar slit into the chest of Scylax. Blood ran down the dark hair on his chest and dribbled across his lean belly.

A shout went up from the spectators.

"They like the sight of blood, barbarian," Scylax said.

"Yours or mine, Thracian?"

"Any blood at all, just so long as it's not theirs."

"Stop that damned conversation and get to work!" Ulpius shouted. He looked at Valens. "Five to three on the barbarian."

"He has great confidence in you, barbarian," Scylax said dryly.

"I'd almost rather die than see him win any money on me."

"I'll give you that wish."

Their blades clashed as they circled around, leaping and parrying blows with sword or shield. Gradually the greater skill of Calgaich, aided by his longer sword, began to give him the edge. Scylax fought steadily, but there was a desperation in his efforts. He fought in the approved style, a style that had given him fourteen victories in the arena, and he hoped that the *rudis,* the wooden sword of retirement, would be his with a few more victories.

Calgaich retreated warily from the persistent attack of the Thracian. Only he, and perhaps Quintus Gaius, knew that Scylax was getting careless in his attack, so desperate was he for a victory.

"Make him fight, Gaius!" Valens shouted. "Use the whips!"

"Coward!" a woman shouted at Calgaich.

Calgaich still retreated. Scylax rushed in, sensing victory at last. His rounded shield took ringing blows while his blade hacked and hewed at Calgaich's wooden shield, so that finally it split from top to bottom.

Calgaich leaped back and threw the shattered shield to one side. They circled again, breathing harshly, with mingled sweat and blood running down their bodies and bare thighs. Scylax's mouth was square as he sucked in air. He was tiring.

"How close are you to the wooden sword, Thracian?" Calgaich asked.

"Perhaps another victory, barbarian."

"My defeat?"

"That might do it."

Calgaich nodded, then suddenly retreated. Scylax rushed in, thrust out his shield to take a blow, and stabbed in hard with his dagger. Calgaich wasn't there. He had leaped aside. He grasped his sword hilt with both hands and brought the gleaming blade down with a solid, sure stroke that struck the Thracian's left forearm just above the wrist. The severed hand and shield dropped to the sand.

Scylax hurled away his dagger. He grasped his forearm above the stump. The blood rushed through his fingers and dripped to the sands. His eyes were wide in his head.

"*Habet! Habet!* He's wounded! He's wounded!" the spectators shouted. They leaped to their feet.

Calgaich turned to look toward the podium. The eyes of the spectators were wide in their heads. Their mouths were open, with the lips drawn back, baring their teeth, like so many animals. Only the tall, gray-haired man who sat alone in the sunlight had not moved.

Scylax looked at Calgaich with sick, uncomprehending eyes.

"There's your retirement, Roman," Calgaich said quietly. "If not that, I would have had to kill you."

Some of the spectators had turned their thumbs down, while many of the others were waving handkerchiefs, and holding up their right thumbs. "*Mitte! Mitte!* Let him go! Let him go!" they shouted.

Quintus looked at Valens. The procurator's face was dark with congested blood. Both Rodan and Scylax had been favorites of his. He had won a great deal of money from betting on them. Now this stinking barbarian had neatly eliminated both of them. Damn Scylax anyhow! He should have beaten the barbarian upstart.

"*Mitte! Mitte!*" the spectators shouted. They were standing now and stamping their feet.

Valens nodded and turned up a thumb, almost as though in disgust. Ulpius held out a hand for the payment of his bet on Calgaich.

Attendants rushed the stricken Scylax from the field to the hospital. Slaves came out on the sand and covered the bloodstains. Calgaich placed his sword on the sand and picked up his tunic.

"Wait, barbarian!" Quintus ordered.

Calgaich turned slowly to look at the gladiator master. He held the tunic against a slight wound on his chest. He looked up toward the podium and saw the murderous look on the face of Aemilius Valens.

Already some of Calgaich's friends were running across the arena toward him. Quintus motioned to the men with whips. They advanced toward the running men, who came to a sudden halt, and then hastily retraced their steps.

"What the hell is this?" Lutorius shouted. "He's beaten two of your best! You bastards!"

Valens stood up. "Get Togatus," he ordered.

"Are you mad!" Lady Antonia shouted at him. "The barbarian has proven himself this day, Valens!"

"Not against Togatus."

"But Togatus will be fresh, while the barbarian is tired and wounded."

"Wounded? That pin prick?" Valens laughed.

"Would you like to have one for yourself, Roman?" Calgaich shouted at him.

It became very quiet in the stands. Valens turned his head slowly to look at Calgaich. "That settles it! Gaius! Send for Togatus at once!" Then he noticed the gray-haired man, looking at him. "It is my right, Senator!" he added harshly. "You know the law as well as I do."

"I said nothing, Aemilius Valens," the senator responded. "However, the man has well proven himself. What more do you want of him? Are you making something personal of this. What has he ever done to you?"

There was no reply from the procurator. He turned away.

They brought Togatus to the arena. He was a burly veteran, a victor in twenty-one combats, who had already refused the wooden sword twice. Rumor had it that Valens had been considering replacing Quintus Gaius with Togatus. It was his right and privilege to do so, for was he not the procurator of the Games, as well as the favorite of the emperor?

A trainer came out onto the field and stanched the flow

of blood on Calgaich's chest by the use of cobwebs and a soothing unguent. "Your time has come, barbarian," he whispered. He did not sound unsympathetic. Togatus wasn't popular at the Ludus Maximus.

Calgaich shrugged. "I've already put two of Valens's pets out of business. If I defeat Togatus, what's to prevent them from sending on others, until they kill me at last?"

"Nothing, barbarian. You might think of your mates here at the school. As bad as the Oak Tree is, he's far better than that bastard Togatus."

Togatus was of the school of *hoplomachi,* or fully armored gladiators, named after the famed early Greek Hoplites. The ranks of the *hoplomachi* were composed of the most enormous and heaviest men of all gladiator types. They wore rounded helmets whose bottom edges came down to rest on their shoulders and chests so as to protect their necks and throats. A thick, ornamented cuirass protected their upper body. They wore a *greave* on their left leg only, and a linked metal sleeve on their right, or weapon, arm. They carried the big curved shields of the legionnaires. Some of them were called *postulati.* They were allowed to carry any weapon they desired. Togatus had selected a heavy mace with a ponderous lead head.

"Nothing can stand before him, barbarian," the trainer murmured over his shoulder as he left the field.

Calgaich took another of his shields from Crates. It would be scant protection against the lead mace. He watched Togatus as the *hoplomachus* was helped into his fighting gear. Only a week ago he had watched from a distance as Togatus had fought at a private showing against three *tirones.* They had tried to fight the armor-plated animal as best they knew how, and when they had run from the field in panic, they had been driven relentlessly back by whips and red hot irons, to be brutally battered to death by Togatus. The drunken spectators had howled with laughter at their antics to escape him. The sand of the fighting area had been dyed a solid crimson when the massacre was over. Calgaich could still hear the merciless thudding of the mace on the armor and bodies of the doomed men, and their hoarse screams of anguish.

Togatus thrust his thick left forearm into the loops of

his curved shield. He grasped his mace and turned toward Calgaich. It was an eerie sight, for Calgaich could see nothing of his face, covered as it was by the faceplate of the helmet. Togatus moved slowly and ponderously toward the line which Quintus Gaius had marked on the fresh sand. He rested the head of his mace on the sand and looked at Calgaich. He said something within the hollow-sounding helmet.

Quintus looked at Calgaich. "Are you ready?"

Calgaich nodded. "What does he say?"

"He wants the fighting space to be limited. Do you accept?"

"Do I have a choice?"

"I can make it so, barbarian."

The sun was blazing down. The heat reflected from the sand. Togatus would soon be stifling in his heavy helmet and armor. The fight could not be settled if Calgaich kept running from him to tire him out.

"Well, Calgaich?"

"Limit it then, and be damned to him."

Quintus came over to check Calgaich's chest wound. "He has a bad left eye," he murmured. "His vision on that side is very limited."

"Why are you telling me this, master?"

The hard eyes of the Roman briefly held those of Calgaich. "You were not to be killed this day. That was the agreement, but there can be no way of stopping Togatus to save you, if that is necessary. Besides, you've made an enemy out of Valens. You made fools out of two of his favorites, and Togatus ranks much higher with Valens than those other two."

Calgaich nodded.

Togatus rumbled in his helmet. "Let's get on with this!"

Quintus smiled a little. "He's getting hot inside his oven."

"Is that why you're stalling?"

"Who? *Me?*" Quintus looked shocked.

One of the trainers laid a long rope on the sand. It was shaped into a circle, hardly more than forty feet across. Several trainers, with whips, were stationed around the perimeter of the circle. They certainly couldn't harm the armored Togatus with their whips but they could cut

Calgaich's hide into bloody ribbons if he tried to escape from the lethal circle.

Quintus held out his arms. "A contest! Between Togatus, *hoplomachus*, with twenty-one victories, and Calgaich, barbarian swordsman, with two victories! To the death!"

Togatus took up his stance in the center of the circle. His tactics were at once apparent to Calgaich. Togatus could stand comparatively still in the center of the circle, while keeping Calgaich moving around him, but within the limits of the circle, and never more than several strides away from Togatus.

Calgaich moved to the left. He reached out with his sword and tapped it against Togatus's heavy curved shield. The veteran's reaction was immediate. He moved with startling swiftness for one of his bulk, and armored as he was. The mace swept down and put a deep crease in the front of Calgaich's wooden shield. Calgaich moved again to the right of his opponent. The mace seemed to leap out, but this time it was deflected from Calgaich's sword, just enough to make it sweep down the face of Calgaich's shield. The good iron of the Sword of Evicatos chimed musically as it was struck.

"He'll snap your sword like a twig!" Someone roared from the side of the arena. "Keep away from him, you damned fool!"

Calgaich grinned a little. There was no mistaking the voice of Lutorius.

Calgaich moved to his left again, making a semicircle about Togatus. He thrust toward the eyeholes of the helmet to see if he could make the veteran draw back from the threat. Calgaich was wrong. It was nearly a fatal mistake, for the mace crashed down with ponderous force against Calgaich's shield and split it halfway down to the metal boss.

Calgaich moved in swiftly, striking against the right side of Togatus's helmet, and then retreating before he could raise the heavy mace for another blow. Calgaich circled to his right. Togatus's reaction was slower. Calgaich battered at the helmet again. He knew he could never shear through the thick metal, but the sound of the blows ringing against it might serve to disconcert Togatus.

The sweat was streaming from Calgaich's face and

body. How must it be for his opponent within that helmet with the sun's heat beating down on it and his stinging sweat running down into his eyes?

Calgaich kept stalking like a lean hunting cat, worrying its quarry. First to the left, then a quick reversal to the right, a savage beating stroke on the helmet, and then a swift race around behind the veteran, to make him turn, and turn again.

"Stand still! Stand still and fight, barbarian!" Valens shouted. "You run around like a mouse in a pot!"

Calgaich stopped moving about. Togatus moved ponderously forward. He raised his mace and slammed it down with terrific force. It struck the split in Calgaich's shield and hooked itself there. Calgaich dragged backward on the shield, and stepped aside. Then as Togatus stumbled toward the rope border of the fighting circle Calgaich swung his sword with all his force to strike the back of the helmet with such power that Togatus fell on his knees atop the rope. Calgaich unhooked his arm from his shield and leaped around behind Togatus. He jumped high and then planted both feet on his opponent's back so that Togatus sprawled belly flat across the rope. His mace was outflung from his sweating hand and it landed ten feet away from him.

Calgaich beat a devil's tattoo atop the huge helmet of Togatus. He stepped back and thrust the tip of the blade into Togatus's rump, where it was unprotected by armor. Togatus screamed hollowly within his helmet.

Calgaich stepped backward to the center of the circle and rested his sword tip on the sand.

Togatus tried to get up, like a turtle who has been placed upon his back. His powerful legs churned at the sand. He dropped flat again. His body was heaving with his exertions.

Quintus Gaius forgot who he was and where he was. "Kill the sonofabitch, barbarian!" he yelled. "Don't let him get up!"

The spectators were excited and blood hungry. *"Verbera! Verbera! Occide! Occide!* Lay on! Lay on! Kill! Kill!" they roared. They began to stamp their feet in unison with their bloodthirsty cries.

Calgaich looked at Quintus Gaius. The gladiator master

nodded. The spectators beneath the awning were like animals howling in the wilderness as they closed in on a quarry that someone had wounded and would soon kill. He saw Morar amidst these human animals. She was standing. Her fists were clenched and pressed up tight beneath her full breasts. Her chin was outthrust and her eyes were wild with the blood lust. The only spectators who were not crying for the blood of the defeated Togatus were Valens, whose contorted face betrayed his feelings, and the gray-haired man who sat alone in the brilliant sunlight. His eyes met those of Calgaich, but there was no expression on his seamed face.

"Occide! Occide! Occide! Occide!" the crowd chanted.

Calgaich thrust his sword tip into the sand. He gripped the fallen Togatus by his ankles and dragged him, belly downward, within the fighting circle. He rolled him over onto his back. Togatus lay still. He knew the score.

Calgaich removed the heavy helmet from Togatus's head. The veteran's head and face were streaming with perspiration. His face was beet red and his mouth was squared as he fought for breath in great wheezing gasps. His eyes met those of Calgaich. Calgaich pointed toward the spectators.

Togatus knew the formalized ritual. He looked toward the spectators beneath the awning. He raised his head and held out his right arm with clenched fist and one finger raised, the sign for mercy.

Almost all of the thumbs were turned down. *"Iugula!* Slay him!"* the cries beat down upon Calgaich and his stricken opponent.

Togatus looked up at Calgaich. There was no fear in his eyes. He was a longtime member of the cult of dying. There should be dignity in it. "Make it quick, barbarian," he requested. "You've killed men before."

Calgaich drew his dagger. He looked at the spot on Togatus's throat where a little pulse showed, beating steadily. That was the place. One sure, hard thrust would do it.

"Kill! Kill! Kill!" the mob chanted.

Calgaich threw the dagger on the sand. He picked up his sword and carried it from the circle. He handed it to the waiting Crates. He turned his back on the howling mob and walked toward the baths.

Sandaled feet beat on the hard earth behind Calgaich. Lutorius came puffing up behind Calgaich. "By the gods!" he yelled. "I've never seen anything like it! Are you mad! They'll have the skin off your back for that, barbarian!"

Calgaich shook his head. "No, they won't, Bottle Emptier."

Lutorius fell into step beside Calgaich. "I've always thought there was a madness in you, barbarian. Now, I am sure."

"Think what you will."

Calgaich looked back toward the arena. "Who was that gray-haired man who sat alone back there?"

"You don't know!"

"I would not have asked, had I known."

"Rufus Arrius Niger, once tribune *legatus legionis*, now a senator of Rome. Your maternal grandfather, barbarian—Old Give Me Another!"

CHAPTER 21

It was the evening of the weekly visit of the whores to the deserving students of the Ludus Maximus. In the anticipation and the bawdy excitement, none of the guards or the inmates noticed that Calgaich and Lutorius were not making their selection of the "girls," as they had done in the past month since Calgaich had won his astounding triple victory in the practice arena.

The sprawling villa of Quintus Gaius nestled in the hollow of a hillside covered with the grayish-green leaves of olive groves. The villa was not far from the city walls and overlooked the yellow flood of the Tiber River on its way to the sea. The sun had died, leaving a purple dusk over the countryside and the city. A cool wind had begun to blow from the sea. The evening wind blew across the garden of the villa and drifted a fine cool spray from the fountain across Calgaich's face and hair. It reminded him of the sea mists of his own country.

"Maybe I risked too much in inviting you and Bottle Emptier here, barbarian," Quintus suggested as he lightly watered his good Falernian wine.

Calgaich shrugged. "Why? You've told us more than once that there is no chance of our escaping from Rome."

"It's not the thought of your escaping that has been bothering me. Valens has not forgotten your triple victory. It put a big dent in his ambitions to get control of the mob in the city. By the gods! We made him lose face, barbarian, and to a man as vain as he is, that can be the equivalent of a death sentence for us. Valens can't stand to lose face! Ever since the emperor left Rome three months ago to put down a revolt in Cyrenaica, Valens has been ruling the city. If the emperor had any idea of what his beloved cousin and favorite was doing here he'd damned well get his ass back to Rome."

Calgaich looked curiously at the gladiator master. "You mean?" He left the thought unspoken.

Quintus nodded. "The emperor is no fool, but he thinks he can hold his throne better by fighting barbarians along the frontiers of Rome, when in reality his worst enemies are right here in the city. Valentinian is a soldier, and a good one, but he is no politician. Why he left the city months ago to go to Cyrenaica, with the political struggle for power that has been going on here ever since Valens became procurator of the Games, is beyond me and every one of his loyal subjects. He will believe no evil of Valens."

"And you say you are one of the loyal subjects of the emperor?"

Quintus nodded. "He personally appointed me as gladiator master and gave me this villa. I tell you this, barbarian: If the emperor had seen you perform that day in the practice arena, he might have pardoned you."

"For what crime?"

"I warn you, Calgaich, your pride will undo you. Without a pardon, you can't escape the arena!"

"You yourself just spoke of loyalty to your emperor. Do you Romans think that loyalty is a virtue only of yourselves?"

"If you and your countrymen enter the arena to fight in the forthcoming Games planned by Valens, you are doomed."

"You're very sure of that."

Quintus nodded. "I *know!*"

They eyed each other like a pair of combatants trying out each other's defenses.

Quintus suddenly turned his head. "Paetina!" he roared. "Have wine and food brought here! Find that damned Bottle Emptier!"

Paetina came from within the house to the garden. She was tall and slender with naked, cone-shaped breasts capped by large nipples. Her breasts were outthrust like shield bosses. Her bluish-black hair covered the top of her head like the curly fleece of a ram. Her eyes were immense and set in a face that tapered almost sharply from her chin to her high cheekbones. Her skin was a velvety bluish-black in color with a soft, oily sheen to it. She walked noiselessly on bare feet with a sensuous feline grace. She couldn't have been more than eighteen years old.

Calgaich eyed the beautiful black woman. "By the gods," he murmured.

"The food is being prepared, master. Will you have the rich Cyprian wine, or perhaps the good yellow Chios with the meal?" Paetina asked.

Quintus grinned. "Bring them both, Paetina. Where is that damned Bottle Emptier?"

The faintest trace of a smile passed across her face. "He was chasing the Syrian through the olive groves, master. He slipped in some goat dung and she got away, leaving her gown in his hands." She turned her head to one side and stifled her laughter.

Quintus lightly slapped her rounded rump. "Go and get him then! Mind you don't let him corner *you*, Paetina."

She grinned. "He can't find me in the shadows."

"Wait until moonrise," Quintus warned.

"By that time he'll be so drunk he won't be able to perform."

Calgaich smiled. "You don't know the Bottle Emptier very well, Paetina." He watched her leave the garden. "Who is she?" he asked quietly.

"A Nubian. The daughter of a great king. She was given to me by the emperor himself."

"A black slave!"

Quintus shrugged. "More like a hostage, barbarian. She was sent here many months ago. Aemilius Valens then, as now, was in charge of the city and the government here at home. He felt that he should have taken charge of her. You know what that would have meant."

"I've heard he likes them young, *very* young, and untouched by other men."

"That was why the emperor sent her to me instead of that whoremonger. Valentinian had given his word to her father that she would not be ·touched. Even though he trusts Valens with almost everything, he knew better than to turn Paetina over to him. She has been here ever since."

"Untouched?"

Quintus nodded. "The honor of the emperor was at stake."

"To a black king in Nubia."

Their eyes met across the table.

Lutorius came through the garden gateway from the olive grove. "I would have had her. Damn it! Why did that goat have to shit right where I was running?"

Calgaich grinned. "He knew you were coming, Bottle Emptier. You were ambushed."

Lutorius dropped onto a couch and reached for the wine jug. "That's the story of my life."

"Don't worry, Bottle Emptier. When you do catch her, you'll be sorry," Quintus said. "She'll break your back in bed. I warn you. I gave up on her months ago. I like them a little quieter, if not less amorous. Besides, there are plenty of others around here, Lutorius. You've got this whole night and the next day to play the satyr. Take it easy! This isn't a whorehouse where you pay your money, hop on and then hop off, and then go home wondering if you really had anything at all."

Lutorius nodded. "You're right, Oak Tree. The night is young. The wine is good. The companionship is of the best. Why worry?" He drained his wine cup and looked speculatively toward the shadowed olive grove. "Still, I *almost* caught her . . ." He looked at Calgaich. "Have you made a choice yet, eh, barbarian?"

Calgaich shook his head. "I hadn't thought of it."

"Perhaps that slender reed of a Nubian?" Lutorius persisted. "Not my style. Those tits of hers would poke a hole into a legion shield, and she's got no width to her rump." His voice died away as he caught a warning glance from Calgaich.

"Crates!" Quintus roared. "Food, by the gods! Move those skinny legs of yours!" He looked at Lutorius. "The Nubian is a virgin, Bottle Emptier."

"I'll take care of that for you," Lutorius offered. "Although I don't like virgins. Give me a broken-in filly like that damned speedy Syrian for my taste."

"Paetina is like one of my own to me. I never had a family. I never knew my own father. My mother died of drink when I was no bigger than a fart. I had no brothers and sisters. The only relatives I ever really had were my comrades in the legion, that is, until Paetina came.

"So, you see, this is my home. My slaves are my family. This is where I can live and enjoy life, at least until I have to go back to that accursed school and train other men to fight and kill each other."

A slave came from the house and lighted lamps which he hung about the garden. Crates and two women slaves brought food and more wine to the table.

"Is there no escape for you from the school, Oak Tree?" Calgaich asked.

"Where could I go? I have a position of importance. I gained my wooden sword because the city mob was always with me. Valens has always wanted to oust me from the Ludus Maximus and has the power to do so. But like every other official in the city, he fears the mob. Still, it is not an easy life, knowing that Valens is always looking for some way to oust me."

"Can't you retire here?" Lutorius asked.

Quintus shrugged. "I have been too long in harness to suddenly drop it altogether and become a gentleman olive farmer. Besides! I think I owe the mob something for what they have done for me. By the gods! Do you know how many boy babies born in the past ten years have borne the name of Quintus Gaius? There are half a dozen wine shops named The Oak Tree after me. They even had a street named after me! It is really through the mob that I gained this place, as well as the favor of the emperor."

"But, if the emperor were here, you'd be safe enough from Valens, eh, Quintus?" Calgaich asked.

"If he were here instead of fighting one of his damned frontier wars again. In Cyrenaica, of all places!"

"And Valens is plotting to take over the throne."

Quintus leaned forward. "It would be worth your life if you said that out in public. He has spies everywhere. He has the palace guard with him and the garrison of Ostia, as well as the powerful naval squadron stationed there. Also the instructors and students of the three other gladiatorial schools."

"A ready-made professional army able to gain control of the city," Calgaich added.

"Can you think of a better one?" Quintus asked quietly.

"But he needs the city mob as well before he could gain control of Rome."

"How popular is he?" Calgaich asked.

Quintus shrugged. "Popular enough. He has done a good job as procurator of the Games. He'd throw his own mother into the arena to please the mob."

"I can see now why he hated us the day I fought," Calgaich said.

"He would have kept at you until you were slain if it hadn't been for your grandfather, barbarian."

"Where does he stand in all this political intrigue?"

"He is loyal. First to Rome, and then to the emperor. Valens hates him and fears him."

It was very quiet in the lamplit garden. Moths fluttered about the oil lamps. The soft splashing of the fountain mingled with the soughing of the night wind through the olive and cypress trees. Quintus suddenly looked uneasy. "Calgaich, take a walk toward the front of the villa, but don't go through the house. Lutorius, scout the olive grove. I'll take a look inside the house. You both know what I mean. The night has ears in Rome."

Calgaich vaulted over the garden wall and padded through the shrubbery toward the front of the house. The faint grinding of wagon wheels on the flags of the road, mingled with the clopping of hooves, came to him on the wind from the winding road that passed along the bottom of the slopes on its way to the banks of the Tiber. The vehicle turned up on the side road toward the villa.

Calgaich faded into the shrubbery. The wagon came to a halt in front of the house. The driver descended from the seat. Quintus Gaius met him at the doorway. There was no mistaking the huge bulk of the gladiator master, even in the pre-moon darkness. A woman laughed shrilly. The house door opened, then closed softly.

Calgaich went back to the garden. Lutorius came through the gateway. He shook his head. "Nothing, not even that damned speedy Syrian."

"There was a wagon at the front of the house."

"I heard it. There was a woman there."

Calgaich grinned. "A city whore, perhaps?"

"I don't know why. The Oak Tree has women in plenty here, enough for him and us. Why another?"

Quintus came from the house accompanied by a tall man clad in a white tunic and wearing gilded sandals.

"By Hercules!" Lutorius cried. "It's the weasel!"

"I must be drunker than I thought," Calgaich admitted.

"Well met, friends!" Fomoire cried.

"You look like you've just come from the Forum, or at least the latrines there," Lutorius said. "They say that's where most of the business of Rome takes place anyway."

Fomoire smiled. "Nothing quite as elegant as that."

Quintus indicated a couch for Fomoire. "Fomoire brings us news."

"You look well, Fomoire," Calgaich said. "How are things in the sty of the Perfumed Pig?"

"I'm still a virgin, if that's what you mean." Fomoire studied Calgaich for a moment. "But you aren't concerned about me, Calgaich. Isn't it the women about whom you're concerned?"

"You're right," Calgaich admitted.

"Morar and Cairenn have gone to the house of Aemilius Valens on the Viminal Hill."

Calgaich narrowed his eyes. "What's that you say?"

"It seems as though Morar wanted to go, and Lucius Sextillius fears the man."

"Did she go with the permission of the Lady Antonia?" Calgaich asked.

"One woman is enough in the camp of Lady Antonia, and *she* must be the one. The Perfumed Pig resisted Antonia's wishes at first, but she placated him by letting him keep Bronwyn."

Calgaich shook his head. Morar meant nothing to him now, no matter what she did, or whom she slept with, but Bronwyn was another matter, an innocent in the hands of the depraved Lucius, whom Calgaich had learned to despise and hate.

"Fomoire, you are too brief in your report. Tell me more. Why did Morar let her stay? Could she be that evil?" Calgaich left his couch and began pacing back and forth between the fountain and the table laden with food and wine.

"Do you really want to hear, Calgaich? Is it not enough to know that Morar and Cairenn have gone to

Valens's villa and Bronwyn is left behind? Do you really want details?"

"*I have to know,*" Calgaich said, pausing at the foot of Fomoire's couch.

"Then, seat yourself and I will tell you."

Calgaich resumed his place on a couch, his eyes on Fomoire. He drank deeply from his wine. Lutorius and Quintus did not move.

Fomoire picked up his wine cup, but he did not drink. There was a faraway look in his eyes as he began to speak, turning the wine cup in his hands.

"I am powerless in the villa of the Perfumed Pig. I can *do* nothing. But I *know* everything that goes on. I am in places I would be killed for even having seen. I have grown to know the gardens and the sweep and spread of the heavy curtains which line the rooms and baths. It is there I spend many hours of my time.

"Two weeks ago, late one afternoon, Lady Antonia and Lucius Sextillius were walking in the gardens. They were discussing Morar. Lady Antonia was telling Lucius that it was politically necessary for him to allow Morar to go to Aemilius Valens. I, too, was walking in the gardens," Fomoire said modestly," and heard everything.

" 'Valens has too much power for us to go against his wishes,' Lady Antonia said. 'We can gain favor by presenting Morar to him as a gift, a token of our loyalty, rather than have Valens seize the golden-haired woman, which he has the power to do.'

" 'He would not have that power if the emperor were in Rome,' Lucius pouted.

" 'He is *not* in Rome. Valens *is*. And he controls the mob,' Lady Antonia said. She called for more wine. I could see from my place behind the shrubs that she was pouring his cup more full than hers. It was not like her.

" 'Besides,' she continued, 'there are those who say her sister is more lovely in her shyness. Morar is too brazen and well deserves the title *Flava Coma*—Yellow Hair.'

" 'She is *not* a whore; she was to be my *wife*,' Lucius said, dashing his cup to the tiles surrounding the fountain.

"Antonia signaled for another cup. 'She will be Valens's betrothed within a week. *She* wishes to go. I have told her she may go.' She paused to allow Lucius to understand that it was already beyond his control. Then she said in a cajoling voice, 'But I have not yet told her of the one condition of her leaving here.'

" 'Which is?' Lucius asked peevishly.

" 'Her sister, Bronwyn, stays.' "

Fomoire stopped speaking to take a sip of his wine. Calgaich and Lutorius were silent. They, too, took deep draws on the fine Falernian wine, but their eyes never left Fomoire's face. Soon he continued.

"That evening Lady Antonia and Lucius went their separate ways—she to a party at her son's *domus,* and he to a reception for one of the emperor's generals, newly arrived in Rome, to bring news of the emperor's victories. I knew that the next morning was when Lady Antonia would speak to Morar. I went to Lucius earlier than usual and gave him his morning draught; then I made myself a part of the heavy curtain in Morar's chamber. Morar had just risen from a heavy sleep and too much wine the night before. She called for Cairenn to summon her slaves and the make-up boxes. She paints herself now in the fashion of the Roman women, puts ochre on her cheeks and lips.

"Then she sent Cairenn to bring Bronwyn to her for company, that they might be painted and dressed together. Cairenn works hard in Morar's service, running here and there to do her bidding, but at least she is safe." Fomoire stopped speaking at the word "safe."

"Continue," Calgaich said softly.

"When Cairenn returned with a sleepy Bronwyn, Morar made her drink a cup of wine to wake her up, and then she sent for fruit and cheese and bade Bronwyn eat because she was growing thin. Next, Morar told the slaves to begin their morning's tasks. Together the sisters sat in chairs as the women began to comb their long golden hair. They did this for at least an hour. The slaves love tending the hair of the sisters, because it is so soft and lovely."

"Do not dwell on it," Calgaich said quickly. Quintus waved the slaves away who had come for the remnants of food.

Fomoire continued, "Lady Antonia entered as they sat there. She did not waste words. 'You are to prepare to leave tonight, Morar. Valens wishes to have you visit him at his villa, and we have generously agreed for you to go.' She stood before Morar and waved away a chair proffered by a fearful slave woman. One could tell Lady Antonia was jealous of the sisters' youth and beauty.

" 'The slave woman,' she gestured to Cairenn who was holding a heavy gold necklace, 'goes with you.' Cairenn never raised her eyes to Lady Antonia, but walked with her head down. I could see that Morar was delighted at being allowed to leave the Perfumed Pig's villa so easily, and already her eyes were clouded with the thought of being in Valens's bed that same night. But Lady Antonia's next words brought her back.

" 'Bronwyn, of course, stays here. Lucius and I have need of her company.'

" 'But I cannot leave her here,' Morar cried, pushing away the woman who was lifting a lock of her hair into place.

" 'Then, you will stay and she will go. Valens would be disappointed for a few hours, but I think he would accept the substitution.'

"Bronwyn just sat there quietly while the two women spat words back and forth. Finally, quietly, she began to cry. But she said nothing until Lady Antonia had left the chamber. 'Morar,' she wept, 'you cannot leave me here. Anything is better than this house. You are more clever than I and have been able to hold Lucius at arm's length as it suits you.'

" 'Quiet,' Morar said, touching her sister's hand; then she sent the other slaves away, telling them they could finish their tasks later. Bronwyn's painted face was wet and streaked. Only Cairenn remained in the chamber. And I," Fomoire said, "but they did not know I was there.

"Morar started pacing back and forth. 'Bronwyn, I have tried to teach you the ways with men and . . .'

" 'I have not the will to learn,' Bronwyn said quietly.

" 'Let me stay in Bronwyn's place,' Cairenn said, coming forward from the bed she had been arranging. She stood behind Bronwyn with her hands on Bronwyn's shoulders. 'Do not leave your sister here. I have heard whisperings in the slave quarters at night, after the screams have stopped. Things you never dreamed and I dare not say.'

" 'You *want* to stay?' Morar asked Cairenn, pausing in her stride.

" 'I want Bronwyn to *go*,' Cairenn replied softly.

" 'Lady Antonia would not allow it.' Morar tore the half-finished headdress from her hair. She again began pacing the room, picking up dresses and flinging them down. She dropped a gold buckle to the tile floor. Finally she turned as if her mind were made up and hardened to what she intended to do.

" 'I will send for you,' she said to Bronwyn. Cairenn gasped, and Bronwyn again began to cry, her hands covering her face, the powder running onto her fingers. Then Morar came and knelt at Bronwyn's feet, and took Bronwyn's hands in hers.

" 'Oh, don't you see. It is the only way. Valens has the power in Rome. When I am in his villa, that power will be mine. And I will send for you.'

" 'It will not be soon enough,' her sister said. Her tears were gone now. She heard Morar's words with a heavy heart, and it was almost as if she knew her fate had been decided in that last moment.

" 'You will see,' Morar said, ignoring her words. Then she stood up and clapped her hands. Immediately the slaves appeared. 'Come,' she said. 'Begin my hair again. I did not like it anyway.' The women rushed to their combs and paint pots.

" 'Cairenn, our clothes must be made ready. Take only the most recent ones. I shall have many more within a few days.'

"Cairenn was helping Bronwyn from the chamber. 'I shall begin packing when I return,' Cairenn said coldly. 'Perhaps you and your sister should say goodbye in private.'

"Morar waved her hand. 'There is no need. I shall send for Bronwyn as soon as I am settled.' She came to Bronwyn. 'You see, little sister, that we have no choice, don't you?' Her eyes pleaded for forgiveness.

" 'You are wrong, Morar; I have a choice,' Bronwyn said. 'And now I wish to return to my rooms.' She left and did not look back." Fomoire stopped talking. The night was darker, and the stars shone brighter in the sky. Calgaich bowed his head. There was nothing he could do. He felt powerless that once again Morar was in control of the destiny of another.

"I will do what I can," Fomoire said softly.

Calgaich looked up. "And Cairenn?" he asked.

"She went with Morar, to be her handmaiden."

"And into the bed of Valens, along with Morar," Calgaich said bitterly.

Fomoire shook his head. "Morar would not allow it. She must always be first with any man."

"How could she stop Valens from having his way with her?" Calgaich demanded.

"She stopped Lucius from doing it."

"Are you sure?" Calgaich asked.

Fomoire smiled. "There is nothing that goes on in the perfumed pig sty of Sextillius that I don't know about. No, Calgaich, the Perfumed Pig never had his way with Cairenn, or with Morar, for that matter."

"And Bronwyn? What of her, Fomoire?"

Fomoire shrugged. "Not while Morar was there, at least."

"And Morar left her innocent sister there, in the power of that animal," Calgaich murmured.

"Perhaps Morar will send for her soon." But Fomoire did not sound as if he believed his words.

"It is probably too late," Calgaich said.

"There is a power struggle going on. Valens wants to be emperor," Fomoire continued. "Senator Rufus Arrius Niger leads the loyal faction. The Lady Antonia Claudius sits in between them, like a hunting cat, waiting to see which way the prey will go. She would have given in to Morar—if Morar had insisted. Lady Antonia is afraid of Valens and would have tried to please him. Morar should have known this."

They sat silent for a time.

"Tell him what Valens has planned for the Games, Fomoire," Quintus urged, to change the subject.

"Valens has been organizing a group of opponents for you and your barbarian comrades, Calgaich. The combat will be an even match. There will be fifty combatants on each side."

Calgaich grinned. "I can hardly wait. Will we have choice of weapons?"

Fomoire nodded. "Your own."

"Then we have nothing to fear."

Fomoire shook his head. "You don't understand, barbarian. Your opponents will be all ex-legionnaires. Veterans—men who had been condemned to the galleys or the sulphur mines, even to death. They will oppose you with legion weapons and tactics. Valens plans to show the type of fighting that has won Rome world domination, as opposed to the wild, free-swinging style of you barbarians that has brought so many of you to death or slavery."

Calgaich flushed, burning with anger.

Quintus held up a big hand. "Perhaps on your native soil you and your tribesmen can be a match, and sometimes more than a match, against the legionnaires. But here you will fight within the confined area of the arena. In addition, your group of barbarians has never fought together. The only thing you have in common is that you *are* barbarians. You have no commander. No unit discipline. You will all fight well. You will all die. There is no way you can avoid that."

Lutorius nodded. "The Oak Tree is right, Calgaich."

"I'll risk it!" Calgaich snapped.

Quintus shook his head. "You can't fight them alone, swordsman. You can't carry the brunt of such a battle on your shoulders. Furthermore, your opponents, who are sure to be victorious, will be given their freedom and a chance to enroll in one of the state gladiator schools as freedmen rather than as condemned criminals."

"And the defeated ones?" Calgaich asked quietly.

Quintus turned down a thumb. "There are to be no survivors."

"Organized slaughter," Calgaich murmured.

"Valens means to regain the popularity he lost with your victory in the practice arena," Fomoire added.

Lutorius drained his wine cup. "I know nothing of the barbarian style of fighting, other than having fought against them myself. To send men such as myself into the arena armed and dressed like barbarians is the same as a death sentence."

"That is what Valens intends it to be," Fomoire said.

"Lutorius was a legionnaire," Calgaich said quietly. "Many of the Dirty Fifty, including myself, had some training in the auxiliaries. I know this: Once the legion shield wall is broken, no legionnaires can stop the barbarian charge."

"Aye," Lutorius agreed doubtfully, "but the trick is to break the shield wall. It will be like fighting in the bottom of a chamberpot in that damned arena, with no room for maneuvering."

"Lutorius might have become a centurion if he could have left the bottle alone," Calgaich continued. It was almost as if he were thinking out loud, oblivious of the others. "We are warriors, and in excellent condition, thanks to the Oak Tree. We have a month to prepare for the combat."

Calgaich looked grimly at the gladiator master. "If you will give us permission, those of us who have little knowledge of legion tactics can be taught them. Then, when the day of the great Games of Aemilius Valens arrives, forty of us will march into the arena armed and trained like legionnaires, the same as those who will oppose us in the fight to the death. The remaining ten will be armed as barbarians."

"You're mad," Quintus accused.

Calgaich dipped a finger into his wine cup, then traced two lines on the table top. "Here are our opponents. Here we are." He drew a shorter line behind the line of barbarians. "Here, nine warriors, to be led by me, armed as barbarians. It will' be up to Lutorius, commanding his forty men, to break through our opponents' shield wall. Once that is done, I can attack that break with my warriors. Once we get in among them . . ." His voice died away.

Quintus shook his head. "It's unrealistic, Calgaich. Lutorius would bear the brunt of the opening attack with his forty men against fifty of the enemy. Forty partially trained men attacking fifty professionals. Supposing they *don't* break through the shield wall?"

"It's either that, or death to us all, Oak Tree. By your own words, we will fight well, but we will all die. I agree to that, *if* we fight using only our own methods."

"You realize how much I would be risking?" Quintus demanded. "My own life would be forfeit to Valens."

Calgaich smiled. "If Valens's group defeats us, that will be the end of you in the Ludus Maximus. Valens will regain the popularity he wants, and he will have his chance at the throne."

"You place big stakes on such an outcome, Bottle Emptier."

"He's right," Fomoire put in. "The mob and the emperor put you here in this villa and made a national hero out of you, Quintus. You, of all people, should know the unstable temperament of the city mob."

Quintus looked at the Druid. "Who are you anyway?" he demanded. "How can you know such things?"

Calgaich leaned quickly forward. "Besides, Oak Tree, it would be one hell of a joke on Valens and the mob. If the arena mob accepts it, what can *he* do?"

The gladiator master rubbed his square jaw. He drained his wine cup and refilled it. He then looked up at the rising moon and murmured something to himself. "You win," he said quietly. "But it will have to be done in the greatest secrecy. I can bring them here in units of ten for the initial training, then it will be up to you, Lutorius. It's a risk. The greatest of caution must be taken. If Valens gets one word of this . . ."

"Is it agreed then?" Calgaich asked.

Quintus extended a hand. Lutorius, Fomoire and Calgaich placed their hands upon it. They nodded together.

Quintus stood up. "Well? Are you ready for your women, barbarians? They are ready for you."

The good wine was working well within Calgaich. The thought of a woman was good. He had bedded a number of the professionals who had been brought to the Ludus Maximus once every week. They were faceless now, only shadowy figures in his unlit cell, and when he had awakened from a drunken sleep they had been gone.

Quintus began to tick off on his fingers. "There is Lepida, the cook. She's getting along in years, but she is broad in the beam and heavy of breast and you'll be comfortable in the saddle with her. There is the wild Syrian; and Lyra, the Iberian housemaid, is as slim as a trout, but she knows a few tricks that might arouse your interest. Ah! Julia, the milkmaid! Young and unskilled, but as tight as a clenched fist. Help yourselves, Lutorius and Fomoire. Only leave the Nubian alone. She is not to be touched, you understand? Not by *anyone!*"

"What about me?" Calgaich asked as he walked toward the house.

Quintus smiled mysteriously, "We have a surprise for you, barbarian. She waits in your room."

Fomoire looked after Quintus. "Can he be trusted?"

Calgaich shrugged. "As much as anyone in this manure pile they call Rome. Still, he may be trustworthy, but he isn't doing all this just for our sakes, priest."

"You sensed that, too?"

"I know men, Druid."

"Whatever he has in mind, it will not harm you or Lutorius."

"*If* we survive the arena."

"Some of us will have to die to help the others to survive."

Calgaich nodded. "For what purpose did you really come here tonight? Does the Perfumed Pig allow his personal slaves to move freely about Rome? Surely you did not come here only to tell us about Valens and his plans for the Games."

Fomoire shook his head. "There is a woman waiting for you."

Calgaich stood up. "Who is she?"

"I can't tell you that."

"Whose idea was this?"

"Hers."

Calgaich started toward the house. "Is it Morar?"

The Druid looked mysterious. "Why don't you go and see?"

CHAPTER 22

Calgaich paused outside the door to his room. He listened but heard nothing. He pushed open the door. The room was dark. The window-hanging had been drawn closed.

She stood with her back to the window, a tall, shadowed figure. She moved slightly as Calgaich entered. The scent of her exotic perfume drifted to him.

"Calgaich?" she queried, her voice soft and low.

"I am Calgaich. Who are you?"

"Does it matter, warrior?"

"I like to know who is going to be in bed with me."

"You'll find out that it doesn't matter, once we *are* in bed, warrior."

"Let me be the judge of that, woman."

"Do you make love as stirringly and as passionately as you fight in the arena?"

Calgaich grinned. "Better."

"Conceit!"

He shook his head. "Confidence."

"Then show me, Calgaich."

Calgaich kept his hand on his hideout knife. Rome was a place of intrigue and sudden death for the unwary.

"Undress me, Calgaich," she requested sweetly.

Calgaich kicked off his sandals. He stripped his tunic from his body and dropped his loincloth onto the floor. He moved so swiftly toward her she had little chance to evade him, or to tease him, had she wanted to. He passed his hands up and down her lightly clad body feeling for a weapon.

"I am unarmed," she whispered. "Did you like what you found?"

He unfastened the clasp that held her girdle up beneath

her breasts. He removed the gown from her body. It was feather light and seemed to whisper between his hands as he handled it. He stripped a thin, knee-length tunic from her. Her breasts were upheld by a band of the finest of soft leather. He unfastened it and threw it to one side. Then he knelt before her and passed his hands down her smooth thighs and slim legs to her ankles. He undid the latchets of her tiny sandals. She stepped free of them to stand completely naked before him.

Calgaich passed his hands up along her body and cupped them under her full breasts. He teased her nipples to harden them. She pressed close to him and passed her hands down his body to his crotch where she grasped him firmly. Gripping her hair with one hand, he drew her head back so that he could kiss her smooth throat and her full, parted lips. She thrust her loins hard against his. Calgaich picked her up and placed her on the bed. "Wine?" he asked.

She nodded. "A great deal."

"There is no water."

"I like it undiluted. The stronger the better."

Calgaich handed her a cup and she clasped her hands about his and the cup and drank greedily from it so that the red wine ran down her chin and across her fine full breasts.

She lay back on the bed and drew him down to her. She pressed her wine-wet mouth loosely against his and thrust her pointed tongue into his mouth. Suddenly she grasped his privates in a hard and painful grip. She was a passionate and hungry bitch. He slapped her lightly across the face and she relaxed her grip.

The pins fell from her elaborate hairdo as she twisted back and forth with the passion aroused by his kisses and his fondling of her. Her breasts rose and fell spasmodically. Calgaich placed a hand between her thighs. She opened her long legs like an unfolding flower.

She guided him into her and then wrapped her legs about his hips and her arms about his neck.

The passionate struggle went on between them, each of them trying to inflict the most pain upon the other, as though they were contending wrestlers rather than lovers, each one seeking victory over the other, but the consummation was exactly mutual. She shuddered and then went limp in his arms.

Calgaich stood up and reached for the wine jug. He drank deeply from it as he looked down upon her. He could hear her erratic breathing and soft moaning as she slowly relaxed.

Calgaich reached for the window hanging. "This damned room is stifling."

"No!" she cried.

But she was too late. Calgaich ripped aside the window hanging. The full light of the moon seemed to pour onto the bed. Her body was glistening with sweat and seemed to be of the smoothest of ivory. Her fine breasts were brown nippled and tipped with gold paint. Her disheveled hair was dark and very long. Her dark eyes were rimmed with antimony.

"You know me now?" Lady Antonia asked lazily.

She was at least in her middle forties, but her firm body was remarkably well preserved for its age. Calgaich could see the enameling on her oval-shaped face, which was now smudged and cut through with tiny channels of sweat. The hair was too dark to be natural and was obviously dyed.

"Are you surprised?"

Calgaich nodded.

"Pleasantly, I hope."

He grinned crookedly. "You'd make a fine whore." He wasn't lying.

She beckoned to him. "Come close."

He bent down toward her. She rubbed her sweat-damp hands across the blue warrior patterns so that the moonlight glistened on them as though they were of fresh wet paint. She seemed to be fascinated by the tattooing.

"You risked much in coming here, Lady Antonia."

"Call me Tonia," she pouted.

Calgaich could hardly suppress a smile at the aging woman's coquettishness. "Tonia then. You must remember that I'm a prisoner of war. A student in the Ludus Maximus." His voice was correctly humble, but he knew he was not deluding her.

"I might be able to change that, my warrior." She stretched her shapely arms up over her head and arched her back so that her breasts were outthrust. She looked sideways at him and smiled lazily.

"How would you like to be one of my body servants?"

"What of your husband?"

She laughed. "He hasn't been between my thighs in years."

"And your son?"

"Ulpius? He's quite busy in his own affairs."

"We have nothing but hate for each other."

"He doesn't live in my house, Calgaich."

He handed her a cup of wine. "Do you still want me to come and live with you?"

"You could have the best of everything, Calgaich. Pure white togas of the finest Milesian wool. Sandals of gilded leather. Jewels. Money. Anything you want, including *me*."

"This would be acceptable to your family? Your friends? Your society?" he asked.

She smiled. "It's a way of life in Rome. No one thinks anything about it, Calgaich. It's considered fashionable!"

The moonlight was full on her face. Calgaich could see the tiny crow's-feet at the corners of her eyes and the thin parallel lines on her forehead that had been concealed by the paint she had worn until her sweat and contact with him had destroyed the masterful make-up job it had been. She smiled a little loosely. A trickle of wine ran from one corner of her mouth and dribbled down a breast to her flat belly.

"It might be the difference between your life and death within the next month," Antonia warned. There was a sharper edge in her tone of voice. "Aemilius Valens wants to make sure you do not survive the arena."

Calgaich laughed softly. "I might do something about that."

Antonia shrugged. "You have such arrogance. Even if you survive the Games next month, what will become of you after that? Valens has great power in Rome. He is the emperor's favorite. Valens usually gets what he wants."

"Including the throne?"

Antonia narrowed her eyes. The soft and subtle beauty that was still hers in the shadows and subdued lighting was gone now. In the full light of the moon her features were revealed to be those of a middle-aged woman, unprotected by skillful make-up. There was a sharpness and an avidity about them now.

"You can die very easily by saying something like that in public, Calgaich," Antonia warned.

"I'm not in public now. I'm with you, a woman who wants me to become a tame stud in her own house. You want great power. You who hate Aemilius Valens because he stands in your way in the political arena."

Her tapered hands closed into fists.

"Do you deny it?" Calgaich asked.

"Just who are you?"

Calgaich grinned crookedly. "A simple barbarian."

"And grandson to Rufus Arrius Niger."

Calgaich nodded. "That too."

"Are you considering my offer?" she asked.

He lay down beside her, passing his hands across her breasts to arouse her again. Teasingly his hands moved down toward the dark triangular mat of hair at her crotch.

"Tell me," she insisted. "Will you consider my offer?"

"Do I have any choice at all?"

She drew him down to her and kissed him passionately. He wasn't quite as ready as she was for another performance. He rolled over onto his belly and reached down to the floor for the wine jug. She got up on one elbow and looked at the raised crisscross cicatrices on his back.

Antonia traced one of the lash scars with a finger tip. "What are these?" she asked quietly.

"From the lead-tipped kiss of the Roman cat," he replied coldly.

She narrowed her eyes. "But why? They are old. They can't be since you've come here."

He shook his head. "Long ago I deserted the Roman Eagles—twice."

"And that is why Rufus Arrius Niger will not save you from the arena."

"You know about that?"

"The story has gone the rounds of Rome." She smiled thinly. "So, you see, that works to our mutual advantage, warrior. If Niger won't save you from the arena and almost certain death, perhaps I can."

"Which would be a double victory for you, eh, Tonia? You would save me from the hands of your one enemy,

Valens, and show up your other principal enemy, Niger, in the Senate."

She eyed him. "It hasn't taken you long to understand the political situation here in Rome." She sneered. "Why, you ignorant barbarian! I've given you a choice between life and death and you stand there playing games!"

He laughed at her. "But you still want me to come with you tonight."

Her moods were like quicksilver. *"Will* you come with me tonight?"

Calgaich was tempted. Her house would provide a measure of safety, at least for the time being. Thus protected—and away from his comrades—he would be free to think only of himself and his determination to escape. Perhaps he could protect Bronwyn.

We have need of you, Calgaich, Guidd One-Eye had said to Calgaich. *If we're to reach Rome and live through the Games, we must have a leader.* They all depended upon Calgaich to lead them in an attempt to escape. It was almost hopeless, he was sure, but they depended upon him for leadership—Guidd, Fomoire, Lutorius, Niall, Chilo, Lexus, Cunori and all the others he had grown to know and like on the long journey to Rome and while in the Ludus Maximus.

"Answer me, damn you!" Antonia shouted. "If you don't come with me tonight, I'll see that you'll be severely punished, you stupid, stinking barbarian!"

She didn't expect the hard slap that caught her alongside the head. She fell sideways and was driven back by another slap on the other side of her head.

Furious, Calgaich forced his knees in between her thighs. She spread her legs to meet him, despite her anger. He drove into her like a breeding stud, until she began to cry out in pain. She tried to push him away from her. There was no escape. The cruel moonlight showed her for what she really was—a middle-aged nymphomaniac who could not hold her liquor.

She bit her lower lip so hard the blood ran down her chin to mingle with the wine stains on her white skin. At last Calgaich withdrew himself from her. He stood up beside the bed with his anger still aflame. She turned her head sideways, moaned a little, and then passed out.

Calgaich dressed himself. He wiped most of the ruined make-up from her face and the hair dye from her shoulders and neck and then dressed her. Once she opened her eyes and looked at him, but there seemed to be no sign of recognition in her eyes. She was dead drunk.

Someone tapped on the door. "Who is it?" Calgaich called out as he reached for his knife.

"Fomoire."

Calgaich opened the door. He jerked his head toward the bed. "There lies your lovely mistress."

"Dead?"

"Dead drunk."

Fomoire looked sideways at Calgaich. "This is our chance. We could take her away in the wagon, then drive to Ostia. Perhaps we could take ship from there."

Calgaich shook his head. "No. We'd be caught. Besides, there are the others, or have you forgotten them?"

"They'll all die in the arena anyway, Calgaich."

"Not if I can help it."

"Did she ask you to go with her tonight?"

Calgaich studied the Druid. "You knew about that?"

"I was never sure. But I suspected as much. There have been many other men in her household. A great many of them. She seems to tire of them quickly."

"And what happens to them?"

"Some of them she accused of rape and then had them sent to the arena. Others just vanished. She is said to be a master of the great Roman art of poisoning."

"Here is one she didn't send to the arena or poison," said the quiet voice from behind them.

It was Quintus Gaius.

"You too?" Calgaich asked.

Quintus nodded. "She needs a boar or a ram to satisfy her." He eyed the unconscious woman. "What was it this time, barbarian? The screwing or the drinking?"

Calgaich shrugged. "Both," he replied. He grinned a little. "She wanted to quit during the second bout."

"And you kept on?"

"*I* wasn't satisfied, Oak Tree. After all, I was entitled to a whore this night."

"And you got the most notorious one in Rome."

"How is it that you survived her, Oak Tree?"

"I was still fighting in the arena in those days, so she couldn't have me committed there to get rid of me. She didn't dare poison me or have me assassinated. I was too well known and more popular in Rome at that time than she was. The mob would have torn her to pieces if they found out she had been responsible for my death. I may be one of the few, if not the only stud that ever got away from her."

"What can she do to me, now that I have refused to go with her?" Calgaich asked.

Quintus shrugged. "Very little, outside of maybe bribing someone to slip a knife into you, or a drop of poison in your wine. No, barbarian, your reputation has already spread all over Rome, and Valens wants you to live long enough to die in the arena to put a shine on his shield."

"What about *me?*" Fomoire asked.

"Don't talk. Watch your back at all times. Be careful of your food and wine," Quintus replied. "Besides, aren't you in the favor of the Perfumed Pig?"

"Not exactly. And besides, it is she who rules Sextillius. He is afraid of her. So I'll be walking on the edge of death from now on." Fomoire looked at Calgaich. "There seems to be no escape."

"You are not alone in that, Fomoire," Calgaich said. "The only difference between you and the rest of us prisoners is that we will *know* when our times comes for death in the arena."

They carried the unconscious woman from the villa and placed her in the light wagon Fomoire had driven from the city. Quintus and Calgaich watched Fomoire drive the wagon down the road.

Quintus looked sideways at Calgaich. "How was she?"

"Good. At least the first time."

"I found her good too. Even with her age, barbarian, she's still one hell of a whore."

They walked together into the lamplit garden. Quintus looked toward the city, ghostly and white on her fabled seven hills.

"Will you miss it, Oak Tree?" Calgaich asked.

Quintus whirled. "What do you mean?"

Calgaich sat down on a couch and reached for a wine jug. "You are not risking your career and your life just to play a rough joke on Valens and his condemned legionnaires. It's far too dangerous a game. If Valens gains the throne, that will be the end of you and of the black girl Paetina. But from what I've heard of Valentinian, he'll fight back, and he will need you with him. He can't afford to have anything happen to his hostage, Paetina."

Quintus sat down heavily. "Just how drunk are you, barbarian?"

"Not as drunk as I intend to get this night."

"Go on, then."

"You can't escape Rome under the present conditions," Calgaich continued. "But, during the forthcoming Games, all Rome will have her attention centered on the combat between my barbarians and the champions of Valens. A perfect chance for you to escape from the city and to join the emperor in Cyrenaica. If you do so, then perhaps your beloved emperor will understand what Valens is doing here in his absence."

Quintus studied Calgaich. "By the gods," he murmured. "There is witchcraft in all you damned Celts!"

"Your secret is safe with me. By allowing us to train as legionnaires, to have a fair chance against our opponents, you've perhaps given us a chance to survive. We owe you much. At the same time, if we cover up for your escape our debt is paid to you."

Quintus nodded. "I believe you, Calgaich. Come, there is still plenty of wine. The night is young. Let's see which of us can drink the other under the table."

CHAPTER 23

It was almost midday in Rome. The sun was blazing; the sky was cloudless, except toward the east where puffed thunderclouds hung over the mountains. The full light and heat of the sun lay heavy upon the great city. The winding streets were almost deserted save for those near the Flavian Amphitheatre. This was the day Procurator of the Games Aemilius Valens had been promising all Rome for over a month. The day when the condemned legionnaires were to show the Roman mob how to slaughter the crude barbarians by dint of superior valor and skill-at-arms.

All morning long the roar of the crowd had surged up at irregular intervals from the Flavian Amphitheatre. All morning the slaves had been busy dragging the bloody corpses of men and beasts from the arena through the gateway of the dead, the Porta Libitinensis, named after Libitina, goddess of burials, to the *carnaria,* the deep burial pits dug on wastelands not far from the amphitheatre. All morning long the living, both men and beasts, had been fed into the bloody maw of the arena. There were some victories for the men; there were none for the beasts.

A slow trickling of victorious gladiators came from the Porta Sanavivaria, the gateway of the living, to the Meta Sudans, the fountain that threw up misty clouds of spray exquisitely tinted in rainbow hues by the rays of the sun. Here the gladiators washed the dust, blood and sand from their faces and bodies. Latecomers hurried past them toward the amphitheatre, calling out the names of their favorites as they recognized them. There, too, were the girls and women who favored these brutal fighting machines and who were willing to do anything to please them.

During the midday lull in the games, the company of

barbarians was marched unarmed from the Ludus Maximus through the Via Labicana to the Flavian Amphitheatre. They wore their traditional clothing, long trousers crossgartered to the knees, and tunics that reached to midthigh. Their attire had been made to the specifications of Calgaich through the orders of Quintus Gaius.

Calgaich looked back at his command as they marched with heads erect and free-swinging strides past the gaping Romans who lined each side of the Via Labicana. There were Lutorius; Guidd One-Eye; Lexus, the giant Gaul; Niall, the redheaded Selgovae; and Chilo, the Greek tutor. Big Loarn, of the Brigantes; Girich, the son of Aengus, the Pict; Conaid, the Little Hound, of the Damnonii; Garth, the Silurian harper; and Eogabal, Muirchu and Crus, a trio of Northern Picts from the tribe of the Niduari, were others numbered among the company. The brothers Catrawt and Onlach were from the border Votadini. Ottar, a young Saxon chieftain, was in the ranks. There were others, a miscellaneous group of border and central Britons, some Gauls, a few Saxons and a Jute. They had been trained rigorously and secretly in legion tactics. Nine of them and Calgaich would fight as barbarians when the shield wall of their opponents was broken. *If* it was broken.

Quintus Gaius marched at the head of his guards, preceding the barbarians. If any man had risked his life in the past weeks of secret training, it had been he. If Aemilius Valens had ever found out what was happening, the life of Quintus would have been forfeit. Perhaps not publicly, for Valens still feared the power of the mob and knew that the gladiator master was far more popular with the city rabble than he himself was. But there were other ways—undetectable ways—by which a man could be assassinated.

The amphitheatre towered above the marching barbarians, dwarfing them and the Romans in the surrounding streets. Swarms of food and drink peddlers, male and female prostitutes, and plump little boys with rouged and painted faces, who rendered their services to whoever desired them, all crowded under the shadowed arcades of the amphitheatre. Grinning Romans, waiting in long lines to enter the amphitheatre, jeered at the barbarians.

"You'll get yours this day, barbarians!" a man shouted. "Well, you don't speak a civilized language, so you don't understand me, anyway!"

"Up your pimply ass!" Lutorius snarled back. "You misbegotten degenerate result of a mating between a diseased *spintrian* and a knock-kneed male camel!"

The crowd roared at Lutorius's retort. "He has to be a Roman with a comeback like that!" a prostitute cried.

Lutorius grinned. "No thanks, sweetheart! I'm a Romano-Briton and proud of it. What's your name and address?"

"Callina! This is my beat!"

"You'll never live to screw her!" an older prostitute shouted. "This is your last day!"

Lutorius gave her the finger as he passed her.

The column came to a halt at the command of Quintus Gaius. Another marching column coming from the other direction had reached the entry gate just ahead of them. They were led by a centurion who bore his vine staff of office.

Quintus looked back at Calgaich. "Your opponents, barbarian."

There was no mistaking them. The stamp of the legion was on them, from their precise marching discipline to the helmet-strap galls on their jaws. Their centurion looked sideways from under the rim of his helmet. His hard eyes met Calgaich's.

"It's that prick Montanas," Lutorius breathed. "I'd give my left testicle to get a crack at him in the arena this day."

"He's yours," Calgaich agreed. "But if you don't make it today, Bottle Emptier, I want him for myself."

They marched through a crowded corridor into the vast, cavernous interior of the immense structure. The air was filled with the miasma of the arena, compounded of fresh and stale perspiration, animal dung and blood. The stench of blood dominated the atmosphere.

The barbarians entered a large, low-ceilinged room. The door was closed behind them and guards took up their positions outside. The odor in the room sickened the barbarians.

"How can men live in such places as this, *calo?*" Calgaich asked.

Lutorious shrugged. "Most of them who come to the arena spend little time in here. They come in living and are taken out dead."

"How long has this madness been going on?" Garth, the Silurian harper, asked.

"For about two hundred and eighty years," Lutorius replied. "As long as the politicians and the emperors satisfy the blood lust of these city Romans, they won't be thinking of revolt, or wondering what the hell is going on in the Senate and the government. It costs cart-loads of *sesterces* every week. But it's better than having the mob come looking for them with blood in their eyes."

"Give them bread and circuses and they'll keep quiet," Calgaich added.

"Half the population of Rome is on the free bread list," Lutorius added. "So, if they haven't any work to do, what else have they? The Games! It's a great life—as long as it lasts, and to hell with tomorrow!"

Quintus came into the room followed by attendants carrying Roman legion helmets, armor, shields and weapons. "You've got about an hour," he announced. He looked at Calgaich and Lutorius and beckoned them out into the corridor. They stepped behind a buttress. "No one seems any the wiser yet," he said in a low voice. "I have your barbarian weapons in another room, under guard. It is rumored that Valens didn't want you to have them. Then someone told him that in order for you to make a good showing you'd need them."

"Who said that?"

"I heard it was Morar. The gossip around Rome is that she has Valens under her spell and is leading him around by his prick, but, of course, that could be only gossip."

Lutorius shook his head. "I believe it."

"But there's another rumor that it was a Roman woman of high rank who suggested it," Quintus added.

"Antonia?" Calgaich asked.

"I've heard it said she hasn't fully recovered yet from her bout in bed with you." Quintus clapped Calgaich on a shoulder. "You're a dangerous man, barbarian."

There was a sudden blasting of trumpets from the arena followed by the roar of the crowd.

Quintus looked up. "The afternoon begins." There was

a faraway look in his eyes. "How many times have I stood here in this very corridor and heard that sound, knowing that within a short time I would enter onto the sands, never knowing whether I'd be hauled out dead by the hooks of the Mercuries, or live to run around the arena holding the palm branch of victory?"

Quintus then led Calgaich, Lexus, Guidd, Girich, Niall, Catrawt, Onlach, Muirchu. Eogabal and Crus to the room where their barbarian weapons and shields had been stored. Quintus closed the door behind himself and pointed to the weapons.

Calgaich's eyes glistened as he saw his sword and spear. He fastened the sword belt about his waist, then withdrew the sword from its scabbard. The light of the oil lamps shone dully on the fine polished metal of the blade. He swung the sword about himself and as he did so, he seemed to be transfigured into someone none of them, with the exception of Guidd, had ever seen before, not even on the day he had won his three victories in the Ludus Maximus.

"Enough, barbarian!" Quintus cried. "Save that for the arena!"

Calgaich seemed to return slowly to the physical world. He tapped the sword against the stone wall. He placed his ear to the metal.

"'Does it speak to you, Calgaich?" Guidd asked in a hushed voice.

Calgaich nodded. He suddenly seemed to be aware of the others crowded into that stifling room.

Calgaich's party then armed themselves with long-bladed swords and daggers. They slid their left arms through the loops of the wooden lime-whitened shields and took long spears from the rack. After weeks of training with the traditional weapons of the arena, a slow and subtle change came over them as they felt their familiar weapons. Calgaich led his party into the corridor. Lutorius marched up behind Calgaich's group. He and each of his men had been equipped with the *scutum,* the big curved shield of the legionnaires. It was constructed of light, tough wood that was covered with leather and reenforced with iron plates. They wore the rounded iron helmet and the *ocrea,* or greave of bronze, on their right leg only, which was advanced while fighting. They carried the famed sword of the legions, the pointed *gladius Hispanicus,* which was about two feet long and several inches wide. It could be used for both cutting and thrusting, but the legionnaires preferred the thrust because it caused fearful wounds. Their sheathed swords hung at their right sides from shoulder belts. A dagger hung at each of their left sides. The legion spear, the *pilum,* was no less famous than the sword. Its slender metal shaft was longer than the wooden shaft to which it was attached. The metal shaft was forged of soft iron, and hardened only at the point, so that once it was hurled in the onset, or charge, the barb would stick in an opponent's flesh or shield, while the soft metal shaft would bend so that it was almost impossible to get it out during the press of combat. Thus the *pilum* would form an encumbrance to an opponent while the legionnaire charged in for close-quarter fighting, which was preferred by the Roman legions.

"Get ready, barbarians!" an attendant shouted down the corridor.

Calgaich looked back along the ranks of his command. He saw no fear on the faces or in the eyes of his barbarians. They were a mixed lot, a mongrel grouping, but they were unified for one purpose—*survival.*

Quintus Gaius came along the crowded corridor. "You're carrying the honor of the Ludus Maximus into the arena this day, barbarians."

Lutorius spat to one side. "Shit," he said succinctly.

Calgaich raised his spear. "The gods help us all, sword brothers. This day we fight together, despite our origins. We are only 'barbarians' to that howling mob out there. It's victory or death for us. Are you ready?"

"We are, Calgaich!" they roared as one.

Calgaich turned to Quintus Gaius. He nodded.

Quintus Gaius then led the way to the gateway that opened onto the sands of the arena.

CHAPTER 24

The shrill sound of trumpets carried into the dimly lit corridor. The unit led by Montanas stood at attention just behind the large double gate which opened into the arena. Quintus Gaius held up his arm to halt the unit of barbarians behind the ex-legionnaires.

Montanas stepped to one side of his command and looked back at the first ten barbarians. He noted that the unit led by Calgaich was armed as he had been told they would be. He smiled slightly, ever so slightly.

Out in the arena a brazen gong was struck slowly three times. Both doors of the entry gate then opened to let in a flood of sunlight.

Quintus Gaius spoke to Calgaich out of the side of his mouth. "Montanas suspects nothing."

Decrius Montanas shouted out his command to march, then stepped out into the glare, which streamed down from the oval opening in the center of the huge awning that covered the amphitheatre. His men tramped steadily after him.

Quintus Gaius turned to Calgaich. "It's all yours, barbarian. May the gods be with you this day." He smiled and placed his right hand on Calgaich's right shoulder while he looked deep into Calgaich's eyes. "This is goodbye, Calgaich. I think you know what I mean."

Calgaich raised his shield arm. He gripped the right wrist of Quintus Gaius with his left hand. "May the gods be with you, too, this day, Quintus Gaius."

The gladiator master stepped back. He cupped his hands about his mouth. *"To the sands!"* he shouted.

Calgaich looked back at his barbarians. "Forward!" His strong voice echoed hollowly within the long corridor and the sound of it was instantly drowned out by the solid tramping of nailed sandals on the flagstones of the corridor.

Calgaich and his command marched out on the saffron-colored sands. The roar of the crowd had swelled as the ex-legionnaires had marched into the arena. Few of those many thousands in the amphitheatre had ever seen a legion unit marching. No legion command was ever stationed in Rome or in the home country itself. It was too dangerous to have such highly trained professionals near the seat of government, particularly if they had a popular and ambitious commander. A number of emperors in the long history of Rome had already been established on the throne by the strength and power of their legions.

The roar of the spectators died away as Calgaich and his nine barbarians marched into the sunlight.

"You barbarians haven't got a chance against our Roman legionnaires!" a drunken Roman shouted.

Ribald laughter rippled throughout the towering tiers. Then the spectators saw the steady marching unit led by Lutorius, those who wore the legion helmets and the *lorica,* a leathern coat strengthened by bands of metal across the breast, on the back and over the shoulders. They saw the big semicircular legion shields, the sheathed swords and the legion spears resting on their shoulders. Lutorius was the very model of a proud centurion.

Aemilius Valens had assumed the emperor's podium in Valentinian's absence. It was an area fenced off from the rest of the seats, and was composed of the first tiers of seats just behind the scrolled iron grating that fenced in the entire circumference of the arena. He stood to take the salute of Decrius Montanas as the ex-legionnaires marched to the area below the podium. The fours wheeled and turned to the right at the centurion's command to form a double rank standing stiffly at attention facing the podium. Decrius Montanas and his men gave the clashing salute of the legions to the procurator.

Valens narrowed his eyes as he looked beyond the legion unit toward Calgaich and his bare-headed, long-haired and mustachioed barbarians. His eyes widened as he saw Lutorius and his pseudo-legionnaires marching along behind the barbarians. Valens gripped the scrolled fencing. "What mockery is this?" he exclaimed angrily.

Calgaich pointed to the right with his spear. His barbarians wheeled into a single line facing the podium and came to a halt. Lutorius barked sharp commands with all the assured authority of a centurion of twenty years' service with the Eagles. His unit fours turned sharply to the right to form a double rank, which came to a halt to extend Calgaich's line of barbarians.

Calgaich raised his eyes. The spectators were massed almost to the very top of the amphitheatre, which was backed by the seatless fourth story. The sunlight beat down through the oval center of the immense awnings of red, blue and yellow which were suspended from cables stretched from the rim of the fourth story of the structure. Thus the audience of more than fifty thousand spectators sat in parti-colored shades of red, blue and yellow, while the combatants fought in the indirect sunlight pouring through the opening in the center of the awnings. The heat within the vast elliptical bowl was almost overpowering from the blazing sun overhead and the body heat of the massed humanity sweltering within the amphitheatre.

Within the podium area were the guests of Aemilius Valens. These were the elite of Rome: the patricians and powerful politicians. Among them was Lucius Sextillius, and beside him sat Bronwyn. Her eyes were blank, staring. The Lady Antonia was there sitting between Mucius Claudius, her husband, and Ulpius Claudius. Morar sat in the front row, beside the seat vacated by Aemilius Valens. She looked down at Calgaich, but her lovely face was immobile, as though painted on ivory. A young dark-haired woman with a fan stood behind Morar. It was Cairenn. She looked directly at Calgaich over the golden head of her mistress. It was the first time he had seen her since the day he had marched toward Rome from Ostia.

The voice of Aemilius Valens had been drowned out by the sustained roaring of the blood-hungry crowd. They wanted to get on with the carnage. Valens's mouth worked in his rage, but not a word could be heard from him.

Fomoire sat in the first tier of seats behind the podium. He smiled at Calgaich and pointed to his left toward a gray-haired man just beyond the fenced-in area of the podium. It was Rufus Arrius Niger.

The howling of the mob died away as they realized something was not quite right about the scene before them.

"Why am I not answered!" Aemilius Valens shouted.

Calgaich stepped forward and saluted the procurator with the great Spear of Evicatos. "What is it that you wish, Procurator?" he asked loudly in impeccable Latin. His voice carried far.

Valens extended a shaking hand to point at the unit of Lutorius. "Who are those men armed as legionnaires?"

The sudden intense hush in the vast bowl seemed unreal. Spectators stood up and leaned forward to get a better look at the strange spectacle on the floor of the arena.

"Answer me!" Valens screamed. He seemed mentally unstable in his great rage.

"Barbarians, Procurator." Calgaich was perfectly straight-faced.

"He looks like he'll burst his stinking brains from within his skull," Niall murmured from just behind Calgaich.

"We can only hope," Calgaich said out of the side of his mouth.

"They'd only replace him with another perfumed prick," Girich put in.

"Those are not barbarians!" Valens shouted. "Those are legionnaires!"

"Look again, Procurator," Calgaich invited. "Study their faces! Those are not Roman swine, but rather barbarians, dressed and armed in Roman fashion!"

A woman laughed at Calgaich's ready and insolent answer. A slight tittering arose from those people seated closest to the podium. The tittering died away suddenly when Aemilius Valens turned to glare at them.

Decrius Montanas stepped forward to look along the line of Calgaich's men, from the ten barbarians to the forty men in Roman uniforms. His face flushed darkly when he recognized Lutorius.

"I'll have those masqueraders whipped from the arena with redhot irons!" Valens screamed. "You and your few barbarians can face the legionnaires alone!"

Calgaich shook his head. "You can't, Procurator. Besides, isn't it our deaths you so eagerly want?"

"Watch that tongue of yours, barbarian, or I'll have it torn out by the roots!"

Calgaich shrugged. "Why bother? If you have your wish, Roman, my tongue will be stilled soon enough."

Laughter spread again through the audience. It was louder this time and more widespread. The long-haired, proud barbarian showed no fear of Aemilius Valens, a man who could not stand to lose face.

"I'll have you cut down now, barbarian!"

Calgaich smiled. "Have you the courage, Roman, to come down here and try it for yourself, man to man?"

Laughter broke out like a gale of wind. It was almost deafening and very raucous, and it spread quickly throughout the huge elliptical bowl.

Valens closed his hands, white-knuckled, on the bars of the scrolled fence.

"You're making a fool of yourself, Aemilius," Lady Antonia murmured sweetly.

"Shut that painted whore's mouth of yours!" Valens snarled back over a shoulder.

Calgaich leaned casually on his great spear. "It's getting hotter by the minute down here on the sands, Roman. Let's get on with the fighting. Isn't that why you've all come here, Romans? If Valens wants to debate the issue with me, we can do it in your Senate."

The laughter reverberated from side to side of the amphitheatre. The spectators slapped their thighs and threw back their heads to roar. This insolent barbarian had the procurator with his testicles in a nutcracker and he was giving them a squeeze.

Lutorius looked sideways at Calgaich. "You've got the audience with us. I don't know how you did it, but you'd better quit while you're ahead."

"Where is Quintus Gaius?" Valens shouted. "I'll have his head for this!"

"Well along the Ostian Road by now, riding for his life, with his beloved Paetina," Calgaich murmured softly. He looked sideways at Lutorius and grinned.

"Fetch Gaius!" Valens snapped at an attendant.

Calgaich could feel the itching sweat running down his body and legs. A trickle of it ran from his temples and down the sides of his face.

"It's like a Roman bath in here," Niall complained.

The attendant came hurrying back to Valens. "Quintus Gaius cannot be found, Procurator."

"On with the games!" many spectators shouted. A muted roaring came from the audience. They began to stamp their sandaled feet in rhythm.

Valens didn't want to give in. By the gods, he did not! He looked back over his shoulder and saw the sweating faces of thousands of the spectators. This was the true semicontrolled mob of Rome. They could be controlled only as long as they were satisfied with bread and circuses. They were not to be thwarted. More than one high official and several emperors had been torn from their lofty positions because of them.

"Get on with it!" Antonia hissed at Valens. "You fool! Do you want to have us all mobbed?"

Lucius Sextillius looked back at the angry mob. "She's right, Valens," he agreed hoarsely. "They'll tear us to pieces!"

Pieces of half-eaten food and fruit arched out from high up in the stands and dropped on the podium. A ripe fig splattered against the procurator's back.

Calgaich grinned crookedly. "Where's your vaunted authority now, Roman?"

"Give the signal," Morar implored.

Valens thrust out his right arm. The audience became suddenly still. The foot stamping died away. Valens reached inside his tunic, took out a white handkerchief and then waved it.

The crowd was instantly on its feet. "Ahhhhhhhhhh! . . ." the massed voices roared.

Decrius Montanas snapped out his commands. His unit wheeled into sets of fours and double-timed toward the center of the arena. Calgaich looked at Lutorius and nodded. Lutorius shouted his commands. His columns of fours marched after the command of Montanas. Calgaich raised his spear. As he turned to follow the lead of Lutorius his eyes caught the eyes of Rufus Arrius Niger. There was no expression on his seamed face.

Montanas and his command had reached the far side of the arena, on the long axis of the elliptical bowl. At the centurion's orders the ex-legionnaires wheeled and turned to face their oncoming opponents in a double line of twenty-five each. Lutorius instantly halted his command about one quarter of the distance between it and the podium, or about two hundred feet from their opponents. He aligned his forty men into a double rank. Calgaich and his nine warriors halted behind the rear rank of Lutorius's unit.

"Forward!" Decrius Montanas commanded. The ex-legionnaires stepped out at the regulation marching pace of the legions, or about one hundred steps per minute.

"Forward!" Lutorius shouted.

The barbarians moved forward, opening their ranks to pass around Lutorius and then closing again when he was behind the rear rank and ahead of the warriors led by Calgaich, in the proper position of command.

There was little sound in the arena now, except for the shuffling of the many pairs of nailed sandals on the sands and the irregular and persistent clinking of metal against metal.

"Charge!" Lutorius suddenly bellowed.

Montanas was caught short. It was not customary for a legion unit to charge so soon, lest the men get out of breath before they closed with their opponents. He had forgotten that he was not dealing with Roman legionnaires, such as himself, but rather with the long-legged barbarians who had been trained from early boyhood to run like hunting hounds.

"Charge!" the centurion shouted.

The barbarians had the impetus with them now. They had reached the middle of the arena with Calgaich and his spearmen loping easily after them.

"First rank volley spears!" Lutorius called out.

The *pila* were launched on the run. They flashed through the sunlit air and struck with deadly precision into the shields of the ex-legionnaires. The long, soft metal shafts bent with the impact and the forward movement of the Romans. The wooden shafts twisted sideways to strike against the shields of other men or were forced under their feet so that many of them tripped and fell headlong on the sands. Here and there along the front rank some men went down with three inches of sharp iron stuck in their unprotected faces or right arms. Some of them fell backward and others forward, so that the second rank crashed into them, or over them, to break their steady stride and disorganize the rank. The whole unit wavered in panic from the sudden and unexpected volley of spears.

The barbarians closed in at a dead run. The front rank drew their swords at a command from Lutorius, while the second rank poised their *pila* and volleyed them toward the wavering lines of Romans. The shower of spears struck into the disorganized legionnaires, who were desperately trying to reform their ranks under the lashing of Montanas's tongue and vine staff.

"*Impetus gladiorum!*" Lutorius roared. It was the feared "Onset with swords."

The second rank of barbarians whipped out their swords and followed closely after the first rank as they closed in on the wavering Romans.

"Ahhhhhhhh! . . . Ahhhhhhhh! . . . Ahhhhhhhh! . . ." the excited crowd roared. They were on their feet now, eyes wide and fists clenched.

The Romans dropped their spears, drew their swords and fell back, fighting for every inch of sand. Bodies fell wounded or lifeless to one side or the other. Some were ground underfoot by the nailed sandals of the combatants. A tired or wounded man who went down was as good as dead. The blood-glistening sword blades flashed in the bright sunlight.

Lutorius ranged like a questing hound behind the ranks of his swordsmen. His eyes were ever on the red-plumed helmet of Montanas, who stood like a rock within the backward bent crescent of his fighting men. He was like a pillar of strength on the field. By sheer force of personality and courage he rallied his men so that a knot of them smashed into the ranks of the barbarian swordsmen. With the advantage of numbers and years of training, the Romans were able to break through Lutorius's unit, while dealing fearful wounds and death on both sides. The rest of their comrades were heartened by the rally and drove back into the combat again.

Calgaich raised his spear. "*Abu! Abu!* To victory! To victory!" he shouted.

Calgaich's great spear spitted a Roman. Calgaich couched the shaft of the spear under his arm and swung the Roman to one side. As the Roman dropped to the bloody sand, one of his comrades stumbled over him and went down on one knee. Before he could regain his feet the blood-wet Spear of Evicatos sank up to the heron feathers in his throat.

Calgaich and his spearmen stopped the Roman onset and drove them back through the reeling ranks of Lutorius's command. Calgaich poised his great spear to hurl it at Decrius Montanas. The Roman legionnaire was not trained to think of himself as an individual, but rather as part of a fighting machine. Kill the leader and the unit could very easily be defeated.

"Montanas is mine, barbarian!" Lutorius shouted as he sank his sword a hand's span into the throat of an opponent, withdrew it and then slashed sideways at another Roman, opening the side of his neck halfway to the spinal column.

The trampled sand was now blood-spattered and covered with wounded, dying and dead men. The heat within the arena was intense. Sweat mingled with the blood on the faces and bodies of the combatants. The din was terrific as sword blades clashed against shields, helmets and other swords. There was no sound from the men, other than the voices of Montanas, Lutorius and Calgaich as they gave their commands.

The barbarian spearmen drove the last of the Romans from the ranks of barbarian swordsmen. Lutorius reformed his broken ranks, as Calgaich and his spearmen dropped behind them.

The Romans came on again, a double rank of hardfighting swordsmen, who seemed to sense victory. Again they crashed into the barbarian ranks. The barbarians dropped back. They began to break under the steady and relentless pressure of the ex-legionnaires.

The Romans saw victory within their grasp. In their excitement they broke their ranks and turned aside to pursue those of the barbarians who were wavering on the verge of panic but did not know where to run. The walls of the arena hemmed them in.

The prophetic words of Quintus Gaius came back to Calgaich: *Perhaps on your native soil you and your tribesmen can be a match, and sometimes more than a match against the legionnaires, but here you will fight within the confined area of the arena.*

Thunder rumbled in the skies over Rome. It reverberated through the seven hills and the narrow, twisted streets of the city.

The melee swirled about in the very center of the arena. One man was hardly distinguishable from another on the opposing sides except for the tall, helmetless warriors led by Calgaich.

Calgaich saw his chance now. The Romans had broken their own shield wall in their eagerness to cut down the barbarians. Calgaich pointed with his blood-bladed spear toward the center of the Roman ranks. He charged, followed closely by Lexus, Guidd, Girich, Niall, Catrawt, Onlach, Eogabal, Muirchu and Crus.

Montanas shouted a command. Some of his men dropped back before the barbarian spear charge and snatched up discarded *pila*. They turned at the command of the centurion and launched a flight of *pila* at short range. Catrawt went down with two spears in his chest. Crus knelt on one knee, sorely wounded. Before he could rise a *gladius* decapitated him.

Lexus took a *pilum* point through his left bicep. He staggered to one side while dragging the pilum with him. "Calgaich!" he cried.

Calgaich dropped his spear, whipped out his sword and slashed clean through the soft iron of the spear shaft so that only the barbed head remained in the arm of the Gaul.

Lexus grinned. "What do I owe you, Novantae?"

Calgaich grinned back as he sheathed his sword, "Kill me three Romans for that, Gaul!"

Montanas's spearmen drove back the barbarians. At a command from the centurion they unsheathed their swords and charged into the center of the barbarian line. They were met by Calgaich and five of his remaining spearmen. Calgaich drove aside the shield of a Roman and sank his spear point into the chest of the man. The spear blade caught between two of the iron plates of his body armor. Calgaich tried to withdraw it, but as the Roman fell he carried the spear down with him.

Calgaich drew his sword. The sun flashed from the magnificent weapon. A great roar went up from the spectators as they saw the weapon. It was already legendary in Rome. Calgaich and Lutorius had not underestimated the fighting capabilities of the ex-legionnaires. They had known all along that the chances of victory rested on a razor's edge. Still, the combat, despite the surprise attack by the barbarians, had been comparatively even. There was one factor that Calgaich had *not* considered—the barbarians, mostly northmen, were not used to the intense heat and windless air of a city such as Rome and the concentration of it within the vast stone bowl of the amphitheatre. On their own ground, in their own countries, the barbarians would have been winning a victory. But here, under the Mediterranean sun and the furious onslaught of the acclimated ex-legionnaires, they began to drop back. There was no panic, but the odor of imminent defeat hovered over the barbarians.

Lexus was badly exhausted from the heat and a second wound. Guidd could hardly raise his spear and shield. Niall was bleeding from three wounds.

The barbarians began to look over their shoulders, a sure sign of impending panic and eventual retreat that would be followed by a merciless slaughter if they broke their ranks. Chilo was battered to the ground, but luckily his excited opponent pressed on for more victims rather than slaying the Greek as he should have.

Calgaich heard the rumbling of thunder over the great bowl of the amphitheatre. He looked into the eyes of his battered, wavering and semiexhausted command. He raised his sword and shook it toward the heavens. "Lugh of the Shining Spear!" he shouted with all his strength. "Help us, your children, in this foreign place of hell!"

The spectators roared with laughter. They stamped their feet in rhythm. *"Occide! Occide! Occide!"* they chanted in unison. "Kill! Kill! Kill!" The hellish roaring of their voices drowned out the sudden and ominous rumbling of thunder over the seven hills of Rome. The Romans were being fed like vampires with the sight of much blood and slaughter.

Suddenly the sky darkened. The sunlight vanished. The interior of the amphitheatre became darkly shadowed. The combatants fought on in an eerie semidarkness. A sudden deluge of icy rain streamed through the oval opening in the vast awning.

The rain was succeeded by a violent downpouring of

hail as big as grapes, which battered down through the opening in the awning or tore great holes into the material. The hail pounded down on the shrieking spectators. The combatants stopped fighting and held their shields over their heads.

Calgaich swung his sword. "Come on, you barbarian sonsofbitches! Do you want to live forever!" he roared.

The revived barbarians shouted and charged forward against the startled Romans. Calgaich's sword splintered shields and struck sparks from helmets. The barbarians were outnumbered, but the very impetuosity of their attack drove the Romans back toward the center of the arena.

Decrius Montanas saw that Calgaich was inspiring the attack. None of his men could get near the mad barbarian whose flashing, reddened sword blade cut men down on all sides. Decrius charged toward Calgaich.

"He's mine, barbarian!" Lutorius shouted.

"Get out of the way, you pig-shit!" the centurion yelled at Lutorius.

Lutorius grinned. "Make me, you privy maggot!"

The two of them stood toe to toe in the very center of the arena. The sun emerged and shone down on them from the oval opening in the awning. Chips of wood and pieces of leather flew from the sword strokes on their battered shields. It was a test of champions of the *gladius*.

The centurion drove Lutorius down on one knee, then raised his sword for a killing stroke. Lutorius rammed his upper shield rim into the Roman's crotch. The centurion's sword blow was deflected, but still it struck Lutorius on the left shoulder between two of his armor plates. Blood flowed. Lutorius staggered to his feet as Montanas bent forward in sickening agony. Lutorius's blade flashed in the bright sunlight as it struck downward with full force and severed the centurion's head from his body. Blood spurted and gushed from the neck to drench Lutorius as the decapitated body took one full step and then crashed to the ground. Lutorius shouted in victory and then fell over the body of the Roman.

The leaderless legionnaires formed a shield wall and retreated, step by step, from the wild, free-swinging assault of the yelling barbarians. At last the rear rank stood with their backs against the arena wall just below the podium.

Calgaich stepped back and held out his arms to halt his maddened warriors. Calgaich was *fey*. His eyes glared. His mouth squared in a battle cry. There was no chance for the Romans now. They had fought well and desperately but they knew it was the end for them.

Calgaich looked up at the vast sea of faces and flourished his bloodied sword. "Romans! I am Calgaich mac Lellan, son of that Lellan who once led five hundred war spears against your legions! I am grandson to Evicatos the Spearman! Do you hear the wild fowl calling! The ravens gather for the flesh of these defeated men! Come to the sword welcoming! *All* of you! Stand not back, you proud Romans! This is a red welcome for a feast of human wolves! Do not stand back, you who sit there on your fat Roman asses looking down upon *fighting* men! Come! Try me! Is my challenge to fifty thousand of you the doorway to sudden death!"

"Damn him!" Ulpius Claudius stood up.

Antonia gripped her son's arm. "Are you mad! Sit down! For the love of the gods and your mother, my only son, do not challenge that madman of a barbarian."

Mucius Claudius looked sideways at his wife. "Let him go, Tonia!" He smiled slyly. He knew Ulpius was not his own son. He had always hated Ulpius, and resented Antonia's love for him.

"Shut your mouth!" Antonia screamed.

"The legionnaires are without a leader," Ulpius argued. "They haven't a chance now, at least with that mad barbarian leading the enemy."

Morar leaned close to Valens. "See that he goes, Aemilius," she murmured.

"It would be like a death sentence," Aemilius prophesied.

Morar smiled. "One enemy less for you, beloved."

The procurator nodded and looked sideways at Antonia. "Perhaps two," he said quietly. "Ulpius is the only human being who ever meant anything to that gilded whore. If he dies, it will destroy her."

Calgaich picked up the great war spear of Evicatos. He held it in his right hand, while the magnificent sword was in his left. He flourished the two weapons and pugnaciously eyed the quiet spectators. "Are you all afraid?" he shouted.

Lutorius sat on the bloodied sand near the body of Decrius Montanas. "There is a madness in you, barbarian. Would you fight all of them?"

Calgaich grinned. "What have I to lose, *calo?* If I survive this day it will only be to ready myself for another slaughter like today, and then another, until at last I, too, will die on these bloody sands."

"Go on, Ulpius!" Valens shouted. "Show that mad barbarian the swordsmanship of a Roman legionnaire!"

"No!" Antonia screamed.

Ulpius vaulted the iron fence that protected the audience from the arena and landed lightly on the sands. The sun shone on the curiously designed Celtic gold arm torque he had taken months ago from the sacred wood. He snatched up a legion shield and sword. One of the ex-legionnaires placed a helmet on his head.

Calgaich thrust the tip of his spear into the sands to hold it. He backed slowly toward the center of the arena.

"Stand still, barbarian!" Ulpius shouted.

Calgaich stopped. "I'm waiting, Roman. I've waited a long time for this day. I will not run from you."

Ulpius raised his sword, then looked up at the sea of expectant faces. "I ask the procurator of the Games the right to champion these Romans! Whoever wins this combat between me and this braggart of a barbarian, this Calgaich, shall thus decide the victory! Romans! Do you agree?"

Aemilius Valens stood up. He looked up at the vast audience. He looked down into the arena, where the last of the Romans still stood with their backs against the wall. The bloodied sands were dotted everywhere with the bodies of the wounded, the dying and the dead. It had been a great show thus far.

Rufus Arrius Niger stood up. "Procurator! The barbarian has been fighting in the arena all this time. The tribune is fresh. Can this be a fair match?"

Calgaich looked up at the hawklike face of his grandfather. "Don't intercede for me, Roman!"

Niger nodded. It would have been what he would have said were he in his grandson's position. "So be it, Grandson!" he cried.

"Procurator!" Ulpius called out.

Valens nodded, raised his white handkerchief and let it drop.

Calgaich smiled crookedly. "I once said, Roman, that somewhere you and I would see between us who has the longest legs to run."

"Always the braggart!"

"I will make good on my bragging."

The tribune moved forward, chin tucked in behind the rim of his shield, sword held low at his right side.

Calgaich moved sideways, lightly beating his sword blade on the rim of his battered shield. He was tired. Further, a sword tip had penetrated into the muscles of his left shoulder, so that he was tiring more and more from holding up his shield. He could feel the mingled blood and sweat running down his back, soaking his tunic and the backs of his trouser legs.

"Stand still!" the tribune snapped.

Calgaich spat to one side. "Come and make me!"

Ulpius launched his attack. He raised his shield high to parry the expected blow of Calgaich's sword and then thrust hard with his *gladius*. Calgaich's sword tip swept under the Roman's shield instead of descending upon it. The tip slit Ulpius's tunic just over the crotch, a finger's breadth from emasculating him. He leaped back in panic. Calgaich's sword blade rang dully on the tribune's helmet. Ulpius blinked his eyes from the shock. He retreated quickly.

"Stand still, Roman!" Calgaich jeered.

The tribune recovered and closed in, shield low and out-thrust, while his sword drove in quickly toward Calgaich's face. Calgaich involuntarily drew back his head. Ulpius's shield clashed hard against Calgaich's to drive it upward. The Roman's sword traced an angry red line across Calgaich's right thigh.

Every Roman in the stands was on his or her feet. The handful of survivors from the recent combat stood back from the two duelists, watching with keen and professional interest each nuance of swordplay, for here were two masters of the art in its varying forms—the professional Roman legionnaire and the wild barbarian from the farthest northern reaches of the Roman Empire.

Ulpius closed in, always pressing the attack against his

tiring opponent. Chips flew from Calgaich's shield. His left
arm was numbing from the strain of holding up the shield
and the intense battering it was taking from the incessant
sword blows. He could feel the blood trickling down his
back and from the slit wound on his right thigh.

A powerful blow split Calgaich's shield from upper
rim to boss. Ulpius grunted in satisfaction. He drove in
hard, smashing his shield boss against that of Calgaich's
parrying sword blade like a smith at his anvil.

Suddenly Calgaich shifted. He darted to one side, risking a killing slash of the *gladius,* and brought down an
overhand sword stroke on top of the Roman's helmet. His
sword rebounded from the helmet and struck Ulpius's
left shoulder a glancing blow. Immediately, blood soaked
through the Roman's white woolen tunic.

An animallike roaring went up from the audience as
they saw the blood. Lady Antonia stood up and approached
the iron fencing in front of the podium. She clasped the
gilded fence and peered between the bars in absorbed
fascination as her beloved only son fought against her most
recent lover.

The two opponents circled. Their breathing was harsh
and erratic. Their sandaled feet were reddened from scuf-
fling through the bloody sands. Sweat streamed from their
flushed faces. Again and again the Roman pressed his
steady, disciplined attack, and again and again Calgaich's
magnificent long sword seemed to be in just the right
place to take the clashing blow of the short, thick-bladed
gladius.

The crowd quieted. They were watching two past
masters of their trade. But surely no barbarian could long
withstand the Roman's skilled and technical assault.

Calgaich's shield was split in two. He cast the pieces to
one side. It had become too tiring to bear the weight of it.

Ulpius Claudius stepped back. His chest rose and fell
erratically. His left shoulder was red with blood. Sweat
dripped from his handsome face.

"Do you want another shield, barbarian?" Ulpius asked.

Calgaich shook his head.

Ulpius searched Calgaich's scarred face for a sign of
weakness. Rather than kill this proud barbarian on his
feet, like a man and a warrior, Ulpius would have pre-

ferred to see him fall to the sands, weak from his wounds and exhaustion, and extend a clenched fist with one finger raised for mercy. He saw no signs of weakness on Calgaich's face.

Calgaich drew his long-bladed Celtic dagger and held it in his left hand.

They circled. Ulpius plunged into the attack. He charged and thrust his shield forward. He slashed out with a sweeping sword stroke. Calgaich parried the stroke with his dagger and brought his sword down over the top of the tribune's lowered shield in a smashing blow that rang on Ulpius's helmet and drew a shower of sparks from it. Ulpius staggered. Calgaich leaped sideways. He thrust his sword under his opponent's and raised it high, while thrusting hard with his dagger behind the inner side of the Roman's shield. They broke apart from each other. Ulpius staggered backward. There was a strange look on his flushed face.

Blood dripped from Calgaich's dagger. Calgaich looked into the eyes of the tribune, seeking the slightest hint of the glazing that shows there from a mortal wound.

"Not yet, barbarian," Ulpius grunted thickly.

They were both close to exhaustion. The heat within the arena was now more intense than it had been before the sudden thunder shower that had momentarily cooled the city and the amphitheatre. The air was thick with humidity, and breathing was difficult for both combatants.

The huge bowl was inordinately quiet. Perhaps it was because for the first time these jaded Romans were actually seeing the type of barbarian warrior who had been hammering at their frontiers for hundreds of years.

Ulpius attacked. This time there seemed to be more desperation than cool skill in his attack. No matter where and how he attacked, however, there was always that pair of flashing blades between him and the set, scarred face of the barbarian. A burning hatred crept through the tribune. This was no ordinary man he was facing. Then, mingled with the hatred, there came a hint of fear, which grew by the moment and almost turned into green panic.

Desperate, Ulpius threw all caution aside. He charged. He thrust out his shield and flailed wildly with his sword. Every stroke of his sword was met by a skilled dagger parry or a sword counterstroke. He fell back. His clothing was soaked with sweat and blood. His legs trembled with fatigue. His chest rose and fell spasmodically. Sweat burned his reddened eyes.

Calgaich began to prowl around the exhausted Roman like a hunting cat. Calgaich was limping now. His left arm was hanging by his side. Ulpius Claudius turned slowly so as to keep facing Calgaich. A chilling fear of this master swordsman had taken possession of him.

"*Verbera! Verbera! Verbera!* Lay on! Lay on! Lay on! *Iugula! Iugula! Iugula!* Slay him! Slay him! Slay him! *Occide! Occide! Occide!* Kill! Kill! Kill!" the mob mouthed in roaring unison as they stamped their feet in time to their bloodthirsty chanting.

Calgaich looked beyond the exhausted tribune up toward the sea of red and sweating faces rising tier upon tier to the uppermost rim of the amphitheatre. A slow realization came to him. The fickle mob wanted *him* to kill Ulpius. They were rooting for him, Calgaich, the barbarian, and *not* for the Roman tribune Ulpius Claudius!

Calgaich looked at Ulpius. The Roman had narrowed his eyes in puzzlement. He took his eyes from watching Calgaich and looked about the vast bowl filled with shouting, gesticulating humanity. *Then he knew . . .*

Ulpius charged so swiftly he caught Calgaich unawares. His sword got in under Calgaich's sword. He slammed his shield upward to hold the sword while he thrust hard with his sword for Calgaich's vitals. Calgaich's dagger deflected the thrust. The sword slid under the flesh over Calgaich's left ribs and then protruded from the rear left side just above the pelvis. Calgaich grunted in savage, sickening pain.

Calgaich wrenched himself sideways. The sword would not tear free from the wound. Ulpius hung onto his sword and was dragged sideways along with Calgaich. The Roman tried desperately to withdraw his sword, knowing full well that if he let go of it he would die instantly. Either way it was a deadly mistake.

Calgaich's dagger came up unseen and penetrated under Ulpius's rib cage to strike into his heart. For a fraction of a second the tribune straightened up. He looked into Calgaich's eyes, only a hand's span from his own eyes. His mouth squared. It poured forth a gushing of thick blood. Ulpius fell backward, releasing the grip on his sword. His helmet fell off. His arms were outflung as he fell onto the bloody sand. He looked up at the sky with staring eyes that did not see.

The Lady Antonia's frenzied scream rose even above the roaring voices of the crowd. She turned and stared upward at the sea of faces with an uncomprehending look on her face and complete and permanent madness in her eyes.

Calgaich withdrew the *gladius* from his side and threw it toward the podium. He raised his sword for a two-handed stroke and brought it down, flashing redly in the bright sunlight, to sever Ulpius Claudius's head from his body.

Calgaich picked up the head by its short-cropped hair. He raised it and turned about so that the vast mob could see it. "*Abu! Abu! Abu!* To victory! To victory! To victory!" he shouted hoarsely. He fell forward over the body of the tribune and lay still.

CHAPTER 25

Calgaich lay in one of the cool, marble-lined chambers of the healing shrine of Aesculapius, located on an island in the Tiber. For at least a week the days and nights had seemed to run together, so that he could hardly distinguish one from the other. He had only the vaguest memories of being taken on a litter from the arena with the palm branch of victory lying across his breast while the roar of the vast audience had dinned in his ears. The uproar had been for him, Calgaich, a barbarian and a prisoner of war, for having defeated a patrician Roman in front of his own people. He vaguely remembered Guidd and Lutorius limping alongside the litter as it was taken through the Porta Sanavivaria. There had been another man waiting for him outside of the gate—Rufus Arrius Niger.

Calgaich had dim memories of shaven-headed priests bending over him. There had been that dull and persistent throbbing in his left side. His left shoulder had been stiff and sore. There had been a burning sensation across his right thigh. That had been days past. Now the pain was gone, but there was a great lassitude within him, so that he could hardly move his limbs or raise his head. He had been drugged, he was sure, by the priests of the shrine.

Several times he opened his eyes to see the grinning faces of Lutorius and Guidd looking down at him. One night very late, he saw a cloaked figure standing in the shadows of his chamber. Superstitious fear coursed through him. He thought it was someone from the afterlife who had come to guide him there. Only when the man stepped into the dim rays of moonlight from a small, high window did Calgaich recognize his grandfather.

The days were long and uneventful except for the visitations of the healing priests and the frequent baths that were an important part of the treatment. He began to look forward each evening to the person who attended him after his bath. She was a *balneatrix*, or bath attendant, a statuesque, ebony-haired Cyprian with lustrous eyes like those of a doe. Each evening she would have him placed on a table of cypress wood covered with white Egyptian cloth of byssus. She would rub him down and massage his naked body with her fine, supple hands, using unguents and perfumed olive oil. She never spoke or smiled.

After his bath and massage he would be carried by attendants to his room where he would most often fall into a dreamless sleep, into a sort of never-never land through which, at times, voices would sound close at hand, but seem to come from disembodied spirits.

There came a day when he felt that he was recovering. The intermittent fevers had left him some days past, but the resultant weakness, coupled with the healing drugs which he was given, seemed to have drained much of his usual great vitality from him. Temple attendants carried him on a litter to the baths that evening and lowered him into the *tepidarium*, or warm water bath. He was left alone, because there seemed to be no other patients in residence in that part of the temple.

The *tepidarium* was lighted dully with a few flickering oil lamps whose flames were reflected in wavering lines on the large pool. Calgaich swam slowly back and forth. He was looking forward with pleasure to his nightly massage and rubdown by the beautiful Cyprian. There were other idle and sensuous thoughts in his head, but something about the beautiful silent creature held him from propositioning her.

She came into the room on noiseless bare feet. She spread the cloth of byssus on the table and placed her pots of unguents and jars of oil on the cloth. She looked expectantly at Calgaich, and then came to the side of the pool to help him out. As she bent down to him he looked over one of her shoulders to see a shaven-headed priest swiftly enter through a side door. The priest brushed past the table in his great haste and one of the pots of unguents fell clattering to the marble floor.

The Cyprian turned quickly at the sound. Her eyes widened. A curious gurgling sound came from her throat. The priest whipped out a *sica*, the short, curved and deadly Roman knife, and ran toward Calgaich. The woman threw herself at the priest. She staggered to one side as his knife rose and fell with vicious force. Blood spread widely on the breast of her white gown, but she threw herself at the priest again. Again the knife rose and fell. Then it was thrust in under her ribs. She fell sideways into the pool, dragging the priest with her.

When the priest surfaced, he found himself staring into the orbs of death—the cold gray eyes of Calgaich. One of his hands gripped the priest's hand that held the knife, while the other closed on the man's throat, crushing his larynx. Quickly he sank to the bottom.

Calgaich swam to the dying Cyprian and pulled her to the side of the pool. He crawled from the pool, and with the last of his strength, pulled her from the water. Later, several true priests came running into the *tepidarium*. They found Calgaich seated on the floor cradling the dead woman in his arms. His eyes were brimming with tears.

The priests of Aesculapius were badly frightened. The bright morning light shone through the entrance of the shrine and reflected from the polished *cuirass* and plumed helmet of the praefect of the watch. They were frightened enough of the officer; after all, they were but meek and peaceful men, who had dedicated their lives to healing the sick. It was the other man who had come with the praefect who had put the fear of dire punishment into them.

"Who was that assassin?" Rufus Arrius Niger demanded harshly. "How did he get unseen into the temple? Surely some of you must have known he was not one of you! Or was one of you bribed to admit him into the temple? Perhaps a door was left unlocked on purpose? Speak up, any of you!"

Salvius, the head priest, spread out his small white hands. "Surely, Senator, you don't believe we would have allowed the assassin to enter the temple? We are men of healing. We have nothing to do with the vice and corruption of the world beyond our island. We allow no armed men within our temple at any time." He looked toward the sword that hung at the side of the praefect.

Rufus nodded to the praefect. "Wait outside, Veturius."

Rufus then followed the head priest to Calgaich's room. Calgaich was sitting up in bed. The memory of the beautiful and silent Cyprian weighed heavily upon him. She had died to save his life and yet he had not even known her name.

To Calgaich, Rufus Arrius Niger had always been a dim and remote figure. Everything he had ever learned about him had come from the lips of others, principally his enemies. They respected him or feared him, but none of them had ever said they *liked* him.

"I am having a guard placed here with you, Calgaich," Rufus said. "I will not rest until you are safe in my house."

Salvius shook his head. "Senator, I have told you we cannot allow armed men in the temple."

Rufus waved a hand. "No fear of that. Yet I have found a guard so fearsome that no man will dare approach Calgaich without Calgaich's permission. A guard who stands watch twenty-four hours a day."

Salvius shook his shaven head. "Impossible, Senator!"

Rufus walked to the door. Calgaich and Salvius heard his footsteps on the marble tiles as he walked toward the front of the great temple.

The priest looked at Calgaich. "I told him we had no knowledge of the assassin who attacked you last night."

Calgaich passed a hand over his eyes. He could still see the bloody face of the dying Cyprian as she lay in his arms.

"Her name was Flavia," the priest said.

"She never spoke to me, Salvius."

Salvius nodded. "She had no tongue."

Calgaich stared uncomprehendingly at the priest.

"She was the slave of a wealthy Roman some years ago. She displeased him. He had her tongue cut out. She came to us for help and we took her in and trained her as a *balneatrix*."

"Why was her tongue cut out?"

Salvius shrugged. "It is said that she laughed at the man and at his intense conceit. She also called him a name he could not bear."

"Who was the man?"

Salvius looked quickly behind himself. He came closer to the bed. "The favorite of the emperor. The procurator of Games—Aemilius Valens—"

Footsteps echoed in the corridor.

Salvius turned. His face paled. "For love of the gods," he murmured. His hands trembled as he backed against the wall.

Bron padded softly into the room. He came to the side of the bed and placed his forepaws upon it. Calgaich gripped Bron about the neck and drew him close. Tears filled his eyes.

Rufus Arrius Niger came into the room followed by Lutorius and Guidd One-Eye. Rufus peremptorily jerked his head at the priest. Salvius left the room in undignified haste for a head priest of the Temple of Aesculapius.

Calgaich was overwhelmed. "This is too much. I thought he had been condemned to the Games."

Guidd shook his head. "The best of the many beasts that are brought to Rome are taken to the emperor's menagerie. Sometimes they try to breed them. That was Bron's fate."

"How did you get him from there?" Calgaich asked.

Lutorius winked. "The head keeper once served with your grandfather. After a few *sesterces* were placed in the right palms it was an easy matter."

Calgaich looked at his grandfather. "I thank you for bringing my hound back to me."

"Guidd told me how Bron had waited for your return to Caledonia. Such faithfulness should be rewarded."

"To what end? Are we still not captives?"

"You, Lutorius and Guidd are in my temporary custody," Rufus replied. "The other survivors were sent back to the Ludus Maximus to be trained as gladiators. None of you can ever leave Rome."

"And so we are doomed to live out our lives in this hellhole of a city, far from the misted hills and the rushing rivers of our homeland."

Calgaich looked at Lutorius. "Who else survived, Bottle Emptier?"

"Lexus, Garth, Girich, Niall, Onlach, Eogabal, Muirchu, Loarn, Conaid, Chilo and Ottar, the young Saxon."

"And how many of the enemy survived?"

"Only ten."

"Were they put to death for being defeated?"

Lutorius shook his head. "The senator put a stop to that. Following your victory Valens was like a madman in his rage. He knew he could not have you killed, after your great victory over Ulpius Claudius, so he tried to take out his vengeance on the ex-legionnaires."

"They fought well," Rufus put in. "I couldn't let them die. The mob was swayed by my appeal to let them live."

"Which must have set well with Valens."

Rufus shrugged. "We have been enemies ever since I returned to Rome."

"A dangerous enemy, Grandfather." Calgaich shook his head. "And is there any news of Quintus?"

"Togatus has succeeded him as gladiator master at the Ludus Maximus," Lutorius said.

At that moment Salvius came into the room. "Your Honor, Calgaich must rest now."

Rufus nodded. "Mind you, priest, if anything else happens to my grandson here, shrine or no shrine, I'll come in and clean out the place myself. You understand!"

"The gods forbid that anything should happen to him!" Salvius exclaimed.

"How soon will my grandson be ready to leave the temple? I want him to recuperate for a time at my country villa."

"A week, perhaps, Senator."

They left Calgaich alone with Bron. Bron lay down on the floor facing the doorway. No one could enter that room now without the permission of Calgaich. Calgaich closed his eyes and dropped off to sleep. Flavia's face passed through his mind. Again he heard the hideous gurgling that had come from her tongueless mouth when she had tried to warn him. He awoke with a start. The room was dark. He had slept all afternoon.

He dropped his legs over the side of the bed and slowly started down the long corridor toward the *tepidarium*. Bron padded beside him. Calgaich stripped and lowered himself into the tepid water. It was quiet and peaceful in the large room. But still the memory of the night before haunted him.

He could see down the long corridor that led to the front

of the temple. Suddenly a shadowy veiled figure, clothed in white, was moving toward the doorway of the *tepidarium*. Calgaich felt the hairs rise on the back of his neck. An icy fingertip seemed to trace a line down the length of his spine. Flavia, he thought . . . The figure reached the doorway of the *tepidarium*. Bron rose to his legs and thrust his head forward, with his ears laid back. He growled deep within his throat.

The woman laughed. "Call off Bron, Calgaich." She spoke in the quick and musical tongue of the Novantae.

"By the gods," Calgaich breathed. He *knew* that voice, but yet he wasn't quite sure. She sounded like Bronwyn.

"I've come to substitute for the *balneatrix!*" she cried. "With the permission of the head priest, of course!"

The woman spread the cloth of byssus sheet across the cypress wood table and then placed her pots of unguents and jars of perfumed oils upon the cloth.

"Bronwyn?" Calgaich asked softly.

The woman's back was toward him but he could see the sheen of her golden hair in the soft lamplight.

"Bronwyn?" Calgaich repeated more forcefully.

She turned. "Why Bronwyn, Calgaich?" she asked. "Won't *I* do?" She stripped off her filmy veil.

It was Morar and she was more beautiful than ever. Her white gown clung to her shapely body so that every curve and line of it was plain to be seen. The subtle fragrance of her exquisite perfume came to him.

"Shall I help you from the pool?" she asked.

He nodded. When he was out of the pool, she dried him with a towel.

"You don't seem surprised," she said.

"Nothing surprises me anymore in Rome."

Her deft hands passed along the newly healed scar on his shoulder and then down to the scar on his left side, just above the pelvis. He lay down on the table as she began to rub him down with oils and lotions.

"Does Valens know you are here?" he asked.

She laughed. "He is down in Ostia. He's been there for a week."

"For what purpose?"

"You should know. He's looking for Quintus Gaius."

"Why should I know?"

"Do I have to answer that?"

"You're in fashion here in Rome. As soon as your husband is out of the way, you seek another man."

"In the first place, he is not my husband, and in the second place, I am *not* seeking you, Calgaich."

"Then why are you here?"

She was skilled in the arts of the *balneatrix*. Calgaich could feel himself relaxing.

"I heard it said that you were recuperating slowly."

"That is not so."

"Roll over," she ordered.

He rolled over and looked up into her incredible blue eyes. "Where is Bronwyn, Morar?"

She shrugged. "With Lucius."

"You left her with him."

She applied oil to his chest. "She wanted to stay."

"You're lying, Morar!"

She stepped back a little. "How the warrior patterns show with oil upon them!"

"Did you make a deal with the Perfumed Pig to go to the bed of Valens on condition that he keep Bronwyn?"

"I don't like your insinuation."

He gripped her by the wrists as he sat up. "That's the truth, isn't it?" he demanded. "You left your own sister in the sty of that stinking degenerate so that you could live with a more powerful man!"

"You're hurting my wrists!"

Calgaich could feel the pressure of her breasts against his arm. The fragrance of her perfume, coupled with the oils she had rubbed on Calgaich's body, seemed to bewitch him. He slid his arm about her slender waist and drew her close to him.

Suddenly Bron growled. Calgaich looked about the dim room. No one else was there. Bron had never taken his eyes off Morar. He evidently sensed something that Calgaich did not.

Morar pushed Calgaich back a little. "Later," she murmured. "Let me finish your massage."

"How did you get into the temple?"

"Next to the emperor, Valens is the most powerful man in Rome. Do you think Salvius would try to keep me out knowing that?"

Calgaich looked beyond her as she bent over him again, rubbing her oils into his thighs. Why had she really come?

She was subtly arousing him, caressing his thighs and pressing her body hard against his at times.

She stood back. "There! Wasn't that as good a job as any *balneatrix* might have done?"

Calgaich shook his head. "Not the one I had before you came here, Morar."

She looked sideways at him. "She was *that* good? Ah, but then, of course, she won't be back again, will she?"

He sat up. "How do you know that?" he asked quickly.

She was not to be trapped. "Salvius told me."

"What else did he tell you?"

"That there had been an assassin here last night."

Calgaich dropped his long legs over the side of the table. He looked into her guileless eyes. "You said that Salvius could not refuse you entry into the temple because you are Valens's woman. Perhaps my assassin used the same method of entry."

She smiled. "It's getting late. I'll help you to your room."

"You didn't answer."

"I told you Aemilius Valens has been in Ostia for a week."

"Which means nothing. He could have given orders before he left for that killer to come here. Then, he would be safe in Ostia if any outcry came because of my being murdered."

She shook her head. "If Aemilius had wanted you to die it would have been easy enough to have it done at any other time."

She had him there. Calgaich stood up. He motioned to his hound. "Go ahead, Bron."

The wolfhound padded softly into the dimly lighted corridor. Calgaich then took Morar by the arm and together they walked into the shadowy corridor.

His room was dim except for faint moonlight coming through the one high window over the bed. Calgaich drew her close and kissed her.

"You have wine?" she whispered.

He nodded. "Cyprian. The best."

"Let's drink then!"

He took the wine jug from the little table and filled his cup for her.

She sipped the wine and then held up her arms. "Calgaich," she whispered.

He lay down beside her. They kissed again and again as she fondled and teased him. Calgaich lay back. He reached for the wine jug and drank deeply.

Morar slipped a hand under the mattress. As Calgaich leaned over her again, fortified by the strong Cyprian wine, she passed her hand quickly across the wide mouth of the wine jug.

She was ready for him with every fiber of her being. She was *too* ready. Slowly he reached up to her throat and closed his hands about it. Her eyes opened fully and she looked into his cold gray eyes. She tried to speak but could not.

"Tell me, you whore," he whispered between his teeth, "why did you come here tonight?"

"I told you," she husked.

He suddenly hated her naked beauty and conniving ways. He tightened his grasp on her throat. "What is the *real* reason, whore?"

She tried to look away from him.

"Would you like to be beaten?" he asked softly. "I can raise welts on that ivory skin of yours that will stand out for days. Tell me!"

"Damn you! You wouldn't dare!" she snarled viciously.

"Who's to stop me!"

"I'd tell Valens!"

He grinned down at her. "He doesn't know you're here. You probably don't want him to know you're here."

"The Ordovician woman is with child!" she gasped.

Calgaich stared at her. "You lie!"

"Why should I?"

Calgaich studied her. "You'd have no reason to lie, it's true. Who is the man?"

"Don't *you* know?" she asked quietly.

He released her and sat up. "Impossible!"

She shook her head. "She told me she had lain with you. There have been no other men with her, Calgaich."

"You're sure?"

"She would not lie to me. I have protected her from Sextillius and Valens."

"Why?"

Morar smiled. "Because I want that child for myself."

There was something twisted in the mind that dwelt behind that beautiful face. She was a devious and conniving bitch. "Why?" he demanded again.

"The child will be *mine*, Calgaich. It will be a boy. I am sure of that. He will be brought up and will rise to great fame in Rome. No woman can ever be empress, but none can stop me from making *my* son emperor of Rome!" Her voice had risen and her eyes had widened as she spoke.

"My son will have the blood of Evicatos within his veins. Evicatos the Spearman! He will have the blood of Lellan within him—Lellan, the leader of five hundred war spears!" She looked triumphantly up at Calgaich. "And his father: Calgaich, son of Lellan, and grandson to Evicatos the Spearman and Rufus Arrius Niger! Calgaich, the greatest swordsman the world has ever known!"

"You're mad!" he said quietly.

She reached out and gripped one of his wrists. "There is a way you might save the woman and the child, Calgaich."

He looked down at her lush body and shook his head. "No, Morar. Not now. Not ever. No child of mine shall fall into your hands to be a tool to further your ambition."

She sat up. "Then, the child will be mine."

"And Cairenn will bear it and then be put to death."

She nodded. "The child must be known as mine."

"You've forgotten something, or have you?" He searched her face with his eyes but he could not see beyond the mask of her beauty, to recognize whatever she was—witch or she-demon.

"What do you mean, Calgaich?"

"I am the child's father. No matter how much power you now have, by your own devices, or through Valens, you can't deny that."

She raised her arms toward him. "Come, Calgaich! Make love to me! Stay here in Rome. There is power for you here. Your grandfather has great riches. Some day they will be yours. Together *we* could rule Rome."

Calgaich moved back from her. Her naked, sick ambition sickened him. "Get out of here, whore!" He turned away from her.

He did not see the look of pure hatred that passed across her beautiful face. She got up from the bed and quickly dressed herself.

"One thing more: If anything happens to my child or Cairenn, I will come to you, Morar, and you'll die under my hands," he warned.

She sneered. "You'll never live that long."

He raised a hand to her.

Morar retreated to the doorway.

"Drink yourself into stupidity!" Morar cried. "Go on! I have offered you myself and the world of Rome and you've turned me down! You'll never get another chance, barbarian!"

Then she was gone.

Calgaich reached for the wine jug. Bron raised his head and growled. Calgaich shrugged. He really had no taste for the wine. He dropped onto his bed, and for a long time stared up at the ceiling. Cairenn was with child and the child was his. He recalled the night he had raped her in the abandoned tower while the wolves had howled out in the bitter cold. He remembered how she had fought for him and saved his life when he had fallen overboard from the trireme *Neptunus*. He closed his eyes and saw in his mind's eye her exquisite heart-shaped face.

Calgaich sat bolt upright. "By the gods! *She is my woman!* How could I have been so blind?" He loved Bronwyn, too. And he would never forget the night she had come to him and risked her life to set him free. But he had thought that she was Morar, or he would never have forced her. She was a sister to him in his thoughts, and now he feared for her sanity. His mind returned to Cairenn, and he felt at peace with the knowledge of his love for her. He must live to tell her.

Calgaich was awakened by Tetius, an attendant, in the morning. He walked down the corridor to the *tepidarium* accompanied by Bron.

Tetius stayed in the room. He grinned to himself as he noticed the faint aura of fine perfume which still remained in the air. He straightened out the bed, while surreptitiously eyeing the wine jug. He tiptoed to the doorway and peered up and down the corridor. It was empty.

Tetius turned back into the room and reached for the wine jug.

Bron rose to his feet just inside the doorway of the *tepidarium*. Tetius walked slowly into the room. He held the wine jug in his left hand. His face was drawn and his right hand was at his throat. Suddenly his eyes widened and with a strangled cry he fell forward. The wine jug crashed onto the marble tiles and was shattered. A thin trickling of wine dribbled along the tiles and into the pool.

Calgaich drew himself out of the pool. He rolled Tetius over onto his back. His eyes stared unseeingly at the ceiling.

When Morar had left the room in a cold rage, she cried out: "Drink yourself into stupidity! Go on! I have offered you myself and the world of Rome and you've turned me down! *You'll never get another chance, barbarian!*"

CHAPTER 26

The formal garden of the house of Rufus Arrius Niger backed onto a precipitous slope of the Pincian Hill. The garden was bordered with myrtle trees in stone jars. The portico of the house was opposite the summer house with a small open space in the middle shaded by four plane trees. A marble fountain sprayed undulating mists of water upward, which descended to overflow from the bowl and water the roots of the plane trees and the grass plot about them.

Beyond the summer house was an exercise area, round like a circus, surrounded by box trees and dwarf shrubs. There in the soft amethyst light of dusk could be seen the naked torso of Calgaich, who was exercising with his magnificent sword. It had taken over a month of constant exercising before he had begun to feel he had regained his old stamina and skill. He was being watched by his grandfather, Guidd and Bron.

"There is none like him," Guidd One-Eye said proudly.

Rufus lay propped up on a couch in the coolness of the summer house. There was a gauntness and an unusual listlessness about the old soldier. "Only the great skills of the priests of Aesculapius saved him from certain death," he said.

"And the help of Lugh of the Shining Spear," Guidd added.

Rufus shrugged. "If you so believe, woodsman," he agreed dryly.

Bron rose from beside the couch to greet his master as he came to the summer house. "Is there cool wine?" Calgaich asked.

"The Bottle Emptier is bringing some from the house," Rufus replied.

Calgaich grinned. "Pray to the gods that it gets here." He squatted beside the low couch. "How do you feel?" he asked.

"I seem to grow weaker each day."

Lutorius came from the house carrying a large tray, upon which were arrayed jugs of wine and cool water, wine cups and a heap of fresh fruit. He was accompanied by a tall, gaunt man with long silvery hair.

"Fomoire comes," Guidd announced.

"Then you did get my message to him," Calgaich said.

Guidd nodded. "I found him in the garden of the house of Lucius Sextillius. He was alone. It was easy to climb to the top of the wall and call to him. I didn't want the Perfumed Pig to know you had sent for Fomoire."

Calgaich introduced Fomoire to his grandfather. "He has some skill as a leech in my country," he added. "I wanted him to see you."

"You are a slave to Lucius Sextillius?" Rufus asked.

Fomoire bowed his head. "I am, sir."

Rufus looked at Calgaich. "Can this man be trusted?"

Calgaich nodded. "With your life, Grandfather."

"Were you followed here?" Guidd asked Fomoire.

Fomoire shook his head. "I was sent on an errand which should have taken me a great deal of time. I hurried to complete it and then came here."

Calgaich looked at Guidd. "Just in case, look around outside, old hound."

Guidd nodded, then vanished in among the trees toward the side wall of the garden.

Lutorius filled wine cups for Rufus and Calgaich.

"Fill cups for yourself and this guest, Bottle Emptier," Rufus ordered.

"I am only a *calo* in the house of my lord, sir," Lutorius responded.

Some of the old fire came back into Rufus's eyes. "Damn you! I'll have the hide off your back, if you refuse to obey my orders!" Rufus roared.

Lutorius jumped to attention. He then filled wine cups for Fomoire and himself.

Rufus smiled faintly. "That may be the only way you understand, *calo*. After all, I must owe you something more than a broken nose for saving my life at Carrhae."

Lutorius grinned widely. "That broken nose was an honor, sir!"

Fomoire had been studying the old soldier all this time. Calgaich slanted his eyes sideways at the Druid. Fomoire shook his head a little.

"Well, leech! What do you think?" Rufus asked gruffly.

"May I examine you, sir?" Fomoire requested.

The Druid looked into the eyes of the old man. He passed his slim hands over Rufus's face and fingered the texture of his hair. He passed a hand across the parchmentlike skin of Rufus. At last he stood up.

"Well?" Rufus asked.

Fomoire looked questioningly at Calgaich.

"Tell him, Fomoire," Calgaich said.

Fomoire turned away. He did not want to look at Rufus. Calgaich gripped the Druid by the shoulder. "What is it?"

Rufus emptied his wine cup. "Merely a fever, eh, leech? I've had them before. Once in Cappadocia . . . Ah, but that was long ago." There was a reminiscent tone to his quiet voice.

"Your food and wine?" Fomoire asked. "Who prepares them?"

"The wine is from my own grapes in the country. My servants and slaves prepare my food."

"You trust them all?"

"Why not? They are my *familia*."

"Damn you, Fomoire!" Calgaich snapped. "What is it?"

"I can bear the truth," Rufus said quietly.

"Slow poisoning," Fomoire told them.

It was very quiet in the garden. A moth fluttered about one of the oil lamps. An owl swooped low over the plane trees and vanished into the shadows.

Calgaich's eyes widened as he saw the owl. He knew the bird was one of ill omen, and a harbinger of impending death.

"How long do I have?" Rufus asked.

Fomoire shrugged. "It's difficult to tell. By that means it would seem to be a slow sickness of some sort or perhaps like advancing age. The doses of poison have been skillfully measured to make the effect long lasting. I don't think it is fatal—*yet* . . ."

"But who? Why?" Rufus asked. He looked at Calgaich.

"You stand in the way, Grandfather," Calgaich murmured.

"Valens?"

"More likely the woman, Morar."

Rufus tightened his hands together. "That golden bitch! But she would not have been able to do it herself."

Calgaich's memory quickened. "Have you been anywhere near her?"

Rufus shook his head. "The gods forbid!"

Calgaich looked toward the house. "Then it *is* someone in your *familia*."

"Impossible!" Rufus snapped.

"Who can be trusted in Rome?" Fomoire asked dryly.

"Who is the newest member of your *familia*?" Lutorius asked.

Rufus shook his head. "I'm not sure. Marcus, my steward would know."

Calgaich nodded to Lutorius. "Don't make it too obvious."

Lutorius walked toward the house, then looked back. "If I find out, do you want me to take care of him?"

Calgaich shook his head. "Not yet."

"I must leave," Fomoire said. "I've been gone too long as it is. If Sextillius finds out I've been here, he'll have the hide off my back."

Calgaich walked with him to a side gate of the garden. "Tell me, how is Bronwyn?" he asked.

Fomoire would not meet Calgaich eye to eye. "I don't like to talk about her, Calgaich."

"Tell me!"

Fomoire paused beside the gate. "She lives life as if she were in a trance."

Calgaich remembered the blank, staring look on her face when he had entered the arena of the Flavian Amphitheatre. Morar must not have sent for her yet. It was worse than her attempt to murder him. Bronwyn was her blood, her sister.

Fomoire continued, "She never smiles. There are nights when I hear her crying out, but no one can help her, not in the house of the Perfumed Pig. There are rumors among the slaves and servants as to what goes on. Some of them are called in by Sextillius to participate, but they will not speak about it for fear of losing their tongues. Sometimes there are beasts involved.

"The *cumal*, Cairenn, sends her messages from time to time, but they do not sustain her. She called me to her chambers a few nights ago, very late, when the orgy with Lucius was over. She asked about you. She did not cry; I think she cannot cry anymore. It is beyond her. She wanted me to sing to her. 'Old songs,' she said, 'from long ago.' I sang as best I could. I did not want her to see me crying, so I held my face away from her. Her torn clothing was strewn around the floor, and silken cords were flung about from when they must have tied her. She had bruises on her wrists and ankles." His voice broke. "I don't want to talk about it, Calgaich."

Calgaich nodded. "I understand."

"It is too late for the girl. She can never be the same. It would be better if she were dead. There are things she has been forced to do . . ."

"The *Book of Elephantis*," Calgaich murmured.

"And worse," Fomoire added quietly.

Calgaich opened the the gate for him. Guidd stood there. He nodded. The way was clear.

Fomoire turned as he passed through the gateway. "Since the death of Ulpius, Lady Antonia has become mad. The two weaklings, her husband, Mucius Claudius, and her brother, Lucius Sextillius, have fawned on Aemilius Valens while seeking his favor. Without the Lady Antonia, they are nothing, and, of course, they now have control of the family money, so they are buying their way into the camp of Valens."

Calgaich looked back through the dark garden toward the lamplighted summer house. "And Morar is seeing to it that Rufus, their foremost enemy in the Senate, will be gotten out of the way."

"If anything happens to your grandfather, your fate and possibly that of all us barbarians will be certain. The time is approaching. We must escape, or die here," Guidd said.

"We'll have to move first and *fast*, Fomoire."

They watched the Druid hurry down the steep shadowed street.

"He risks much," Guidd murmured. "If Sextillius learns that he has been here . . ."

As Calgaich approached, Rufus rose from his couch. Standing at the wall of his garden, he looked down upon the lights of Rome.

"Wine, Grandfather?" Calgaich asked.

Rufus nodded.

Calgaich filled two cups, and handed one to the old man. Rufus drank deeply. He looked sideways at Calgaich. "It is what I feared most—a slow and unclean death. A soldier should die in battle, with reddened blade in his hand and his eyes on the victorious Eagles."

"Then why do you stay here, Grandfather?"

"I am a senator, an honored servant of the Empire."

"That's not an answer."

"Don't talk that way to me!" Rufus snapped.

"You can retire from the Senate, with honor, as you did from the legion."

Rufus nodded with reluctance. "At any time."

"Then why not do so?"

"Your questions wound me like the point of that sword of yours."

"You haven't answered them honestly."

Rufus turned to look into the scarred face of his only living relative. "You have your grandmother's way of seeing through a person, Calgaich."

"I think you, too, must have that same quality."

Rufus nodded. "And it has gained me many enemies in Rome. The politicians here are corrupt and deceitful. They know no loyalty to anyone or anything."

"Perhaps you should have stayed in the legion, Grandfather."

"The long years change the perspective of a man, Calgaich. There are times when we are living at our best and utmost and yet we are too blind to see it." He placed his wine cup on the parapet and rested his hands on either side of it while he looked down the long dark slopes of the hill below the garden. It was as if he were trying to look into the past, perhaps to the time when he had been a highly honored soldier of Rome stationed in Britannia, with a beautiful young barbarian for a wife and a little daughter who had been an almost exact copy of her mother. He had asked little of life and less from Rome, other than to serve her and her emperor. He had not married until his later years, convinced that he first had to be fully dedicated to the Empire and none other.

For a few brief years he had been happier than ever before, almost placing Rome second in his affection for his wife and daughter. But he lost both of them, his wife to an early death, his daughter to Lellan, chief of the wild Novantae. After that he had tried to forget by rededicating his life to the Empire. It had never been the same.

"Rome is doomed," Rufus murmured, almost as though talking to himself. "The legions form a thin crust of defense on the farflung frontiers, to protect the inner core of the Empire that is rotten with softness and corruption. Those people in the Flavian Amphitheatre are never satisfied with the rivers of blood in that unholy place. More! More! More! they cry. Half of the city lives on free bread and wine. If an effort is made to cut them off they will rise against the government. The politicians make sure the mob is fed and their interest is diverted to the arena and the chariot races so that their political connivery and corruption can go unheeded.

"Today the legions are composed almost exclusively of barbarians who have never seen Rome. Some day those legions might have to be recalled here, to defend Rome against the hundreds of thousands of wild barbarians battering always at the frontiers."

"All Rome is a fortress, Grandfather," Calgaich added quietly. "Prisoner of her own ambition, Rome. She conquered the known world and in so doing wove a tight net of barbarians about herself. It is only a matter of time before that net will close in on her and strangle her to death."

Rufus looked quickly at Calgaich. "Are those your own words?"

"They were spoken to me by a woman who had heard them spoken many times in her childhood."

There was a strange look on Rufus's gaunt, seamed face. "Who was she?" he demanded.

"My mother, your own daughter, Lydia."

Rufus nodded slowly. "She, too, understood."

"She often told me that she would not live to see the Romans driven from Britannia. But she said the time would surely come. It was inevitable."

"Is that all she said?"

Calgaich shook his head. "She also said that Evicatos, my paternal grandfather, had tried to drive the Romans from Britannia and had failed. My own father, Lellan, a great warrior, also tried and failed. She prophesied that my time, too, would come when I would lead the war spears south to Londinium as my grandfather and father had done before me."

"She was said to have the 'second sight.' Did she say you would succeed?"

Calgaich shook his head. "She did not know. But she did say that if by chance I did not succeed, my son might."

"But you have no son, Calgaich. You are a prisoner in Rome. The odds are that you will never have a son. So you see, Calgaich, your mother, the gods rest her soul, was quite wrong."

"Only the gods know that, Grandfather."

Rufus nodded. "One likes to think so," he said dryly.

Lutorius and Guidd brought food and more wine to the summer house. Lutorius caught Calgaich's eye. Later Calgaich waited for Lutorius in the shelter of the boxwood trees.

"Marcus told me that Nepos, an Iberian fisherman, is the newest slave in the house," Lutorius said.

"You think it might be he?"

Lutorius shook his head.

"Who else then?"

Lutorius glanced toward the house. "Marcus was too quick to point out the Iberian."

"You mean?"

"There is a cook, perhaps a little fat and somewhat greasy, but kind to me in her own way, you understand. I think she loves me. So I gave her a promise. She hinted that it was Marcus himself who is doing the poisoning."

"But the man has been with my grandfather for many years!"

"All the more reason he would go unsuspected."

"Do you think he has been bribed by Valens?"

"More likely by Morar."

"The cook will warn us if anything further happens?"

"Yes."

They walked toward the summer house.

Calgaich looked sideways at the *calo*. "What was the promise you gave the cook, eh, Bottle Emptier?"

Lutorius grinned. "I would marry her when I got my parole."

They were still laughing when they reached the summer house.

Rufus pushed back his plate. He looked down at the great wolfhound. "Where is a loyalty such as his to be found in all Rome? The assassin's dagger, or the cup of the poisoner, are never far removed from the few men such as myself who stand up against the foul corruption that thrives like maggots in a latrine here in Rome. Is there no one I can trust?"

Calgaich nodded. "You have Lutorius, Guidd, Bron and myself here with you now."

Rufus smiled a little. "A drunken ex-legionnaire, a one-eyed barbarian huntsman, a savage wolfhound and a wild barbarian of a grandson."

"We four barbarians may be all you have. You can depend upon us, Grandfather, even though we are considered to be barbarians, and enemies of Rome," Calgaich vowed.

An owl hooted softly from the deep shadows of the trees.

CHAPTER 27

It was the week-long festival of Midsummer Day, the summer Saturnalia, in honor of Saturn, god of the sown and sprouting seed. The schools were on holiday and all public business was halted. The law courts were closed and all offenses, short of the gravest, went unpunished. Plebeians and slaves were allowed liberties and license with their superiors and masters. The streets, squares and houses of Rome were filled day and night with revelers.

The flames of torches and bonfires could be seen in the streets at dusk from the Pincian hilltop mansion of Rufus Arrius Niger. The sounds of music and singing filled the streets and the houses of Rome, but the house of the senator was quiet and dimly lighted. His servants and slaves had been given leave to join the merrymakers on the last night of the Saturnalia. Only Marcus, the steward, and Nepos, the Iberian slave, were still within the mansion.

There was to be no revelry that night in Rufus's house, for he was slowly dying.

Calgaich and Lutorius sat with Rufus in the dim, lamp-lit atrium of his garden pavilion. Rufus lay on a couch. The old man had been drifting in and out of a coma for two days.

Lutorius got up and walked to the rear of the pavilion to overlook the Gardens of Sallust far below.

Calgaich came to stand beside him. "What is it, *calo?*"

"Listen to them down there. All Rome is drunk tonight."

"And you wish you were down there with them, eh?"

Lutorius shook his head. "Not with Old Give Me Another dying." His eyes glistened with tears.

Calgaich rested a hand on the shoulder of the *calo.* "We learned too late of the treachery that will bring about his death. There's nothing we can do for him now."

361

"Not for *him*. But for those who plotted and executed his poisoning. *That,* we can do something about!"

"The time is at hand. The whole city is drunk. I have heard that Valens and Morar are having a great festival at their mansion on the Viminal Hill. Lucius Sextillius is said to be one of the guests. If we can slip into the gardens, perhaps disguised as revelers, we've got a good chance of killing all three of them."

Lutorius nodded. "When do we leave?"

"Not until the old man dies."

"That might take hours!"

"We will wait!"

Rufus stirred. "Calgaich!" he called.

Calgaich and Lutorius hurried to the side of the old man. "Are you feeling better?" Calgaich asked. It was a senseless question, he knew.

"I have only a little time left. I am no longer concerned about myself. My time has come. It is you I'm thinking about now.

"With my death you will be hounded down by Valens. The power struggle here in Rome has passed into the hands of Valens, the woman Morar and that pig Sextillius. Of the three, I consider the woman the most dangerous. After she has used Valens she'll get rid of him, one way or another. If Valens becomes emperor she'll control him like a puppet on a string.

"Everything I have is to be left to you. You will never be able to use that wealth here in Rome. You are not a Roman citizen and you can never become one. Should you survive the plotting of Valens and that Morar, they will see to it that your wealth is stripped from you. Most of my wealth can't be liquidated without long legal involvements. Therefore, cash money to take with you is the best wealth I can give you."

Rufus smiled faintly. "I know that you've had it ever in your mind to escape from Rome with your barbarian comrades. Somehow your gods saw to it that Cunori, the Gaulish seaman, was recommended to me by Aulus, the sailing master of the trireme *Neptunus*, to command my small vessel, the *Lydia*.

"I have sent six bags of *sesterces* down to Ostia in the

care of one of my most trusted servants. He entrusted it in turn to Cunori, my sailing master.

"Your grandfather, Evicatos, led a great invasion into Britannia and almost reached Londinium. Your father Lellan tried, too. They both failed. It is likely to be your destiny to lead the next invasion of Britannia. But you will also fail, if you repeat the errors made by your grandfather and father.

"There are four steps that must be taken in order for you to succeed," Rufus continued. "You will need many allies to achieve your objective—the Novantae, the border tribes, certainly many Picts, and perhaps even the Saxons. You must organize and unify your invading force. You will be facing the best trained and most victorious soldiers in the world—the Roman legions. You can't defeat them leading a rabble, a mob of wild-eyed barbarians, where each man fights as though the whole battle is a personal matter, wherein he seeks great honor only for himself. You must have a leader, *one man,* whose decisions are final and who can achieve the first two steps. Perhaps that is yourself, Calgaich, but only the gods know that now." His voice seemed to fade.

Calgaich and Lutorius bent over the old man. His breathing was harsh and irregular. After a time he opened his eyes. He smiled faintly.

"I'm not done yet, Grandson," Rufus murmured. "The key to all such endeavors—*financing . . ."*

"The money you sent down to the *Lydia?"*

Rufus nodded.

"I don't understand. You, one of the most honored soldiers and senators in the history of Rome, are giving me the funds with which to finance an invasion of Britannia." Calgaich shook his head in mingled wonder and puzzlement. "Why, Grandfather?"

"This is not the Empire for which I fought for so many years. I told you some time ago that the Rome I have known all my life is doomed. I would prefer that you barbarians regain that which is rightfully yours."

Lutorius filled a wine cup with strong Corsican wine and held it to the lips of the old man. Rufus lay back against some pillows and closed his eyes.

"Who took the money down to Ostia, sir?" Lutorius asked.

"Marcus, my steward."

Lutorius looked at Calgaich over the head of Rufus. He raised his eyebrows.

Rufus opened his eyes. "Grandson, give me your knife." Calgaich shook his head.

"A man has the right to open his veins rather than to die an unclean or dishonorable death. That is an unwritten Roman law. This I have chosen to do. Further, you must make your escape attempt this night. Once my death is made public, your chance will be gone forever."

Calgaich nodded. It would have been his choice had he been in the same situation as Rufus. He withdrew the short Roman *sica* from within his tunic. He placed it in Rufus's hands.

Rufus drained his wine cup. He looked about the lovely shadowed garden. "I shall miss this place."

Guidd One-Eye appeared from the side gate. "Calgaich!" he called. There was urgency in his voice.

"Lydia," Rufus murmured. It was the last thing he would ever say. Calgaich turned away.

They did not look back as they ran toward the gate.

Fomoire stood within the gate with his back against the garden wall. His head was bent and his right hand was enveloped in a bloody bandage. There was a bandage covering his left eye.

"What happened?" Calgaich demanded.

Fomoire slowly raised his head. "The vengeance of Lucius Sextillius," he whispered. He sagged sideways and was caught by Guidd and Lutorius. "I might have been followed here."

"Get him into the house," Calgaich ordered.

He opened the gate and looked up and down the narrow, shadowed street. It was empty of life. He closed and barred the gate and hurried into the house.

Fomoire was lying on a bed in the small room shared by Lutorius and Guidd. He was sipping greedily at a wine cup held to his lips by Guidd. Calgaich could see that Fomoire's right hand was fingerless.

"The eye?" Calgaich asked.

"Blinded by a hot iron."

Calgaich shook his head in horror. "Can you talk?" he asked Fomoire.

"You must leave this place," Fomoire whispered. "Morar found out somehow that I had been here to see your grandfather. She knows of my skill as a leech. They know your grandfather is dying. They plan to have you arrested as soon as the old man dies."

"Why did they maim you, Fomoire?"

"It was because of Bronwyn. She was living a life of hell with Sextillius. Drugs and aphrodisiacs turned her into an animal. A few times her mind seemed to clear itself, and then she would appeal to Morar for help, to no avail. It was as though she didn't exist in Morar's mind.

"The Perfumed Pig held an orgy composed of the most licentious and depraved men and women of Rome. At the height of the evening Bronwyn appeared. She was as naked as the day of her birth, painted and gilded like a peacock, and performed the most suggestive dance I have ever seen. At its end she threw herself to the floor and crawled to the feet of Sextillius, to fawn upon him and then perform an act of fellatio on him. While she was doing this Sextillius beckoned to Murranus, a gladiator and beast in human form, who thereupon aproached her from the rear and sodomized her."

Calgaich raised a hand as though to strike Fomoire. "Enough!" he shouted hoarsely. His eyes were wide in his head.

Fomoire drew back in alarm and weakly raised his hands to defend himself. "It was not my doing, Calgaich!" he cried.

"Let's get on with this!" Lutorius snapped.

Calgaich nodded. "I'm sorry, Fomoire."

Fomoire smiled faintly. "When one sees the battle flame in your eyes . . . To go on—the depraved sex acts being performed before the others excited them into a frenzy. They coupled with each other, men and men, women and women, whoever was next at hand, and in the middle of the debauchery Sextillius had his slaves release some of his trained hounds into the room. The last I saw of Bronwyn was when she was under a huge stud of a hound." His voice died away as the horror of the scene came back to him.

"Calgaich," Guidd pleaded, "we must leave!"

"You and Lutorius find Marcus. You know what to do."

"And Nepos?"

"He's done us no harm."

"He can talk though," Lutorius put in quickly.

"Use your own judgment. We can take him with us. His life will be forfeit here anyway."

Lutorius and Guidd drew their knives and left the room.

Calgaich looked down at the Druid. "Tell me the rest," he said quietly. The fire was gone from his eyes. His features were as though carved from stone. No emotion showed in them, but Fomoire knew what hatred and vengeance must be stored within Calgaich's mind like bitter gall.

"Just before dawn light," Fomoire continued, "Bronwyn crawled into my cubicle in the slave quarters. 'If living is this horrifying, dying must be easy,' she said. I nodded as I took her into my arms." His voice died away on a broken note.

"And you showed her how to die?" Calgaich demanded.

Fomoire nodded. "Forgive me, Calgaich. Had you seen her, the terror in her lovely eyes, and the loathing with which she considered herself when she realized what Sextillius had done to her."

"Poison, Fomoire?"

"The best, or worst. There was no pain."

"Go on."

"I carried her to her rooms."

"And Sextillius discovered you then?"

Fomoire shook his head. "By the gods, when he found out what had happened to his golden whore, as he called her, he became almost mad. He didn't know how she got the poison."

"An easy enough commodity in Rome."

"Yes. But he suspected me."

"Why did he not kill you?"

Fomoire smiled a little. "I was too valuable a slave. He said, 'We will remove the fingers of the hand that might have helped Bronwyn die, and one of your eyes as a warning that the other eye may be taken at any time.' I couldn't escape until this evening, and came directly here. They will be looking for you and the others, Calgaich, as well as me."

"We're leaving here tonight. Are you strong enough to travel?" Calgaich asked Fomoire.

"I barely made it here. Go on without me. They will not find me alive."

"Or dead. You're coming with us if I have to carry you on my back all the way to Ostia."

Marcus, the steward, was in his darkened room. The leather bags he was handling were heavy with *sesterces.* He grinned to himself. There was a fortune in those bags. He would leave the house that night, while Calgaich and Lutorius were fully occupied in the death watch of the old bastard, Rufus Arrius Niger. Marcus had already taken two of the bags from their hiding place in his room to bury them on the hill slope behind the mansion garden. It would be easy enough to retrieve them some dark night after the old man's death.

Now he lifted two more of the bags and tiptoed to the door of his room which opened onto a balcony that over-looked the atrium of the house. He peered down. Faint lamplight shimmered on the surface of the large *impluvium,* or pool, centered in the atrium.

"Where are you going, Marcus?" Lutorius asked softly out of the darkness at the far end of the balcony.

Marcus dropped the two money bags. He ran in panic to the stairway at the other end of the balcony and plunged down the steps.

A shadowy figure stood near the vestibule at the front of the atrium. "What's your hurry, Marcus?" Nepos suddenly asked.

Marcus whirled. He splashed through the knee-deep water in the *impluvium.* He scrambled out of the pool.

Another man stood near the rear of the room. "Where are you going, Marcus?" he asked.

Marcus backed slowly into the center of the pool. He could feel the little fish in the pool nibbling at his bare legs. He looked back over his shoulder. Lutorius leaned against a pillar while fastidiously cleaning his fingernails with his knife. Nepos squatted at the edge of the pool. There was a half grin on the face of the Iberian. He had always hated Marcus. The one-eyed barbarian was standing at the edge of the pool with bared knife.

"Did you take the good *sesterces* down to Ostia, as your master asked you to do, Marcus?" Lutorius asked. "He trusted you above all others, you know."

Marcus nodded quickly.

"*All* of them, Marcus?"

"Yes," Marcus blurted.

Lutorius slanted his eyes upwards toward the balcony. "You left your own savings up there then. Is that so?"

"Yes! Yes!"

"By the gods, you were a frugal man, steward."

"That is so!"

Lutorius sauntered to the edge of the pool. He squatted there. "How many bags did you have, eh, Marcus?"

"Only four," Marcus replied.

"Search his room, Nepos. He dropped two bags on the balcony," Lutorius said.

While Nepos searched the room, Guidd and Lutorius thoughtfully watched the steward. It was very quiet in the beautiful atrium.

Nepos came down the stairs, laden with four heavy bags. "These are all I could find, master."

"Now will you let me go?" Marcus pleaded.

"Of course."

"It *is* all of the master's money."

"*All* of it, steward?" Puzzled, Lutorius scratched his head. "It seems to me that *six* bags of *sesterces* were to be delivered to Ostia."

The man was a devil. Marcus smiled wanly. "There are two more bags hidden on the slope behind the garden, at the base of the largest oleander there."

Lutorius nodded. "There is one other matter, Marcus," he said quietly.

Marcus stood by the edge of the pool. "What do you mean?"

"Your good master is dying this night. He was poisoned," Lutorius continued relentlessly.

"By Nepos!"

"Nepos?" Lutorius asked, looking at the slave.

The Iberian shook his head.

Marcus turned to run. Guidd merely thrust his knife out

in front of himself and as the steward ran into it, he pushed it into the man's plump belly and twisted it. Marcus fell sideways into the pool with outflung arms. His blood began to tint the water.

"Good hunting, woodsman," Lutorius said. He dragged the steward from the water. "Wipe up the blood on the tiles." He then lifted the steward across his shoulders and dogtrotted out into the garden. He pitched Marcus over the parapet. Lutorius then dropped over the wall, found the largest oleander, and dug up two plump money bags. He hid them at the base of the wall and then returned to the garden.

Calgaich was shearing off Fomoire's long hair when the others came into the bedchamber. He had already shorn off his own long mustache and hair. "Guidd," he said over a shoulder, "get rid of that long, barbarian hair and mustache. You'll have to look like a Roman at least until we escape from Ostia."

They worked swiftly. Calgaich got his sword and spear and wrapped them in a bed coverlet to conceal them. Guidd, Nepos and Lutorius armed themselves with short swords they found in the house. Calgaich shoved the hair-cutting shears and a razor inside his tunic.

Outside they helped Fomoire to the parapeted wall at the rear of the garden. Guidd then dropped over the wall with Nepos. They caught Fomoire as he was lowered to them. Calgaich then lowered Bron over next.

Lutorius rested a leg on the parapet. "Are you ready, barbarian?" he asked.

Calgaich shook his head. "Take my sword and spear. There is something I must do, Bottle Emptier. I'll meet you at the bottom of the hill."

Calgaich walked through the darkened, echoing house. He found some large jars of lamp oil and carried them to the pavilion.

Rufus Arrius Niger, once tribune *legatus legionis* and senator of Rome, lay still in death. His eyes were open. The knife lay on the tiles beside the couch. Calgaich closed the eyes of the old soldier. He thrust the knife inside his tunic. He gathered furniture from other rooms of the pavilion and stacked it around the couch. He drenched the furniture and the coverlet of the couch with the lamp oil.

For a moment or two he stood there looking down at his grandfather. Tears trickled slowly from his eyes. It was eerily quiet in the garden.

Calgaich struck a light and held it to the edge of the couch coverlet. The flame ate eagerly into the oil-soaked material and lighted the calm, hawk-like profile of Rufus Arrius Niger. Soon a chair caught fire. Tongues of flame licked along the dry wood and set fire to a fine table of cypress wood. Calgaich tore loose a piece of the flaming coverlet and cast it upward so that it caught in the dry latticework which shaded the open-roofed room. The oil-soaked furniture was now all aflame and eerily lighting the stiffening body of the old soldier.

"*Ave*, Tribune," Calgaich murmured.

There was a sudden loud thudding at the barred front door of the mansion. The sound echoed hollowly through the building. The door crashed open just as Calgaich dropped from the wall to join his comrades.

When the subpraefect of the guard ran through the house followed by his men, he saw the glowing of flames within the pavilion. The garden was empty of life. They watched as the latticework roofing collapsed and sent up a roaring pillar of sparks and smoke. The illumination lighted the steep slope of the Pincian Hill and the dense shrubbery that covered it. There was no sign of life to be seen.

CHAPTER 28

Calgaich, Bron and his four companions stood inside a dark doorway on the side street next to the Ludus Maximus. No sounds of revelry came from within the high, vine-covered walls of the gladiator school.

"There are not too many students in school," Lutorius whispered. "Maybe ten or fifteen outside of our barbarians. The *veterani* and the instructors are probably out in the streets or in the wineshops."

"Would the students, outside of our comrades, give the alarm if we enter the school?" Calgaich asked.

Lutorius shrugged. "Who knows? They might, to curry favor with Togatus."

"How many guards might be on duty tonight?"

"Ten maybe. Twenty at the most. Those off duty would be in the guardhouse or in their quarters."

"What about Togatus?"

"He's probably in Quintus's old quarters."

"On such a festive night?" asked Fomoire.

"Why should he leave the school, weasel? He has the best of everything in there, as Quintus did. Fine food, excellent wine and perhaps a whore or two. Anyway, he'd be a damned fool to roam the streets during the Saturnalia. He's not too popular in Rome."

Calgaich handed his sword and spear to Nepos. He turned to Lutorius. "We'll need the keys to the armory and the outer door of the prisoner barracks."

"Quintus always kept them in the anteroom of his quarters."

Calgaich looked at Fomoire. "Lutorius, Guidd and I will go over the wall. If the alarm is sounded and we are seen, escape any way you can. Nepos here knows the city. You'll have plenty of money with which to grease any palms if you want to escape from Rome."

"And what of you?" Fomoire asked quietly.

Calgaich grinned wryly. "We escape, or we die."

"If you die, there will be no escape for us. We can't make it alone, Calgaich."

Calgaich pointed toward the school. "And what of our comrades? I won't leave Rome without them."

"We'll need a place to meet once we get out of the school," Lutorius added. "There is a deserted temple two blocks away, at the foot of the Street of the Pear. It was once dedicated to Dionysius, but has been abandoned since he went out of favor many years ago."

Calgaich nodded. "Nepos, do you know where it is?"

"Yes, I think so."

"Good! You and Fomoire hide the money bags there. As our comrades escape take two or three of them at a time to the temple. Tell them to wait in the temple until we are all there."

"And if you don't show up?" Nepos asked.

Calgaich shrugged. "Then you're on your own. You know of my grandfather's boat at Ostia?"

"The *Lydia?* Yes."

"Cunori, her master, is one of us. Try to reach her."

Nepos grinned wryly. "With a maimed man, a savage wolfhound and six bags of *sesterces?* You honor me, master!"

"I am *not* your master! There are no masters here! We are all comrades this night and henceforth until we escape or die. One more thing: If you are caught, you must tell no one our plan to escape. Do you understand?"

Nepos nodded. "Yes."

"You must not talk about the boat!"

Calgaich, Guidd and Lutorius then crossed the street. They kicked off their sandals. Calgaich climbed the vine-covered wall. He reached the parapet and poked his head up over its rim. The guard walkway was empty. He whistled softly to his two companions.

Lutorius came over the wall followed by Guidd. The large quadrangle and the practice area were shadowy expanses in the darkness. Faint yellowish light showed through the slit windows of the guardhouse which was in the base of one of the guard towers where the main gate was located.

They let themselves down from the guard walkway to the tiled roof of one of the barracks.

"Quiet!" Calgaich hissed.

They dropped flat on the large tiles.

Nailed sandals beat a little unsteadily on the walkway. A dim figure showed in the darkness. The guard passed within fifteen feet of the three prone figures on the roof. The man hiccupped. In a little while his unsteady footsteps died away.

Lutorius grinned. "He's full of Saturnalia wine."

Calgaich hung from the tile rain gutter of the roof and then dropped lightly to the ground. Lutorius and Guidd landed beside him. They crouched in an arcade, peering into the darkness.

Calgaich gripped Guidd by the shoulder and pointed toward the gate. Guidd nodded. He vanished silently into the shadows of the arcade.

Calgaich and Lutorius catfooted across the wide quadrangle. Calgaich started for the door to Togatus's quarters. Lutorius gripped him by an arm and shook his head. They froze in position under the arcade.

Sandals thudded on the hardpacked earth of the quadrangle. Two men passed just beyond the arched openings of the arcade and within a few feet of the two motionless figures in the deep shadows.

"Damned if this isn't the quietest night I've ever spent in this place, Ostorius," said one of the men. "Meanwhile, Rome is one big wineshop and whorehouse."

"True, but what have we to worry about? Togatus wants company. He's got plenty of wine, food and three women in there with him, Aelius. By Zeus, one of them is a Greek whore that could shake your reason just to look at her. Tits on her like a cow and an ass as broad as a spear shaft is long."

They opened the door to Togatus's quarters, then closed it behind them.

Guidd came silently across the quadrangle. "The guards are deep into the wine jugs. There are only two of them on watch. One in each gate tower."

Calgaich drew his dagger. "I'll get the keys."

"Remember who you're up against, barbarian. Three of the best."

"You'll hear soon enough if I need help, *calo*."

Calgaich eased open the door. An oil lamp flickered dimly in the anteroom. The door into the quarters of the gladiator master was slightly ajar. He could hear the sound of men talking loudly and the shrill laughter of drunken women.

The draft from the outer door blew out the oil lamp. Calgaich cursed beneath his breath as he searched for the ring of keys. Finally his hand closed on the key ring on a wall hook. He unhooked the key ring and turned quickly to leave the room. The heavy keys swung in his hand and knocked a vase from a table. It shattered to pieces on the tiled floor.

The sound of voices and laughter suddenly stopped.

Calgaich jumped into a corner as the inner door swung open to admit a flood of lamplight from the quarters. A tall, broad-shouldered man was framed within the doorway. At that instant Lutorius suddenly appeared in the outer doorway with his knife in his hand.

"By Hercules! It's that damned Bottle Emptier!" Aelius shouted. He drew his dagger and plunged toward Lutorius.

Calgaich brought the heavy cluster of keys down across the back of the head guard's thick neck. Aelius staggered forward to meet the point of Lutorius's knife. He fell face downward on the floor just as Ostorius came plunging through the inner doorway with his dagger ready.

Calgaich swung the keys to smash them across the face of the instructor. Ostorius staggered back against the wall, half-blinded by the blood that spurted from his face. Calgaich's dagger flashed in the light from the open door and finished off Ostorius.

A broad and powerful figure in the inner doorway was framed by the light from behind him. Togatus was as drunk as a priest of Dionysius. His eyes widened as he backed slowly into his quarters. The whores screamed in shrill unison.

"Shut the outer door, *calo*," Calgaich ordered.

"He's mine, barbarian," Lutorius claimed.

Lutorius crossed the room in three great strides. Togatus threw a wine jug at his face. Lutorius fended it off with his left forearm and closed in on Togatus. Togatus took one knife thrust to get his bearlike arms about Lutorius. The two of them stood there straining against one another.

Calgaich kicked a screaming whore out of the way. He snatched up a chair and brought it down full force on the rounded head of the gladiator master. Togatus merely grunted and tightened his grip. Lutorius gasped from the terrible pressure.

Calgaich stepped in close and drove his dagger into the back of Togatus, who stiffened and relaxed his hold on Lutorius. He staggered backward and Lutorius slid his knife in up under the ribs of the gladiator master. He swayed sideways and crashed onto the bed.

The whores had stopped screaming. They huddled together in a corner of the room.

Lutorius looked slowly at the three women. "Well, Calgaich?" he asked softly.

"They haven't harmed us."

"As soon as we leave they'll scream an alarm."

"We can lock them in."

"We can't risk letting them live, Calgaich," Lutorius insisted.

Calgaich walked quickly from the room. "Lock them in!" he snapped over a shoulder.

Guidd was waiting outside. "Did you get them all?"

Calgaich nodded, leading the way along the arcade to the armory, where he unlocked the door and with Guidd's help selected swords and daggers with which to arm the other barbarians.

They unlocked the outer door of the prisoner barracks. The dark hall was quiet.

Calgaich looked back over his shoulder. "Where's that damned Bottle Emptier?" he hissed.

"I'll get him, Calgaich."

Lutorius softly closed the outer door to Togatus's quarters. Calgaich had left the key in the lock. Lutorius locked the door. He drank deeply from a wine jug and then wiped the blood from his knife onto the thick vines which hung from the roof of the arcade.

Guidd came silently through the darkness. He whistled softly. "Calgaich wants you, *calo.*"

Lutorius handed the jug to Guidd. "Have one on me, woodsman."

Guidd drank deeply. He wiped his mouth. They walked across the quadrangle. Guidd looked sideways at Lutorius. "How were the whores?"

Lutorius nodded. "Not bad. Not bad."

"Perhaps they might make an outcry."

Lutorius looked back over his shoulder. "Not a chance, woodsman, not a chance. . . ."

The cells did not have locks, but were held shut by thick wooden bars placed across the doors and resting in metal supports. Calgaich paused outside the first cell door. He could hear the occupant moving softly about. "Lexus?" Calgaich whispered.

"Yes. Who is it?"

"Calgaich."

There was a moment's pause. "Is this some cursed Roman trick?"

Calgaich lifted the bar from its supports and opened the heavy door. A huge figure stood in the center of the cell. Lexus gripped Calgaich in a bear hug.

"By the gods, Gaul, let me go!" Calgaich gasped. "Show me where the rest of our comrades are."

They released the other prisoners. As each of them passed out into the opening quadrangle Lutorius handed them a sword and a dagger. Guidd then guided them to the stairway which ascended to the wall. At the bottom of the wall Nepos guided them by twos and threes to the abandoned temple of Dionysius. There, Fomoire instructed them to shear off their long hair and scrape off their mustaches.

They were all there when Calgaich, Lutorius and Guidd came into the temple. Lexus, the giant Gaul; Garth, the Silurian harper; Conaid, the Little Hound, of the Damnonii; Chilo, the Greek tutor; Loarn, the daring Brigantes; and Niall, the redheaded Selgovae. There were also Ottar, the quiet young Saxon chief; Girich, the Pict, who was the son of Aengus; Onlach, of the border Votadini; and Eogabal and Muirchu of the Northern Picts, the fierce and untamed Niduari.

Calgaich looked from one to the other of the silent shadowy figures of men. "You are free now, at least from the Ludus Maximus. The Saturnalia will be over by dawn tomorrow and then your escape will be discovered. There is a boat down at Ostia, the *Lydia,* which was my grandfather's and is now mine. You all remember Cunori, the Venetus seaman. He now commands the *Lydia.* We plan to escape from Ostia on the *Lydia.* You can travel one by one, or in twos, but no more than two together down to the Emporium, the warehouses on the bank of the Tiber, where a boat can be stolen with which you can go down the river to Ostia.

"You will have to move fast and not arouse suspicion. Any of you who are caught must not talk. You know nothing of this plan. Probably not all of you will make it to the Tiber or to Ostia. That rests in the laps of the gods. Go now, while you still have darkness and time on your side."

None of them moved.

"Well?" Calgaich demanded.

"Aren't you coming with us, Calgaich?" Lexus asked.

Calgaich shook his head. "There are things I must do first."

"What do you mean?" Loarn asked.

"You all know of my woman, Cairenn. She is a slave to Aemilius Valens and the woman Morar. She is now in their house at the top of the Viminal Hill. I am going there to get her."

"This is madness!" Chilo cried. "What is one woman more or less? Would you jeopardize your chance for freedom and perhaps your very life for a slave woman?"

"She is with child," Calgaich replied quietly. "The child is mine. I mean to take Cairenn back with me to my own country."

It was very quiet in the dank temple.

"This Valens, and the bitch-woman Morar," Niall put in softly. "Do you mean to let them live, Calgaich?"

"No, Niall. They must die."

"You'll not go alone then to do this thing."

A low murmur spread amongst the men.

"I'm going with him," Lutorius said.

"And I," Guidd added.

"Count me in, Calgaich," Lexus added.

Calgaich shook his head. "I will take only four men with me—Lutorius, Guidd, Girich and Conaid."

No one spoke. They knew the voice of command when they heard it.

Calgaich looked at Nepos. "Do you know the way to the Emporium, Nepos?"

The Iberian nodded. "I have been there many times to buy food and staples for my master."

"Lead the rest of the men there. Take care of Fomoire. Find a barge on the Tiber embankment to steal. Send a man back to meet us at the main gate of the Emporium. If we are not there in two hours, you must leave for Ostia. Otherwise, the dawn will catch you on the river."

Nepos led the men from the temple. Lexus helped Fomoire.

Calgaich took his sword and spear. He looked at his four comrades. He nodded. They left the temple with great Bron padding beside his master and started up the slope of the Street of the Pear toward the top of the Viminal Hill.

CHAPTER 29

The mansion of Aemilius Valens stood at the very crest of the Viminal Hill. The rear wall of its sumptuous garden overlooked a steep slope that descended to the next street. The slope itself was thickly overgrown with tall oleander bushes. Within the dark shelter of the oleanders just below the rear wall of the garden, Calgaich, Lutorius, Girich, Conaid and Bron now waited for word from Guidd, who had gone ahead to scout the situation. They could hear the faint sounds of revelry coming from the garden and from the other great homes on the Viminal Hill.

Guidd came noiselessly down the slope. "There are no guards about the garden and only one in the house," he whispered. "He is the porter at the front door and he's drunk."

"And inside?" Calgaich asked.

"There are not too many people there now. I overheard some of them saying they were going to the Baths of Trajan."

"Valens? Morar? Cairenn?"

Guidd nodded. "I saw Valens and Morar. They were not together." He grinned. "Valens was with a young boy who was painted like a whore. Morar was naked in the bushes with two men. The Perfumed Pig is still there. He was with a drunken manservant. They went into the house together. I left the rear garden gate unlatched before I came over the wall. It will be easy to hide in the shrubbery."

"You didn't see Cairenn?"

Guidd shook his head. "But the house is very large. There are many rooms and outbuildings. There is a summer house like your grandfather's at the rear of the garden. I didn't get into it because I heard voices in there."

"Let's go," Calgaich said.

They ascended the slope. Guidd eased open the gate. Quickly they moved into the garden and took shelter among the many ornamental trees and shrubs. It was immense, a veritable park of rare trees, beds of flowers, ornamental shrubs, pools of fish and water plants, and a number of fine fountains. Tiled pathways stretched across the green lawns. There were many statues and busts. A large pavilion of glistening white marble shone ghostlike from amid a border of plane trees and shrubs. Here and there lamps had been hung in the garden, but there were dark, hidden little glades concealed in the shadows of the trees and shrubs.

Wine cups and bottles and jugs lay strewn about on the grass. Under a table heaped with dishes and remnants of food, a drunk lay fast asleep. Concealed by a thin row of ornamental trees and plants a fat man lay on top of a nude woman whose legs were outspread to receive him, but there was no motion from either one of them—they evidently were both dead drunk. A half-dressed man lay in a pool of his own vomit.

"Rome," Calgaich murmured. "The Imperial City. The center of the world."

Calgaich leaned his war spear against the garden wall and unsheathed his sword. "Guidd, Lutorius, come with me. Girich and Conaid, keep guard here in the garden. We'll call for you if we need you." He looked down at Bron. "Stay here."

Guidd led the way toward the mansion. Once, as they passed a thick cluster of trees and shrubbery they heard a woman laugh. Guidd looked back at Calgaich. They both knew who it was.

They halted just behind the mansion. Calgaich sheathed his sword and drew his dagger. Guidd motioned to Calgaich and Lutorius to follow him. They passed beneath a portico and entered the *peristylium,* a column-girdled open court. A fountain played in the center of a large shallow pool surrounded by emerald-green grass. There were several beds of bright rare flowers and a few tropical plants. A single tree towered through the open top of the court. Above and on three sides of it was a balcony with rooms opening onto it.

Guidd entered into a dark hallway on one side of the house. They passed a large library and a kitchen. No one was in either room. The end of the hallway was closed with a heavy drapery.

Guidd eased back the drapery. There before them was an immense atrium, a magnificent court paved with elaborate mosaics. Four elegant Corinthian columns in blue-veined marble supported the roof around a wide opening, or light-well. Directly below the light-well was a complicated fountain where bronze dancing nymphs and bearded tritons were shooting jets of water into a pink marble basin, in which grew luxuriant water plants. On the inner sides of the doors which opened onto it were statues of marble and bronze standing upon carved stone pedestals.

The doorways around the room were covered by heavy curtains in rich colors of saffron, blue, purple and olivine. The walls were decorated with elaborate frescoes in brilliant colors. A few lamps lighted the interior of the room.

Calgaich pointed toward the rooms which opened onto the atrium. Lutorius and Guidd nodded. They catfooted into the courtyard. Calgaich pulled back a drapery. Two naked women were making love to each other. The next two rooms were empty. Calgaich met Guidd and Lutorius at the other end of the chamber.

Guidd shook his head. "Nothing, Calgaich."

Footsteps sounded hurriedly on the floor in the passageway from the *peristylium*. Guidd, Lutorius and Calgaich faded into the shadows behind the pillars. An old fat woman shuffled toward the front of the room. As she passed, Calgaich stepped quickly behind her and slipped a crooked arm about her throat. He rested the point of his dagger against her fat back.

"Don't look at me," Calgaich warned. "If you do, you'll die. Where is the barbarian slave woman Cairenn?"

"In the big bedchamber at the front of the house next to the vestibule," she quavered.

"Is she alone?"

"She was the last time I saw her."

"How long ago was that?"

"Perhaps an hour ago."

"Are there any other servants in the house?"

"Just myself, one man servant and the door porter. He's

dead drunk within the vestibule. The rest of the servants and some of the slaves are out in the streets for the last night of the Saturnalia. The other slaves were locked into their quarters at sundown."

"Where were you going?"

"I had been working, preparing the summer house for my master and his woman. I was going to bed. I am too old for drinking and whoring this night."

Calgaich looked at Lutorius. Lutorius drew a finger across his throat. Calgaich shook his head. Guidd bound and gagged the serving woman. He and Lutorius placed her in one of the empty rooms.

"Bind and gag those people in the bedrooms," Calgaich ordered. "No killing! You understand? Then stand guard at the rear of the house until I return. Let no one surprise me from behind."

Calgaich peered into the vestibule. The porter was asleep on his pallet, snoring gently and dead to the world. He didn't even move when Calgaich rolled him over and bound his wrists together.

There was a faint chink of light to one side of the heavy drapery which covered the doorway of the room on the right of the vestibule. Calgaich parted it enough so that he could see into the room without being seen himself.

Cairenn stood with her back to the wall beside the bed. She was naked. Her long black hair hung down forward of her white shoulders and covered her bare breasts. Her stomach was rounded, full with his child, thought Calgaich. Her clear white skin stood out in sharp contrast to the frescoed wall. On the floor in front of her was her nightgown, ripped in shreds.

"Get out of here, pig!" she snapped.

The man to whom she was speaking was also naked. He was short and rolls of fat hung above his hips. His fat little rump was beaded with sweat. Lucius Sextillius shook his head. "There is no one in this house who will stop me, barbarian bitch. They are all drunk or making love."

"The Lady Morar will have you cut into little bits!"

"She is too busy fornicating in the garden."

"You know I am with child!"

"That doesn't bother me."

Cairenn reached for a vase on the table beside her. Lucius crouched a little and moved slowly toward her.

"It bothers *me*, pig," Calgaich said quietly.

Lucius whirled and stared uncomprehendingly at Calgaich. His chin dropped. A little drool crept from a corner of his mouth.

Calgaich moved catlike toward the quaestor.

Lucius moved with surprising swiftness. He spat full into Calgaich's face and then leaped up onto the bed. He plunged across it and jumped down on the far side of it. He darted through a side door and was gone.

Calgaich wiped the sputum from his eyes. "Get dressed, Cairenn." He followed after Lucius.

Lucius was running through the atrium. He looked back over his shoulder and saw Calgaich closing in on him. He darted into one of the two passageways that led back to the *peristylium*. He raced through the hallway and burst into the court. He rounded the large pool and started toward the portico, then stopped short. Two men had appeared out of the shadows of the portico. The quaestor knew them well. He backed up. His heels caught on the rim of the pool and he sat down hard on his fat buttocks among the exotic water plants, with the fountain jets spraying over his head.

"Remember me, pig?" Lutorius asked with a fearful grin.

"And me, pig?" Guidd added.

Calgaich rounded the pool with his bared sword in his hand.

"What is it you want?" Lucius whined. "I'm a rich man now! I'll give you anything I have, only don't hurt me!"

"I should cut off the fingers of your right hand and blind your left eye as you did Fomoire," Calgaich said grimly.

Lucius screamed like a stricken mare. "I was *always* kind to him! Let me live! You *must* let me live! What have I done to deserve this?"

"*Bronwyn*," Calgaich answered quietly.

Calgaich's sword flashed once in the dim lamplight. Lucius's headless trunk fell back into the water.

Cairenn was ready when Calgaich came back for her. She rested her head on his chest and began to cry great

wrenching sobs. As he drew her close, he could feel the
swell of her stomach where his child grew. He calmed
her, and as he did so, a missing part of him seemed to
be fitted back into place. He seemed a whole being again.
He could hardly wait to tell her so, to tell her what she
meant to him. But now was not the time.

"We're going home, Cairenn," he murmured.

Calgaich took her from that house of hell and led her
to the garden gate. "Guard her well, friends," he said.
"There is something I must do in the summer house before
I can leave."

"Will you need help?" Lutorius asked.

Calgaich reached for his war spear. "Only this and
Bron."

"You don't know how many of them are in that summer house."

"It doesn't matter. This is something I must do alone.
You understand?"

Calgaich and Bron moved silently into the deep shadows
of the plane trees which surrounded the summer house.
He could see within the central room of the building.
There was no one there. He entered the room and parted
the draperies of a bedchamber. An older woman, painted
and rouged like a prostitute, lay naked in bed with two
younger men. All three of them were in a drunken sleep.

The sound of a crooning voice came from the next
chamber. It was the voice of an old man who lay in bed
with a plump little boy. He was fondling the child and
singing softly to him.

Calgaich padded down a hallway toward the rear of
the pavilion. Bron raised his head and growled a little. The
wind was moving a drapery that closed off a chamber at
the rear of the building. A faint line of light showed now
and again as the drapery moved.

Calgaich paused just outside the room. No sound came
from within the chamber. Calgaich reached out with his
spear and used the tip of it to move the drapery to one
side so that he could see into the room.

Morar laughed.

Faint lamplight illuminated the richly furnished room.
Morar and Valens were in bed together. Calgaich watched
them with sickness in his heart. Was this the pure and

golden girl he had known and loved during his naive youth? The naked, sweating back of Aemilius Valens was now toward Calgaich as he rode the white body of Morar.

Calgaich poised his great *laigen,* the mighty war spear of Evicatos. "Morar!" he cried as he approached the bed. He wanted her to know he was going to kill her.

Morar turned her golden head sideways to look past Valens. Her painted face was contorted with lust and dripping with sweat. Her great eyes widened in disbelief as she saw the grim, scarred face of Calgaich, the deadly war spear and the savage wolfhound Bron. Valens turned his head to look into the icy eyes of Calgaich. He opened his mouth, just as Morar screamed, but before he could utter a sound the spear was thrust into his back and through his body to plunge into the heart of Morar.

For a moment Calgaich stood there looking down upon the transfixed pair and then he withdrew the dripping spear and wiped it on the white silken sheets. He ran silently from the summer house with Bron at his heels.

CHAPTER 30

Lutorius pointed to the vast complex of buildings across the street. "The main gate to the Emporium," he whispered over his shoulder. "The warehouses border on the Tiber where it has been embanked as quays for the barges that come upriver from Ostia with cargoes from the ships."

"Have you seen the others?" Calgaich asked.

Lutorius shook his head.

"I told them to leave if we didn't get here in two hours."

"We've seen no one in the streets of the Emporium. The warehouse workers are probably all in the city celebrating this last night of the festival."

"All the better for us, *calo*."

Lutorius shook his head. "There is always a watch patrol on duty."

"Maybe they're all drunk like the rest of Rome this wild night," Conaid suggested.

"They wouldn't dare. This place is too important to Rome. If anything happened here all Rome would go hungry."

"How often do they patrol?" Calgaich asked.

"I think every two hours."

Guidd appeared at the main gate.

"Did you find the others?" Calgaich asked.

Guidd nodded. "They have found an empty barge."

"Did you see the watch?"

Guidd shook his head. "It's a large place, Calgaich. There are many streets."

He led the way across the street into the complex of streets and buildings. Tall grain warehouses loomed on either side of them. Their light footfalls echoed back from the surrounding walls. Soon they began to smell the river.

The sound of nailed sandals striking the pavement in rhythm came from somewhere behind them. A lantern flickered in the dark street.

"The watch!" Lutorius cried.

They cut around a corner and ran toward the nearby river.

Calgaich looked back over a shoulder. He could see the faint flickering of lantern light against a wall. "Guidd and Conaid! Take Cairenn and Bron to the barge! Run!"

Lutorius, Girich and Calgaich slowed their pace as Guidd and Conaid each took Cairenn by an arm and helped her toward the river. They turned a corner just as the watch marched into the street where Calgaich, Lutorius and Girich had taken shelter in a doorway. Calgaich and his two companions could not move. If they stepped out into the street they would be seen.

The low murmuring of voices came from the watch. Now and again a door would be rattled to check if it was locked. The guards came closer to the three barbarians.

Calgaich peered around the edge of the doorway.

"How many are there?" Girich asked.

"Ten or twelve."

"Good enough odds, Calgaich."

"We'll have to make a run for it," Lutorius whispered.

Calgaich nodded. "Girich first. Lutorius next. I'll follow. Go!"

Girich leaped out of the doorway and ran toward the river followed by Lutorius. Calgaich came last.

The street echoed with the shouting of the watch. Their sandals beat on the pavement as they pursued the barbarians. Girich rounded a corner and disappeared. Lutorius turned to follow Girich. His foot slipped and he went down. His head struck the pavement. His sword clattered from his hand. The watch closed in.

Calgaich turned. His spear was ready in his right hand. The approaching lantern light shone on him.

Fabatus, the watch commander, recognized Calgaich. "It's the barbarian, Calgaich!" he shouted.

The watch formed a rank from one side of the street to the other. They walked slowly toward Calgaich with their spears extended beyond their shields.

Lutorius moved a little and groaned.

This is the end then, Calgaich thought. What better way to die than in defending a fallen comrade?

The watch charged.

Suddenly Garth, Girich and Bron appeared out of the darkness behind Calgaich. The two men had become great friends during their months in captivity. "We've come to stand beside you, Calgaich!" Girich shouted.

The three barbarians closed in on the twelve Romans as though they were going to a festival.

A Roman died with two inches of Calgaich's spear sticking in his throat. The watch commander parried a wild blow from Girich. His skilled counter-stroke struck the Pict flat-bladed alongside the head and sent him down beneath the trampling feet. Calgaich was driven back by the press of the watchmen, leaving Garth standing alone over Girich with flailing sword.

Calgaich's spear was dragged from his hand by the falling body of a watchman whom it had penetrated. Calgaich drew his sword and laid about himself to clear some space to get back to Garth, who was fighting singlehanded against three watchmen.

Lutorius got up onto his feet and reached for his sword. He staggered a little as he turned toward Calgaich. A watchman closed in on the hazy Lutorius. Bron charged. He leaped into the air and came down on the back of the Roman, who was carried to the ground by the weight of Bron. A quick thrust of Lutorius's sword kept the Roman down.

Sandals beat on the pavement as a knot of barbarians charged from the river embankment to reenforce their comrades. Calgaich led them back toward where Garth was still holding his own. Garth's sword pierced a Roman's throat. Before he could withdraw his blade a Roman spear drove into his back. He gasped and went down across the body of Girich.

Ottar the Saxon charged past Calgaich. His sword lashed out like strokes of lightning to fell two Romans. The remaining Romans turned to flee.

"After them!" Calgaich shouted. "Let no one escape!"

The fleet-footed barbarians easily ran down the slower Romans. It was all over in a matter of minutes.

The barbarians stood in the street, breathing hard and grinning at each other.

"Into the river with them!" Calgaich commanded. "Keep their shields, helmets and weapons! Wipe the blood from the pavement!"

Calgaich turned to retrieve his spear from the body of a watchman. Girich stood there with Garth in his arms. There were tears in the Pict's eyes. "He died for me, Calgaich," he said brokenly. "I will not throw his body into that stinking river as if it were Roman shit!"

"Take him aboard. We'll bury him in the clean sea, *if* we get that far."

The river barge, *Isis of Geminus,* was moored to the embankment. The Tiber had been steadily rising all that day because of severe summer thunderstorms in the foothills of the Apennine Mountains. Its yellow, turbid flood, swollen with rainwater, swirled in strong currents.

"Fray those mooring lines through to make it look as though they broke from the pressure of the current against the barge," Calgaich ordered.

They were all aboard now. Ten oarsmen took their seats, five to a side. They looked expectantly at Calgaich.

Calgaich took the tiller. "Nepos! Get up forward and warn me of any dangers ahead. Cast loose the barge! Fend off forward and aft! Out oars! Give way together!"

The rushing current caught the clumsy flat-bottomed barge and swung it out into the middle of the yellow river. The long heavy oars dipped into the water and the barge seemed to lurch forward with each strong stroking of the blades. The *Isis* shot past the wharves that lay downriver from the stone embankment of the Emporium.

Lutorius looked up at Calgaich from his position at port stroke. "Will we make it before dawn, barbarian?"

"We have to, Bottle Emptier."

Cairenn came up from below. She came aft to stand beside Calgaich.

"It's not safe up here, woman," Calgaich said.

"It stinks down below, Calgaich."

"The stink of the river is not much better."

"But the air is fresher," she argued.

"Go below!" Calgaich snapped.

She shook her head and smiled sweetly. "In *my* condition, Calgaich, for which *you* are truly responsible, it's not easy to keep one's stomach down. I'll stay right here."

Calgaich looked away from the grinning faces of his oarsmen. Cairenn sat down at his feet and rested her back against the low railing of the barge. She had lived through too much to return to the role of a pampered woman as she had been in her father's *rath*. The many weeks she spent fleeing with Calgaich, first from the Picts and then from the Romans, had left their mark on her. The months lived in the service of the treacherous Morar had taught her the value of freedom and independence. She would *choose* to stay by Calgaich when she felt it right. It was right that she stay near him now.

The creak and grind of the oars mingled with the expelled breaths of the oarsmen. Now and again Calgaich would look back over his shoulder toward the east, looking for, but hoping he would not see the first faint traces of the false dawn etching the serrated tops of the great Apennines.

Suddenly Nepos waved his arms. "Ostia looms!" he called.

The farms and villas on the banks of the river began to give way to the outlying buildings of the port city.

The river banks were now confined between houses and other buildings. Boats and barges were moored to the banks. No one was to be seen. No lights showed. The city seemed to be asleep.

It was still dark when they eased the *Isis* into a mooring place in the inner harbor of the port city.

Calgaich went quickly over the side of the *Isis*, followed by Lutorius, Chilo and Nepos.

Nepos led the way with a catlike sureness through the twisted, narrow streets of the slum area of the city. They reached the place where Calgaich had last seen the graceful *Lydia*. She wasn't there.

"We'll have to take another vessel," Lutorius said.

All of the moored vessels were larger, heavier and clumsier-looking than the Greek-built *Lydia*. Calgaich looked up at the sky. It had lightened almost imperceptibly. "Lugh of the Shining Spear," he prayed. "Help us this day. Help us to find the *Lydia*." He closed his eyes for a moment.

"Calgaich," Lutorius called softly. "There she is."

The *Lydia* lay moored just forward of an immense grain ship that had thrown her into deep shadow. Ahead of the *Lydia* was a swift-looking, double-banked rowing galley.

Calgaich dropped lightly onto the deck of the *Lydia*. He walked to the small cabin built over the afterdeck and quietly opened the door. The cabin was dark. While easing in through the doorway, he felt something sharp press against the small of his back.

"Don't move," Cunori warned. "What do you want?"

Calgaich grinned. "Take the knife point from my back, Dolphin, and I'll tell you."

Cunori gripped Calgaich by the shoulders. "Thanks to the gods," he murmured. "Have you come here with your grandfather?"

Calgaich shook his head. "He's dead. Some of us have escaped from the city under the cover of the Saturnalia. There isn't much time. It will soon be dawn."

"I can't believe this! After all these months!"

"It's true. Is the *Lydia* ready for sea?"

"Always! Those were the orders of your grandfather."

Calgaich nodded. "He knew far more than I expected he did."

Calgaich sent Nepos and Chilo back for the others.

"Look!" Lutorius cried. He pointed to the east.

The faintest of graying light showed over the heights far to the east.

Calgaich and Lutorius worked swiftly under the instructions of Cunori to prepare the vessel for sailing. Chilo came back to the *Lydia* followed by Cairenn, Bron, Lexus, who helped Fomoire along, and Guidd One-Eye. By the time the *Lydia* was ready to leave, all the others were aboard. The last to board had been Girich, bearing the stiffening body of Garth, the Silurian harper.

Cunori shook his head dubiously. "We'll need more food stores and water, Calgaich. I never expected you to bring so many passengers."

"We can't afford to take the time now."

"Once we leave here, Calgaich, the alarm will be out. We won't be able to touch land for stores and water until we've passed through the Pillars of Hercules. Perhaps not even then, for Hispania is occupied by the Romans."

"We leave now! Rather die at sea from hunger and thirst than to risk capture here today!"

The moorings were cast loose and the *Lydia* was fended out from the quay. The harbor was still in darkness but here and there lights showed on some vessels and from buildings along the long quays.

"What ship is that?" a harsh voice suddenly cried from the high stern of the bireme moored ahead of the *Lydia*.

Cunori cupped his hands about his mouth. "The *Lydia*, of Ostia, bound for Nicaea, sir!"

"On what business?"

"Pleasure, sir. This is the private vessel of the honored senator Rufus Arrius Niger."

"Is he aboard?"

"He is, sir."

"Let me speak with him."

Cunori laughed softly. "He'd have my head on a platter if I awoke him at this hour. Too much Saturnalia, you understand?"

"Have you reported your sailing to the harbor master?"

"Yesterday, sir."

There was a moment's silence. "Well, get on with it then! See that you don't wake up the whole harbor in the process!"

"No fear of that," Cunori said out of the side of his mouth.

"What ship was that?" Calgaich asked quietly.

"That's the naval bireme *Fortunata*, the fastest galley in these waters."

"Faster than the *Lydia*?"

"Not under sail, but with her oars and sails together she'll outrun any vessel in these waters."

There wasn't a breath of wind stirring in the predawn hush. The sweep oars of the *Lydia* ground in their locks as she was rowed out of the congested inner harbor through the narrow channel into the larger outer harbor. There wasn't a ripple on the water as the *Lydia* forged toward the harbor entrance. The eastern sky was lightening more rapidly now. It was very quiet except for the creaking of the oars and the chuckling of the water at the prow.

Cunori looked sideways at Calgaich. "I still can't believe

it. All these past months I thought I would be here at Ostia the rest of my life, serving some Roman."

Calgaich shrugged. "We're not even out of the harbor yet."

"Aye," Cunori agreed, "but we are free of these cursed Romans. We may never reach the open sea beyond the Pillars of Hercules, but we can die at sea before we let the Romans take us prisoners again."

Calgaich looked into Cunori's serious face. He looked at the faces of the oarsmen—Lexus, Conaid, Chilo, Loarn, Lutorius, Niall, Ottar, Girich, Nepos, and Eogabal. None of them, or those others who were hidden below decks would let themselves be taken alive.

The *Lydia* met the slow and easy swell of the open sea as she passed the colossus beyond the harbor entrance and then rounded the southern tip of the separate curved mole that protected the channel entrance.

The stroking of the heavy oars had an uneven effect and the harsh breathing of the oarsmen was louder and more irregular. The *Lydia* began to plunge a little as she met the low, smooth onshore swells. The sea was lightening with the coming of the dawn. The sun slowly tipped the mountains and the sea became golden in color.

"How long before the alarm reaches Ostia?" Cunori asked suddenly.

"It's thirteen miles by road, Dolphin. A fast horse can make it in an hour. Why?"

"Look behind you, Calgaich."

They were a good two miles beyond the outer mole by then. A large vessel was rounding the southern end of the mole. Her double bank of oars dashed against the water throwing up glittering spray.

"A merchantman?" Calgaich asked.

Cunori shook his head. "A naval craft."

"The *Fortunata?*"

"I think so."

"Maybe she's going elsewhere?"

"No. I know now that I made a mistake back there at the harbor entrance."

"How so?"

"I left the harbor by the southern end of the outer mole."

Calgaich was puzzled. "So?"

"Nicaea is to the north and west. We were seen leaving the harbor by the tower lookouts on the outer mole. Probably, they signaled the *Fortunata* as she came out of the harbor. As soon as her commander knew we had left by the south entrance he would know damned well we weren't heading for Nicaea."

"Can she catch us?"

"Yes. The galley is double-banked, as you know, and her oarsmen are fresh and more skilled in their trade than our barbarians, who are tiring. There is no wind to fill our sails."

Cairenn and Fomoire came up on deck. Cairenn helped the weakened Druid to a seat. She chatted with him and managed to bring a wan smile to his gaunt face. Her laughter rang out and some of the oarsmen turned their heads to see her. She turned to smile and then lifted her eyes to look at Calgaich. A stab of intense pain seemed to shoot through Calgaich. It was nothing like one of the many wounds he had suffered in his warrior life. It was a sickening feeling that seemed to well up from deep within him. If the *Fortunata* caught up with the *Lydia,* Calgaich himself would have to put Cairenn and her unborn child to death before he died on the deck of the *Lydia* with reddened weapon in his hand.

The sun rose higher and higher. Its heat smote mercilessly down on the sea and the bodies of the toiling oarsmen. The *Lydia* moved sluggishly across the smooth swells of the sea like an ant crawling through a pool of honey.

Cairenn took the tiller of the steering oar while Cunori and Calgaich spelled some of the more tired oarsmen.

The *Fortunata* crept closer and closer. There was no doubt in the minds of the *Lydia*'s crew that the bireme was pursuing them.

Hour after hour the chase went on. White puffs of clouds appeared in the sky as the hours dragged past. In the distance could be seen the sails of Ostia-bound becalmed sailing vessels dotting the sea.

The *Fortunata* was almost within hailing distance when the smooth surface of the sea was ruffled by cat's-paws of wind coming from dead astern of the two vessels.

Cunori cupped his hands about his mouth. "Hoist the

mainsail and the foresail! Step lively or we'll have the Romans spitting on our afterdeck within the hour!"

The sails were hoisted and began to fill, a little fitfully at first. After a time a steady breeze began to blow and the sails swelled. The oarsmen stayed at their stations, although some of them were so tired they seemed asleep, moving back and forth in rhythm like automatons.

The *Fortunata* hoisted her sails. But by then the lightness and swiftness of the *Lydia* had become apparent. Steadily she pulled away from the ungainly *Fortunata*.

"In oars!" Cunori commanded.

The oarsmen pulled in the heavy oars and stowed them fore and aft. Man after man collapsed on the deck and lay as though dead.

Cunori pointed aft. "Calgaich, they are tiring, too, but they must keep rowing to keep up with us. Pray to your gods that the breeze keeps up."

Calgaich shrugged. "These are Roman sea gods around here, Dolphin, and I doubt if they can hear us."

Lutorius had been appointed to dole out the food and water. When his duty was done, he came aft. "When is our landfall, Cunori?" he asked.

"We must pass between two great islands, Sardinia and Corsica, before we can set our course for the Pillars of Hercules. Why do you ask?"

Lutorius looked over his shoulder. "We've used up far too much water today. It couldn't be helped because of the great heat and the exertion of the rowers."

"How much is left, Lutorius?" Calgaich asked in a low voice.

"Perhaps enough for two days, on short rations."

Cunori whistled softly. "Now I know why you asked about a landfall. We can't land on either Sardinia or Corsica, not with the *Fortunata* dogging us."

"And beyond the straits?" Calgaich asked.

"Nepos!" Cunori called out.

The Iberian came aft. "Yes, master?"

"What land is beyond the straits between Sardinia and Corsica?"

"The Balearic Islands. The nearest one is about two hundred and fifty miles or more."

Cunori rubbed his jaw. "We can make about one hundred miles per day under sail. Providing we get a good wind."

"You'll be against the currents all the way, master."

"Two and a half to three days to the Balearics, then," Cunori murmured. "But we don't even know what kind of a reception we'll get when we land there."

It was very quiet aboard the *Lydia*.

"There is water closer than that," Calgaich said quietly.

"Where?" Lutorius asked.

Calgaich looked aft through the darkness. A faint light showed far behind the *Lydia*. "The *Fortunata*," Calgaich replied.

"She has a crew of well over a hundred," Cunori warned.

"Most of them are galley slaves, who are chained to their oars."

"And an afterguard of marines," Lutorius added.

Calgaich nodded. "Who must sleep at night."

Lutorius stared at Calgaich. "You mean? . . ."

"Board her."

"This is madness!" Cunori cried.

Calgaich looked at him. "We have no other choice. They will have plenty of water on board for their galley slaves. That's the *one* thing they can't deprive them of, mates."

"They'll see us coming," Nepos warned.

"There's no moon tonight. We can turn back. When near them we can lower our sails to keep from being sighted."

"It can't be done," Cunori argued.

Lutorius shrugged. "How do you plan this madness, barbarian?"

"I'll need at least seven men besides myself. They must all be good swimmers. We turn back in the *Lydia*. Out of sighting distance, we lower the sails. Then the boarding party enters the sea, armed only with daggers. We wait there while the *Lydia* returns on her original course. When the *Fortunata* approaches we board her. Once we have control of her, we signal the *Lydia*. Cunori brings her back. We transfer the water and stores to the *Lydia*. Then we strip the Roman's sails from them for our own use, and take any other gear we may need."

Lutorius grinned. "And then we sink the *Fortunata*?"

"With those galley slaves chained to their oars?" Calgaich shook his head. "Of course we could always release the galley slaves and let them take over the *Fortunata*."

"By the gods!" Lutorius cried. "Now you've said it!"

Cunori shook his head. "To what end? They'd be tracked down in time. There would be no escape from the Roman sea for them. You know what would happen to them if they were caught."

Lutorius shrugged. "Well, it's a good thought all the same."

The late night sky was a dark blanket of blue sprinkled with ice-chip stars. The sea was dark. It moved with slow and sinuous swells. The only light to be seen was on board the *Fortunata*.

Cairenn came up on deck as the boarding party prepared themselves. Now and again her great emerald eyes would slant sideways to where Calgaich stood. He could not look at her. She meant so much to him, he could not bear the thought of parting from her.

They were ready now—Calgaich, Ottar, Lutorius, Chilo, Girich, Lexus, Niall and Eogabal.

Cunori brought the *Lydia* about smartly. The sails were lowered, but not furled. Oarsmen took their positions, three to a side at their muffled oars.

Calgaich walked aft to Cunori. "If we take her, we'll hoist three signal lamps in a vertical line, and lower them immediately. Get to us as quickly as you can. We may still need help."

"And if you don't take her?"

Calgaich looked forward. He could just see the dim figure of Cairenn beside the mast.

"Calgaich?" Cunori asked.

"Then you must go on without us." Calgaich placed a hand on the shoulder of the seaman. "Take Cairenn back to my country. The Novantae must be told that the child she bears is mine. If it is a boy and the gods are willing, he should be a chieftain of the Novantae some day."

Cairenn could not restrain herself any longer. She came running aft to Calgaich with outstretched arms. "You can't leave me like this without a farewell." Calgaich drew her close. She rested her head against his broad chest. He stroked her long black hair. "I'll be waiting for you. You *will* return!" she insisted.

He looked down at her and smiled. "Who said I wouldn't?" he cried. He raised his head and looked into the knowing eyes of Cunori. They both knew the odds.

Cairenn looked up into Calgaich's face and then turned her head toward Cunori. "You will return!" she said fiercely. Calgaich could feel the strength her spirit and will put into her arms. "You'll crack my ribs, little hare," he said softly. He *would* return for this woman who was to be his wife and the mother of his child. He kissed her gently and pushed her toward Cunori. "I'll leave you now, Cairenn, but only for a little while. Guard her well, Cunori and you others. She bears my child within her. I will return."

The boarding party came aft. One by one they let themselves down into the sea. Calgaich was the last into the water. His eyes met those of Cairenn for a moment, and then he was gone. The *Lydia* moved slowly away from them, then turned back to her westerly course again. Soon she vanished into the darkness.

The only sign of life on the darkened surface of the sea was the faint light of the *Fortunata* as she moved slowly and steadily toward the eight barbarians who were in the water and directly on her course.

CHAPTER 31

Calgaich and his men could hear the steady grinding of the *Fortunata*'s oars as they swung back and forth in their oarlocks. Soon they could distinguish the dark shape of the large square sail looming up above the galley's long hull.

Calgaich looked at his comrades. "She has a ram at her prow. Eogbal, Chilo, Niall and Lexus will board her there —two to a side. Lutorius, Ottar, Girich and I will board her further aft. Lutorius and I on the starboard side, Ottar and Girich on the larboard side. We'll float under the lower bank of oars and try to board her at the last oars on the side. Niall, you'll lead the boarders at the ram. Once on deck, wait until you hear us aboard, then two of you work your way aft, leaving two on guard on the foredeck. You must get the guard's weapons. We've got to get control of the deck at once."

"What if some of us miss getting aboard?" Lexus asked.

"Then you'll have a long swim."

"And if those on deck don't get control of the ship?" Chilo asked.

"Then we either die on deck, or join those in the water. In that case, the *Lydia* will not come back for us."

The galley loomed high out of the darkness. The ram appeared, with a frothing of foam about it as it parted the water. Niall, Lexus, Chilo and Eogbal grabbed at it as it reached them. The galley seemed to shoot past the other four boarders.

"Now, Bottle Emptier!" Calgaich snapped.

They reached up and caught onto the last lower oar. Calgaich swung himself up on top of it, but Lutorius lost his grip. Calgaich gripped him by his hair and hauled him up. Calgaich worked his way up to the upper oar and rode back and forth on it. He made out the dim figure of the helmsman at the tiller.

Calgaich heaved himself over the railing and lay flat on the deck. A moment later Lutorius dropped on top of him.

A man came aft. He turned to look forward, as if he had heard something. Calgaich clamped his hand over the Roman's mouth and stabbed him in the back. He then lowered him to the deck. He withdrew the Roman's sword from its sheath and handed it to Lutorius while Calgaich took his dagger. Lutorius eased the dead Roman over the rail.

They faced the side of the wooden fighting tower, that was just forward of the afterdeck cabin. They crawled across the deck to avoid being seen by the helmsman. Calgaich flattened himself against the side of the tower and looked around the corner. A tall, dark figure moved quickly toward him.

Calgaich took a chance and softly identified himself. "Calgaich."

It was Ottar, with Girich close behind him.

"Take the after door, Girich," Calgaich whispered. "Lutorius, subdue the helmsman. Lash the helm to hold the galley on her course. Then back up Girich. Ottar, come with me."

The fore door of the tower was closed. Calgaich tried to open it. It was bolted from within. Ottar pressed his hand against Calgaich's chest and pushed him backward. The Saxon then lifted his foot and drove it at the place where the bolt should be. The door crashed open.

Calgaich was first inside the tower. The deck was crowded with marines who had been startled out of their sleep. Before they could reach for their weapons, Calgaich and Ottar were in amongst them, striking right and left with their daggers. Some of them bolted for the after door of the tower and opened it, but Girich met them face to face.

Calgaich and Ottar snatched up swords. There was hardly room within the tower for such a melee. Five marines were downed when the remaining five pushed their way through the forward door, fleeing in panic from the three madmen who had crashed in on them. The Romans started to run forward. Niall and Lexus met them head-on. The marines were caught in a vise. Two went down in death; two leaped over the side to escape. The last of them was lifted bodily from the deck by Lexus and tossed over the side.

The clashing of blades came from the afterdeck where Lutorius had taken over the helm. The Bottle Emptier had his hands full, fighting three swordsmen at once.

"Close that after hatch!" Lutorius shouted as he withdrew his sword from the body of a marine. "There's many more of them down there!"

Lexus slammed the hatch down atop the head of a man who was rising up from below. The Gaul then stood on top of the hatch while he swung his sword at three Romans who had come up from another hatch. It was as if he were cutting grain. One man went down with his head half-severed from his body.

Ottar came up behind the two men Lexus was fighting. One hard, sure thrust disposed of one of the Romans. Ottar's blade went into the back of the third man at the same time Lexus's blade pierced his chest.

They slammed shut the door of the after cabin. The decks were slippery with blood.

Calgaich grinned. "An easy victory, comrades!"

Niall shook his head. "Chilo was struck by the ram and went down under the galley. We couldn't save him."

"Where's Eogabal?"

Niall jerked his head. "Up forward, standing guard."

"Find me two lamps!" Calgaich snapped.

Calgaich carried the two lamps forward. He stumbled over something on the foredeck beside the ship's altar. He looked down into the face of Eogabal. A pool of blood had formed beside him.

Niall came up behind Calgaich. "There was no one here when we boarded the galley."

Calgaich silently pointed to a small open hatch. He placed his two lamps on the deck and jerked his head at Niall. Together they walked silently forward and looked over the bow railing. Just below them was a white terrified face. The Roman was balancing precariously on the slippery ram.

Calgaich turned back to the lamps. "He's all yours, Niall."

Calgaich strung the two lamps below the lamp that hung from a foreshroud. He waited a moment and then lowered them. He wiped the sweat from his face and leaned against the mast.

The *Lydia* came ghosting through the darkness. As the boat pulled alongside, Calgaich could see Cairenn at the railing, her face white and drawn. Finally, she saw him and raised her hand in a gesture of homecoming.

Lines shot over from the *Lydia* and the *Fortunata* was

made fast alongside. Most of the crew of the *Lydia* came swarming aboard.

They emptied the galley of most of her water and food stores and stripped her of her sails.

Calgaich went down into the stinking hold. The *hortator* had been bound to the mast where it protruded through the two decks. His dark eyes followed Calgaich as he walked between the rows of galley slaves. Most of them lay asleep beneath their oars. Some of them looked dead from exhaustion.

"If you release them, master," the *hortator* warned quietly, "they'll kill everyone aboard. This is a Roman sea. There can be no escape for them."

Calgaich nodded and drew his knife to cut some of the bonds that held the Roman to the mast. It would be some time before he could work himself loose and by that time the *Lydia* would be gone into the enveloping darkness.

"Calgaich!" Lutorius shouted down the after hatchway. "There is a light astern! It might be another naval ship!"

Calgaich climbed back on deck. His men had returned to the *Lydia*. Calgaich leaped aboard her.

"Cast off!" Cunori commanded. "Fend off! Out oars! Give way together! Hoist the main and foresail!"

The *Lydia* moved slowly away from the drifting *Fortunata*. Her oars dashed against the water, and her sails filled. Soon the dim shape of the bireme was lost in the darkness. All that could be seen was the faint light of the unknown vessel coming up astern of the galley.

There would be no sleep for the crew of the *Lydia* that night. One of the great oars of the galley was set up as a jury mast in a hole chopped through the afterdeck of the *Lydia*. Stout braces were fashioned below the deck to hold the improvised mast in place. Shroud lines were fastened to the top of the mast and made fast to the railings. Cunori cut up the large spare mainsail of the bireme and fashioned a smaller sail for the after mast of the *Lydia*. The sail was hoisted. It filled with the freshening breeze and the craft surged ahead with her lee rail so low the oarsmen had difficulty working their oars, but they could not be allowed to stop rowing. The *Lydia* must put as many miles as she could between herself, the *Fortunata* and the unknown vessel, which by now must have found the drifting galley.

CHAPTER 32

The storm-battered *Lydia* was on a northeasterly course off the west coast of Britannia, fighting her way through a fall storm. The wind was rising again. The cold gray sea was churning itself into waves whose crests were torn off by the whining wind and driven like stinging hail against the vessel and her crew. For two gloomy days and pitch-black nights the storm had driven the *Lydia* toward the great firth, or estuary, which cut deeply into the land of southwest Caledonia.

Calgaich mac Lellan stood in the bow. Just an hour past they had been sighted by a Roman patrol galley which had passed so close that an archer on her deck had driven an arrow into the right arm of Cunori while he had been steering. Lugh had aided the *Lydia* and her crew by bringing clouds and mist between the two vessels. Still, the patrol galley must be close at hand.

Calgaich looked back over his shoulder. A human chain composed of most of the crew was bailing steadily, ever since a plank had given way and a leak had started below the waterline. Some of them were standing knee-deep in bilge water. Cairenn lay in the after cabin bunk, attended by Fomoire. The violent pitching and tossing of the *Lydia* had brought on premature labor.

Calgaich could see the powerful figure of Ottar as he steered the *Lydia*. The Saxon chieftain was a born seaman who had often raided the east coast of Britannia with his sword-brothers in the days before he had been captured and taken to Rome.

Cunori raised himself in his bunk, which was opposite to Cairenn's. "How does it go, little one?" he asked.

Cairenn was swathed in a spare sail so that only her

403

pale, heart-shaped face, framed in her thick and lustrous black hair, showed against the weathered material of the sail. "The pains are stronger now, Cunori. Let's hope Nodons doesn't claim my baby as a sacrifice for our safe passage to Caledonia."

Cunori shook his head. "Do not say such things!"

Fomoire looked up from where he sat on the deck. "Sometimes Nodons is not to be denied when he's in such a rage. We'll be lucky if he doesn't take the *Lydia* and all of us with her," he prophesied gloomily.

Cairenn looked quickly at Fomoire. "No!" she said firmly. "I bear the son of Calgaich! Nothing must happen to him!"

Fomoire nodded. "Nor to Calgaich," he added quietly. "The *Lydia* and the rest of us don't really matter. But Calgaich must return to Caledonia to take over his chieftainship and he must have his son with him so that he, in turn, will succeed to the chieftainship. *That is written . . .*"

"Where?" Calgaich asked dryly from the doorway.

Fomoire smiled weakly. "In the stars. Those same stars by which we steered a true course here from the Pillars of Hercules."

Calgaich squatted beside Cairenn's bunk. He passed a sword-calloused palm across her brow and then cupped his hand under her chin to raise her head a little so that he could look into her eyes. She, in turn, could see the pain in his eyes. She knew he was suffering almost as much as she was.

"How much farther, Calgaich?" Cunori asked.

Calgaich shrugged. "I've seen no landmarks in this hellish weather, Dolphin. But we can't be far from land. That Roman patrol ship could not have been far from the coast."

"It's a long coast," Fomoire put in.

Calgaich looked through the doorway. He could see the bent backs of the crewmen as they mechanically took the containers of water from the men in the hold and then threw the water over the side. How many of them would still be alive when they reached Caledonia? He shook his head as he thought of the comrades who had been left behind as sacrifices so that the *Lydia* might win her way to Caledonia.

Cairenn rested her hand on his forearm. "It couldn't be helped, Calgaich," she murmured.

He looked quickly at her. She had an uncanny way, sometimes, of reading his mind. "What about those who died in the arena that we might be free? Or Garth, who died in the filthy streets of the Emporium with a watchman's spear in his back? What of Chilo, who was swept under the ram of the *Fortunata* and drowned, and Eogabal, who died on the foredeck of that same galley? Both of them died so that we might have water and stores to continue our escape. And Nepos, who guided us to water in Hispania and was recaptured by the Romans? How many others shall be lost before we can reach our home?"

Cairenn had no reply.

Calgaich stood up. "A terrible price to pay."

Cairenn twisted suddenly in great agony. Cold sweat broke out on her pale face. "Fomoire," she gasped. The pains were greater than she had expected. Were they pains of life or death?

"Leave us," Fomoire said to Calgaich. "I think her time has come."

Calgaich stood in the doorway uncertainly. Cairenn's breath was coming in gasps, and she was writhing beneath the rough sail. Her belly heaved as if she were herself a sea. He did not want to leave her, but Fomoire gently pushed him out onto the deck.

The *Lydia* shuddered as a great wave struck her. It was followed by another. Some of the crewmen were swept into the lee scuppers. The men below decks cursed savagely as they were pitched about like pebbles in a shaken cup.

Lexus was laughing as he hauled one man after another to his feet and shoved him back toward the hatch to resume bailing. Little Conaid had gone partially over the side and was clinging to the railing. Lexus leaned toward him to help him get back aboard.

No one saw the enormous grandfather wave rise smoothly from the depths. It swept cleanly over the amidships of the *Lydia* like a moving wall of blue-gray stone. When it passed, little Conaid was still clinging desperately to the railing, but Lexus was nowhere to be seen. Nodons had taken his sacrifice.

Cunori reeled from the cabin to give Ottar a hand at the

tiller. The two of them fought to bring the *Lydia* back on her course.

"Head her into the wind!" Ottar shouted.

Cunori shook his head. "We'll never make it! We've taken too much water aboard!"

"Bail, damn you, bail!" Calgaich roared at the badly shaken crew. "Do you want my son to drown as he is born! Bail, damn you, bail!"

They were in a wild, watery world of the sea and flying spindrift. It was almost as if they had sailed off the earth onto an unknown planet composed entirely of water. The *Lydia* plunged and wallowed. She took the waves solidly over her sides so that at times the deck was knee-deep in water from railing to railing. The laboring craft staggered under the repeated liquid blows of the sea as Nodons exerted all his powerful and terrible strength to founder the *Lydia*.

Yet the *Lydia* drove on, fighting like a living thing to survive. She would plunge deeply into the water until it seemed as though she would never come up. After a nerve-shattering hesitation she would begin to rise, shake herself off like a wet hound, only to dive again into the next wave.

There was a wide grin on the face of Cunori. "See how she fights the sea! Nodons shall not take her!"

Ottar looked quickly backward over both shoulders as though Nodons himself might have heard the Venetus. "Be careful," he warned.

Calgaich worked his way forward. He drove the point of his war spear into the deck and held onto the shaft with one hand, while steadying himself by holding onto the forestay with his other. There seemed to be nothing ahead of the *Lydia* but a deceptive gray opaqueness. Calgaich narrowed his eyes. There was a faint difference in the grayness off in the distance, the most delicate of nuances, and hardly perceptible, *but it was there* . . . He shook his head. Perhaps it was a trick of Nodons to lure the unwary into his watery world. Calgaich stared fixedly into the distance. Then he knew where he was!

He turned, jerked his spear from the deck and pointed it toward the barely discernible coastline. "There she looms!" he shouted into the teeth of the wind. "Albu! Albu! Albu!"

Suddenly the wind slackened and died away.

The *Lydia* forged on, driven by the powerful inshore current.

No one looked up from their bailing. There wasn't time.

The dim arms of two bay headlands showed through the grayness. They were entering a large bay off the firth that Calgaich knew was but half a day's march from Rioghaine.

The faint cry of a baby came from the after cabin.

All eyes turned to look toward the cabin.

Cairenn came to the doorway. She extended her hands while holding the newborn babe.

"Calgaich!" she cried in a voice of utter joy. "I bring you a fine son, sired by you and brought into the world by this great storm!"

CHAPTER 33

It was almost dusk. Calgaich stood on a hilltop with Lutorius, Loarn, Niall, Onlach and Conaid, looking down on the *rath* of Rioghaine and the Dun of Evicatos. His other sword-brothers had stayed with Cunori and Ottar while the two seaman repaired the *Lydia* in order to guard Cairenn and her infant son.

Calgaich turned as Bron came through the grove of birches. "Guidd comes," he said.

A wolflike, two-legged shape came noiselessly through the woods. Guidd threw back the wolf's head that covered his own gray poll and grinned.

"Well, Guidd?" Calgaich asked.

Guidd reached inside his wolfskin coat and withdrew an earthenware jug. He handed it to Calgaich, who passed it to Lutorius.

"My *crannog* den was untouched, Calgaich," Guidd said.

"Were you at the *rath?*"

Guidd nodded. "I was welcomed by our people because of the news I brought them yesterday, that Calgaich, the son of Lellan and the grandson of Evicatos, had returned to claim his chieftainship."

"They'll back me if I attack the Dun of Evicatos?"

Guidd shook his head. "No need, Calgaich. When they learned of Bruidge's treachery to you, and that Lellan had died at the hands of the Red Crests in a Roman fort, they turned against Bruidge."

"He still sits drinking in the *dun?*"

"Yes, but alone. One by one his hirelings deserted him."

Lutorius handed the jug to Calgaich. "How so, woodsman?"

"Some of them fled into the forests. Others just vanished. Like this!" He waved his hands sideways.

408

"With a Novantae spear in their backs?" Loarn asked.

"Who knows?" Guidd asked. He grinned.

"Has anyone told Bruidge I have returned?" Calgaich asked Guidd.

"No. The people say he believes you died. Paralus, the Greek trader, came this way some time past. He brought the news that you had been sorely wounded in the arena. He did not say that you had survived."

"Good! I'll bring him that news myself."

"We'll go with you, barbarian," Lutorius said.

"No. I must go alone. Guidd will take you to his wolf den. Wait there. If all goes well, I'll send Bron for you."

Calgaich strode through the birches with Bron at his side. He stopped when he was out of the woods and looked up at the towering *dun*. Not a light showed. He looked back at the woods. There was no sign or sound of the others. He heard only the soughing of the dusk wind through the pines, conifers and birches.

Calgaich started up the slope, then stopped short. There was something missing. Then he knew what it was—it was the first time in his years at Rioghaine that he had not heard the sound of the night-hunting wolves in the dense forest that bordered the dark loch and the shadowy hills. Was it an omen? An eerie feeling crept through him. He gripped his great spear and strode on up the rocky slope.

The dark *dun* loomed high above him. Calgaich paused at the thick, rough-hewn door. He reached out with his spear and pushed it open. The door creaked open on rusty hinges. The narrow passage beyond it was as dark as the pit.

Calgaich stepped inside. He catfooted through the passageway. The antechamber of the main hall was dark except for the faint dusk light that came through the high loopholes pierced into the drystone walls. Some small creature scuttled across Calgaich's feet in order to escape. Bron growled.

The door to the great hall was closed. Calgaich placed his ear against it. He heard the faint sound of a voice. The ball butt of his spear bumped against the wall and the sound of it echoed in the antechamber. The voice stopped short.

Calgaich pushed the door open with his left hand while

he held his spear ready for a quick thrust. The door creaked open and struck against its stone stop.

A deep bed of ashes and embers lay in one of the large stone fireplaces situated to one side of the hall. The draft from the opened door fanned across the embers and brought the fire back to a temporary life. Flickering flames flared up and formed dancing patterns on the walls.

The muttering voice came to Calgaich again. It came from a huge hunched figure sitting in the great chair behind the massive table; the chair that had once been the seat of Evicatos and later that of Lellan.

Bruidge of the Battle-Axe had his head bent over his large drinking horn. The rising firelight reflected from the silver mounting of the horn and on the crescent blade of the battle-axe that hung on the wall behind him.

Calgaich went toward him, treading on the filthy dried rushes and bracken that covered the floors. He threw wood and bracken onto the fire. The dancing flames flickered eagerly over the fresh fuel, and the firelight grew.

Calgaich walked back to the center of the hall and leaned on his spear. Bruidge raised his drinking horn. His eyes fell upon the tall warrior. His jaw dropped a little and a thin trickle of saliva drooled from the corners of his mouth.

Once, long months past, Guidd One-Eye had spoken of Bruidge: *Once Bruidge of the Battle-Axe was a man to be reckoned with in battle but now he is a coward. He fears everything, including his own people, and, mark you, he sees things in the darkness of his own bedchamber and hall* that no one else can see. *Therefore, he is never alone.*

Bruidge slowly extended a shaking hand and held it in front of his eyes. "There is no one there," he muttered to himself.

The rising evening wind moaned softly through the high slit windows of the hall.

"Calgaich is dead, slain by the Red Crests," Bruidge reassured himself. He nodded. "Yes, that's so."

Bron raised his head and growled.

Bruidge gripped his drinking horn. He did not look up. "The great wolfhound Bron is dead. My brother Lellan is dead. *There is no one there . . .*"

Calgaich looked quickly behind himself. The hairs

prickled on the back of his neck. Why had Bruidge mentioned Lellan? By the dark gods! Was it possible that Lellan *was* there, but unseen by Calgaich and only seen by Bruidge? Calgaich looked down at Bron. The hound was looking up and to one side, away from Calgaich, as if he were looking up into the face of someone he loved as much as he now loved him.

Bruidge slowly stood up. His shadow loomed large on the wall behind him.

Bracken snapped and crackled in the fireplace. A burning branch flew from the fire and landed on the dried rushes. The eager flame began to eat quickly into them.

Bruidge held out a shaking hand. "Go," he ordered.

Calgaich and the hound did not move.

"My brother! My nephew!" Bruidge cried in a hoarse voice. "Go! You are no longer among the living! Leave this hall! It is mine now!"

The fire ate its way through the rushes toward the pile of firewood and bracken. It licked at the bracken and began to take hold.

Bruidge turned quickly. His large, veined hands gripped the thick shaft of his battle-axe. He whirled with the great weapon upraised in his hands. Then he bent forward in acute pain. His mouth squared from an inner agony. Cold sweat burst from his forehead.

Calgaich walked toward the table.

"Stay back!" Bruidge roared.

Calgaich shook his head.

Bruidge swung the axe up over his head. He screamed hoarsely as he brought it down in a tremendous stroke. The keen iron bit deeply into the table. Greasy plates and cups leaped into the air and then clattered down again. The beer from Bruidge's drinking horn flowed across the surface of the table and dripped at Calgaich's feet.

Bruidge gasped and then fell forward to lie on top of the table beside his great axe. He did not move again.

The firewood was flaring upward as it gained strength. A chair was catching fire. Runnels of fire stretched out into the dried rushes in all directions from the burning bracken.

Calgaich gripped Bruidge by his thick gray hair and turned the head sideways to look into staring eyes that would never see again.

Calgaich walked to the door of the hall. He turned. He looked about the hall as it now was, for he knew he would never see it like that again.

Bron whined deep in his throat. He was looking at something, or perhaps *someone*, he alone could see or sense.

An eerie feeling came over Calgaich. There was a presence there. But he knew he had nothing to fear.

Calgaich closed the outer door of the great *dun*. Smoke was already leaking thickly through the high slit windows of the towering structure. The flickering of rising flames could be seen reflected in the thick smoke.

Calgaich turned on a heel. With Bron beside him he strode down the long rocky hill toward the forest of birches at the foot of the slope.

Calgaich did not look back.

EPILOGUE

It was late spring and the trees were budding. Here and there in the hollows and on the shaded slopes were patches of snow which shrank visibly every day. The sky was bright and clear with a warming sun shining down upon the land. The wind was fresh and cool.

Calgaich rode up the long reverse slope of a hill which overlooked the Wall of Hadrian. He carried the great war spear of Evicatos slung across his back. Cairenn rode beside him, cradling their infant son, Evicatos the Younger. Bron trotted beside Calgaich's horse.

Calgaich drew rein at the crest of the hill and looked across the shining river. Beyond it was the Great Wall. The sunlight flashed now and then from the polished helmets and spear points of the auxiliaries who manned the watch towers and mile castles. "Give me our son, Cairenn," he requested.

He held the infant in his powerful swordsman's hands. "Look, Evicatos. There is the Great Wall of Hadrian. You will not remember it now, but in the later years to come you will know it well and learn to hate it as all our people hate it."

The others of Calgaich's party rode up beside him and Cairenn. There were Guidd One-Eye, Fomoire, the Druid, Lutorius, the Bottle Emptier, and Cunori, the Dolphin. Niall, the Selgovae, Loarn of the Brigantes, Onlach of the Votadini, and Ottar, the Saxon, stood slightly apart from the others. It was time for them to leave Calgaich and his people for their ride to their homelands in the east. Two days earlier Girich, the Pict, Conaid, the Little Hound, of the Damnonii, and Muirchu, the Niduari, had left Rioghaine for their own homelands. They had each borne a message from Calgaich, chieftain of the Novantae: "The time is nearing when all the tribes of Caledonia must unite to drive the Red Crests from Britannia. I ask each and all of you, Pict, Damnonii and Niduari, to join me in this last and greatest campaign to rid Britannia of the oppressors. Let me hear from you on this matter before the spring is gone from the land." Niall, Loarn, Onlach and Ottar each bore the same message for deliverance to their people.

A message was being flashed along the wall, from mile castle to signal tower, on and on as far as the eye could see to the west and to the east. The Romans had seen the barbarian horsemen standing out clearly and boldly against the skyline.

"Go now, sword-brothers," Calgaich suggested with a smile. "The Romans are alerted."

Those still on the hillcrest watched as the easternbound party went their separate ways and disappeared into the forest.

"Here they come, barbarian," Lutorius warned.

A *turma* of Dacian auxiliary cavalry hammered down the slope across the river and thundered out onto the wooden bridge. Infantry could be seen double-timing along the wall toward the mile castle nearest the bridge.

"There are a lot of them," Guidd said thoughtfully. He grinned like an old grizzler of a wolf.

"The long arm of Rome," Fomoire added.

Cunori spat to one side. "Let them come!"

Calgaich handed Evicatos the Younger to Cairenn. "Take him back." He looked at the others. "Get off the skyline," he added.

Calgaich remained alone on the crest. He held the Spear of Evicatos in his right hand. The fresh wind ruffled the heron's feathers at the base of the blade.

Roman auxiliary infantry formed their ranks at the far end of the bridge while the cavalry hammered up the long slope toward the lone horseman. At a command from their centurion the foot soldiers double-timed across the bridge.

The young centurion who led the cavalry drew his sword and waved it. There was a smile on his face. He was new to the frontier and he badly wanted to blood his virgin sword.

The veteran decurion of cavalry suddenly recognized the

lone barbarian horseman. "Centurion!" he shouted. "Wait!"

The centurion looked back over his shoulder. "Why?"

"Don't you know who that barbarian is, sir?"

"I don't give a damn! I want him for myself!"

"That's Calgaich the Swordsman!" the decurion shouted.

The centurion's horse dug its hoofs into the soft turf as his reins were abruptly hauled back. He reared and nearly threw his rider. The centurion was hardly a hundred feet from Calgaich.

Calgaich made no motion; the only movement about him was the wind-fluttered heron's feathers at the base of his spear blade.

On the same ridge, far to the left of Calgaich, sat a figure on a horse, holding a bundle in her lap. Cairenn and Calgaich had been parted too many times in the past, and they would be apart in the future as the tribes of Caledonia banded together to fight the Romans at the hated wall. She would not leave him now. Patiently, Cairenn waited for him to turn and see her there. Then he would smile and ride toward her and their young son. Together they would begin the journey home.

The centurion turned in his saddle. He thrust up an arm to halt the infantry coming up the slope. He turned again to look at Calgaich—the great barbarian swordsman who was a legend in his own time.

Minutes passed.

The centurion slowly raised his sword and saluted Calgaich. He then turned his horse and led his troops back to the bridge and across it to the Wall of Hadrian.

The centurion looked back as the mile castle gate was opened to admit his troops. Calgaich was still there. The centurion ran up the steps to the wall walkway and again looked across the river. The hillcrest was empty of life.